Cause Celeb

Also by Helen Fielding

BRIDGET JONES: THE EDGE OF REASON

BRIDGET JONES'S DIARY

HELEN FIELDING

Cause Celeb

Viking

VIKING
Published by the Penguin Group
Penguin Putnam Inc., 375 Hudson Street,
New York, New York 10014, U.S.A.
Penguin Books Ltd, 27 Wrights Lane,
London W8 5TZ, England
Penguin Books Australia Ltd, Ringwood,
Victoria, Australia
Penguin Books Canada Ltd, 10 Alcorn Avenue,
Toronto, Ontario, Canada M4V 3B2
Penguin Books (N.Z.) Ltd, 182–190 Wairau Road,
Auckland 10, New Zealand

Penguin Books Ltd, Registered Offices:
Harmondsworth, Middlesex, England

First American edition
Published in 2001 by Viking Penguin,
a member of Penguin Putnam Inc.

3 5 7 9 10 8 6 4 2

PUBLISHER'S NOTE
This is a work of fiction. Names, characters, places, and incidents either are the
product of the author's imagination or are used fictitiously, and any resemblance
to actual persons, living or dead, business establishments, events, or locales is entirely
coincidental.

LIBRARY OF CONGRESS CATALOGING IN PUBLICATION DATA
Fielding, Helen, date.
Cause celeb / Helen Fielding.
p. cm.
ISBN 0-670-89450-8
1. British—Africa, North—Fiction.   2. Africa, North—Fiction.   3. Food relief—
Fiction. I. Title.
PR6056.I4588 C38   2001
823'.914—dc21   00-043367

This book is printed on acid-free paper. ∞

Printed in the United States of America
Set in Bembo

For my father, Michael Fielding

ACKNOWLEDGMENTS

With thanks to Gillon Aitken, Dr. John Collee, Richard Coles, Adrienne Connors, Will Day of Comic Relief, Nellie Fielding and family, Paula, Piers and Sam Fletcher, Dr. Osma Galal, Georgia Garrett, Kathrin Grunig of the Red Cross and Red Crescent, Roger Hutchings, Mick Imlah, Tina Jenkins, Paul Lariviere of UNHCR, John Lloyd, John Magrath of Oxfam, Judith Marshall of the Natural History Museum's Department of Entomology, Harry Ritchie, Dr. John Seaman of Save the Children Fund, Jane Tewson of Comic Relief, Sarah Wallace, Jane Wellesley for help, advice, expertise and much kindness; and to Comic Relief, Médecin sans Frontières, Oxfam, the Red Cross, the Save the Children Fund and the Sudanese Commission of Refugees.

With appreciation of Peter Gill's *A Year in the Death of Africa* (Paladin), John Rowley's *Grasshoppers and Locusts: The Plague of the Sahel* (Panos), Ben Jackson's *Poverty and the Planet* (Penguin) and Nigel Twose's *Cultivating Hunger* (Oxfam).

And with special thanks to Richard Curtis.

Cause Celeb

One

*J*t used to seem extraordinary to me that someone like Henry could actually exist, extraordinary that a person could be transported into an environment so alien to his own, and remain so utterly unaffected by his surroundings. It was as if he had been coated with a very strong sealant, the sort of thing they use to paint on oceangoing yachts.

Henry was spreading thick cut luxury marmalade from a Fortnum and Mason's jar on a piece of Nambulan unleavened bread.

"Got up this morning, didn't Boris Believe it—family of eight outside my hut wanting to move their tent nearer the river. I said to the chap, 'I thought this was a bloody refugee camp, not a holiday camp, but you go ahead, mate, by all means. Never mind the old malnutrition—you go for the view.'"

Breakfast was taken in Safila, just after dawn. It was a quiet time, the hour before the heat became intolerable, with the silence broken only by the rooster and Henry, who was incapable of shutting up except when he was asleep. I was particularly annoyed by Henry that morning, because I suspected he had started an affair with one of our more emotionally fragile nurses, Sian. She was sitting next to him now, giving him a look you could have spread on a piece of toast. Sian was a sweet-natured girl who had joined us two months ago, after returning early from night shift to find her husband of eighteen months in bed with a Turkish minicab driver. Her therapy was being continued via correspondence.

Betty was talking about food as usual. "Do you know, what I could *really* eat now is a pudding. Mind you, I say that. Bread-and-butter pudding. Oooh, lovely, with raisins and a bit of nutmeg. I wonder if Kamal could do us a bread-and-butter pudding if we made that biscuit tin into an oven?"

It was five-thirty in the morning. I got up from the table, walked outside and sighed. How the tiny irritations of life filled the mind out here, keeping the big horrors at bay. I dipped a cup into the water pot, and walked to the edge of the hill to brush my teeth.

Our compound was behind me, with its round mud huts, showers, latrines and the cabana where we took our meals. Before me was the sandy basin which housed Safila camp, a great scar in the desert. The light was very soft at that time, the sun pale, just clearing the horizon. Clustered over a pattern of hummocks and paths, leading down to the point where the two blue rivers met, were the huts which housed the refugees. Five years ago, during the great mid-eighties famine, there were sixty thousand of them, and a hundred a day were dying. Now twenty thousand remained. The rest had gone back over the border to Kefti, to the mountains and the war.

A gust of hot wind made the dry grasses rustle. I was bothered by more than Henry that morning. A rumor was circulating in the camp about a locust plague back in Kefti, which was threatening the harvest. There were often scare stories in the camp of one kind or another: it was hard to know what to believe. We'd heard talk of a new influx of refugees on their way to us again, maybe thousands.

Sounds were beginning to rise from the camp now, goats being herded, laughter, children playing, contented sounds. Once, the great swathe of cries which rose to us here were those which went with starvation and death. I bit the side of my thumb, and tried not to remember. I couldn't think back to that time again. Footsteps were coming from the cabana. Henry was sauntering across the compound and back to his hut. He was wearing his favorite T-shirt, which featured a motif set out like a multiple choice questionnaire for relief workers.

(a) Missionary?

(b) Mercenary?

(c) Misfit?

(d) Broken heart?

Henry had ticked (b), which was a joke since his family owned half of northeast England. Me? I was a c/d hybrid and soft in the head to boot.

In London in the summer of 1985 I was afflicted by a crush, which is a terrible thing to happen to a woman. I met Oliver, the object of my rampant imaginings, at a gala performance of Vivaldi's *Gloria* at the Royal Albert Hall. I was what was known as a puffette: a publicist in a publishing company, Ginsberg and Fink. I wiggled around in short skirts, legs in sheer black tights crossing and uncrossing in meetings, then kept going on and on about people not being interested in my mind. Funny how at twenty-five you worry about not being taken seriously and take being a sex object for granted. Later you take being taken seriously for granted, and worry about not being a sex object.

Our company chairman, Sir William Ginsberg, liked to put together little gatherings of the arty and the talented from all walks of life, not revealing to the guests in advance who the other guests would be. For all the ill-informed like me these gatherings were a total nightmare. You feared to ask anyone what they did lest they turned out to be the author of *Love in the Time of Cholera,* or one of the Beach Boys.

I had been to three dinner parties at Sir William's house. I wasn't sure he remembered quite who I was. He employed several young girls and always used to invite one or two of us along because of our fine minds, presumably. I spent the evenings in a state of awed nervousness, saying very little. But I liked meeting these creative interesting people. I wanted to fit in. This was the first time I had been invited to a large-scale party, and I was most excited.

Sir William had organized a little soirée before the concert:

drinks for a hundred in one of the Hall's hospitality suites; fifteen boxes hired on the company; then a sit-down dinner for a chosen dozen and the rest of us could piss off.

I arrived deliberately late at the Albert Hall, inspected my reflection in the ladies' powder room, and made my way along the deep red corridor to the Elgar Room. A uniformed attendant checked my name on a list and swung open the dark wooden door into a burst of light. The room was golden and all-a-glitter, the black-tied guests spilling down an ornamental staircase in the center of the room, and leaning on the gilt balustrades of the higher level. It was bizarre being in a room full of celebrities—you felt as if you knew everyone, but nobody knew you. I set off towards the table where drinks were being served, catching snatches of conversation as I squeezed my way along.

"Frankly, I have to say, it's not coming off the page . . ."

"You see the trouble with Melvyn . . ."

"Jerome, have you got the mobile?"

I felt a hand on my elbow.

"*Mmmmm!* The most gorgeous girl in the world. Oh, dear heaven, you look absolutely divine. My heart's going to go this time, I swear it. Absolutely convinced of it. Give me a kiss, my darling, do."

It was Dinsdale Warburton, one of my major authors, and an ancient giant of the English stage. Dinsdale had recently written his memoirs for us. He had a worried face, was queer as a coot, and unfailingly kind.

"But, my darling!" Dinsdale's brows were almost meeting in horror. "You do not have a drrink. But let us get you one! Let us get you one at once!"

Then his eyes were caught by something over my shoulder. "Oh! The most gorgeous man in the world. Dear boy, dear boy. You look absolutely divine. You know, I did love your whatever it was you did the other night. You looked so *exquisitely* clever and pretty."

Oliver Marchant was the editor and presenter of a successful and right-on arts program called *Soft Focus*. His reputation as the thinking-woman's man preceded him, but I had no idea he was going to be quite so devastating. Dinsdale was speaking to me: "Have

you met this gorgeous man, my darling. Do you know Oliver Marchant?"

I panicked. How were you supposed to answer this question with
famous people? Yes, I've seen you on the telly? No . . . in other words,
I've never heard of you. "Yes, I mean . . . no. Sorry . . . pathetic."

Oliver took my hand. "And this is?"

"Ah. The most gorgeous girl in the world, dear boy, absolute
goddess."

"Yes, but what is her *name,* Dinsdale?" said Oliver.

Dinsdale looked flummoxed for a moment. I absolutely couldn't
believe he'd forgotten my name. I'd been working very closely with
him for two months.

"I'm Rosie Richardson," I said apologetically.

"Pleased to meet you . . . Rosie Richardson," said Oliver.

He was long, lean and dark in a navy suit with an ordinary tie,
not a bow tie, loosened at the neck. I noticed very precisely the way
his black hair fell against his collar, the half shadow on his chin.

"Rosie, my darling, I'm off to get you a drink this second. On
my way. You must be *fainting* with thirst," said Dinsdale and hurried
off looking sheepish.

I turned to Oliver, to find he was now talking to a gray-haired
newsreader. The newsreader had his teenage daughter with him.

"How's it going, mate?" said the newsreader, clapping Oliver on
the shoulder.

"Oh, same old shit, you know. How are you, Sarah?"

Oliver spoke charmingly to the girl, who was getting even more
flustered than I was. He glanced across and smiled at me as if to say,
"Hang on."

"Bye-bye, Sarah," said Oliver sweetly, as the girl and her father
prepared to move off. "Good luck with those exams." He gave her
a little wave. "Dirty *bitch,*" he said to me in an undertone, looking
at the departing teenager. "Dying for it." I laughed. "So," he said,
"are you having a lovely time?"

"Well, I find it very odd, to be honest," I said. "I've never been in
a room with so many famous people before. They all seem to know
each other. It's like a club. *Do* they all know each other?"

"You're right. I've always thought it was more of a new aristocracy, but you're absolutely right. It has more open membership. It's the Famous Club. The only membership requirement is that the public know who you are," he said, glancing disparagingly round the room.

"No, no, *you're* right, it *is* like an aristocracy," I said eagerly. "You know, the country estates and the hunting, and it's hereditary now: Julian Lennon, Kiefer Sutherland, Charlie Sheen."

"It also inhabits every single first-class lounge and awards ceremony you ever pass through. But, actually, it *is* more like a club with its rules. You have to know the form. He who is less famous must wait to be approached by he who is more famous," Oliver said.

At this, Lady Hilary Ginsberg, Sir William's wife, interrupted him, rather knocking down his theory. "Oliver, I'm so thrilled to see you. How is the Lorca coming along?"

Oliver looked blank just for a moment. He didn't recognize her.

"Hilary Ginsberg, so pleased you could come," she said hastily, her back slightly turned to me, excluding me. "Have you met Martin?"

Lady Hilary was a tragic name-dropper. I had often bent with her over her dinner party celebrity lists, which were like a Dow Jones index of fame, with artists, actors, writers, journalists, moving up and down, depending on fashion, acts of God, or their own greediness for exposure. Lady Hilary seemed to have embraced this index as a yardstick for her entire life. I once heard her discuss, without irony, why a certain name was not a particularly good one to drop. Even her closest women friends would be invited to dinner parties with Sir William only when their value was up, otherwise it was lunch alone with her.

Oliver was continuing with the Famous Club theory. "You put two of them in a room full of noncelebs, they'll end up talking to each other, whether or not they've already met, providing . . . providing the more famous of the two approaches the other one first," Oliver went on. Everyone was laughing by this time. "Come on, Martin, you're a celeb, you must know it's true." As Oliver finished his sentence he turned his eyes to mine and kept looking.

Sir William appeared, booming behind us, startling everyone.

"Come along, come along, heavens above, we're ver', ver' late, going to miss the trumpets," and seizing Oliver and the novelist by their elbows like an old hen, he bustled them out.

Oliver was seated behind me in the box. I spent the entire performance in a state of almost unbearable arousal. I fancied I could feel his breath on my neck and back in my low-cut dress. At one point his hand brushed my skin as if by accident. I almost died.

When the music stopped and the applause died down I daren't look at him. I stood surveying the emptying Albert Hall as everyone left the box, trying to calm down. I heard someone moving down the steps behind me. It was him. He bent and kissed the nape of my neck. At least I hoped it was him.

"I'm so sorry," Oliver murmured, "that was just something I had to do."

I looked round at him, trying to raise one eyebrow.

"I could murder a pizza," he whispered urgently. "Why don't you turn into a pizza?"

"Because I don't want to be murdered."

"I didn't mean murder . . . exactly."

And thus the obsession began, and a chain of events which was to lead me surely but circuitously to a mud hut in Africa. There are people, particularly in times of prominent famine, who become almost reverent when you say you are an aid worker. Actually, the reason I first got interested in Africa was because I fancied someone. That's about how saintly I am, if you really want to know. If Oliver had asked me out that night in the Albert Hall, I'd probably have never even heard of Nambula. As it was, Sir William interrupted us. "Oliver, Oliver, wherever have you got to? Come along, come along, grub's up!"

Typically, my employer ignored me. Oliver took an elegant-enough leave, but I still had to face the fact that he had allowed himself to be whisked off to dinner with the chosen few, after kissing my neck, without so much as a what's-your-phone-number.

For about a week after the Vivaldi Works Outing I was in a state of sexual overexcitement, convinced that Oliver would find out who I was and call.

But Oliver didn't ring. He didn't ring. I reached out for any form of contact possible. I started arranging an unnatural number of evenings with a friend who had worked for him four years ago. I watched *Soft Focus* three times a week. I rang the *Soft Focus* press office for the list of the next three months' programs to see if any of them had anything remotely to do with any of our authors. I went to exhibitions on Sundays. I started reading extraordinarily dull articles in the arts pages about East European spatter-print painters. No luck. Zilch.

Two

I lay naked, with nothing above me but a sheet. My body was a perfect, cleansed and silken thing. Oliver knelt on the bed, slowly drew back the sheet and looked at me. He touched my breasts as if they were rare fragile artifacts, ran the palm of his hand luxuriantly down my stomach, until I caught my breath. "Oh, Jesus, Rosie," he whispered. "I want to fuck you so much."

Then the door opened, and Hermoine Hallet-McWilliam burst into the office. "Have you done that memo? Sir William's asking where it is."

For all her well-connected background, Hermione was badly challenged in the manners department. "Nearly finished, Hermione," I said brightly, turning back to the computer.

"Can't imagine what you've been doing," she said. "Told you to do that an hour ago." Then she picked up the phone and dialed a number. "Candida. Hi. Smee. Listen, you going to be Larkfield at the weekend? That's *completely* brilliant. Ophelia's coming with Hero and Perpetua. Well, fairly smart, I suppose. Absolutely. Quite agree. No, you're quite right. Well, say hello to Lucretia for me. Bye."

One of these days she would answer the phone to someone called Beelzebub.

Suddenly I was all softness and radiance in a powder-blue wrap. The sun was streaming down on us as we sat at my kitchen table. It was our first breakfast together.

"People can be really quite different from each other, can't they, Oliver?" I said.

"Sorry, darling?"

"I, for example, like a warm currant tea cake for my breakfast. You, on the other hand, might prefer muesli, or scrambled eggs with smoked salmon, or bagels perhaps, with a range of cheeses," I said, opening my immaculate fridge to reveal an array of tempting foodstuffs.

"Rosemary." Hermione was standing above me, staring at me furiously. "I am not. Going. To ask you. Again. May I please have Sir William's memo?"

I turned back, under Hermione's gaze, to the computer and started typing out the handwritten memo which lay on the desk. It was another of Sir William's mad attempts to make himself more famous.

23 JULY 1985
To: ALL MEMBERS OF THE PUBLICITY DEPARTMENT
FROM: SIR WILLIAM GINSBERG
RE: CORPORATE PROFILE-RAISING

We are looking very very hard for ways of increasing public awareness of the socially responsible aspects of the company and myself as its chairman. In the light of the recent Live Aid concert it is very very important Ginsberg and Fink are seen to be doing their bit.

Suddenly the first birth pangs of an idea twinged in my brain. Startled by the sensation, I reached for the list of forthcoming *Soft Focus* programs, which was lying in a pile of papers on my desk. I scanned the list. There it was:

PROGRAM 25: *In the wake of Band Aid and Live Aid, Soft Focus investigates the new phenomenon of charity in relation to popular culture, and looks at the contribution of various areas of the arts world to aid for the Ethiopian famine.*

I reckoned it ought to be possible to get Sir William onto the program, although, obviously, it would have to involve a lot of consultation with the producer.

"Books." Sir William banged his fist down on his large mahogany desk. "Ver' good idea. Take 'em some books. Books all over the shop, clutterin' the place up. Take 'em out in an airlift. Ties in smooth as a sewin' machine. Ver' good angle for an arts program."

"Don't you think the Ethiopians would rather have something to eat?" I said.

"No, no, no. Books. Just the ticket. Every man jack in the whole ruddy shootin' match flyin' out food. Need somethin' to read while they're waitin' for it."

"In fact, although naturally food is the pressing concern, there may actually be something interesting for us in the books concept." Eamonn Salt, the press officer for the SUSTAIN charity, pulled at his beard. Sir William pulled at his beard too.

"Really?" I said.

"Yes, indeed. We're trying to get away from the dehumanizing of the indigenous African in the media famine coverage," Eamonn went on in his flat monotone. "Introducing the notion of the learned African person, the intelligent African thirsting for knowledge to replace what we call the Starving Monkey Myth. Your idea might well have a role to play in increasing public empathy, though many of my colleagues would disagree. It's a different school of thought. Though, of course, we'd be up against public outrage about waste of resources, charity for luxury. I'm sure you're familiar with the arguments."

"Ver' good. Arguments. Books. Just the ticket to get the *Soft Focus* lot goin'," said Sir William.

"But would the Ethiopians be able to read the books if they're in English?" I said.

"Ah, well, remember, the famine covers the whole of the Sahel. Your best bet might be to send them to the camps on the border between Abouti and Nambula. There are refugees from Kefti there who are highly educated. The Keftians have an excellent British-based education system," said Eamonn.

"Where's Kefti?" I said.

"Rebel province of Abouti, bordering Nambula, North Africa. The Keftians have been pursuing a somewhat bloody war for independence from the Marxist regime in Abouti for twenty-five years. Highly organized culture. The Sahel famine has hit them probably harder than anyone—it is impossible for the NGOs to get food aid to them because of the war and for diplomatic reasons. There is a major exodus from Kefti at present over the border into Nambula. Very, very severe malnourishment there."

"What about taking out food with a few books thrown in?" I said.

"Ruddy good idea," said Sir William. "First rate. Good thinkin', gel."

Fired up with unaccustomed zeal, I started organizing an appeal among the staff of the corporation for the food, rounding up remaindered books, looking into sponsored flights. I rang up *Soft Focus* and fixed up a meeting for a week's time with Sir William, Oliver Marchant and me. A vision of Africa, with its tribes, drums, fires and lions, danced and twinkled. I thought of Geldof, I thought of purpose and meaning, I thought of relief workers being passionate, poor and self-sacrificing, saving the grateful Africans. But mainly I thought of Oliver.

CHAPTER

Three

"Where's my Kit-Kat?"

Henry was standing outside the cabana, looking around indignantly. The staff had finished breakfast and were wandering around the compound getting ready to go to the camp. Sian hurried over to Henry.

"My bloody Katerina Kit-Kat. I left it in Fenella Fridge and somebody's Sophia Scoffed it."

Sian was talking to him in a low voice, soothing him.

"Henry, you're blind and stupid," I called across. "It's under the antibiotics. Go and have another look."

"Ding *dong!*" he said, turning round and raising his eyebrows suggestively. "I do so *love* it when you get all strict," and he sauntered back into the cabana, as Sian hurried after him.

The sun was starting to burn now. The first trails of smoke were beginning to rise above the camp and figures were moving slowly along the paths and across the plain: a boy leading a donkey carrying two bulging leather sacks of water, a woman with a pile of firewood on her head, a man in a white djellaba walking with a stick balanced on his shoulders, arms hanging lazily over the stick. In a few hours' time the light would be blinding white and the heat would become claustrophobic. It was easy to imagine you were going to suffocate and stop breathing.

Betty came bustling across the gravel towards me. "I don't want to intrude before you've started your day properly, dear," she said, "though . . ."—she opened her eyes very wide and showed me her watch—"it is six o'clock. But I wondered if I could have a little word in your ear."

Betty was round and in her late fifties. I knew what she wanted to have a little word about: Henry and Sian. She wouldn't be up front about it. She wouldn't say, "I don't think you should let your assistant behave promiscuously with the nurses." What she would do would be to tell me a little story about someone I'd never heard of who had once run a relief camp in Zanzibar or, perhaps, Chad. This person, surprise surprise, would have allowed their assistants to sleep with the nurses—and guess what? It would all have ended in an AIDS outbreak, earthquake or tidal wave and they would have decided that everyone should sleep in their own mud huts in future.

"Can we have a chat later?" I said, suddenly remembering the toothbrush and holding it up. "When I've finished my teeth?"

I finished the brushing, and scrunched across the gravel to my hut. I had a lot to do that day. I was the administrator of the camp, doing the organization for SUSTAIN, the charity which employed us all. I had been at Safila for just over four years. For the first two I had been assistant administrator, then I'd taken over the main job, with Henry joining as my assistant. I had to oversee supplies of food and drugs and medical equipment, the vehicles, the drinking water, the food—and the staff, which seemed to take up more time than anything.

I opened the piece of corrugated iron which served as a door, and stepped inside my hut. My home in Safila was a thatched circle of wood and mud, about twenty feet in diameter with a hard earth floor covered in rush mats. It smelt of dust. I had a metal-framed bed with a mosquito net, a desk, shelves for my books and files, two metal armchairs with hideous floral foam-rubber cushions, and a Formica coffee table. Everything was covered in sand. It got between your teeth, into your ears, your pockets, your pants. I was fond of my hut, though I think it was the privacy rather than anything else about it which held the appeal.

I say privacy, but two minutes later there was a halfhearted rattle at the door and Betty poked her head round, giving an understanding upside-down smile. She came in, without being asked, gave me a hug, and plonked herself on the bed. There was a scuffling in the ceiling, the ceiling being a large canvas sheet, which was there to catch creatures that would otherwise fall out of the thatch into the room.

"Hello, little friends," said Betty, looking up.

Oh, no, oh, no. It was a bit early in the morning to have Betty in your hut.

"You're worried, Rosie, aren't you? And, do you know, I think you're right to be worried."

Here we go, I thought, Henry and Sian.

"It reminds me of when Judy Elliot was running Mikabele back in 'seventy-four. She'd had several arrivals in a very poor state, sent a message to head office asking for reinforcements and got her head bitten off for overreacting. Two months later there was a massive influx, a hundred a day dying during the worst of it, and of course she didn't have the staff or the equipment."

So it wasn't Henry and Sian. It was the locusts.

"What have you heard? Do you think there's anything in it?"

Over the four years I had been in Safila there had been several famine scares, hordes of refugees about to flood over the border bringing plagues of cholera, meningitis, elephantiasis, God knows what, but it had never, in all the time I had been in Safila, come to anything serious. Sometimes we suspected it was just a refugee ruse to get more food.

Betty gave a little toss of her head, offended. "You mustn't think I'm in any way trying to tell you your job, Rosie dear. You know I have the greatest admiration for everything you do, the greatest admiration. But, you know, we must always listen to the voice of the African, the voice of Africa."

Suddenly I wanted to bite Betty, or just sort of pummel her face for quite a long time.

"I'm worried too, Betty, but we can't go raising an alert if we've nothing concrete to go on. Have you heard anything I haven't heard?"

"They, the people, are our barometer, you know. And the Teeth of the Wind as the African calls them"—she paused for approval—"the Teeth of the Wind can be absolute shockers. They fly all day, you know. Miles and miles, they cover, thousands of miles."

"I know, that's what they were saying down at the distribution yesterday, but have you heard anything else?"

"When Mavis Enderby was in Ethiopia in 'fifty-eight there was a plague which gobbled up enough grain to feed a million people for a year. Of course, the thing that really worries me, as I was saying to Linda, is the harvest. Miles and miles across, these swarms are, blotting out the sun, black as soot."

"I KNOW," I said, more loudly than I meant to, which was stupid, as this was not the time to initiate a Betty-huff. "Has anyone said anything else to you?"

"They can eat their body weight of food in a day, you know, it's really very worrying and what with the harvest due, and they can move so fast, great clouds of them . . ."

There was so much to do this morning. I simply had to get Betty to go, so I could think. "Thank you, Betty," I said. "Thank you so much for your support. It is extremely worrying, but you know . . . a trouble shared . . . Now I really must get on, but thanks for bringing it up."

It worked. Splendid. She took this as a cue to roll her eyes with affected modesty and rush over to give me a little hug. "Well, we'd best get down to the camp if we're going to be back and ready in time for Linda's new doctor," she said, and gave me another little hug before departing.

That was the other thing. We had a new doctor arriving today, an American. Betty was leaving in three weeks' time and he was going to replace her. We were supposed to be having a special lunch to welcome him. Linda, who was one of our nurses and rather up-tight, had apparently worked with this man in Chad two years ago, but she wouldn't tell us anything about him. All she did was make it very clear that she had been corresponding with him, and go all coy every time his sleeping arrangements were mentioned. I hoped he was going to be all right. We were such a small group, stuck together, all the relationships were finely balanced. It was easy to knock them off-kilter.

I sat down on the bed, and thought about what Betty had said. For all her annoying little ways, she was a very good doctor, and she did know her stuff as far as Africa was concerned. She seemed to have been working here since the early nineteenth century. There was an awful logic to these rumors. Kefti had just had the first good rains for several years. One of the cruelest ironies of Africa is that the first decent rains after a drought produce ideal conditions for locusts. Because they did, indeed, move so fast, a plague at harvest-time was one of the few things other than a war which could create an instant mass exodus.

I got up, fished out a file, and started looking through it. We tried to run an early-warning system for Kefti, but it wasn't much help, because no one was allowed to go up there. We were banned from going by SUSTAIN because it was a war zone, and banned from going by the Nambulan government because they wanted to keep things sweet with the Aboutians, and the Keftians were fighting Abouti. All the information we had was in this file. It was full of charts about grain prices in the markets near the borders, graphs of the height and weight of children, sightings of movements of people over the border. I had looked at it two days ago. There was nothing out of the ordinary. I was just making sure.

I really needed to decide on a response quickly, because Malcolm was supposed to be arriving at eleven o'clock with the new doctor. Malcolm was the SUSTAIN field officer for the whole of Nambula. He was a bit of a prat, but if we were going to raise an alarm this was a good chance to do it. I decided to go down to the camp and talk to Muhammad Mahmoud. He would know what was up. I was feeling panicky. I had a drink of water, and tried to calm down.

When I stepped out into the white light, I saw Henry having an intimate chat with Sian outside her hut. He was chucking her under her chin in a cutesy-pie manner. She saw me watching, blushed and shot back inside the hut. Henry just raised his eyebrows and smirked—the arrogance of that boy.

"Henry Montague," I said strictly. "Go to your room."

He grinned gleefully. Henry had a smile which was almost too big for his face, in a widemouthed, upper-class way. He was always rather elegant, with dark hair hanging over his forehead in a foppish fringe, which presumably had been trendy when he last saw South Kensington. I was constantly trying to get him to fasten it back with a hair grip.

"I shall have words with you later," I said. "In the meantime you can put the two cold boxes that are just inside the cabana into the Toyota. I want to go down to the camp and get back before Malcolm arrives."

"Halliaow! Ding! *Dong!* Mistress Efficiency!" he said, putting his arm round me in a manner which denoted no respect whatsoever. There would be no point in talking to him now about the Sian business. Any criticism or caution would be shaken off like drops of water from a high-spirited puppy after a swim.

We set off in the Toyota pickup in amiable silence. I decided not to bring up the locusts with Henry until I had talked to Muhammad. Muhammad Mahmoud was not an official leader in the camp. He was just brighter than anyone else, us included. Driving left no room for chat, anyway. Concentration was required, even if you weren't at the wheel. Shaken and bounced around as if in a tumble dryer, you had to make your body relaxed but tense enough to react when you got thrown up off the seat and hit your head on the roof.

"I say! Hope you've got a sturdy bra on in there, old thing!" bellowed Henry. He used to say this every single time, imagining he had just thought of it.

We were winding down the steep sandy track into the camp now, looking over the huts, the white plastic arc of the hospital, the square rush-matting shapes which housed the clinic, the ration distribution, the market, the school. Over the last four years misery had gradually been replaced by mundanity for the refugees, and for us too. But by and large it was a contented mundanity. We drew from each other—the ex-pats and the refugees. We went to their parties at night, with the drums and the fires, thrilling to the Africa of our childhood fantasies. We gave them the drugs, food and medical knowledge they needed. We rowed down the river, played with their kids and felt adventurous, and they took pleasure from our energy and naïve excitement at being in Africa. "We came out of the tunnel of our despair to find that we could not only live, but also dance," Muhammad once said to me, in his absurdly poetic way. We had come through a crisis together and now we were happy. But the refugees here were entirely dependent on food from the West. It made them vulnerable.

"Bloody hell!" Henry yelled as two boys ran in front of the Toyota, playing chicken. They were not supposed to do this. As the hill leveled out and we entered the main area of the camp, a whole group of kids were running after us, waving and shouting, "Hawadga!"—white man.

As I swung open the door and jumped out of the cab, the heat hit me like the blast from an open oven door and the kids surrounded us. God, they were lovely, the kids: the rough ones running around, shouting and laughing; the shy ones standing like kids stand everywhere in the world with one leg hooked behind the other, rubbing their eyes and then putting their fingers in their mouths, as the health workers had spent the last five years teaching them not to. Two of them were wearing glasses made of straw, modeled on our sunglasses. I bent down and tried them on. They all screamed with laughter as if it was the funniest thing that had ever happened.

We usually had lunch at twelve but I had asked everyone to be back up at the cabana by eleven-thirty, ready to greet Malcolm and the new doctor and have the lunch. At ten-fifteen I was through with my jobs and ready to talk to Muhammad, but then there was a problem in Sian's eye clinic because some of the patients had started demanding five Nambulan sous to have their eyelids turned inside out. They said that people in Wad Denazen, which was another, bigger camp about fifty miles away, got paid five sous to have their eyes examined like this.

"They say it should be the same here," said Sian despairingly.

"Typical Wad Denazen," I said. There were some Italian relief workers there who were pretty overemotional and lazy. The French were bad but the Italians were worse.

"What shall I do? It's dreadful that they're asking for money when we're trying to help them."

"Tell them if they don't want their eyes examined you won't be able to find out what's wrong with them and they'll go blind. And die." I said. "Horribly."

"I can't tell them that," said Sian, wide-eyed.

"Just be firm about it," I said. "They don't really expect the money. They're just trying it on."

"But it's dreadful to—"

"They're only human. You'd try it, if you were that poor."

I looked at her troubled face. Actually, maybe she wouldn't. Oh dear. I remembered what it was like when you first arrived. There were lots of things which rather let you down with a bump. I wanted to stay and talk to her but I had to get on.

Someone came running over from the hospital to say they wanted some IV fluids quickly, which, for some reason, were locked in the other Land Cruiser, and only Debbie had the key. Debbie was a vast girl from Birmingham, with a dry take on life who had been at Safila since the first time I came out. She was brilliant with the refugees. As I hurried along the path to where she was, looking at my watch, I heard a voice behind me saying, "Rhozee." It was Liben Alye sitting under a little tree holding Hazawi and smiling at me lovingly and hopefully. I felt a stab of irritation, then another one of guilt for having had the stab of irritation. I loved Liben Alye, but he never understood about being in a rush. When I first saw him, sitting with a group of old men during the bad times, I had noticed him because of the way he was holding this baby, stroking her cheek and smoothing her hair. It turned out that all his children, six of them, and all his grandchildren except Hazawi had died, which was why he always kept her with him. I squatted down beside him and shook his hand and touched Hazawi's cheek at his invitation and agreed that it was indeed very soft. And I admired her long eyelashes and agreed that they were indeed very long. I turned my wrist so I could see my watch and realized that I was indeed going to be very late for Malcolm. Ah, well.

It took me ages to find Debbie, and then she couldn't stop what she was doing because she was in the process of extracting a Guinea worm from someone's leg. "I can't stop," she said, "or the bloody thing'll come off my matchstick."

I watched while she wound the yellow, stringlike creature very, very slowly round a match, pulling it out of the skin.

"Bloody long bugger, this one," she said to the woman, who grinned proudly.

She carried on winding delicately with her chubby fingers until the end of the worm came out and it hung, squirming, on the matchstick.

"There you are," she said, handing it to the woman. "Fry it up with a bit of oil and some lentils," and she acted out an eating movement, so that the woman laughed.

"What d'you reckon with Linda and this doctor?" said Debbie, as we hurried back to the vehicles. "Is she going to be shagging him or wot?"

"Search me," I said.

"Her mouth's as tight as a choirboy's arse," said Debbie.

"Sure is," I said. "Well, um, not that I'd actually know, of course."

The kids were running along with me again as I walked to Muhammad's shelter. Most of them had their heads shaved with just one little tuft left in the middle. They all chose different shapes for their tuft so it looked quite funny if you were taller than them. I rounded a corner, and there was Muhammad, standing at the entrance to his shelter.

The kids melted away. Muhammad was a striking man with a shock of fuzzy black hair which was almost Kenneth Kaundaesque in its verticalness. He wore a djellaba so white as to be absurd.

"Rosie," he said. "You have been very industrious today. Have you decided to increase your productivity?"

It was a relief to get inside his shelter where it was cool and quiet. Most of the refugees lived in huts, but Muhammad had managed to get hold of the materials and the space to build himself an exceptionally airy and elegant establishment. It was like our cabana, an oblong building with rush-matting walls, designed so that a breeze ran through. In places, harsh white points of light broke through from the outside. I settled down on a low bed, waiting for him to make tea before we could talk. He had a bookshelf leaning against one wall. The Ginsberg and Fink remaindered books were still there.

It was twenty past eleven but there was no explaining the need for haste to Muhammad. There was no hurrying the arrival of the tea; no question of abandoning ceremony and proceeding in an expedient manner. Especially if I was late for something.

Muhammad moved in stately fashion, to and fro, fetching tiny cups, two more sticks for the fire. Sugar. More water. A little more tea. Another twig. A spoon. Damn him. He was doing it on purpose now.

Eventually, finally, with a self-satisfied glint in his eye, he presented me with a tiny cup of tea, obviously too hot to drink, and settled himself down.

"So."

"So."

"You are very excited this morning." Muhammad had a thin, reedy voice and a deep laugh.

"No, I'm not."

"Yes, you are," said Muhammad.

With extreme difficulty, I maintained a lofty silence.

"So," said Muhammad eventually. Ha! My point. "So what is the cause of this agitation? Is it the new doctor?"

He was *such* a pain. "No, of course it isn't the new doctor, for God's sake."

He gave his deep laugh, then looked serious. "So then perhaps it is the Teeth of the Wind," he said dramatically.

"Oh, God, Muhammad. Call them locusts, please."

"You have no poetry in your soul. It is tragic," he said.

"Come on, Sylvia Plath, what have you heard?"

"I hear that there are swarms five miles across, blotting out the sun, plunging the earth into blackness," he said.

"And what have you really heard?"

"It is not good," he said, serious now. "There is no food in the highlands. The rains have been poor for many years now. The people are living on nothing and only trying to survive until the harvest."

"But the harvest will be good this year?"

"Yes. For the first time in many years. Unless the locusts come. Then there will be very bad famine and the people will come here."

"*Is* there a locust plague? Are they swarming?"

"They are not flying, but I have heard that they are hatching in three areas. You know that they begin as grasshoppers and then they march—in a vast, seething, living carpet?"

I looked at him levelly. "Yes. Muhammad, I know."

"If the people had the pesticides then they could spray and destroy them, but they have nothing. Even if they had the chemicals it would not be possible to spray from the air because of the Aboutian fighter jets. Soon the winds will be blowing east–west and will carry the swarms across Kefti and into Nambula."

"And do you believe all this?"

He shrugged and raised his hands. Then he looked down and said, "It is possible."

It is possible. I felt a surge of panic again. Usually he dismissed these rumors as nothing. "How can we find out?" I said.

"For now we must wait, reflect and discuss."

I wanted to stay and talk this through, but it was eleven-forty. I had to go. "Malcolm's going to arrive any minute with the new doctor," I said, getting up.

"I have something to show you," Muhammad replied.

Of course he had something to show me, given that I was late. He took me out through the back of his hut. There, growing in the mud, were three spindly tomato plants bearing a handful of tiny tomatoes of the type which are particularly expensive in supermarkets at home. He knew he was not supposed to do this. The refugees were forbidden to cultivate. That would have turned a relief camp into a permanent settlement.

Muhammad picked one of his six tomatoes and gave it to me.

"Thank you," I said, touched. "I'll have it stuffed."

Then he put his hand on my shoulder and gave me a look. What was it—friendship, solidarity, pity? I got all brisk and flustered. "I'd better go," I said.

When I got back to the Land Cruiser it was locked and Henry had the key. It was twelve o'clock now and everyone else had gone back up to the camp on time as I had asked them to. I drummed my fingers on the front of the car and waited, hoping Henry had not gone up with the others and forgotten that he had the key. What I hadn't told Muhammad was that we were already short of food in the camp. We were supposed to have had a delivery a fortnight before but the UN had sent a message over the radio to say that the food would not be coming for a few weeks because the supply ship had not arrived in Port Nambula. We were going to have to start cutting down everyone's rations anyway, even without writhing living carpets covering the whole of Kefti, and massive swarms of giant-fanged locusts blotting out the sun.

I looked at the group of kids running round the Land Cruiser, giggling, trying to jump up into the back, and remembered the feeding centers of the last famine. We used to have one shelter for the kids who could feed themselves, one for those who were too weak to feed themselves but might live, and one for those who were definitely going to die. I suddenly wanted to burst into tears. I hadn't toughened up as much as I'd thought.

Four

I dreamed of bumping into him in Safeways: walking along the aisles side by side, making jokes about the other customers, scampering about buying absurd foodstuffs to make each other laugh, tinned meat pies, blancmange, packets of dried chicken curry. Unbelievable that at one time in my life I spent hours and hours thinking about this, working out the fine detail of the fantasy.

Once an actual real meeting had been arranged with Oliver my head was completely taken over, like a nest with a cuckoo in it. I used to attempt to ban him from my mind by reading a book, and I'd read the same sentence four times without noticing. I would watch the news and not take in a single word because I was thinking of him. All I could concentrate on was my new Africa project, because it was infused by Oliver with sexual promise. On the Saturday morning before the meeting, I persuaded myself that I really did need to go to Safeways: not the one where I lived, but another, several miles away in the King's Road (where Oliver lived), since their range of handmade pasta was more extensive.

It was tragic, really. I dressed and undressed several times in preparation for the expedition. I did not want to look too dressed up; I wanted to look stylish yet casual, as if I always looked like that on Saturday mornings, and also thin. I put full makeup on, then suspected you could see the foundation in the hard daytime light, so washed the foundation off and settled for eyeliner, mascara, lipstick and blusher, then started again without the eyeliner and lipstick. I wore new white underwear, then changed it to black. I asked myself if it was weird to wear stockings and suspenders under jeans and was unable to see my way to a clear answer.

After I had spent over an hour in Safeways, and returned again to Safeways to purchase a bag of frozen scampi of which I had neither need nor want, and he still did not appear, I cursed the heavens for conspiring against me. "Your behavior is insane and sick," my friend Shirley said when I confessed all this. "If I hear the word 'Oliver' once more this evening I shall bite your head."

Oliver himself became sick. He lay, feverish, in his flat which was vast and airy with white pillars. I tended him. I washed the sheets, made him shepherd's pie and brought it on a tray with flowers in a little square white vase. Then I changed the pie to grilled trout with watercress, and new potatoes steamed in their skins, because shepherd's pie is too heavy if you are sick. His mother arrived. She was glamorous and rich and she was just popping by with some champagne. She didn't have a clue about caring for him, none. He had never known true love and care. But she took to me like nobody's business. "I've never seen him so happy with anyone, my darling," she whispered to me, in her gravelly Sobranie smoker's voice, with a conspiratorial wink.

The meeting was scheduled for six o'clock on Wednesday. At five-thirty on the Tuesday Hermione banged down the phone particularly huffily. "Sir William wants you to go upstairs. Oliver Marchant's up there. He was in the area, apparently, so he wants to have the meeting now instead of tomorrow."

It was a disaster, a complete disaster. I had set aside that whole evening to prepare for the meeting: to go to an aerobics class to clean off those extra few ounces; to have a steam bath and soak myself in scented oils; to prepare my outfits. In fact, had the meeting not been brought forward a day, I might have missed it altogether, since the toiletry preparations and outfit choices might have prevented me leaving the flat at all. As it was, I considered Oliver's premature arrival one of the worst misfortunes which had ever befallen me. I only just had time to get my makeup on.

As I walked into the room and saw Oliver sitting there my brain emptied completely and my mouth went dry.

"Ah," said Sir William, "Oliver. This is our representative from the publicity department, ver' ver' good, Rosemary ah . . ."

"Richardson," finished Oliver, smiling in a fatherly way. He got up and shook my hand. At his touch, chemicals began to charge around crazily in my body shouting, "WARNING WARNING, sexual alert, all systems to pulse."

"How are you?" said Oliver.

"Fine, thanks." My voice came out unexpectedly high. We were still looking into each other's eyes.

"Glarrrh," said Sir William, clearing his throat, "glahum, well . . ."

"So. Still not turned into a pizza?" said Oliver, which was quite cheeky considering my boss was still standing looking at us going "Glahum."

"What's that?" said Sir William. "Wantin' a pizza?"

"Maybe later," said Oliver to me, but looking back at Sir William.

During the meeting Oliver did most of the talking and directed most of what he said to me, which went straight to my head, naturally.

"It's a phenomenon which fascinates me," he was saying. "Celebrities have been promoting causes since the First World War, but you watch: this will become huge. In five years' time no cause will be complete without an accompanying star to promote it."

I made an odd noise. Sir William glanced at me disconcertedly.

"Ver', ver' interesting," he huffed. "Course, celebrities come from all walks of life. Not just a question of world of entertainment, all sorts of areas, prominent figures, benefactors."

"Quite so," said Oliver. "Business, publishing even, as with yourself."

Sir William pulled at his beard, gratified. I was still embarrassed about the odd noise. It had been meant as a murmur of agreement.

"But what this program is actually about," said Oliver, "is the way Third World aid is entering the mainstream of popular culture. Before Geldof it was dreary, it was a question of black and white envelopes plopping onto the doorstep. Now giving is becoming hip and synonymous with a good time."

"Ver' true, and as we've bin sayin'. Goin' out there meself, with the books. Bit of a mercy dash," said Sir William, then looked at me. "Glahum," he said, nodding at me. "Glahum."

"Oh. Do you think it's likely you might want to feature Sir William's trip to Nambula on your program?" I said very quickly.

Oliver smiled and winked at me. "It's certainly an interesting angle for us, with the combination of Sir William and Nambula and the books. I take it these are the Keftian camps we're talking about?"

"That's right," I said, drooling at his knowledge of world affairs.

"Well, I certainly think we should discuss it further," said Oliver. "When things are a little more developed."

Afterwards, as Oliver and I stood on the steps of the Ginsberg building with the golden evening light falling onto us through the trees, he said, "Do you want to come for a drink?" just like in the fantasies. I couldn't believe it. I was wildly happy. Then a split second later I remembered I hadn't done my legs and wondered in a panic if there was any way of shaving them in the ladies' loo.

Even in the car it was like a dream, his hands on the wheel, his thigh in soft dark blue suit material next to my knee in its sheer black—tragically—tights. The doors of the car were cream leather and the dashboard was walnut. The instrument panel twinkled and glowed as if we were in an airplane. We didn't go to a pub, we went to the sort of restaurant where if I had asked for a razor the waiter would have brought me one on a white octagonal china plate, without question or comment.

"Oh, Lu-*ee*-gi."

As Oliver and I were being shown to our table, the actress Kate Fortune was making a noisy flappy entrance, bearing down on the maître d'hôtel, her long dark silky hair swinging everywhere.

"Luigi! *Wonderful* to see you again! Mwah, mwah."

"Actually madam," he said, "it's Roberto."

I'd seen Kate Fortune on television only the night before, in a miniseries about a female explorer who was unexpectedly keen on lip gloss. She was often to be seen in magazines, dressed as a fairy or crinoline lady with accompanying features called "Fortune at Forty." The worst was when she had appeared in one of the color supplements made over as a series of famous film stars, one from each decade since the nineteen-twenties. It seemed an unfortunate self-promotional blunder, only stressing the abyss between Kate Fortune and Marlene Dietrich or Jane Fonda. Tonight she was dressed more in Dallas mode. I had long suspected her of hair-flicking and, sure enough, as she bore down on us, cooing, "Oliver! Heavenly to see you," she took hold of the whole left-hand side of her hair and threw it back into the eyes of Roberto.

Oliver rose gallantly to his feet to receive her kisses, and now had a little circle of peach lip gloss on each cheek. I got to my feet too, but she behaved as if I was the invisible woman, so I sat down again.

"Lovely," she was saying to Oliver, fingering his lapel. "You will try and come and see me doing the Shaw? Can I leave you tickets next week? You will try and put us on your lovely program?"

"Oh, darling, I don't want to come and sit through some *dreary* play," said Oliver. "Why don't you take me out to lunch instead?"

Kate Fortune rolled her eyes, threw back her hair, and said, "Terrible man. I'll get Yvonne to call Gwen tomorrow." Then she disappeared off to her table, casting a gay, coy look behind her. I was surprised she didn't flick up her skirt and show him her pants as well.

Oliver ordered champagne. We had just begun to talk about our earliest sexual experiences, as you do, when Signor Zilli burst into the restaurant. Signor Zilli was a big cult figure at the time. He was a volatile Italian buffoon, played by a huge comedian called Julian Alman. It was very strange seeing him in the flesh, out of costume and character.

"Oliver, hi! Blast!" said Julian Alman, lumbering towards us. "Look, can you come and have a word out here, my car's been clamped. Blast!"

"What do you expect me to do about it?" said Oliver, staring at him incredulously. "Unclamp it with my teeth?"

"No. Look, the thing is, I want you to talk to the clamping men."

Julian Alman seemed completely unaware that everyone in the restaurant was looking at him.

"But if you've parked on a double yellow line you will be clamped. Is this your new Porsche?"

"Yes, the thing is, you see, I was still in it."

"You were still in it?"

"Yes. I was trying to get out."

"Julian," said Oliver. "This isn't making a lot of sense. What was preventing your getting out?"

"Well, you see, it's a bit small for me."

"So why did you buy it?"

"Well, I really wanted this model. You see, they've just been released so there's only three of them on the road, so, you see—"

"Oh, Jesus Christ, Julian, can't you see I've got more important things to do?" he said, gesturing towards me.

"No, that's fine. Go and help him. I don't mind," I said.

"Oh, great. Look, sorry, that's really good of you," said Julian, turning to try and peer out of the window. "Blast."

So Oliver went out to sort out the clampers. He returned ten minutes later looking extremely smug to tell me he'd managed to talk them out of it.

Then we were straight back onto the early sexual experiences. "So the next term I turned up to my Blake tutorial and the tutor was her . . . the same woman I had given the love bite to."

The food was tiny, which was fortunate as I had no appetite. When Oliver had finished his sexual anecdotes from Cambridge, I told him about getting caught naked with Joel in the sand dunes by a policeman, who then asked if he could join in.

"So who was Joel?"

"He was my boyfriend when I was at college."

"Where were you at college?"

"Devon."

"Thank God it wasn't Cambridge," he said, smiling indulgently. "That explains the horny accent. And what did you study in Devon?"

"Agriculture," I said, and giggled.

"Agriculture. Agriculture." He threw his head back and laughed. "You're like something out of Thomas Hardy. Did you ride horses and wear petticoats and frolic in haylofts?" He leaned over and pretended to look up my skirt hopefully.

"No, I read books about crop rotation."

"And was Joel a farmer as well—no, don't tell me, he was an army sergeant with an enormous flashing sword. No? A school-teacher? A reddleman?"

"He was a poet."

"No! This gets better and better. What did he write? 'She was only a farmer's daughter . . .'"

"He didn't write very much when I knew him. He drank a lot, smoked a lot of dope and went on about patriarchal capitalist societies. My brothers couldn't stand him."

"How many brothers have you got?"

"Four and one sister."

"Jesus, I'd better watch my step. So was Joel from Devon as well?"

"No. He came from London and he had a publisher in London. Ginsberg and Fink, actually. I thought he was wonderful."

"Wonderful? I hate Joel," Oliver said. "So what happened to the farming? Why aren't you struggling with lamb's afterbirth and moaning about hedgerows and subsidies?"

"I did work on a farm for a few months after my finals, but then I missed Joel and went up to London to live with him in a commune in Hackney. I worked in a pub and then got a job doing market research on deodorants."

"And what was Joel doing? Knitting lentil stew and smoking joss sticks?"

"Pretty much. He was out of his head most of the time."

"And you were earning the money?"

"Not very much. Anyway, after I had been there for eighteen months I went to a party with Joel at Ginsberg and Fink and Sir William Ginsberg took a shine to me."

"I bet he did, dirty old devil."

"No, it wasn't like that," I said indignantly. "He asked if I would like a temping job for the summer with the company, so I took it."

"When was that?"

"Last summer."

"So is Joel still around?"

"Well, no. It was awful really. My grandmother left me a bit of money so I put it down on a flat. And Joel said I had reverted to my capitalist patriarchal roots and that I was a worthless, superficial trollop."

"A worthless, superficial trollop," he said. "I see. And when was all this?"

"I bought the flat in January."

"Ah, thank you, Roberto."

Having finished the champagne Oliver had ordered a bottle of red wine. I was feeling light-headed already and couldn't drink any more but Oliver seemed completely sober. People in the restaurant kept looking across at him, and an elderly gentleman came over apologizing lengthily for interrupting us, said he knew this must happen all the time and asked for Oliver's autograph for his daughter who was studying at the Slade. Oliver was charming and gracious but got rather cold when the man didn't have a pen, and then extremely cold when the man started saying that the daughter would like to talk to him about working in television. The man left looking bewildered and sad. I took off one of my earrings, which was hurting.

Oliver ordered us brandies and then he spotted another celebrity, Bill Bonham, sitting across the room and went off to talk to him. Bill Bonham was an actor who usually played intelligent thugs in TV plays. He was a director as well, and was always appearing on chat shows, making it clear he didn't suffer fools gladly and swearing a lot. He was almost bald and had cut the rest of his hair very short to match. He always wore a leather jacket and jeans which fitted below his paunch and often seemed on the verge of showing bottom cleavage. I watched in admiration as Oliver chatted to him intensely. Then the two of them disappeared to the loos together.

"I don't think Bill is more famous than you."

"Well, maybe Bill isn't but Julian is," Oliver muttered, and sniffed a few times.

"No, he isn't. Have you got a cold?" I said tenderly.

"Oh, he is. It's completely unfair but he is," said Oliver morosely, sniffing again with one nostril.

"He's a different sort of famous. You're an arts commentator and Julian Alman's a film star."

Oliver was on his third brandy now. His tie was loose, and the top three buttons of his shirt were undone so I could see his dark chest hair.

"But what you do is far more worthwhile," I encouraged. "People see you as an authoritative, intelligent figure."

He wrinkled his nose fondly and squeezed my knee under the table.

The waiter was clearing up the crumbs with a minivacuum, and I realized that he had scooped up the earring I had taken off. I was too shy to say anything to him so I whispered what had happened to Oliver and he roared with laughter and masterfully sorted it all out.

When the bill came I got out my checkbook and offered to pay half, and Oliver leaned forward, tweaked my nose and got out his gold American Express card. He then performed a tour of the restaurant, saying good-bye to all the famous people, with me on his arm.

When we got to my door Oliver stopped the car, turned off the ignition, loosened his seat belt. "So. Are you going to ask me in for a coffee?" he said.

I was nervous and dry-mouthed again as I climbed the stairs with Oliver following. I was proud of my new flat. I thought it rather Parisian. But once inside he burst out laughing. I laughed along gaily trying to join in the joke but it went on too long for me to sustain. "What's so funny?" I said eventually.

"It's so small and twee," he said. *"Sweet."* He wandered into the kitchenette. "This gets better and better," he said. "You have *mottoes* on your wall." He was looking at a picture my mother had given me which said, "Dull Women Have Immaculate Houses."

"Hmmm. I see what you're trying to justify." He was in the living room now. "God. You'd drive me mad with all this mess."

"What mess?" I said, genuinely puzzled.

"Your cassettes are all out of their boxes and your books are all over the place and what's this?" he said, picking up a hair elastic that was wrapped round itself. "It looks like a ringworm."

I was crushed. I had been brought up to think that people who had a place for everything, and no buttons and pencils in dishes, were a bit odd. "I'll make the coffee," I said. I felt oddly depressed when I went into the kitchen. It was all the unaccustomed booze, which didn't seem to have affected Oliver at all. He followed me into the kitchen and, as I was plugging the cord into the kettle, came up behind me and put his arms round my waist. I forgot everything I had been thinking, turned round to face him and we kissed properly. It was ecstasy to be able to touch him, when I had so much longed to touch him for so long. After a while his hand moved to my waist, down my thigh and started to lift up my skirt. I didn't want him to undress me because I was wearing tights with a stout reinforced top, and white knickers which had been in the wash with a blue sock, so I took his hand away and put it on my breast, for want of somewhere better to put it. We kissed some more but I was slightly unbalanced and thought I might lurch over. Oliver brushed his mouth against my cheek and whispered, "Can I stay with you tonight?"

"I'm not sure." I was suddenly nervous.

He started kissing me again. "Come on, don't be silly."

Then I was worried that I seemed immature, so I said, "Mmm, I'll go and get ready," which I considered would be a very adult thing to do and had the added advantage of giving me a chance to do my legs and get rid of the blue knickers. I shot into the bathroom and grabbed off my clothes, shoving them in the airing cupboard, to be tidy. I couldn't use hair-removing cream—no time, vile smell. I thought I had a razor, frantically emptied everything out of the cupboard under the sink, couldn't find it. I heard Oliver going through to the living room and knew a full leg shave was out of the question. I ran my hand down my shin, it wasn't too bad if you ran the hand down not up. I washed. I put perfume on key areas. I brushed my teeth. I realized my powder-blue wrap was in the wash, wrapped a towel round me, put my head—only—round the door, saw him, gorgeous in my living room, smoking, in my chair.

"Ready," I said, beaming excitedly. He looked up. I dived into the bedroom, put the bedside lamp on the floor, and got into bed with the covers up to my chin because I was shy.

He came in, stumbling slightly, carrying the ashtray, put it down on my dressing table. He stubbed out his cigarette and sat down. He was turned away from me, bending to unlace his shoes, like a husband. It seemed rather unromantic not to acknowledge me, but still . . . He stood up and took off his shirt, lifting it over his back without undoing the buttons. I watched the line of muscle which ran from his arm to his waist. I was watching him bit by bit, not taking in the whole. He undid his trousers and stepped out of them, with his back to me. He folded the trousers, and put them on the chair. Then he folded the underpants, which alarmed me momentarily, placed them neatly on top of the trousers and climbed under the duvet.

I turned to face him and we kissed and it was fantastic to be naked against him. He moved down and kissed my breasts. I gasped, ecstatic. Then he rested his head on me and I stroked his hair and he lay quite still on top of me with his arms on either side.

After a few moments I became puzzled as to what was going on. I shifted position slightly and he lifted his head and moved up to my mouth and started kissing me again. His breathing was very heavy. He heaved himself over, easing my legs apart with his knee, kneeling between my thighs. He put his hand down and then he slipped himself inside me, straight in. I was longing for him so much, beside myself, arching my back, crying out, writhing with pleasure. But slowly, in the midst of the excitement I began to realize that Oliver was not moving at all. He was resting his weight on my body and his head in my neck, completely motionless. Gradually I stopped moving so that I was lying quite still too. And then he began to snore.

Once I had got over the shock, I laughed. I thought of the people downstairs listening. "Oh, oh, oh, oh, HGNUURGH, oh oh, HGNUUURGH. Oh." I had to wake him to move after a while. I thought I was going to be asphyxiated. His mood was very black now, his brow furrowed. He got up and went into the bathroom and I heard him go into the living room. After a while he came back in and started getting dressed.

"What are you doing?" I said.

"I'm going home. I've got an early start tomorrow."

A set of kitchen knives fell down through me from my throat.

"Don't even *think* about it," I said. "Get back in the bed."

"But—"

"But nothing. First, you just don't *do* that, second, you are beyond drunk and if you go anywhere near your car I shall ring the police, third, you have just fallen asleep on top of me at the start of what was meant to be a first night of passion. And you snored. Now get back in this bed."

This was before Oliver had broken my spirit and turned my sexual confidence into a wizened little pea. His mouth tightened. He was staring at me oddly, then he started nodding, as if agreeing with one of his own thoughts. He moved the duvet and looked at me. Then he undressed again to reveal, astonishingly, a new erection, and climbed back onto the bed beside me. And when it was over I was full of pride and joy because I, Rosie Richardson, had made Oliver Marchant come.

Some time later, when he had fallen asleep, I lay awake looking at him, with his long dark eyelashes resting against his cheeks like two furry caterpillars. I was happy now, all misgivings pushed to the back of my mind. I couldn't believe that Oliver Marchant was actually in my bed. I knew instinctively that he was one of those men who was disproportionately protective about their sleep, but still I risked a little kiss on the cheek and snuggled up to him affectionately.

"Oh, for God's sake, you're behaving like a five-year-old," he said, and turned his back on me.

The lure of the bastard—I was a sucker for it. "Changeable women are more endurable than monotonous ones," I read somewhere. "They are sometimes murdered but seldom deserted"—exactly the appeal of the male bastard. You know they'll never tie you down or silt you up. It's the excitement and absorption of pursuit: pitting yourself against their harsh nature, trying to turn it around. Even when I discovered what his nature really was I still thought I could transform Oliver. I thought he just needed a bit of love and care and he'd soon get the hang of things. I thought I could love him out of his character.

My friend Rhoda, who was older than me and American, said that I was suffering from a dangerous addiction and shouldn't touch someone like Oliver with a barge pole.

"OK, so long as he can touch me with his barge pole," I said giddily.

Later she said that Africa was just another version of my masochistic bastard complex and I should stay in England, learn to love myself and go out with bores. But I said she'd been reading too many American self-help books, and should get a few drinks down her and lighten up.

Five

*T*he start of an affair can be a dodgy time for everyone: it's like learning to water-ski—once you get up it's fine but there's far more chance of falling over and getting wet and cross than getting up. Picture the scene, three days after that night with Oliver. No phone call. Zilch. But being young and in awe of him, I failed to think the sensible thing, which was "What a rude man." I wasn't *quite* stupid enough to sit at home in the evenings and do psychopath eyes at the phone. But it would have been acting equally neurotically to leave the answerphone off. So I had the crisis of coming back to no message when I got home at the end of the evening. Or coming back to three messages, and finding two of them were from Rhoda, and the other was from Hermione, asking why, in heaven's name, I hadn't told her that Cassandra had left a message that afternoon saying Perpetua wasn't coming to dinner.

Finally on day four in the office, his call came, in a manner of speaking.

It was an irritatingly kindly female voice.

"He*llo,* is that Rosie Richardson?"

"Yes."

"Hel-*lo,* Rosie. This is Oliver Marchant's assistant, Gwen."

His *assistant?* Why his assistant? Within seconds I was into an Oliver-in-hospital fantasy.

"Oliver was wondering if you were free tonight."

"Yes." There was a delicious, tempting rush in my stomach.

"Good. He was wondering if you would like to come to the Broadcasting Society Awards at the Grosvenor House tonight."

"Yes, that would be—"

"Super. Black tie six-thirty for seven. Oliver will pick you up at six-thirty. Could you let me have your address, Rosie?"

This style of romantic follow-up to a sexual encounter is the kind of thing crushes allow you to put up with, which is why they are monstrous afflictions to be fled from like vengeful beasts.

We were seated at a round table in a vast hotel ballroom. Above us, four gigantic chandeliers twinkled down on the mass of bare shoulders, sequins and cummerbunds, the TV lights, the giant screens, and the production staff scurrying round holding yellow scripts, looking self-important, verging on hysterical. The proceedings had not yet begun. Everything was already running late. On-stage a troupe of sparkling dancers were practicing, rushing at the audience doing starburst jumps, then turning and high-kicking off in the opposite direction, heads still turned towards us over their shoulders with air-hostess smiles.

On my right was Vernon Briggs, a portly man with a broad Yorkshire accent. He was an executive at Channel Four, the company televising the awards ceremony. On my left was Corinna Borghese, Oliver's co-presenter on *Soft Focus*. Corinna's thin dark-red lips were pressed together with visible high pressure. Her pale face under its sunglasses and spiky hennaed crop was trembling like the steel ropes of a suspension bridge. *Soft Focus* had been nominated for an award and Corinna, to Vernon's disgust, was insisting she go up and collect it with Oliver.

"The point is, I have as much creative input as he does. I ought to have a producer credit anyway, but the point is if he goes up there on his own for it then it's like Oliver Marchant is the face of *Soft Focus,* right? And I simply don't think that's representative."

"Listen, love, shall I tell you what you do in your job? You sit on your little arse in front of the autocue and you read out what it says." Vernon was leaning towards her with his enormous red face and bulging eyes, wagging a finger. "Reading out loud, that's what you do. Like in school. Oliver is the editor of the program."

"Oliver has a penis is what you mean, right, and I will not be addressed as love," she managed to get out from between the clamped lips.

I was having a lot of trouble keeping my dress under the table. It was part of a converted bridesmaid's dress, silk with a springy, sticky-outy skirt. Once, the dress had been long and peach and worthy of Kate Fortune, but I had had it dyed and altered so that now it was short and black. I had suffered a panic attack while getting dressed. When the doorbell rang I was standing on the bed, trying to see myself full-length in the mirror, wearing a black lycra miniskirt over a swimsuit. At that precise moment, and at that precise moment only, the bridesmaid's dress seemed a good idea. I realized later that one must never, ever go anywhere looking even faintly reminiscent of a shepherdess, even a shepherdess who has just been in a coal hole. The skirt misbehaved continually, springing about in an unmanageable manner. It was now protruding on either side of me, and interfering with the knees not only of Corinna Borghese but also Vernon Briggs, who had now turned his back on both of us.

"Sorry about this," I whispered conspiratorially to Corinna. "I wish I hadn't worn this stupid frock. I tried on about eight things before I came out and panicked. Do you do that?"

"Actually no," said Corinna. "I try to keep my clothes simple."

Dinsdale, who was sitting across the table, gave me a sympathetic look and offered me a cigarette, which I took, though I did not usually smoke.

"Please do not smoke next to me," said Corinna.

The evening had not started well. Oliver had not arrived to meet me. Instead he had sent a driver in a hat, who told me that Oliver was running late in the studio and would meet me at the Grosvenor House. I had twenty minutes of horror in the celebrity-stuffed foyer. People were staring at me, but I knew it was with pity because of the insane dress. It was Dinsdale who rescued me again.

When he caught hold of my arm I had been to the ladies' twice, stared at the seating plan for eight minutes, pretending it took that long to find "Oliver Marchant and Guest." Only then did it occur to me that Oliver must have known he needed a date for this occasion weeks ago. Could it be that I was a last-minute fill-in? Had some other girl dropped out? Some beautiful, accomplished critic perhaps, an authority on the death of Essentialism in the Mittel-European novel, with a bottom like two snooker balls.

An old stand-up comic, Jimmy Horsham, had started talking to me and wouldn't go away. The fact that he had a room in the Grosvenor House for the night had already come up several times. When Dinsdale appeared he slunk off sheepishly.

"My darling, my darling. Whatever are you doing with that filthy old bore? Whatever can he be thinking of? Preposterous idea. Come along, come along. Let's go and nibble at the canapés. I'm trying to avoid Barry," he whispered confidentially. Barry Rhys was another theatrical legend, and Dinsdale's best friend. "He's got that absolute sea elephant of a wife with him. Who are you here with? Is it that dirty old devil Ginsberg?"

"No. I'm with Oliver Marchant," I said, happily.

"But wherever is he, my darling? Why has he left you here to be prrrrryed on?" Dinsdale stared at me ferociously, his brows almost covering his eyes in consternation.

"He's late in the studio."

"No, my darling. No no no. He is over there, look," said Dinsdale, concern oozing from every facial feature.

I felt a stab of hurt. There was Oliver, dark-suited and tieless, sharing a joke with Corinna Borghese—well, telling a joke more like. He was leaning over her, waving a hand expressively. Corinna was staring straight ahead, with an indulgent half-smile playing on her lips. Dinsdale caught hold of my hand and started pulling me along towards them.

"There he is, my darling. Come along. We'll soon have you sorted out." I felt like a child whose parent hadn't turned up at school to pick her up.

Oliver looked startled for a second when he saw me. "Rosie. Hi, how are you? I was looking for you." He smiled, and bent to kiss me. The scent of him brought heady thoughts of the night of passion, but Oliver gave no sign that he remembered. "Do you know Corinna Borghese?" he said.

"Nice to meet you," I said. I was getting the hang of Famous Club introductions now.

"Thank you," said Corinna.

There was an uncomfortable pause.

"So how are you?" said Oliver.

"I'm fine, how are you?"

"Fine."

That was about the level of it.

An hour later everyone was seated for dinner and I was praying Oliver wouldn't look across at me and see that I was failing to talk to anyone. He looked across at me, and saw that I was failing to talk to anyone. I tried to smile but it was a most unnatural smile. It felt like the smile of a devil child, with bits of bread roll in the teeth and yellow eyes.

"You OK?" he mouthed. I nodded gaily, and decided I'd better have another go with Corinna.

"Well, this looks nice," I said brightly, looking at the menu. It offered Gravlax, Chicken in Its White Wine and Cream Sauce with Its Ravioli, or Fresh Tuna Steak with Pommes Parmentière, followed by White Chocolate Mousse in Its Sugar Cage.

"Pommes Parmentière—I suppose that means instant mashed potato," I said.

"This is utterly ridiculous," said Corinna.

I thought she meant having to sit next to me.

"A vegetarian cannot eat this meal. Where is the waiter?"

"Do you not eat fish?" I said. "There's tuna."

"Tuna?" she said with venom, looking at me incredulously. "You do *know* what happens when they catch tuna, don't you? You've heard about the dolphins?"

Our conversation did not improve. It was a relief when, as the last of the Sugar Cages were being cleared away, the big TV lights snapped on. The assembled celebrities rustled, swelled and settled themselves like a flock of pigeons. I was thrilled. I had watched these occasions so often at home on the television, and now I was here. There were trumpets, there was a shouty announcement, more trumpets, and a short fat floor manager, wearing an earpiece and a lot of electrical equipment strapped to his bottom, started clapping his hands bossily in the air while bending his chin onto his chest and talking into a microphone. Everyone applauded obediently. Noel Edmonds strode onto the platform and stood behind a lectern, motioning us to stop clapping.

Meanwhile a thin dark young man with glasses had come up to Corinna.

"Hi. How are you?" he said in a low, confidential voice, kissing her, his eyes darting around the room.

". . . is someone who has been delighting audiences on both sides of the Atlantic for many years . . ." went Noel Edmonds.

"*Dire,* isn't it? Have you spoken to Michael? Howard's over there. Jonathan's going to get it. Definitely. Just going to talk to Jean-Paul about his intro."

"I'll come with you. I'm not staying here if he's going to go up and get it. Blatantly sexist," said Corinna, and stood up and left.

The applause was just beginning to die down after the director's acceptance speech for the Best Drama.

"Great. Fucking great," muttered Bill Bonham. "He thanks the writers, he thanks the lighting cameraman, he thanks his fucking wife, and then, only then, he thinks of mentioning me. Great. I only played the fucking lead. I mean, great. Thanks."

The Lord taketh away even as he giveth. Our table of resentment seethed and sizzled with those blessed, as if by a laying on of hands, with riches and fame, yet blighted by bitterness at those who got a bigger share.

Onstage, Vicky Spankie, a young RSC actress, was accepting her Best Actress Award. She was slight, extremely pretty, with dark hair cut in a bob, and was wearing jeans and a leather jacket. She had recently been all over the tabloids after her marriage to a rain forest Indian.

"You give, and you give, and you give, and you give, and all the time this terrible fear is eating away at you, and you want to shout, 'Look, I am human. I am afraid,'" she was explaining.

"Oh, puh-lease," said Corinna, who had decided to come back, and had maneuvered herself into the seat next to Oliver.

Vicky Spankie was still going on.

"I wonder if something really kind of spiritual could happen here? Where we could all think for a moment and send some kind of waves of love and sanity out to the Brazilian government, who are allowing, every single day, thousands of acres of forest to be cut."

On the big screen above her, which showed the live TV output, the shot cut to the husband, Rani, back at the table looking bewildered. Instead of tribal robes now, he was wearing black tie, but he still had the disk in his bottom lip. In the interview I'd read, the reporter had asked Vicky if Rani took the disk out at night, which had not gone down at all well.

"Come on up, Rani, this is for you too," she was saying. The bemused Rani was being pushed towards the stage, helped up the steps by a young lovely in a glittery sheath. Then everyone was getting to their feet, giving Rani a standing ovation.

Vernon Briggs had grabbed the fat floor manager's microphone and was talking into it in a low furious voice. "Get her to shut up," he was saying. "Marcus, get the Indian *off* the stage and get her to shut up *now*. Get the stupid tart to shut *up*. We are one hour and forty minutes over, Marcus. Get the Indian *off* the stage now."

Just then the cameraman came to our table and started to focus on Oliver, which meant that Best Arts Program was coming up. Corinna leaned towards him into the shot. For a fleeting second, I saw him look furious, then he started talking to Corinna in a low voice. Corinna was biting one side of her bottom lip and kept looking up at the camera.

The image on the big screen cut to the Best Arts Program logo. Vicky Spankie's microphone was cut, and a girl holding a script hurried over to her, ushering her and Rani apologetically off the stage. Vicky put her head in the air, and swept towards the exit, with Rani following her, clutching the award and beaming, as far as it was possible with the disk in his lip. As she passed our table, he caught her arm. "Oh, sod off, you stupid fuckbrain," I heard her mutter under her breath.

Oliver and Corinna were tense. The last of the clips from the four nominations was running. Kevin Garside, a folk singer with a skinhead cut, was performing miners' protest songs. They were his own compositions performed to his own tambourine accompaniment. He was being watched by a group of Guatemalan peasants in a hut, wearing expressions of polite embarrassment.

The red light came on from the camera opposite Oliver. Onstage, Ian McKellen was opening the envelope. The screen was divided in quarters. In one of them was Oliver with a relaxed smile, and Corinna still biting her lip.

"And the winner of Best Arts Program is Sof—"

On the screen I saw Corinna breaking into a smile, and just beginning to rise from her seat.

"—Sofama Kuwayo for *The Dispossessed, a Lament.*"

Oliver's smile stayed till the light behind the camera clicked off.

Onstage, Sofama Kuwayo had taken his award and was finishing his speech: ". . . in your Audis, your Mercs, your BMWs, spare a thought for those, many of them younger than your own kids, without homes to go to. It's *their* words, *their* experience, the poetry of *their* lives which created that program. This award is for them."

"Well, you made a prat of yourself there, Corinna, didn't you?" said Oliver.

About half an hour later we were making our way to Pizza on the Piazza in a little group made up of a studiedly modest Bill Bonham, Corinna and someone called Rats, who was apparently the bass player in the group EX Gap, a still-tearful Vicky Spankie, minus Rani, a comedian called Hughie Harrington-Ellis, and lastly Oliver, with his arm around me.

"Oy, Hughie," a group of boys yelled from a traffic island, "abso-bloody-lootely." This was one of Hughie's many catch phrases. "Absobloodylutely," went the boys. Hughie gave them a gritted-teeth smile and a wave.

"This must happen to you all the time," I said.

"Oh, no," said Hughie dryly. "First time it's ever happened to me."

In the restaurant everyone turned to stare. All the tables were full, but the management somehow managed to move some kids and make them split up and share on three other tables. Within minutes we were all sitting together at their table with the waiters flapping around us.

"Oh, God, this is so embarrassing. It must happen to you all the time. You don't mind, mate, do you?" said a young boy, shoving a bit of paper under Hughie's nose.

"Of course I don't," said Hughie, adding under his breath, "you little tit."

Vicky was signing a photograph, which she just happened to have in her handbag, for the waiter.

A girl came up to Bill Bonham. "I'm sorry, would you mind? This must happen to you all the time."

I was praying for someone to come and ask Oliver, because I could feel him descending into gloom again. Then, thank God, another pair of girls appeared and asked Oliver to sign their menu. "Sorry, you'll have to get used to this," said Oliver smiling smugly.

There was a commotion at the door and Terence Twinkle burst in. "Hi, everyone," he shouted across to our table. "God, it's a nightmare out there. Why can't anyone leave me alone?" He was wearing a floor-length white mink coat.

Six

𝓘t was twelve-thirty when we turned the jeep into the gates of the compound. Malcolm's Land Cruiser was already there, plastered in stickers. A small procession was making its way towards the latrine unit. The procession was headed by Betty, dressed in pink, who was gesturing and laughing beneficently as if hosting a royal visit. Our team had all changed into their best clothes—ludicrously garish pantomime outfits: dresses, shirts and harem pants with brightly colored spots and stripes, run up by the tailors in the camp. Malcolm was wearing a yellow T-shirt and a hat, which looked as though it had something stupid written on it. And next to him, looking away from Betty and across to the camp, was the new doctor, who was of medium height and dressed in dull colors.

At the sound of our vehicle the whole procession slowly turned round and stared accusingly. Sian appeared from the cabana as we climbed out. "I told them there was probably a bit of a crisis down at the hospital," she said conspiratorially. "I think they're all fine only, well, Betty . . ."

There then followed a rather awkward moment as Henry, Sian and I walked across to the latrine procession, with no one quite knowing what to do except smile fixedly. Fortunately, Henry's breeding carried us through. "Malcolm, dear boy!" he started bellowing as we approached. "Great to see you! Hi! You must be the new doctor, great to see you, great! Great to have some more old buggers around the place to dilute the totty."

By this time we had reached the group, but Henry was still on autowitter. "Sorry not to be here to give you the old welcoming committee—bit of an old blood bag crisis down the black hole of Calcutta."

The new doctor looked somewhat taken aback. He seemed pleasant, but dull. Pity.

"Hi," he said mildly. "Robert O'Rourke." His voice was unusually deep and sounded as though it was coming from a long way away.

"Henry Montague, marvelous," Henry was bellowing, meanwhile shaking hands energetically. "Great to have you on board. And this is our great white memsahib—Rosie," said Henry. "I know she looks like a sex object but she's really very strict."

"Strict but fair, I hope," said O'Rourke.

"You mustn't mind Henry," said Sian. "It's his upbringing."

The ice was broken now. For all his absurdity, Henry understood what good manners really mean.

"Nice to have you here," I said. "Malcolm, nice to see you."

Malcolm did his silly teeth-together beam, and waved both hands on either side of his head.

"Have you and Dr. O'Rourke had something to drink?" I asked.

"Well, no, we rather thought Doctor might like to have a good nosey round," Betty interrupted. "After all, this is going to be home sweet home for our new friend for quite some time." She lowered her voice. "Actually, Malcolm, when you have a moment I really would like to have a little chinwag."

The doctor was looking at Betty intently. There was something rather purposeful about him.

He looked at me and gestured towards the camp. "This is a beautiful place." Bewdaful. I couldn't place his accent.

"Very beautiful," I said. Then I looked down and saw his white socks. Ugh.

O'Rourke walked with a slight limp. As Linda took him off to his hut, I tried to look at his leg discreetly without him seeing. Perhaps it was a wooden one. Apart from his medical bag, he seemed to have just one canvas holdall, like an overnight bag. It seemed like traveling light taken to ridiculous extremes considering he was here for two years. I hoped he wasn't going to start wanting to borrow everyone else's shampoo.

The rest of the team were looking so clean and smart that I thought I'd better sort myself out. I went to my hut and glanced in the little mirror hanging above my desk, which is something I rarely did. I remember it because that was the moment when I saw, apart from my red nose and mad hair, the first line on my face, just beginning, heading from the edge of my nose down to the corner of my mouth. It must have been the light at that time of day which caught it. It gave me a shock. I always thought that aging should happen the other way round. Life would be so much more optimistic if you began it as a wrinkly old crone and became younger, more vibrant and beautiful as the years rolled by, secure in the knowledge that at the end of your life someone would be happy to play with you, change your nappy and push you round in a pram till you turned back into an egg. Trying to push unpleasant existential thoughts to the back of my mind, I stepped out into the hot light and headed for the cabana.

The lunch was over and there was a scene of intense absorption, furious tearing of envelopes, silent, urgent reading. It was hard to overestimate the importance of the mail in Safila, the arrival of a letter, or its nonappearance, could bring about massive mood swings. I looked around and saw that neither Betty nor Malcolm was there. She was probably lecturing him about the Teeth of the Wind. I had better make sure she didn't put him off. With some self-control, I ignored the small pile of mail, including a parcel which was for me, and stepped outside.

Betty looked up guiltily as I approached. "I know Rosie will say I'm a silly old moo," she said, "but, Malcolm, I really do think it is beholden on us to respond."

Something peculiar happened to Betty's vowels when she was showing off. Be*heow*lden, res*pund*.

Malcolm already looked desperate to get away from Betty's re-*spunses*. He required delicate handling. He was efficient, so long as everything was logged and predictable: which simply wasn't the way things worked here. He also had the sort of mind which loved to walk in very slow circles around things, looking at them without getting too close.

"Has Betty explained to you about the rumors?" I asked him.

"Yes, yes. It's, er, I have heard something of this in Sidra. It's an interesting development. I think we must wait and see, er, see what develops." Sidra was the nearest town, where there was a UN office, and telephones that worked on odd occasions.

"Well, the thing is if it does develop, it'll happen so fast we won't be able to deal with it. We're short on stocks anyway. You know the UN have told us we can't have the delivery? Do you know when this ship's going to arrive?"

"I, er, well, actually, I was just hoping to get back to Sidra quickly to talk about that sort of area of things and other, er, related matters. So I *think,* if it's all right with you here, and there are no other matters to be gone over then I will make a hasty departure, as there is a great deal, as I say, to be gone into in Sidra."

I decided I had better tell him what I knew, but it did all sound a bit thin. As far as I was concerned the strongest piece of evidence was that Muhammad believed there was a problem. But when I tried to convey this to Malcolm, it sounded suspect, almost as if I was in love with Muhammad Mahmoud and expecting twins by him.

I made Malcolm promise to radio back to me about the food, and alert head office in London. He said he would discuss the matter with the UN High Commission for Refugees, who gave out the food. He didn't sound particularly enamored of the idea. I was not convinced that he'd put the whole force of his personality, such as it was, behind it.

"Ah," said Malcolm, interrupting me, looking over my shoulder. "Don't suppose I could have my socks back before I go, could I?"

I turned round to see O'Rourke, who looked surprised and then said, "Sure," and bent down to take off his shoes and socks. Both his feet were real. He straightened up and looked at me, rolling the socks and handing them to Malcolm. "I knew I'd forgotten to bring something," he said. "Guess I'll have to, er, weave some." He had an unexpected smile which came and went very quickly.

I followed Malcolm to the gate to wave him off, feeling that I'd got it wrong. Malcolm had refugee settlements on every border in the country to oversee. I hadn't convinced him to do much about us. I walked a little way along the track and stood where I could see his vehicle making its way across the plain, raising a plume of dust behind it. The sun was high now. I watched for a long time, till the engine noise died away, till it became a tiny speck and disappeared and the only sound was the cicadas. I felt a big burst of loneliness. Sometimes there were moments like this when the insulation of our little society crumbled away, and I remembered we were just camping in the wilderness. We were like one of those small out-crops of huts you spotted from the airplane on the way from England, surrounded by a thousand miles of desert on every side. Doing or getting anything was blocked by a swathe of distance and time. It took three hours even to get to Sidra.

Back in the cabana I was distracted by my mail. There was a new pair of trainers from my mum in the parcel: black ones, like little boots. I had been waiting for two months for them to come. Also there were new cotton knickers, five pairs in black. There were five letters, three of them from Mum, two from friends in London with handwriting I recognized.

I turned to the first one to cheer me up. I adored my mum's letters. This one began, as usual, *"I was just having a cup of tea and a coffee ring and I thought, I wonder how Rosie's doing? . . ."* and then there was a commotion outside, coming from the direction of the main gate.

I was at the far end of the cabana, so by the time I'd arrived at the gate the others had formed such a tight-knit circle it was impossi-ble to see what they were looking at. Then the group broke up and I saw O'Rourke gesturing everyone away with great politeness, as if trying to move a party of guests through from drinks to dinner. Slumped against the wall of Betty's hut were a Keftian family, ema-ciated, filthy and exhausted. A woman lay on the ground with the stick limbs, tufted hair and unseeing expression of the badly malnourished. Beside her, the father of the family was holding a child in his arms. It was only when I got closer that I realized that the child was dead.

I froze completely. Back in the old days, when we lived with this all the time, we had found a way of dealing with it, a robust, worka-day distancing which enabled us to do what had to be done. But this had caught me with my defenses down. I tried to remind my-self how to be: don't think about the implications, how they feel, what's going to happen, just decide what needs to be done, then do it, one thing at a time. I went into the cabana, found rehydration salts, high-energy biscuits. The mother needed a drip, and O'Rourke and Betty organized that while Henry and I brought the vehicles round. We drove down to the hospital in convoy with Henry and me following in the third vehicle with the father and the dead child. The father was crying. There was something particularly har-rowing about that simple response—your family is starving, your child is dead and so you cry.

It didn't take long to find people who knew the family because the camp had been laid out like a map of Kefti so that all the people from the same villages could stay together. I desperately wanted to talk to the father to find out why they had come. Was it the locusts? How many more were following? I knew I had to leave it be, till the burial was over. I decided to go back to the compound to see if I could get Malcolm on the radio in Sidra.

I couldn't get a connection. I was shouting, "Safila to SUSTAIN Sidra, Safila to SUSTAIN Sidra, Safila to SUSTAIN Sidra," but all there was was crackle. Nothing. No contact. I started saying Safila to Sidra again, then put my head on my arms and tried not to cry. I heard the sound of a vehicle drawing up and tried to pull myself together. This was ridiculous. I was going to be no use to anyone if I flopped around like this. I had to toughen up. The door opened. It was Debbie.

"Have you got the key for the vaccine fridge?" she said, then saw my face and hurried over to me. "Are you all right?"

"Yes, I'm fine. It's just . . . it reminds me of—"

"I know," she said.

"Are *you* all right?"

"Yeah . . . but . . . Well. *You* know, don't you?"

I had to get a message to Malcolm, tell him what had happened, before he left Sidra. It was only one family, but this hadn't happened for so long, they were in such a bad state, there were all these rumors: he had to know about it before he went back to the capital. I climbed into the jeep to drive to Safila village. There was an office there with a radio—the local branch of the Nambulan Commission of Refugees. COR was one of the plethora of acronyms which filled our talk: COR, UNHCR, RESOK, NGO. We were supposed to report all new arrivals to COR. Possibly their radio would be working so I could get a message to Malcolm. I climbed into the jeep and drove along the track to the village. The heat had gone out of the day now, the sun was starting to soften.

The COR office was surrounded by a high rush fence and a scruffy yard. A pig was snuffling around in a pile of rubbish in the corner. A girl with a cloudy eye was sitting on a low bed, picking at her foot, Hassan's girl. She was wearing a pair of my earrings. She jumped up, beaming as I arrived, eyeing the earrings I was wearing and showed me into the office.

"Hassan maquis," she said. Hassan is not here.

Hassan was the COR officer. I sat down and tried Sidra on his radio. There was the same empty crackle. The girl reached over and fingered my earring. I shook my head and pointed to the ones I had given her last time. She smiled sheepishly. I fiddled with the dial to try and get El Daman, the capital. There was nothing there. I kept trying. Nothing.

When I left the office it was six o'clock and already dark. The darkness came swiftly out there, once the sun had set. The lights of the vehicle picked up crazily shaped plants sticking out of the sand dunes. I passed the others coming back from the camp just before I reached the hill and stopped opposite them leaving the engine running. Henry was at the wheel with Sian, Debbie, Linda and Betty squeezed inside.

"What's happening?" I said to Henry.

"All doing fine, old girl."

"Have any of the arrivals said anything about locusts?" I said.

"Not as far as I know. Did you get through to Sidra?"

"No. Nothing."

"Bloody hell. Bad luck. See you up there, old thing."

"We'll have supper waiting for you," said Betty. "Kamal's doing us a chicken."

The camp felt very different at night, foreign and inaccessible. The huts were closed up. Here and there, I could see a candle through the darkness but almost everyone was already asleep. There was nothing to do without the sun. I pulled up at the hospital, which was an arc of white canvas supported on a metal frame. I went in through the flap and stood just inside, watching. Halfway down the row of low wooden beds was one with a drip set up above it. O'Rourke was adjusting the bag on the end of a length of tube.

The mother was asleep, breathing noisily and unevenly. O'Rourke signaled a cautious thumbs-up at her and gestured me back towards the door. We walked together without speaking and then stepped outside. He needed a shave.

"You OK?" he said, first of all, putting his hand on my shoulder. I obviously hadn't pulled myself together as much as I thought.

"Yeah, I'm fine," I whispered back. "How are they? What did they say?"

He said the family were seventy-five percent malnourished, which was pretty bad. The child had died of a diarrheal disease, but it wasn't cholera.

"And the father? Where's he? He was all right, wasn't he?"

"He'll be all right."

"Did you talk to him?"

"I didn't have the chance."

"I'll go and find him, then."

"Give me two minutes. I'll come along."

I waited for him and we set off towards Muhammad's shelter. Away from the lamps of the hospital you could see almost nothing. We walked in silence. O'Rourke seemed relaxed here. He was going to be fine. Muhammad greeted us, waiting for us at his door. He led us to where the family were staying. We stood a little distance away while he went to the hut. A candle was burning outside. The father came stooping out adjusting his robes; he looked weaker than he had that morning. He and Muhammad talked in low voices. Muhammad called us over and the father took O'Rourke by the hand, shaking it and talking emotionally. Then he shook my hand too, and other members of the family followed and joined in. It was a bit like being a celebrity in the West.

Finally we all went inside. There was one lamp, made out of a dried milk can. A woman was making coffee over some embers. O'Rourke and I sat on the bed. Muhammad sat opposite and began to question the father. Three sleepy toddlers were sitting in a line on the floor. They didn't move or make a sound for forty minutes. I couldn't imagine kids doing that in England. I once asked Muhammad why the children were so well behaved here. He said if they made a noise in the home they got hit with a stick.

The man spoke rapidly, in short bursts, his eyes focused on the middle distance. Every now and then he paused and made a little humming noise in his throat.

"He is saying that he left his village because his child was sick. The rest of the people have no food but they are waiting for the harvest. Only he has seen that the locusts are hatching around the riverbed and so he is afraid that these locusts will come before the harvest."

"And what about the other villagers?"

"They are afraid but they are making ready to protect the harvest with sticks and with fire."

"Don't they have any pesticides at all?" I asked.

"No. None."

On the way back, O'Rourke said, "I think they've been sent here to raise the alarm, and got sicker than they thought on the way. I don't have the impression he needed to come."

"Not yet, anyway," I said.

"You may be right," said Muhammad.

When we got back to the Toyota, a small crowd had gathered. Word had evidently spread about the arrivals. There were two officials of RESOK, the Keftian relief association, wanting to talk to me. They spoke to Muhammad first.

"They want to know what it means for them," he said.

"Of course."

"They do not want their brothers to be turned away, but there is not enough food. They want to know when the ship is coming."

I wanted to know when the ship was coming too. This was not the time to be running low on supplies.

"Could you say that I see things very much as they do and will do what I can? There is no need to be afraid."

At this O'Rourke let out a disapproving tsking noise, which surprised me.

There was more point-making from the RESOK guys. The mood was restless and uncomfortable.

"I don't think this is the moment for a discussion group," I said quietly to Muhammad. He nodded and said something to the group and they let us go. As we started up the hill I caught sight of Liben Alye standing at the side of the road, still holding Hazawi, who was sleeping now. He held up his hand and waved.

"Oooh, I haven't had pâté for eighteen months and then it was more of a terrine, which I'm not so keen on. It's the lumps of fat I can take or leave," Betty was gushing.

The pâté was a present from O'Rourke. It turned out that he had brought a large crate of goodies as well as his one bag. The fridge was now full of exotic cheeses and chocolates from America. There was Earl Grey tea on the shelf, good olive oil, and several bottles of wine. He'd done pretty well to get those past Customs. O'Rourke was clearly a success. It was as if a rooster had arrived in a farmyard sending everyone clucking and flapping into the air. Henry seemed rather thrown. He was used to being the only man round the table.

After about half an hour of food talk O'Rourke was getting fidgety.

"What's our situation now in terms of supplies?" He said it quietly, just to me, but everyone turned to listen.

"Not good," I said. "We missed the delivery before the June rains because the ship from France didn't come in time. By the time it arrived the trucks couldn't get through to us."

"That's because of the mud, huh?"

"And the rivers," said Debbie. "The water just comes rushing down in a torrent. You can't get through it."

"So what did you do?"

"We had to go on half rations for August," I said. "The trucks got through at the start of September but the UN had sent some of our consignment to the South so we only got two months' rations instead of five."

"So where does that leave you now?"

"We should have had another delivery at the beginning of October but the ship is late again. I've been cutting down the rations so we've got enough for a few weeks, maybe four or five, but not if we start getting new arrivals."

"And the rations come from UNHCR?"

"Yes."

"Can't you get emergency food from SUSTAIN?" said O'Rourke.

I smiled wryly. O'Rourke was probably used to the big U.S. agencies who were able to throw money at a crisis.

"SUSTAIN are supposed to supply staff here, not food. They're good. They'll help if they can but they're just one little agency with no money."

There was silence.

"It'll probably be all right," I said. "The ship'll come soon."

"You reckon?" said O'Rourke. Then he said, "Shall we have some cheese?" and, realizing the irony, he smiled. "Well, that's the starving taken care of. Pass the Brie, will you?"

"Quite so, quite so," said Henry. "Let them eat Brie."

After a while O'Rourke got up and went to bed and Linda followed soon after. There were lots of meaningful looks exchanged.

But they were not particularly satisfying as meaningful looks go because nobody quite knew what they meant.

"Anyone want any more cheese while it's still here?" said Henry, handing it round, leaning his arm across Sian's shoulder.

"Rosie, do you remember Monica Hutchinson—used to run Dessie in 'seventy-three?" said Betty.

Well, obviously I didn't since I had only just entered my teens at the time.

"It's funny, I don't know why, I was thinking about her today."

"Oh, really?"

"Yes. She was a lovely woman."

Silence, everyone continued to pick at the cheese.

"Lovely—but just a bit too easygoing. Oooh, they had terrible trouble in Dessie. The staff used to indulge in relationships, which I've always felt is most unwise in a small community, I'm sure you agree. Anyway, Monica just used to turn a blind eye to it, you know, people will be people. But they ended up in a most terrible situation with fights and dreadful scenes and in the end two of the nurses had to be sent home. But the worst of it was, they had complaints from the Ministry of Information office who'd seen it Going On."

"Seen what going on?" I said.

"Well, you know," said Betty.

More silent eating. I daren't look at anyone.

"I must say, Betty, I didn't realize ministers of information extended their line of duty to old Vera Voyeurism," Henry remarked.

A laugh spurted out of Debbie which she turned into an only quite convincing cough/sneeze hybrid.

"She was a super girl was Monica." As if she hadn't heard, Betty went on trying to convince us this wasn't a parable. "Married Colin Seagrove who was CMO at Wadkowli in 'seventy-seven."

I wanted to stay talking with everyone. It was reassuring, all the normal stupid chat, but they all started getting up and going to bed so I went and sat on the edge of the hill for quite a long time, thinking. Debbie came over after she'd had her shower and we chatted for a bit about the arrivals, and then did a bit of nodding and winking in the direction of Linda's hut. When I got into my hut I'd forgotten to tuck the net in round the bed and there was a spider on the sheet, a brown one with thick legs covered in lumps. I flattened it with a copy of *Newsweek* and chucked it outside. I checked the bed with the hurricane lamp but it still wasn't nice getting in. I couldn't sleep because I kept seeing the family slumped against Betty's hut. The dogs were barking. Sometimes they used to bark all night, those bloody dogs. I wondered if Linda really was in bed with O'Rourke. I started to feel lonely, then reminded myself that there are worse things than being on your own.

Seven

g was crying in my bed beside him, but I think he didn't know. A thin wet line was trickling across my face into my ear. It was Saturday night, two months since I had first slept with Oliver. I got out of bed, and crept towards the door, trying to avoid the floorboard that creaked. I stretched out my hand for my dressing gown and as I reached across I knocked a glass off the dressing table next to it.

"What the fuck are you doing?"

I froze, said nothing.

"What time is it?"

"I don't know. It's dark," I whispered.

Oliver picked his watch up off the bedside table and threw it down. "Jesus Christ, it's five o'clock in the morning. I've only been asleep half an hour. Thanks."

I stayed where I was till he settled down, then carried on towards the door. It was closed. I turned the handle very, very slowly and pulled. It let out a long, loud creak.

A book flew across the room. I slipped out and shut the door behind me.

In the kitchen I made a cup of tea and went through into the living room, where my tapes and books were now arranged in alphabetical order.

I had been looking forward to Saturday night all week. That was my date with Oliver. He was a busy man. He liked to sleep with me, and seemed keen on me, but he didn't have time to see me more than once a week. I understood, of course I did. I was lucky to be sleeping with Oliver Marchant. Hermione was positively green. Sex was all the more wild and exquisite because I was unsure of him and had to wait. It was the fruit of days of fantasies. I used to feel him inside me and think I was still dreaming.

The relationship seesaw: What would you do if it was perfectly balanced? I thought. Sitting there, suspended boringly, legs dangling in the air. Much better to be slightly at a disadvantage; so much more fun that way, swinging to and fro trying to get a bit higher. Much better to have those passionate, tantalizing thrills than endless boring TV suppers, sitting snuggled on the sofa in jeans and an old cardi, not caring what you looked like because inside you were so sure he loved you just for you. I looked at the trail of stockings and suspenders on the living room floor and burst into tears again. What you don't want is to be on a seesaw with a maniac like Oliver, who keeps lifting you up high then banging you down on the tarmac, so that all your most sensitive inner parts are bashed about and broken. I knew that I should dust myself down, thumb my nose at him and walk away. I couldn't do it.

On the Friday he had called me at the office and said he was sorry, he'd forgotten, he had a party on Saturday night.

"Oh, great. That'll be nice, whose party?"

"Rosie, the thing is, it's just a small do, invitation only. I mean I don't really want to go but . . ."

So I couldn't come. Saturday night was off. Every time he did this I thought he meant it was over. Hermione was listening.

"That's fine. No problem," I said, trying to sound nonchalant.

"Look I'll call you tonight. OK?"

"I thought you were busy tonight?"

Why couldn't we go out tonight instead?

"Look, I just need a night in, all right, it's been a long week." So why not have a night in with me, watching telly on the sofa? I said nothing.

"I'll call you tonight." He was angry now. I had offended the mysterious unwritten code.

"I might go out tonight."

"Who are you going with?" he said angrily.

I said nothing, startled by his tone.

"OK, if that's the way you want to play it. I'll call you in the morning. Bye." Slam.

"All right, that'll be great. I'll see you then. Yes, lovely. Talk to you tomorrow," I said to no one, smiling at no one, looking up at Hermione. "Bye, sweetheart."

That night I went round to Shirley's and moped a bit, had a bottle of wine with her, giggled about men—"Men? Can't live with 'em, can't live without 'em"—tried clothes on, went home in a taxi and a good mood.

When I got in there was one message on the answerphone.

"Hello, my little Devon plumpkin. Just wanted to hear your voice. Sorry I was so vile this afternoon. It's been a filthy week. I'll tell you about it. Mmmmm. Wish you were here now. Give me a ring when you get in if you like."

I was a bit drunk. I called him. He was sweet, we talked dirty. We arranged to have lunch on Sunday. We talked dirty some more. I felt romantic. Poor old thing, with his pressures and horrible work and social demands. He said, "I'll tell you what. I'll come round after the party tomorrow. I won't be late. It's just a duty job." And I thought, Why not?

On Saturday I spoke to Rhoda. She was going to the same party as Oliver. It was in an old church in Notting Hill. Five hundred people were expected. Maybe he didn't realize. Maybe it didn't seem like that on the invitation.

"Ditch him, girl," said Rhoda.

I stayed in. I thought he'd come round before midnight. At eleven, I slipped into a little black silk teddy and stockings. He really liked stockings, Oliver did. At one o'clock, I got into bed, still in the stockings. I slept in fits and starts. I was awake at three when the doorbell rang. He was rolling drunk. This time, even when we were having sex all over the living room, I was annoyed.

When we lay in bed afterwards I asked him about the party. "Were there a lot of people there?"

"Yeah, er, no, actually. Not really."

"Who was there?"

He told me about it as if he was telling a story.

". . . and it was then Vicky Spankie rather fell for my charms."

"What do you mean? I thought you didn't like her."

"Hey, hey, come on, I was just dancing with her and talking to her. She's a sweet girl. It's completely absurd her being married to that opportunist Indian idiot. I'll give it three months. He'll take her for everything she has."

"I thought that was what she'd done to him."

"Do I detect a note of jealousy, my plumpkin? No need, no need. She has got nice tits, though."

He fumbled drunkenly at my breasts. I felt cold as a lump of dough.

When I crept back to bed from the living room at six he didn't wake. He didn't wake when I got up at eleven either. I faffed around the flat for a couple of hours, trying to read the papers, not settling to anything. The only thing that cheered me up was a piece in one of the tabloids, called "Twenty Facts You Never Knew about Rain Forest Indians." There was a composite picture of Vicky Spankie and Rani at the top of the page with Vicky looking in the direction of Rani's loincloth with an expression of some dismay.

Oliver still wasn't awake at one. It was a lovely hot day outside. I imagined all the other people in London, all happily paired off, girls with lovers who wanted to go out with them, lying in parks in the sunshine reading the papers, holding hands, jumping into cars and driving off to country pubs. And here I was, creeping round my own flat in my powder-blue wrap, alone but trying not to make a noise in case I woke him and made him furious, unable even to wash my hair and get dressed.

Sod this, I thought. I started running a bath. I heard the sounds of stirring in the bedroom. I went to get the hair dryer and my clothes.

He was under the duvet like a beast in a lair. His eyes were red, his chin was covered in stubble. He looked at me as if he hated me.

"I am *trying* to sleep," he said.

I picked up the clothes and the hair dryer without a word.

I sat miserably in the bath. I was fed up, fed up, fed up. I hated my job, I hated Hermoine, but most of all I was angry. I had no strength. I had to fit in with what he wanted or he would leave me. I had no bargaining power except to leave him and I couldn't do it because I was in love with him. I got out of the bath, put on my makeup, got dressed, and dried my hair.

I decided that I had to make myself ditch him. I would go out and walk around in the sun, then I would come back and wake him up and throw him out. I was just writing a note when he appeared in the doorway, wearing trousers and no shirt. His cheeks were flushed and his black hair was all sticking up on top, like a little boy's. I saw him clock my mood. He came and knelt on the floor in front of me, nuzzling my breasts. Then he took my face in his hands and stroked it with his fingertips.

"Rosie," he said, quietly, earnestly, "you are such perfection." I was weakening. I didn't want the pain of leaving him, I wanted warmth and love.

"I'm going out," I said uncertainly.

"Going out? Why?"

"Because it's a beautiful day."

"Darling, darling, I'm sorry. I was a horrible dormant beast. You look wonderful. Come on, let's have a cup of coffee and sit on the terrace."

I stomped into the kitchen and started making coffee. I did not know what to feel. I felt one thing and then I felt another thing. When I went into the living room he had tidied up all the things from the floor and he held his arms open wide to me. He was a very, very beautiful man. Still I did not respond. He got up, took the coffee cups out of my hands, put them down, took me in his arms and started crooning in a French accent. "You must reeemember zeees, a keees is just a keees, a smile is just a smile." I didn't want to laugh but I did. Then he swept me up and carried me to bed. It is hard to believe that someone does not want you when they make love to you as if they love you.

This time when we lay back on the pillows he did not light a cigarette and I did not snuggle up to him. I was in the after-sex state where your whole body feels as though it has undergone a fabulous, glorious chemical change. Part of me was still entirely besotted with him, part of me wanted to throw my arms round him and tell him I loved him so much. But the rest of me was still hurt and filled with foreboding.

I could tell he wanted me to lie on his chest like I always did. He reached out and tried to put his arm round me, but I pulled away.

"What's the matter?" he said.

"Nothing." I was so frightened he would stop being nice that I couldn't explain.

He stroked my hair and mumbled something which sounded like "I love you."

"What?" I said.

"I love you," he said. It was the magic formula, the lure, the bargaining counter: the overloaded phrase which meant everything and nothing. It did the trick, as he knew it would.

"I love you too," I said, because it was true.

That afternoon we spent a lot of time talking about Oliver's problems, his pressures at work and why he found it so difficult to have relationships. I cooked him a nice supper, listened to him, and sympathized, and it seemed that things would be better between us. He just needed a bit of love and understanding, I decided. We spent the next night together too. It was the first time we had spent two nights together on the trot.

"Ah. Come in, come in. How's it goin'? Any news from Marchant?"

"I . . ." I could swear Sir William knew what Oliver and I had been doing last night. I had a vision of Oliver coming towards me under the duvet, ready to take me.

"What's the matter, gel, cat got yer tongue?" The trouble was Sir William's literary mercy dash had become a taboo subject between Oliver and me.

"I don't think they're going to come out and film in Africa," I hedged, "but I think they might include you in the discussion. We should get some decent coverage in the papers anyway."

"Hmm. When's it supposed to be?"

"Six weeks' time."

"Well, if the damn thing's not going to be on TV there might not be a lot of point in me goin'. Might have to send you out on your own."

"What?"

"Might have to go on your own, gel, and see to the photographs."

This was the first he had mentioned my going at all. I wasn't sure if I wanted to. I'd never been outside Europe before. But over the next few weeks, the idea began to seem more and more alluring.

"Ah, it's about tonight." It was Oliver's assistant, as usual.

"Oh, hello, how are you?"

Hermione looked across at me and sniffed.

"Fine, thank you. Now about tonight. It's dinner at Richard and Annalene's for the Dalai Lama."

"Sorry, Richard—?"

"Richard Jenner. You've seen his film?"

"Not all the way through. I mean, actually no."

"Oh. Well. Don't worry. I'll see if I can have a cassette biked round to you. How about that? So Oliver will pick you up at eight. He said don't overdress."

Oliver rang me half an hour later, pretending it was just to chat, but I suspected it was to check on what I was wearing. It was two weeks after we had spent that whole Sunday together, and this was our first formal outing as man and girlfriend. He said he would come round at eight-fifteen. When my doorbell rang, it was eight o'clock. I was still drying my hair, and only halfway through my dinner party homework watching Jenner's truly terrible film which featured his girlfriend Annalene as a Polish waitress. I was nervous as hell. I was gulping at a gin and tonic to calm myself. When I got to the front door there was no Oliver but another driver in a hat.

We drove for a long way down into Docklands, stopping in a narrow alley between black warehouses. At the entrance to the building, an arch had been cut away and replaced by glass. Inside was a flag, which said, "Show Flat," stuck in a pot full of tropical plants.

I pressed the bell marked "Jenner," and became aware of a lens pointing at me out of the bell paraphernalia: a video entryphone. After a while a female voice said, "Hello?"

"This is Rosie Richardson. I've come with Oliver Marchant but he's running late in the studio."

"Come on up, it's the third floor."

It buzzed, but I pushed instead of pulled and missed it. I had to ring again.

"Hello?"

"I'm sorry, it didn't—"

The buzzer went again and I still didn't catch it in time, so I had to ring again, getting an extremely exasperated voice on the other end. This time I made it in—into a foyer which smelt like a hotel and had gray carpet climbing up the walls. When I stepped out of the lift at the third floor I could hear party sounds coming from an open door along the corridor to the right.

It led onto a tiny platform at the top of a spiral staircase. Below was a cavernous space with one wall made entirely of glass looking out onto the Thames. The whole floor was suspended on metal poles and surrounded by railings with another floor below. In the center you could see down to an unusually long thin swimming pool. Everything else was painted white.

There were about thirty people on the platform, a little group of them looking out over the river, another group peering down at the swimming pool, and the rest seated in a circle in some very, very odd chairs, which were like wrought-iron sculptures with cushions. From above it looked like a surrealist painting, with the guests molded into unusual shapes and forms by their chosen seat. I could see Richard Jenner, a tiny, wizened pixie of a man, lying on a peculiar chaise longue that positioned him with his legs higher than his head.

I set off down the wrought-iron staircase making too much noise with my heels. When I got to the bottom I didn't know what to do. I could see several famous faces, but no one I knew. The groups looked pretty locked in, with large expanses of floor between them. No one was wearing any shoes. I stood there awkwardly, then Jenner caught sight of me, did a sideways roll out of his chair onto one leg, and scurried towards me, grasping my hand, talking in a low, nasal voice.

"Hello, my darling, have you got a drink? Hazel—drink, drink, drink," he said, gesturing to a girl in a French maid's outfit standing by a table full of colored drinks. "Come in, come in, sit down, meet some people, now you are?—tell me remind me."

"I'm Rosie Richardson, I was invited by Oliver Marchant."

"Of course, my darling, of course, we've met before, of course." We hadn't. "Lovely to see you again. Here you are, one of my specials." He handed me a peach-colored cocktail. "Oliver has just called. He won't be long. Now, my darling, would you mind taking your shoes off? We don't want to mark the floor."

In fact I minded very much because there was a hole in the toe of one of my stockings, but I took off my shoes obediently, feeling suddenly small and dumpy, and handed them to the waiting maid.

"Thank you, my darling. I'm afraid the Dalai's having a bit of a nightmare fitting everything in and he's probably not going to make it. But we will have Mick and Jerry—fingers crossed—and we've already got—Blake, Dave Rufford and Ken," he said conspiratorially, waving a hand towards the window. There indeed, in a little group all on their own, were a pushy young Liberal MP, the drummer from a seventies rock band, and a commercials director who had just made the leap to the big screen with a movie set in the drains beneath London.

My appointed seat was a giant version of an ordinary kitchen chair, cast in wrought iron. I had to climb onto it, and I sat feeling like a baby in a high chair, swigging at my cocktail. It was black-frock house, as far as the women were concerned. Colors other than black did not feature in the outfit choices. A woman sitting below me craned her neck round, framed her mouth into a smile which had no effect on her eyes and was kind enough to ask me what I did. "I'm in publishing."

"Oh, really? What do you do?"

Her interest was not able to surmount the fact that I was only in publicity and after a stilted exchange she turned away with a distracted smile. The only other conversation I had until Oliver arrived was thanking the cocktail waitress. It was impossible to communicate with anyone else in that position, but climbing down was too much of a performance to entertain. So I just sat quietly and listened.

Hughie Harrington-Ellis was perched uncomfortably on the edge of a cast-iron stool, talking to another seventies musician who seemed to be called Gary. I couldn't place him precisely but I knew he was from a band who still performed together in spite of middle age. To look at him, he could have been a bank manager. Dave Rufford came to join the group with his wife. He was tall, with a long gaunt face. He was wearing sunglasses, and a dark-green baggy suit. His wife, who was around forty and extremely smart, was holding a baby.

"Hello, mate," said Gary. "How's it going?"

"Survivin', survivin'," said Dave. " 'Ere, this is Max. Ugly little blighter, in'e?"

Hughie had got up with exaggerated cordiality to greet the couple. He was surveying the baby with a show of fascinated detachment.

"You see, what is so marvelous about infants is that they don't recognize celebrity at all," he said. "You simply have no idea, Maximilian, do you, who you are surrounded by?"

"Right," said Gary.

"Ugly little blighter," said Dave.

"'Ere, d'you get that 'orse?" said Gary.

"Yeah. It's a bastard."

"Dave's taken up hunting," said Gary to Hughie.

"My *dear,*" said Hughie.

"He thinks he's the lord of the manor," said the wife, in a genuinely posh voice.

"Where you keepin' 'im?" said Dave.

"We're 'avin another stable block built 'cos I've been keepin' the Ferraris in the stables so we're 'avin this new block built all in the style of the old one. I'm gonna put some of me wine in there as well 'cos I'm not happy about the cellars in the Rectory. I 'ad this bloke come round and 'e said it was too damp for it down there, so we're 'avin another cellar under the new stables that's all, like, the right temperature."

"I do hope the horses don't crap in your Château Margaux, dear boy."

"Right," said Gary. "Huh huh. Yur."

"He wouldn't notice the difference if they did," murmured the wife.

"Do you drive the Ferraris?" asked Hughie.

"Nah. Well, a bit. It's more for the investment. No capital gains. Nah, I drive the Aston usually, or the Roller. 'Owbout you? Got a decent motor?"

"Ooooh, no, no. No, I just bang round in an old Ford Fiesta," said Hughie. "I have so much trouble you know being 'spotted.' I simply can't get anywhere in a more ostentatious vehicle."

Dave Rufford looked utterly crushed for only a moment. "Yeah, well, I 'ave me windows tinted," he said.

One of the waitresses came and bent over Richard. He talked to her, looking distressed, then stood up to address the group with the air of a man about to announce the death of a child.

"Everyone, everyone, a moment, please. I'm so sorry. Mick and Jerry can't be with us. They have a problem. I am so sorry, my loves. They send you all huge hugs."

When Oliver appeared I had been sipping away nervously for quite some time. He came down the staircase looking gorgeous in a large soft navy overcoat and a very white shirt. He looked around the room and burst out laughing as Jenner scurried towards him.

"Richard, you mad fucker, what on earth are you doing to your guests? It looks like something by Hieronymus Bosch." He shook Richard's hand, allowed himself to be relieved of the coat and declined the offered cocktails. "I'm not touching one of your concoctions, Richard, I've been had before. I'll have a Scotch if you've got one." Then he came straight over to me and kissed me on the lips. "Sweetheart, I'm really sorry, I just got caught, how awful for you. Has Jenner been looking after you? Richard, how dare you put her on this insane chair?"

He took my hand and helped me to my feet. When I stood up, I noticed that I was drunk. Fortunately Richard had whisked Oliver away so perhaps he hadn't noticed. I stood rooted to the spot, terrified.

Someone announced dinner. There was a display of wriggling and leaping as the guests extracted themselves from the chairs and set off in the same direction. We were all going to have to go down another spiral staircase to the next layer.

My brain was starting to revolve now, really quite fast. Trying to control a rising panic attack, I concentrated very hard on the stairs, counting the treads. As long as I didn't fall over or say anything then no one would know. There were many round tables with white tablecloths. I got into my chair, somehow. There was a white hexagonal plate in front of me with a tiny bird on it, trussed up with one of its eggs next to it. Oliver was at the other side of the table. He was next to Jenner's girlfriend. She seemed to be about twelve. She was beautiful, all dressed in black, and talking to Ken Garside, the movie director who had made the film about the drains.

I stared at them, trying to focus my eyes. Snatches of their conversation drifted over. Her voice was a Miss London singsong with every sentence dropping to the same note.

"What? No? Ree-*ly?*" Apparently something disgusting was happening, drainwise, downstairs and Things kept being released into the swimming pool. "It's reelye *bad,* you know. D'you think we should, like, take the whole pool out?"

She seemed to feel that Ken Garside should know all about plumbing because of the drain movie. He looked very puzzled. I drank some water, hoping it would clear my head, but instead it set my stomach off. I felt a shift inside, followed by a wave of nausea.

Oliver had rescued Ken Garside from the drain discussion and was talking to Annalene about Jenner's film. "Seriously, Annalene . . . very, very impressed . . . get away from this old bastard . . . spread your wings." I couldn't understand why he was being so enthusiastic. The girl was really wooden and stupid. The film was total rubbish, but I could hear him enthusing: "Definitive . . . seminal . . . key."

The chap sitting on the other side of me touched my arm, making me jump.

"Could you pass the butter, please? Hi, I'm Liam." I knew. He was another celebrity.

"Hello. I'm Rosie." I concentrated hard on passing the butter.

"Are you OK?"

"Yes, thank you, I'm fine." I wasn't fine. I squinted at the Irish actor. He had been in a film the year before about the IRA. There were interviews with him in the papers saying, "I can't take this sex appeal stuff seriously," and extolling the virtues of married life. He used to be pictured with his two babies and a sensible-looking wife whom he'd been with since school. Recently there had been stories about him having an affair with a model. He'd been pictured putting two fingers up and telling the photographers to fuck off.

"Do you know lots of these folks here?"

"No, no."

By now, I really didn't want anyone to talk to me. It simply wasn't wise. If I could just stare quietly at a piece of bread then all would be well.

"Me neither," he said. "I've never fockin' met any of them before. I've never met Richard Jenner. He just rang me up. It's fockin' mad."

"Why did you come, then?" I said, trying to get my brain to stay still.

Just then Hughie Harrington-Ellis came and sat on the other side of me.

"Shall we eat?" he said. The thought of food was not good at all. I stuck my fork into the bird's tiny little egg feeling like a child murderer. I took a bite and there was a vile taste in my mouth which mingled unpleasantly with something sweet on the quail's skin. My stomach heaved, then settled.

Hughie turned his back to me and started talking to the Irish actor. I could hear the Irish voice, full of indignation: "Tabloids . . . filth, scum . . . reptiles . . . none of their fockin' business."

"You didn't say that when you were doing all those profiles with your wife and baby, did you?" I slurred.

"As Oscar said, 'In the old days men had the rack, now they have the press,'" said Hughie, ignoring me, "the lowest form of life, 'unable to discriminate between a bicycle accident and the collapse of civilization.' That's Shaw."

". . . vindictive . . . gobshite."

". . . 'avin a fireplace put in next to the bath, made out of bits of this ancient Greek pillar."

I could hear Oliver across the table. "You see the problem with Melvyn . . ."

"Fockin' scombags."

"Sold two Ferraris."

". . . two hundred grand . . ."

". . . seen her show? Total embarrassment."

". . . seems a bleedin' lot for a fireplace, but . . ."

". . . Renaissance man delusions . . ."

". . . lookin' at ancient history when you're 'avin a bath an' a fag . . ."

Suddenly, I knew I was going to be sick. Where was the loo? I looked round the room. Whiteness, black dresses, and very bright ties against very white shirts danced and crossed each other. The floor was not attached to the walls, it was another of the platforms. I was going to have to walk fifty feet across that wooden floor before I could even start on another spiral staircase. Oliver looked across at me. I felt the vomit rising, started to get to my feet, sat down again, politely cupped my hands over my mouth and threw up into them.

When I finally laid my head on my pillow that night, I wanted to die. At first Oliver had been kind. He came over to me like a shot, gave me napkins and whispered, "It's OK, it's OK, I'll get you out of here, come on." He placed himself between me and the faces, put his arm round me and propelled me to the staircase. He counted me up the stairs, "Come on, come on, next one, next one." I looked down, the faces were still all there, pink, like piggies.

After a while I was in a bathroom, which was hospital white. I washed my mouth and face and lay down on the cool floor, wanting to stay there, possibly live there, perhaps even marry the cool floor. I could hear Oliver and Richard Jenner outside. Oliver sounded angry.

When we got outside he was not being nice anymore. I was being sick again in the flower beds outside the flat. "It's like going out with a fucking puppy," he said. He lit a cigarette and leaned against the wall.

"I'm sorry, I'm sorry," I whispered.

"You should never drink the cocktails at Richard's house. He does this every time. It's completely ridiculous."

"Why didn't you warn me?"

There was a pause. "So. It's my fault, is it?" he said pleasantly. "It's my fault. Of course. But then you didn't need to knock them back, did you?" A wild look came into his eye. "You didn't, did you? You didn't need to knock them back. How many did you have?"

I was getting the hang of what to do when he was like this—nothing. If you neither did nor said anything he had nothing to react to.

"How many did you have?" he said again as we walked to the car. I didn't respond. He suddenly spun round to face me, towering over me.

"How—many—drinks—did—you—have?"

He glared down, his mouth contorting. There was a post box beside us. He brought his fist down on top of it, hard. It must have hurt him but he didn't react. Then he turned back and opened the car door. "Get in."

We drove along in silence.

"Rosie," he was quiet now, controlled, "I asked you how many drinks you had. How many drinks, Rosie?"

The vomit was on its way up again. I gulped, violently.

"You're *not* going to be sick *again*. Shall I stop the car?"

I shook my head.

"How many drinks did you have?"

Silence. Driving.

"How many drinks did you have?"

We continued in this vein until King's Cross. As we hit the Westway he grew calmer.

He stopped the car outside my house. I looked across at him. He was beautiful. He was a lunatic: his brows furrowed, his mouth twisted.

"I'm not coming in with you," he said.

Fair enough. I looked down, sorrowfully. My coat had regurgitated food all over it.

"I finally did it," I said.

"What?"

"Turned into a pizza."

I did not expect Oliver to ring after that. I had let myself down, I knew. I was a danger to myself and everyone around me. The hangover took three days to clear. I went round to Shirley's with Rhoda on day four, Saturday night, and lay in front of the TV eating Milk Tray. For the first time since I had met Oliver, I began to believe life was possible without him; that it might be nicer even. Previously I had begun to fear that there was something secret and horrible about me which I didn't understand. That would explain why sometimes Oliver was nice to me and loved me and sometimes he didn't want me at all and was vile and distant.

"It's not *you* that's horrible, it's *him* that's horrible," said Shirley. "We love you all the time."

"I wouldn't go over the top about it," said Rhoda.

"But it can't be all his fault," I pointed out.

"Look. Shuddup. You have no judgment," said Rhoda.

"OK, you threw up in his car—" said Shirley.

"I did not throw up in his car."

"OK, you threw up on his friend."

"I did not throw up on Hughie Harrington-Ellis. I threw up in my hands and a small portion of it strayed onto Hughie Harrington-Ellis."

"I think it was a perfect symbolic gesture."

"An existential act."

"You have *no* idea what that means. You are just too tragic," I said.

When I got home I was in high spirits. I had made a mistake, I'd fallen for the wrong guy. So what? Sort of thing that could happen to anyone. No harm done. Live to see another day. Make mine a large one—oops, it's down me trousers. Harhar. Free. Free as a bird, free as a fish. Then the phone rang.

"Hi, plumpkin. It's podge-o here."

It was no use, I loved him. I loved the texture of his voice. I loved his posh vowels. I loved his funny little ways.

"Podge-o," I whispered. Contact, warmth, friendliness, relief: an end to enforced feelings of hatred.

"Are you all right, plumpkin? I've missed you. I've told everyone that line: 'I finally turned into a pizza.' You're so *sweet.* Listen, guess where I am?"

"Where?" I said, trying not to be too friendly.

"Notting Hill Gate."

It was only five minutes away. I said nothing.

"Listen, sweetheart, I'm sorry I was so angry the other night. I was drunk. I was thinking maybe we could go away for a few days together. I do love you, you know."

"Do you?" I said, softening. "I'm sorry too—I was repulsive."

"I'll be round in five minutes, then," he said.

The following week, the day before we were supposed to go away, he canceled. He said he was feeling trapped because we were getting too serious. Two days after that we had a wonderful night together, and he asked me how I felt about moving in with him. It was stop, go, stop, go. I'd just start to get my teeth into the pain of breaking up, and he'd turn up and offer to stop the pain. I should have just walked away, but I couldn't release myself.

If only your mind was washable. There have been so many times since then when I have wanted to lift off the top of my head, like the top of a boiled egg, take out my brain and rinse it under the tap like a dirty sponge, squeezing it over and over again, until the water ran clear. Then I would take a hosepipe and flush out my empty head with it, getting out all the gunge, pop the nice clean brain back in, give the top of the head a bit of a hose round and pop that back on too. Then I would not be sad anymore, not hurt, not disillusioned, but clean, naïve and jolly again.

In the absence of a brainwash option, I began to view the Africa trip as an escape. I thought of the vast, empty, open spaces, the deserts, the savannas and thought that perhaps in Africa life would be simpler: pure, unsullied, uncompromised, full of meaning.

CHAPTER
Eight

*T*wo days after the family had arrived at the camp I was sitting in the offices of the UNHCR in Sidra. Kurt, one of the younger officials, was talking on the phone in a high-pitched voice, from time to time letting out an irritating, scoffing, gurgling laugh, jabbing his thumb excitedly on the knob at the end of his pen.

"No! I don't believe you! But you know I think also that he is not so good with the local staff. No, really. I have seen him with Kamal. They say he is racist, you know. I don't know but, really."

I shifted in my seat impatiently. Kurt mouthed, "Won't be a moment," and carried on. He was wearing the ubiquitous UN navy-blue cardi with a crisply ironed white shirt underneath, short-sleeved, no doubt.

"No!" Another gurgle of laughter. "Listen, I have someone with me. But listen, what about the weekend? Do you come to Port Nambula? We can go diving, if you like."

Click, click, click went the pen. I wanted to rap him over the knuckles with it.

"But listen. I think Francine told me they have Gouda cheese at the duty-free shop. . . . Yes. Real Gouda, you know with the little red cover." More giggling. "Fifteen U.S., I think. You can bring me some? Bring me four. And you can get some beer?"

I stood up and sat down again. The previous morning I had driven down to the camp to find that four more families had arrived during the night, and that they were in a worse state than the first. All that day new refugees kept coming. We had a hundred and ten new arrivals now. Five deaths. The radio still wasn't connecting, so I had packed up the jeep and driven to Sidra.

Kurt put his hand over the mouthpiece. "Just a few minutes."

"I've got a lot to do, Kurt. I'm in a hurry. I've got to talk to you."

He was back on the phone again. "But I don't *believe* you! And when did this happen? Friday? Oh, no. But you know he is going to have to watch it or he will be out. But what do you say about the diving? You want to come?"

I told Kurt I would come back later and strode out of the building, heading for my vehicle. The person I really needed to speak to was André, the head UNHCR man in Sidra, but André wasn't there, only useless, stupid Kurt. It was twelve o'clock and I had achieved nothing whatsoever. This morning had felt like running through treacle. It was always like this when you came to town and started trying to have meetings, but this time it mattered.

I set off to drive back across town again to the Sidra regional COR office, feeling a knot tightening in my stomach. I had to get this sorted out, report the problem, request emergency food, find out what was happening with the ship, and get back to the camp. As I approached the souk, I braked to avoid a goat and the car behind drove into me. It was a taxi-truck with fifteen people in the back. No one was hurt. One of the headlights was smashed and the front was a bit dented but that was all and it was his fault. Nevertheless long conversations had to be gone through and a huge crowd gathered.

We were close to the meat market. An alarming smell was emanating from a pickup which was parked next to us, piled with sheep's intestines. Men, goats, dogs, kids and bicycles gathered around. Everyone I knew in Sidra seemed miraculously to be there, and an elaborate greeting ritual had to be gone through with each one.

"Klef?" (Good?)

"Klef." (Good.)

"Domban?" (Good?)

"Domban." (Good.)

"Dibilloo." (Good.)

"Del dibilloo." (Good indeed.)

"Jadan domban?" (So all is good?)

"Domban." (Good.)

"Dalek." (Good.)

I once worked out that I had spent three hours and seventeen minutes during one day just saying "Good?" to people.

All sides of the accident were discussed, with a growing number of interested parties. It kept being agreed that it wasn't my fault, but then somehow the conversation would start off again from square one. It was getting very hot. I had sand in my mouth and my ears, and my legs were sliding against each other in the heat. And I didn't have a hat with me.

Then the atmosphere turned ugly. This was always a moment you had to watch out for in Nambula, when things turned the corner and started to range out of control. The driving laws here were almost as dangerous as driving. If you killed anyone in an accident then the family had the right to kill you on the spot. I decided the moment had come to report the accident and have it dealt with officially. I jumped back in the cab, ignoring the protests, and drove back to the UN. This time André was there, thank God.

"You had a collision with a *carr*? What a *night*mare. You need a drink."

"Double Scotch. No, a treble."

André fetched me a Fanta. He was a Canadian, about the same age as me, medium height, straight, light-brown hair, an aquiline nose in a broad face and very white teeth. He smiled all the time. He was flip, but pretty good.

After we'd done the necessaries with the accident I started to tell him about the arrivals. He listened attentively, asking the odd question, nodding, saying, "Uh-huh. OK, fine. Uh-huh." André dotted everything he said with "OK, fine."

"OK. Fine. Yes, I have heard of these rumors. Fine. OK, so we have a problem. No. We have a question mark. A possibility of a problem."

"When's the ship due?"

"OK. The ship is expected to arrive Tuesday week, OK? But this is the position. We have a situation where, because of various confusions and delays in Europe, we are effectively one delivery behind. What that means is the whole area is on short rations which will run out in between three and six weeks. OK, fine. The ship arrives. We distribute the food, which could take two weeks, and we start with the camps which have the lowest stocks. OK? So even the settlements which are on zero by the time they get a delivery should be able to go back immediately to full rations and in theory everyone should then have full rations for at least two months."

"Say that again." He obliged. I still couldn't follow it.

"So we'll be fine if the ship brings what you're expecting it to bring," I said doubtfully.

"Yes."

"And if it's on time."

"And if it's on time."

"What's the problem with it?"

"Honey, I wish I knew, but I think . . . OK, fine. Let me just say that Nambula's connections with Iraq are not helping us here."

"So we're all skating on thin ice?"

He looked at me.

"Aren't *you* worried?" I said.

"OK, fine. Let me tell you how I see it. The situation is not as it should be, which is why I have been bashing the telex machine and going up and down to El Daman for the last month. The locust story is something which has come up here within the last few days, and something I am treating with a degree of skepticism, given that it is in the interests of the Keftians to get us scared."

"But it's not just talk. We've got a hundred and ten arrivals in a very bad state."

"OK. What are you saying to me about Safila is something I do not want to hear at this moment, OK? What I am going to do is inform El Daman and Geneva that we are getting apparent confirmation of these rumors, and I will ask them to get the situation inside Kefti checked out from the Abouti end. You've told COR?"

"Not yet."

André and I drove together to COR. The Nambulan Commission for Relief couldn't do much about this problem themselves, because they didn't have any money or resources, but they could put pressure on the UN and other Western agencies up in the capital. The trouble was, the commissioner in Sidra did not run the most organized of organizations.

We were shown into his office where he was talking on the telephone, standing up and walking about with a masterful air. He was dressed from top to toe in stone-washed denim, with oddly bulbous trousers. He waved us to sit down with his customary manner which said, "It's all right, you're in the hands of an educated, reasonable, massively intelligent, up-to-the-minute man." This was Saleh's little vanity.

"Wellyboo. Foonmabat, da dirra bellbottom," he was shouting into the receiver, his voice going high with indignation. I couldn't understand more than the rudimentaries of Nambulan, but I liked the sound of the words.

"Fnarbadat. Birra bra. Dildo baboon," Saleh shouted, rolling his eyes at us as if to say, "Look at the idiots I have to deal with here."

When the phone call was over, he placed his hands flat in front of him on the table and smiled with his eyes closed. "So," he said. "What can I help you with?"

André started to tell him, but he said, "Just one moment, please," in a suddenly serious, authoritative voice. At this point a protracted search began through each compartment of the briefcase which was opened on the desk, then carefully through every file on the desk, each drawer. Nothing was said.

This was not unusual. In Nambula, time wasn't a precious commodity. Most people had far too much to fill, and it wasn't considered rude to waste other people's. The search lasted fifteen minutes. At the end of it nothing was found, nothing explained. Saleh merely closed his briefcase, cleared his throat lightly and said, "Go on."

André began again.

"One moment, please," said Saleh. He got up and walked out of the room. We could hear him talking in Nambulan to a woman outside.

After fifteen more minutes he came back in and sat down. We got a good long way into the discussion this time. Saleh adopted an expression of sepulchral gravity. "I see, I see. Oh, this is most serious. I am most concerned. Our radio contact with Safila is malfunctioning, you see, otherwise I am certain my fellow there, Hassan, would have been informing me."

"Yes. That is why I have come to Sidra. I've spoken to Hassan. We must raise an alert, you must put pressure on the donors," I said.

"Ah, Miss Rosie. Of course you know we cannot be raising appeals any more for these Keftians. Our friends in Abouti would not countenance that. Their problems are largely of their own making."

This was bad news. Hitherto COR had been more than willing to help the Keftians once they'd come over the border. There must have been some change of policy within the government. We pressed Saleh to find out what was going on, but he merely smiled. "My friends, I am not at liberty to discuss this matter."

As we left Saleh I turned round to see that the search had begun all over again, starting once more with the briefcase.

We stopped back at the UN office to try to phone Malcolm in El Daman, but the line which had worked so efficiently for Kurt with his mindless babble was now as dead as a post. I drafted a letter instead, which André promised to have delivered to Malcolm in the next El Daman pouch.

I left the UN compound and drove through the wide, straight streets of Sidra, past low sandstone buildings, and headed out beyond the tarmac towards the weird, red Sidra mountains. They rose up sheer from the desert like giant molehills, worn into their smooth sculpted shapes by the wind and the sand. As the truck bounced over the stones and dents of the track which led to Safila, I was filled with foreboding. After the last time, there was so much talk: a famine would never be allowed to happen again, everyone said. And now all the warning signs were there, and no one seemed able to do anything about it.

It was four o'clock when I got back from Sidra, and the compound was deserted. I backed up the truck and drove straight down to the hospital. It was the scene as I remembered it from five years ago: every bed full, the smell of diarrhea, the sound of crying. The whole ex-pat team was there, bar Henry, and five of the Keftian health workers. O'Rourke was bent over a child, feeling below its rib cage.

Betty was upon me in a moment. "I'm afraid you picked an awfully bad moment to go away. We've had seventy more since you left, four more deaths. And we've got cholera. Did you have a good time?"

So that was a hundred and eighty arrivals. Nine deaths. And cholera. Jesus.

"It's been dreadful, absolutely dreadful," Betty continued. "Remember what I was saying yesterday morning? Heaven knows how many more are on their way." She got out a tissue and dabbed at her eyes.

O'Rourke saw me, started to get up, saw Betty and sat down again.

"Have you opened the cholera hospital?"

"Yes, of course. They're in there with Linda."

"And are all the arrivals in here? Have you isolated the others?"

"No, no. Dr. O'Rourke has tested them, and we let the ones who are clear go to their village. It didn't seem fair. He's awfully good, you know."

"Are they from the same area as the others?"

"Yes, no. Well, I'm not sure, actually."

I went round the hospital. Sian was measuring a baby, pushing the thin little legs out flat on the ruler, working out the weight-for-height ratio. She pinched the skin on the little thigh. It stayed for a moment where she had raised it, like peaks of meringue left by a whisk. I went and stood behind O'Rourke. He was absorbed, trying to find a vein in the scalp of the child to get the drip in.

"Hi, Rosie," he said, without looking up.

"Hi," I said quietly.

"Damn." He leaned back and wiped his forehead, then started again. He did it at last.

"OK, let's talk."

He guided me a little distance away. "You've spoken to Betty?"

"Yes."

"It's pretty bad, but contained."

"Are they still coming because of locusts?"

"Yes, but they're all from the same area. It could just be a pocket, touch wood."

"What about the cholera? Don't you think we should be isolating the lot?"

"They've been tested and they're clear. I don't think we should fill up the isolation unit with people who don't need to be there—"

"I just think we've got to be very careful, you know how these things can happen. Have you started immunizing for measles?"

"We were going to," Betty chipped in, joining us, "but Dr. O'Rourke said—"

I glared at him. He was being a bit too bossy, considering he'd just arrived. "We have immunized," I said, "every single refugee against polio, measles, diphtheria, pertussis, tetanus, TB. The last thing we want is an epidemic. We should do all the new arrivals today."

"Dr. O'Rourke said the health workers should do it," Betty concluded breathlessly. "It's done."

Henry had opened up the feeding center again. The mothers were sitting in lines on mats, feeding the children out of orange plastic cups. These were the worst cases. The three gigantic metal cooking pots were out again, and Henry and Muhammad were talking to the cooks.

I put my hand on Henry's elbow. "How is it going?"

"Ah, Rosie, old stick. Fine, fine. Forward to the breach, all hands to the pump, etcetera, etcetera," but he wouldn't look at me. He was very pale, with bags under his eyes. Muhammad was standing behind him. There were beads of sweat on the brown skin of his temples. We all knew how easy it was for things to slide out of control, for disease to start wiping people out like flies.

"Have the health workers told the new arrivals about defecation zones? Are they keeping them away from the river?"

"All been done, old girl."

"We must talk to RESOK, Rosie," said Muhammad. "The serpent of fear is slithering amongst them."

I shot him a look.

"I'm sorry. I mean, they are a little nervous."

I wanted to check the pharmacy to see how we were doing but it was locked, so I walked back to find Henry and asked him to deal with it and then I went to Muhammad's shelter and sat waiting for the RESOK people to arrive. It would be a tricky meeting. RESOK were the Keftians' relief organization, and not supposed to be political, but they were very tough, and keen on their rights. My back was aching from the journey. I could feel sweat trickling down it. The only thing which was good was that the system in the camp seemed to be working well. Everything was organized and under control.

Muhammad came back with O'Rourke.

"He wanted to be at your side for this," Muhammad said to me with a sly look. O'Rourke looked uncomfortable.

The meeting was a heavy, long-drawn-out affair, with coffee first, then slow conversation, interpreted on either side by Muhammad. O'Rourke was not saying anything. He was sitting opposite me behind a table, giving me a look or a nod from time to time.

I decided to give it to them straight, and told them the situation just as André had told it to me. This created some uproar.

"The feeling is that if certain areas have food for six weeks and no new arrivals then some of that food should be here now," said Muhammad. "They are asking why you have not brought it with you."

I tried to explain, but they all started shouting again. I couldn't blame them. I tried to imagine what would happen if the food ran out: all these bolshie young guys changing into starving stick people. Muhammad starving. I couldn't allow that to happen—but how could you single out one life as more important than another?

There was another outbreak of shouting, most of it directed at me. Suddenly O'Rourke banged his fist on the table and stood up.

"Jesus Christ," he yelled. "Don't give the woman a hard time. She's doing everything she can. You've seen the way it's worked to-day—like clockwork. That's down to her. Yes, you're right, it is ridiculous that we haven't got a food convoy arriving this after-noon but it's not her fault. Where is your sense of decorum?"

There was a stunned silence. O'Rourke coughed, looked down and gave a wry look and a wave of his hand at Muhammad. "Do translate."

Muhammad translated. There was silence.

"Carry on, Rosie," O'Rourke said.

I was rattled. The ex-pat women tended to be treated as hon-orary men by the refugees, but still it was sometimes a struggle to maintain authority, and O'Rourke's playing the knight in shining armor was the opposite of helpful. I carried on anyway. I told them, with more confidence than I felt, that if the arrivals stayed steady we'd be all right till the ship came. Muhammad stood up and made a speech. There was much murmuring and nodding amongst the RESOK officials. Then the meeting was declared over and they filed out, shaking my hand politely, and clapping O'Rourke re-spectfully on the back.

When they had gone I turned to him. "Thanks," I said, "but I don't need you to fight my battles for me."

"Oh, Jesus. I'm sorry. I'm such a clod. I just thought you had a lot on your plate. I was trying to help."

"Stick to your own job, buster," I said, then smiled, and he smiled too. It was fine, really.

Just after the sun had set I had to drive back up to the compound. The whole of the sandy basin was radiating a peach glow which seemed to come from the earth itself rather than the sky. The wind had dropped, the smell was of earth and smoke. Figures were mov-ing about contentedly, goats being herded, a man trotting along on a donkey—too big for the donkey, feet almost trailing on the ground. A camel was making its jerky way across the plain, the long neck and jutting chin moving in and out. Shouts came over from the camp, kids playing, laughter, goats. I remembered how it used to sound, and how it used to be. I thought back over the last four years, the feeding, the building, the training, the immunizing, all the work which had gone into making this happy valley. And above, against the reddening sky, a heavy mass of cloud was funneling towards a point, like an omen.

It had been at the same time of day that I had first looked out over Safila, back in November 1985. I was on a hurried mercy dash with Sir William's books. I was like a tourist, taken from airport to air-conditioned hotel, and then being given a tour and shown the sights. There were no huts then. The refugees lived in tents, which had been wrapped in white plastic during the rains so that sand hung in the folds and the effect was very soft. I remember thinking, from a distance, how beautiful it was. I remember simply being happy to be in Africa and away from home.

CHAPTER

Nine

I've fallen in love with you but I'm not *in* love with you."

"But you said you loved me."

"I adore you."

"That's not the same thing."

"You could say it is a love affair."

"So you've *fallen* in love with me but you're not *in* love with me, so while you were falling you sort of swerved off and landed in something else."

"Rosie, if you're going to start being stupid . . ."

It was a mad, familiar dance, where Oliver would duck and dive and twirl, hold his fluctuating feelings above my head, drop them near my hand and whisk them out of reach. What was I doing? Trying to pass or fail? As if the way he felt had anything to do with what I was worth. As if love was something you earned like a merit star, and if I followed every single instruction in every single magazine that month, took in only raw vegetables and hot steam, cleared all cellulite, dressed in Nicole Farhi, made my own pasta, studied advanced sexual gymnastics, never crowded him, always supported him yet was a self-sufficient person in my own right, excelled in my career without being intimidating, dyed my eyelashes, read all existing books on Cubist painters, and dressed up in naughty bus conductress's outfits, Oliver might decide he was *in* love with me rather than just having fallen for me, even if he didn't exactly altogether love me just yet. Of course love doesn't work like that, otherwise nobody but girls in adverts for small hatchback cars would have boyfriends.

We had started a row about where our relationship was going, just after the moment when we should have left for a Famous Club lunch at Julian Alman's. This was one of our favorite ways of making ourselves unhappy. It was always me who started these conversations—mainly because Oliver's behavior made me so insecure. If you ask where a relationship is going too often the question has a habit of turning into where the relationship went. Unfortunately, however, God has given women an inbuilt irresistible urge to insist on knowing where their relationships are going, and to force their partners to discuss the matter at length whenever they are late for something.

Having reached an inconclusive impasse on the love front, Oliver and I moved on to clothes, and in particular my outfit for today. Oliver did not like my clothes. He never said so in so many words, but it was clear. Oliver had excellent taste and lots of money. I had always been unsure about what I was wearing on every occasion but had never seriously bothered about it before. I just lived with it, the way you live with always thinking you are overweight. But now the clothes issue nattered away at me, giving a spoiling tinge to every meeting with Oliver. He had helped out by buying me a little black Alaïa dress, in order that I should look more exactly like all the other women at the functions we attended. Although this was a casual Sunday lunch I ended up squeezing myself into the Alaïa corset-style garment, just for the sake of confidence.

"Do you think I look fat?" I said.

He sighed. "No."

I climbed up onto a chair and inspected an imaginary roll of fat in the dressing table mirror.

"YOU ARE NOT FAT," he shouted through clenched teeth, as I twisted round to try to look at my bottom.

What happened to my generation of women? Who doomed us to spending our entire lives wishing we were half a stone lighter? I wasn't anorexic, bulimic, or anything else you could put in a textbook but I still managed to see everything I ate as an indulgence, and eating it an act of weakness. God, what a thing to remember now.

In the car, mentally bruised and exhausted like ancient warring beasts, we moved on to major-row-trigger number four, which was me going out to Africa. The more miserable I became, the more eager I was to go and the more determined Oliver was to stop me. I couldn't understand why at the time. Partly, I think, he just didn't want me to go away for a fortnight. Given that he claimed not to love me or be in love with me or whatever was going on in his head, he was inconsistently jealous, both of all the other men in the world, and of my time. But most of all I think he wanted me to stay as I was, with my life totally revolving around him, backing him up, with nothing that I was doing particularly important to me. He had sensed that if I went out to Africa then all that would fall apart and crumble away. He was very astute.

The row raged on in the car. Every couple has rows. Rows when you're tense because you're late, rows when you're drunk, rows when you're fed up, rows when you're tired, rows after parties when one of you gets jealous of the other for flirting. Rows don't need to matter. But Oliver was so clever, so eloquent and so cruel that our rows would completely destroy me, and leave me feeling that my personality and everything I believed in had been taken away. I used to want to tape-record them and play them back to someone else to prove that I wasn't mad. I was terrified of him when he was in row mode. When we got to Julian Alman's, I sat shrunken down in my seat, staring straight ahead, not saying anything, hoping he would simply go away.

Oliver said, "Fine, if you're going to be like that you can sit in the car," took the keys and went inside. I sat there limp with misery for half an hour before I could rouse myself to get a taxi home. Later that evening he came round and started talking about how much he'd like to have children with me. Two days later he stopped calling, without explanation, and didn't answer my calls for four days. When he eventually rang, he told me he loved me and I asked when we would meet. He said he couldn't find his diary and disappeared for another two days. The following week it was all on again.

Sometimes it is hard to remember why I loved him so much. He was clever and funny and beautiful and I fancied him with the sort of driven chemical desire which won't lie down. Oliver was unstable but he was never, ever, a bore. And although I grew to hate it, in the beginning it was fun going out with a celebrity. It was fun feeling smug when we were out and everyone wanted a little piece of him, and I was the one on his arm. It was fun knowing that Hermione was jealous. It was fun telling my mum I was going out with a man on the television. It was glamorous going to all the dos and meeting all the people. If I hadn't gone to Africa I would probably just have accepted Oliver's lunacy and carried on.

I was in and out of Nambula within four days on that trip in 1985. Just four days.

Once Sir William knew that *Soft Focus* wasn't going to film the trip he decided against coming, but he did put a lot of his own money into buying the food. All I had to do was make sure that the Ginsberg and Fink logo featured in all the photographs. It was plastered on the food sacks, stuck on the sides of the food lorries. I had boxes of carrier bags and bookmarks all sporting the company logo.

On the way from El Daman airport I watched from the taxi as we drove past failed idea after failed idea: the ornamental park by the river with walkways and archways all covered in sand, the enormous painted sign, festooned with leopards and lions, saying El Daman Municipal Zoo with a gaping hole in the fence beside it. We passed the deserted Municipal Crazy Golf overrun with goats. I looked at the taxis with doors hanging off, the piles of rubble by the side of the road, a group of women walking along arm in arm, laughing, dressed in torn dirty robes and shoes with the straps hanging off them, the El Daman Municipal Ministry of Works with the driveway cracked, the pillars of the entrance broken and smears of mud all over the once-white interior. I felt liberated. I thought that here was a place where it was all right to be only all right; to have grandiose fantasies which came to nothing.

I was driven from office to office that day, with Malcolm introducing me and organizing my permissions. I sat in his jeep, pulling
my dress from my body to let the air in. I leaned back, fuzzled and
exhausted with the heat and I thought that you couldn't ask too
much of yourself or anyone else here. You didn't have to dress up,
make up, look perfect, be whizzy, marry a handsome prince, succeed.
You could have a go at things without a whole world of people who
were charged up, fine-tuned to performance pitch and better than
you at everything, staring coldly at your every hiccup and stumble.
A part of me that had been lying scared in bed could at least get up
and walk around outside here. It was entirely selfish. I was thinking
that Africa could do a lot for me.

Even when I first arrived at the camp, I didn't understand what
I was dealing with. I stood admiring the view for a while, then
walked back to join the photographer and the SUSTAIN people
who were standing talking just by the entrance to the compound.
A lorry was driving towards us on the road. It was brightly painted
with an open rear surrounded by metal rails, to keep the cargo in.
A terrible sound of human voices was coming from it. As it passed
us, I saw that the back was packed like a cattle truck with human
beings, who were so thin that their heads were like skulls. As it was
driving away a body slipped out between the slats around the back
and crumpled onto the ground, and a woman still in the lorry gave
a cry and stretched out her arms towards the body, while the truck
carried on driving away. The body lay in the road near to us: the
neck was broken and the head bent to one side.

For a long time afterwards, I tried not to remember those two
days I spent in the camp. I had been shocked when I watched
the BBC coverage of the Ethiopian famine in November 1984,
Michael Buerk's terse, haunting script: "Dawn, and as the sun breaks
through the piercing chill of night . . . it lights up a biblical famine,
now in the twentieth century. This place, say workers here, is the
closest thing to hell on earth."

I was shocked when I watched Live Aid, and saw the footage of
a starving child trying to stand, with the Cars song playing in the

background. But that was a safe breed of shock: something was being done, the stars were on the case, you could send your fifty quid and know that you cared and you were doing your bit. It was never going to be allowed to happen again.

This was the shock of feeling for the first time that the world had no safety in it, that it was not governed by justice, and that nobody who could be trusted was in control. It was the shame of feeling that I shared responsibility for this horror and of breaking down, and ceasing to function in the midst of an emergency where I could have helped. It was impossible to eat. It was impossible to sleep. Panic had seized me. I felt that I had the guilt of the whole world on my shoulders. I thought I was going to be found out, blazoned across the newspapers, sent to prison. It was as if I had glimpsed a corner of some massive, dark crime in which I was implicated and punishment would follow.

Back in London the panic did not end. It was Christmas time, and I sat in festive houses feeling like a small child at grown-up parties, hearing the voices drift farther and farther away, feeling incapable of talking. The city seemed to be strangling itself, a maze of streets choked and jammed with too many cars, too many shops, too many restaurants, too much of everything. It made me claustrophobic. It made me want to scream. I used to incense Oliver by going outside to sit in the car. I used to sit, watching the rain on the windshield thinking of the African night, of the big sky, rich with stars, and wanting to go back.

In short, I became a complete pain in the arse.

"Champagne?" Julian Alman held up the vintage bottle cheerfully. "Merry Christmas," he said. The price tag was still on it: £27.95.

"I'll have a glass of water, please."

Oliver sighed.

"Sparkling or still?"

"Out of the tap, please."

Julian closed his refrigerated mahogany drinks cabinet and disappeared into the kitchen.

"I wish you would stop this," said Oliver.

I sank on to the rock hardness of the Biedermeier sofa. "I'll drink what I want to drink."

He walked over to the fireplace, and looked at the van Gogh above it. "Ugly, isn't it?" he said. "It was the only one he could afford."

The whole room was ugly. The walls were dark green. The furniture was antique and heavy. The floor was marble. The van Gogh was set behind thick double-glazed glass with a burglar alarm flashing behind it. The windows had bars.

Julian reappeared with a glass of water. "Shall we go upstairs?"

He lived alone in this tall, thin, five-story house in Fulham. It was full of applied architectural features. We ascended the eight flights of stairs, with their ornate, curling banisters. We passed dark-paneled doors, unfathomable items of occasional furniture, heavy-framed paintings with red flashing lights beside them, and stiff, ruched curtains, reminiscent of posh rubber-lined babies' pants. Finally we reached a room at the top which was completely undecorated. There were papers all over the desk, a huge seventies brown-corduroy sofa with a spring sticking out, bare floorboards, beanbags scattered about and Pink Floyd posters on the walls. This was where Julian spent all his time. Often he slept on the sofa because his seventeenth-century four-poster gave him backache. "Blast," he said, "I've forgotten the cigarettes," and set off downstairs again.

I stepped behind the desk and looked out of the window, under the sloping eaves. It was dark, and raining. I watched the cars moving in two steady streams below, the white Georgian houses opposite.

The phone rang. Oliver picked it up. It was a switchboard phone with a line of buttons marked "Kitchen," "Garage," "Laundry Room," "Second Floor Bathroom."

"Hello? Janey." Janey was Julian's new girlfriend. "Oliver here, how are you, sweetheart? Are you after the old beached whale?"

Julian's voice boomed up the stairwell. "Put it through . . . Kitchen, will you?"

"Hang on, Janey." Oliver went to the top of the stairs and yelled, "How do I put it through?"

"Press . . . then press Kitchen."

"Press what?"

"Hold."

"Hold then Kitchen?"

"Yes. No, Hold, then Kitchen, then transfer."

"OK." He came back to the phone. "Just transferring you to Julian in the kitchen." He pressed the buttons. "Damn." He walked to the stairwell again. "I've cut her off."

"What?"

"Cut her off."

". . . God's sake . . ."

"Call her back. It's Janey."

"Who?"

"Janey."

Never had a man been more debilitated by wealth than Julian.

Images from Africa were going round and round in my head. I couldn't stop them. I thought I was going mad. Lights flashed on the phone. I moved from the window and sat down on a beanbag, holding my knees, resting my head on the holes in my jeans. Oliver came back into the room.

"Rosie, I wish you wouldn't come out in those jeans. You look like a member of a teenage girl band. What's happened to all your nice clothes?"

"Sold them," I said, still with my head down.

"You've what?"

"I've taken them to a shop called Second Thoughts. They'll get five hundred quid for them and I'm sending it to Oxfam."

"How naïve can you get? What the fuck difference is that going to make? How are you going to live life here if you can't dress appropriately?"

"It's what's inside you that counts, Oliver."

"Oh. Is it really? Is it? Thank you. Thank you, Mother Teresa, you have shown me the light."

I kept my head down, saying nothing.

"Jesus, Rosie, when are you going to snap out of this? Look, *I'll* send Oxfam five hundred quid if you feel that strongly about it. Go and get the clothes back. When did you do this?"

"You can send them five hundred as well."

"I'll send them a grand, all right? You get the clothes back, then everyone will be better off."

I straightened up and looked at him. "And what would I have done?"

"Got a grip at least."

"You can't buy me out of what I believe."

"Oh, God, spare me the violins. Someone pass her an onion." He saw my look. "OK, sorry, I know. I know. But could you just try to keep at least *some* hold on reality, however tenuous?"

Julian's heavy, lumbering tread was approaching up the stairs. He came in, flung himself on the sofa and lit a cigarette with an air of aggrievement.

"Margarita is stealing from the fridge."

"Who?" said Oliver.

"The lady who looks after me. You've met Margarita. I had six bottles of Moët in there and now there are only four. It really isn't on. I'm more than generous to her. I have her son clean the cars five times a week and then he leaves fleck all over them. What shall I do?"

"Cut off their heads," I said.

"Shut up," said Oliver.

Oliver had come round to look at the scripts for an advertising campaign for British Telecom that Julian had been offered. Julian was worried that the character he was playing wasn't funny enough.

"How much?" Oliver said, as Julian handed him the scripts.

"A hundred grand."

"Not enough. You should ask for two."

I got up and walked out. I stamped down a flight of stairs to the fourth-floor guest room bathroom. It was the size of my flat and lined with mirrors. The floor looked as though it had been cut from a single piece of jade, and in the center, standing on wrought-iron eagles' talons, was a mock Victorian Jacuzzi bath. The loo seat matched the floor. I put the lid down and sat on it. I stared into the gilded mirror opposite seeing the starvation lorry and the body falling out. My face didn't look like my face. There was a marble stool at my feet with another of the switchboard telephones on it. Two fluffy toweling bathrobes hung on a brass eagle's head behind the door. I got up and went out onto the landing.

Julian's voice boomed, "You could always do it better, couldn't you, Oliver?"

"Have you ever had one good word to say about *Soft Focus*? Ever?"

I walked very slowly up the stairs and into the room. They both looked up nervously as if they had a lunatic in their midst. I sat on the chair behind the desk. Once I was settled they looked at each other, picked up their scripts gingerly, and started talking about the advert again.

Amongst the papers in front of me was an invoice with Leighton Health Club written on top. I picked it up. "Julian Alman, one year membership, full and social, £3,500," it said.

"Ahem." They both looked up.

"Why have you done this?" I said.

"Leave Julian's papers alone."

I held it out to them. "Three thousand five hundred pounds. Why?"

"I need to lose weight."

"Three thousand five hundred pounds to lose weight?"

"Rosie," Oliver said. "Will you stop being so fucking sanctimonious?"

"Do you know what this would buy out in Africa?"

"I know, but I *do* give money to Africa." Julian looked apologetic. "I just don't give all of it. And of what I keep, what does it matter what I spend it on?"

"Well, exactly," said Oliver. "Exactly what I'm telling her. Either you give it away or you don't and if you're not going to give it away it makes no difference what you spend it on. Whether it's horses, stocks and shares, Picassos, microwaves—it's all the same."

"We do not have a right to live in luxury and make token gestures when half the world is poor."

"A hair shirt does not suit you, darling."

I got up dramatically, swept over to the window and turned my back on them.

"She's just gone loopy. Ignore her."

"Waste and excess. Waste and excess. It eats away at the soul," I said, turning to look at them like Lady MacBeth. Then I turned again and banged my forehead on the window three times.

I thought I heard one of them giggle. When I turned round they were both looking at me like small boys, as if they didn't know what to do.

"I'm going outside for a bit."

"You are not going to sit in the car again. It's ridiculous."

"I'm going for a walk."

"Actually I'd rather like to go for a walk," said Julian.

"It's fucking pissing down."

"Well, you stay here, then." Julian looked very concerned. "In fact, that'll be much better, Oliver, because then we won't have to set the burglar alarm." So, of course, Oliver immediately decided he wanted to come for a walk in the pouring rain too.

The three of us stood shivering in the porch for some time while Julian tried to set the burglar alarm. "Blast. Hang on. I'll just have to go inside again." He opened the door. The loudest bell I'd ever heard pealed out above our heads. Julian sprinted along the hallway, slipping on the Indian rug on the polished floor, his huge form crashing against the radiator. "Blast," he said, careering off again. The bell was still going strong. Five minutes later it stopped and Julian reappeared, panting.

"Right." He started fiddling with the little box by the doorbell again.

"Come on, Julian. What are you doing?"

"Hang on, it's just my mother's date of birth, then my bank card number." He straightened up and looked at us. "The thing is, you see, it's jolly good because if you key the wrong code in, it won't let you do it again unless you put another code in first, which is jolly good because it stops people taking pot luck. Oh, blast."

The bell had started ringing again.

In the end, the walk was an unexpected success. We all felt bad about the last few hours and were making an effort, so the chemistry altered and a bad time turned into a good time. Julian and Oliver were hungry and I refused to go to a restaurant and made them go to the pub. It was a lovely pub, with a roaring fire and Christmas decorations. They were serving a full Christmas dinner for £4.95, which I deemed acceptable. I lightened up and even managed to eat a bit of Oliver's turkey. It was odd with Oliver. Always before I had felt I was on such thin ice that if I didn't focus all my attention on trying to please him, he would be off like a shot. Now I was routinely behaving with no regard whatsoever for what he wanted. I kept expecting him to explode and disappear. A lot of the time I wanted him to. And he didn't.

Quite quickly I grew less deranged. I had begun the process of calming down, assimilating and compromising, which is necessary to live comfortably in the world as it is, and probably is why its imbalance never changes But underneath, my idea of life was completely altered. It took me a while to realize what that would do to me and Oliver.

Ten

It was 1:00 A.M., Saturday night, Sunday morning, my flat. Oliver got up from the sofa with a face like thunder and started putting his coat on: the big, soft dark-blue overcoat which I used to love.

"What are you doing?"

"I'm going home."

No, no, I thought, as I always did. Please, please, don't go. He had done this so many times before. I knew what it meant: flopping into bed in floods of tears, lying awake half the night miserable, waking up on Sunday morning with no one there, no sex, no fun, pointless croissants in the fridge, pointless ironed duvet, pointless best-pant choosing. No Shirley or Rhoda to cheer me up till the morning. Pain, rejection, everything all over with Oliver.

Traditionally at this point I would burst into tears, throw my arms round him, apologize for whatever had slighted him, beg him to stay. All the familiar feelings began, the tears were welling. I got up, heartbroken, moved towards him, looked up at him, saw the anger in his face, and then, all of a sudden, I stopped. The feelings had vanished. It was as though a giant fuse switch had been pushed and pushed and then finally gone, clicked down. OFF.

"Bye, then," I said. "Make sure you shut the door properly downstairs."

I put the telly on. It was *Carry On Up the Khyber*. There was a

Christmas stocking full of chocolate items which my mother had sent lying on the table. I suddenly wanted a Rolo, and ate the whole tube.

The doorbell rang. I gave it lengthy consideration and then decided to open the Maltesers. It rang again. Then again. Then continually.

BZZZZZZZZZZZZZZZZZZZZZZZZZZZZZZZZZZ. This can't go on, I thought. BZZZZZZZZZZZZZZZZZZZZ. It has to stop. BZZZZZZZZZZZZZZZZZZZZZZZZZZZ.

It didn't.

I padded over to the entryphone.

"Yes," I said.

"Sweetheart, I'm sorry. I'm coming back up."

"No."

"What?"

"No."

"I can't hear you through this thing."

"No. You wanted to go home. Go home."

Silence. BZZZZZZZZZZZZZZZZZZZZZZZZZZZZZZ. Then more silence. I went back to the Maltesers and *Carry On Up the Khyber*. For the first time since I got back from Africa, I was properly, ravenously hungry. I ate the Milky Way, then after a while I remembered the croissants. Chocolate croissants. I went to the kitchen, put three croissants on a plate and took them back to the living room. Then I heard the key in the lock. Shit. I had given him the key when I went to Africa.

Oliver was holding the sort of bunch of pink and yellow flowers you get from petrol stations for £2.95 with imitation white lace on the edge of the cellophane.

"Plumpkin," he said, holding them out to me.

"I said, no."

"Hey, hey, come on." He held his arms open to me, smiling, confident.

"You said you were going home. Go home."

He stared at me, disbelieving. "Come on, it was just a row."

"You've done this to me just once too often."

"Rosie, please." He came towards me and tried to put his arms round me. "Please. It's two o'clock in the morning."

I disengaged myself from him as coldly as he had disengaged himself from me so many times. "You think you can turn me on and off like a tap. When you want me I'm there. When you don't want me, that's fine. I'll still be there for next time. Now go on. I mean it. Out."

"Don't do this," he said, anguished. "It's too . . . it's too . . . wretched."

"Too wretched?" I said. "Too wretched? Was it too wretched when you did it to me half an hour ago? Was it too wretched after Bill Bonham's party? And after we'd been to *ET*? And after we had dinner with my brother? And when I said I didn't think your Lorca thing was the best program ever made? Was it too wretched then? Did it matter what I felt like in the middle of the night on my own? Here take a croissant for the morning. Chocolate. Very good." I took a bite and munched it.

The thunder look crossed his face again. "Don't push it, OK?" he said dangerously. "I am extremely tired and I'm beginning to run out of patience."

"Mmmm," I said. "These are delicious."

He strode towards the door, furious, then his face crumpled. "It'll be too grim if we part like this. Please. Just think about it. Think what it means."

"I've had to think about it plenty of times," I said quietly. "Now just see how you like it."

"I don't understand why you're doing this." He was practically in tears.

All the things he used to say came back on cue. "Look, I have made it as plain as I possibly can that I want to be on my own tonight, all right? And don't come on at me like that. I'll call you in the week, OK? Now, please, let go of me. You're behaving like a spoilt child who can't have what he wants. Good night."

When I finally got him to go he was crying. He was pretty plastered. He slipped as he was going down the stairs. He tried to come up again. And it felt so good. But after the first rush wore off I felt mean and cheap. And somewhere in my head I heard my mum's voice saying, "Two wrongs don't make a right."

The relationship limped on for a while but it was no good. Once the scales had fallen from my eyes it couldn't work. The whole thing had been based on my desire to win him, which made all his inconsistencies and cruelties seem like obstacles to be overcome, rather than the unappealing flaws which now stared me in the face. I was horrified at my own coldness of heart. Had I been in a less extreme mood then perhaps I would have thought harder about love, about how it means taking the whole package, good and bad. How it had been my fault, too, for letting our peculiar dance begin and continue as it had, without standing up to him before. But everything looked black and white to me now. The switch had been thrown.

I had been staring at the computer screen for ten minutes. I was trying to write a press release but I couldn't do it. Hermoine kept glancing over at me, nervously. She was being much nicer to me since I'd got back. Sir William knew who I was now. He was very concerned that I was thin and weird and could only interpret it as a stomach bug. I suspected he had told her to go easy on me. Or maybe it was just the peculiar reverence people have for someone who has been to a horror zone.

I stared furiously at the screen, trying to force myself to concentrate. Thankfully, the phone rang.

"Ah, hello, it's Gwen here. How are you feeling now?"

"Fine, thank you."

"Now, it's about tonight." I suddenly felt really annoyed with him for always making our arrangements through his assistant. It was just too grand for words. Often I suspected it was to stop me asking questions.

"No offense to you, but is there any reason why Oliver can't ring me himself just now?"

"Ah, Er. Well, you know how busy he is."

"Yes, but what is he doing at this precise moment?"

"Er—he's, er—he did say he was busy."

"I see. What is the message?"

"He says he won't be able to come round until ten o'clock because he has a meeting. Oh, and he won't want to eat, so go ahead and eat without him."

"Fine, thank you."

This one again. An unexpected meeting till ten, with food, which he daren't tell me about himself. Great. I had spent my lunch hour buying our supper in Marks and Spencer's. Who was it? Vicky Spankie? Corinna? Someone else? I'd sit in all evening, wondering, and then he'd turn up pissed and guilty at eleven-thirty. No, he wouldn't, though. Not this time.

"Hermoine?"

"What is it?"

"Would you do a favor for me?"

Hermoine looked at me warily.

"What?"

"It's nothing much. It's just to ring this number, say you are my assistant, and that I'm sending my apologies to Oliver. I won't be able to make it tonight because I have a meeting which will go on till one."

"Don't be absurd."

"Oh, go on. Don't be a bloody old bore." I winked at her. I really didn't care what she thought. I hated the stupid job now anyway.

"Go on. Please," I said, holding out the piece of paper with Oliver's number. "He's always doing it to me."

"Oh, all right, then," she said. And afterwards she shrieked with laughter. "Perfect! Oh what a scream! I *must* tell Cassandra. That was completely brilliant. Jolly well serves him right."

And when my phone rang again a few minutes later, she snatched it up before I could get to it and told Oliver I was in a meeting. Unfortunately, though, she got rather carried away.

"Yes, of course I'll give her the message but she's frightfully busy. I really don't know if I'll catch her. Why don't you ring back in a couple of months?"

She banged down the phone and looked gleefully across for approval. But I was horrified.

"A couple of months? Oh no."

"Oh, for heaven's sake, don't be so wet. Do him the world of good. Fancy coming down to Larkfield this weekend?"

When I got out of work he was waiting across the road for me with a bunch of red roses. The seesaw had definitely swung. My flat was starting to look like a flower shop. I couldn't have turned things round better if I had planned it in months of therapy. The trouble was, though, it wouldn't have worked if I was pretending. Never does.

It was Valentine's Day, the day of Julian Alman's wedding to Janey. Oliver was best man. It had been a whirlwind romance. Julian had collapsed gratefully and needily into Janey's abundant offerings of beauty, warmth and normality. Sometimes you could see Janey three times a night on the TV, advertising bras or deodorants. Tall, blond, willowy, with almond eyes and cheek bones to die for, she was the epitome of sophistication and chic until she opened her mouth. Then she was, well, loud, coarse, hilarious, fun, kind—but definitely not chic. In the Claridge's ballroom, Janey's East End clan were mingling confidently with Julian's star-studded guest list, knocking the booze back and roaring with laughter. Janey, however, was in tears.

"Dad's not makin' a bleedin' speech 'cos 'e's too embarrassed in front of this lot."

Glancing round at the assembled show biz establishment I could see Mr. Hooper's point. But still. It was a wedding. He was her dad. Who was going to talk about Janey when she was a little girl?

"Can't we talk to him? Or maybe one of your brothers would do it."

"No, I want me dad." She burst into sobs again. "But that's not the bleedin' worst of it. Julian says he's not gonna make one either."

"But why not?"

"'E says 'e thinks Oliver's going to be funnier than 'im."

Oliver and Julian were in different corners. I could see Oliver bent feverishly over his little cards, practicing his anecdotes. Julian was walking round in circles in his morning suit, looking this way and that, muttering, his big hands clasping and unclasping feebly: Julian at his most bewildered and miserable on his wedding day.

I went over to Oliver's corner and put my arms around his waist. "Oliver."

He didn't look up. "I'm trying to rehearse my speech, as you can perfectly well see. Do you mind?"

"Not at all." I turned and started to walk off.

He came after me, put his hand on my arm. "Sorry, sweetheart, sorry. I'm just preoccupied. Do you want me to read you a bit?"

"No."

"I'm sorry I snapped, plumpkin. What did you want?"

"Do you know that Julian's told Janey he's not making a speech because he's worried that you will be funnier than him?"

"Well, that's his problem, isn't it? He shouldn't have asked me, if he was going to be like this."

"Oliver, it's his wedding day."

"Exactly. It's *his* wedding day. He should have thought it through."

"Go and talk to him. Tell him you won't upstage him."

"Can't avoid it, probably. Anyway, he's the famous comedian. He can look after himself."

"How long has he been your friend? You know he can't write his own jokes. Give him some of yours. Tell him you'll just say something short."

"I can't do that. People expect things of me."

"If anyone drops out it should be you. Go and talk to him."

But he didn't, the bastard. He'd been working on that speech all week and he brought the house down. And Julian lost his nerve, and his audience, stuttered and stumbled and sat down looking traumatized. Nobody mentioned Janey once. The silence on the way home in the car was one of our filthiest ever.

✱

What was I to do? I felt as though the whole platform on which I had been building my life was crumbling away. I had thought that finding the sort of consuming passion I had found with Oliver was the answer to everything. He was Captain von Trapp to my Maria. I had thought that being accepted in a glitzy, whizzy world would thrill me. I was on a career ladder within that world now. I had thought climbing it would be satisfying. But instead I was swimming around in air and nothingness. I couldn't find anything to put my foot on. I talked to my mother a lot on the phone.

"You haven't found yourself yet," she said. "You can't do it with Oliver. People are either drains or radiators and Oliver's a drain. Do something. Take control. Act."

The trouble was, I was scared of him. Though I was determined to leave him, I didn't want to wound his pride and incite vengeance. I didn't want us to hurt each other any more than we had done already either. I hatched up a plan which I thought was perfect.

"I think we should get married," I said.

It was Saturday evening. Oliver was working frantically at his desk trying to finish a script before we left for the theater. He didn't need to finish it till Wednesday. He was just creating a crisis. We were already late.

He stared at the word processor. Then he turned around very slowly. "What did you say?"

"I think we should get married. We've been going out for eight months now. I can't carry on unless I know where our relationship is going. Unless you're really serious about me."

Pressure, emotional demands. I saw them working in his face, saw the mouth tighten, the face twist.

"You've been counting, have you?"

"Yes."

"So we've been going out for eight months and twelve days. And you think that means I have to marry you?"

"I need commitment."

"Ah." He got up and walked across the polished floor, stopping to straighten an architectural magazine on a glass shelf as he passed. "You need commitment." He went and stood by the window with his back to me, still quiet, the early calm. "Eight months, and I have to marry you." I saw the shoulders stiffen. He started striding around the room. "Fuck it, Rosie. Fuck it. I don't need this. I never wanted to be with you in the first place. I didn't even particularly want to sleep with you."

I knew he was only saying it to hurt me, but it worked.

He slammed his fist down on the white table next to him. "Jesus. What's the matter with you? Are you some sort of emotional cripple? Hmmm? Is that what you are?"

"That's such a cliché. That's not fair."

He was staring at me, with that wild look in his eye. "Is that what you are? Hmmm?"

He was coiled energy across the room. I sat down near the door, glanced at where my bag was.

"Answer me. I am telling you to answer me. Are you an emotional cripple or are you not?"

"I'm sorry. It's just the way I am. I need love, I need reassurance. This is what I need."

Bang. The fist again. "This is what you need? This is what you need? Am I hearing this? Am I responsible for what you need now?"

Another push now. "Julian and Janey got married."

"Oh, so that's it, is it? We have to do what Julian and Janey did. We have to be Julian and Janey. Well, maybe Julian feels differently about Janey. Maybe Julian wanted to be with Janey in the first place. Maybe Julian wanted to marry Janey."

"And you don't want to marry me?"

He looked at me incredulously. "No, Rosie. No. I do not want to marry you. What on earth gives you the idea that I would want to marry *you*?"

"And you never wanted to sleep with me in the first place. You never wanted me. I've just forced you into it all. How does that make me feel?"

Bang. Crash. His script hit the floor and splayed across the polished wood.

"I can't stand any more of this. I've had enough!" he yelled.

Right. He'd said it, I was out. I picked up my coat and bag, moved towards the door. Damn. It was all happening too fast. I could see him starting to panic. He was softening now, coming towards me.

"It's horrible to think that I've been with you on sufferance, Oliver. I'm sorry. I just loved you too much. You're much too good for me. I don't want to be a burden to you." Feeble, weak. Perfect. He paused for a moment, the trace of a smirk began on his face. Had to get out now. Quick quick. Turning to the door. Opening it. "I'm sorry to have taken up your time," I said sorrowfully.

Then I shut it and ran. Down the stairs. Reached the hallway. Heard him yelling, "Rosie, for fuck's sake."

I opened the door, closed it, ran, got to the end of the street, glanced round, saw him running after me, saw a taxi, hailed it, got in.

"Camden Town, please."

Shirley's place. Not home. Not for a few days now.

Eleven

Why do you want to do this?"

Mrs. Edwina Roper, head of personnel for SUSTAIN UK, gazed at me coolly from behind large, tastefully glamorous spectacles.

"I want to help."

"You realize there are lots of ways of helping without rushing out to Africa. You could help us with fund-raising, or with publicity."

"I want to do something meaningful with my life."

"I think you will find that relief work in Africa is not as straightforwardly meaningful as you imagine. What is wrong with your life now?"

I looked out of the window, where the rain was teeming down on Vauxhall. There was a row of grisly shops opposite: a newsagent, a secondhand bathroom-fittings outlet. A bath with no taps and a toilet with no seat were leaning on the wall below the window.

"There's nothing that I like about it. There's no point to it."

"It puts rather a lot of pressure on the poor of Africa to give a point to Rosie Richardson's life."

"I thought you would be grateful," I said, sheepishly.

"I know. But this is not about gratitude. You are asking me for a job—a very interesting job."

"I know you've got a job that needs filling in Safila. I want to do it. I'd be good at it."

"What makes you think you'd be good at it?"

"Because I would, I've got a degree in agriculture."

"Agriculture is one thing you won't be called upon to do in Safila."

"I know. But I know about water and, er, drainage."

She raised one eyebrow.

"I'm good at organizing . . . land, and I'm good with people and I've got lots of energy and I really, really want to do it. Why does anybody want to do it?"

She looked down at my CV. "I think you would be of more use to us here in a voluntary capacity."

"But that's not what I want to do. If you don't want me, I'll go to another agency and somebody will take me. I know everyone needs staff at the moment. I've been there. I know what it's like."

She got up and leaned against the front of the desk. "I think anyone who sets too much store by what Africa will do for them risks becoming a liability in the field. Have you recently ended a relationship, Rosie?"

I was completely flabbergasted. How did she know?

"Well, yes," I said. "But that's not why I want to do this. It's the other way round. I broke it off because I wanted to change my life, and do something worth doing."

"Are you sure *you* ended the relationship?" she said knowingly, leaning forward.

I couldn't believe this. Could Oliver, possibly, conceivably have got to her?

"Do you know Oliver Marchant?"

She went and sat back down at her chair, and leaned her chin on both her hands, smiling in a motherly way.

"No. But I have been in this job for a very long time."

I said nothing.

"If you really want to do this, you should take some time before you decide. The job in Safila has been filled, temporarily at least.

SUSTAIN runs a course in disaster relief near Basingstoke. It's a six-month course. If you want to do it, I'll be happy to recommend you."

I sloped back to my flat, dejected, to find messages on the answerphone from everyone under the sun: Julian Alman, Bill Bonham, even ghastly Vicky Spankie, saying they'd heard Oliver had ditched me, and asking if I was all right. Clearly, Oliver had gone round regaling everyone with his story. Fine, I thought. I didn't mind being humiliated if it meant peace.

The only person I called back was Julian. Of course, he instantly tried to transfer me and cut me off. He called me back. "Sorry, just, er, got cut off."

"I rang to thank you for your message. That was really nice of you."

"Oh, I, er, well, Janey and I, you know. Are you all right?"

"I'm really fine. It might all seem a bit strange to you, but I'm going to be much better off without Oliver."

"Ah, well. Hmm. Yes. I can see that."

"Did you have a good honeymoon?"

"Um. Well, I . . . you know, I think, relationships are quite difficult, um, aren't they?"

Oh dear.

"You're telling me. Listen, don't worry about me. And send my love to Janey."

"Yes, but we just wanted to say, you know, we're very sorry and if there's anything we can do we're always here for you."

"Thank you. I'm going away for a bit. So keep well, and see you soon, I expect."

"Yes. Where are you going?"

I nearly said Basingstoke, then realized it didn't quite have the required air of mystery.

"Just away. But I'll be in touch. Love to Janey."

"Ver' sorry to hear this. Ver' sorry. Sher'?"

"Thank you."

Sir William was pottering around trying to deal with the de-
canter and pull on his beard all at the same time. "Bin thinkin'. Bin
thinkin'. Maybe gel like you needs a bit more . . . to get the old
teeth into."

"I think I do need a complete change at the moment."

"Well, I blame this pill."

"I'm sorry?"

"Pill, contraception. Catastrophe. Chap doesn't recognize responsibility anymore. Doesn't know a good thing when it's starin'
'im in the face."

I gulped. Could Oliver possibly have told him the story as well?
Was there no escape from his influence? Sir William handed me the
sherry.

"I'm sure I don't know what you mean," I said, "but I've enjoyed
working for you very much. I appreciate the break you gave me.
And I'm sorry to have to leave."

"Wondered about movin' you to another bit of the corporation,
what about that. Up to Scotland. Ver' good time of year for grouse.
Introduce you to some splendid fellows up there. Shootin' types.
No nonsense."

"You're very kind, but I've already made my plans. I want to go
and work in Africa."

"Yes, heard a bit about that. Roper's wife was on about it." So
Edwina Roper knew Sir William. Nothing was private anymore,
apparently. "Ver', ver' worthwhile thing to do. Have to say. Wish could
go off there m'self and do m'bit. Too many ruddy commitments."

He looked into the distance for a moment and I tried to imagine Sir William chucking it all in to go and live in the bush.

"Still, don't want to rush into these things, y'know."

"I'm not rushing into it."

"Mind made up, eh? Like to see resolve in a gel. Well, all right, all
right. When do you want to go?"

"As soon as you can release me. I think I'm supposed to do a
month's notice."

"No, no no. Bugger that. You bugger off when you want to. Off
you go, off you go now. Ver' good. Press on."

A week to the minute after I had walked out of Oliver's flat the trouble began. The doorbell rang on the Saturday night at six-forty-five. I knew it was him.

"Hello?"

"Hi, plumpkin. It's me."

"I'll come down." I didn't want him in the flat.

He was standing on the doorstep in the dark-blue overcoat. Very white shirt, no tie. Beautiful, beautiful Oliver. He took me in his arms, and the familiar warmth and scent nearly undid everything.

"Go and get your coat."

"No, Oliver."

His face crumpled like a little boy's. He looked so hurt, so defenseless. Oh, Oliver. Oliver, whom I had thought I loved so much.

I went to fetch my coat.

"Where are we going?" I said as I climbed into the car.

"You'll see."

We were driving through Hyde Park in the rain, in a slow stream of traffic listening to the moan of the windshield wipers. Oliver was completely silent now. One side of his mouth was twitching. He put his hand on the horn and held it there in spite of the V signs from the car in front and I realized only then what a risk I was taking. We turned right at the lights, passed the ugly red brick buildings which bordered on the park. Then we turned into the Albert Hall car park. At least this was a public place.

"Are we going to a concert?"

"I said, you'll see."

In we went, through the glass porch into the dingy circular corridor where concertgoers were hanging around aimlessly, into the lift, up the stairs and along the deep red corridor to . . . the Elgar Room. A uniformed attendant greeted Oliver and swung open the dark wooden door into a burst of light. The room was golden and all-a-glitter, but completely empty. The door closed behind us. I suddenly wanted to scream with terror.

"This was where we first met, wasn't it?" He was calm, danger-ously controlled.

"Yes."

I hoped the attendant was still outside the door. I had a vision of the man being bribed to dispose of my body. Wheeling me out im-passively in a canapé trolley.

Oliver took my hand. I decided to stay calm, keep him calm, go along with whatever it was. He led me, trembling, across the red carpet and up the gilt ornamental staircase. There was a table in the center of the room, draped with a red cloth with a bottle of cham-pagne in a silver bucket and two glasses.

He led me to the table. Then dropped dramatically to his knee, whipping a little box out of his pocket, flicking up the lid to reveal an enormous diamond.

"Will you marry me?" he said. . . .

"Rosie, I am asking you to marry me."

I was standing at one end of the table with my head down. The voice was calm still, level. "I am asking you to marry me."

Silence. I could sense him twitching.

"I have asked you a question. Will you marry me?"

"We've just been through all this. You can't undo what you said last week. You said you didn't want me. It hasn't worked between us. I've made my plans now. I'm going away."

"I am asking you to marry me."

"You know how stormy it's been for us both. Relationships shouldn't be like that. I've had enough and so have you. We'll both be better off on our own."

He was gripping the other end of the table very, very tightly so that the red cloth was bunching up in his grip and the ice bucket was starting to slide towards him.

"Can you hear me, Oliver? Don't you understand what I'm saying?"

"I have asked you a civilized question and I expect a civilized an-swer. WILL—YOU—MARRY—ME?"

"No."

One of the glasses fell over as the tablecloth slid.

"Oliver, please, don't do this. Come on, let's go. We can talk somewhere else."

"I am waiting for an answer. WILL YOU MARRY ME?"

"No."

The other glass fell over now. The ice bucket was nearly in front of him. I looked up at the softly twinkling chandeliers.

"Rosie, I AM ASKING YOU TO MARRY ME."

"Oh, shut up, you silly old fool, just shut *up*," I said, and ran for it again.

Back home I had to disconnect the buzzer with a screwdriver. His car stayed outside the house for an hour. Then the phone rang. The car was still there. Maybe it was Shirley. I picked up the receiver.

"I love you."

"You love me."

"I love you."

"Are you sure? You're sure it's not adoration? Or falling for me but not in love with me, or a love affair where you don't actually love me? Or hurt pride?"

He slammed the phone down. It rang again immediately. I reached down under the table and pulled the little plug out of its socket. Then there was silence.

The car stayed outside all night. It was still there when I got up at 4:00 A.M. It was still there when I was brushing my teeth in the morning. I called Shirley and asked if I could come and stay again. I started packing a bag. At ten o'clock there was a battering on the door of my flat. Someone had let him in. I grabbed the bag, went out on the balcony, climbed over, knocked on the next-door French window and Simon, the thin bespectacled engineer who lived in the next-door flat, appeared looking very surprised. The knocking was still going on.

"Would you be very sweet and let me come out through your flat?"

An idiotic gleam came into his eye. "Aha. Are you having an-other of your Stormy Rows?"

"Come on. This is serious. Let me out."

"What's going on?" He was leaning over the balcony, trying to look into my living room. The knocking was still going on.

"Be quiet there, will you? Some of us are trying to sleep," shouted Simon, smirking. The knocking stopped.

I shot through his room, out of the door, down the stairs, out, round the corner, another corner, into another taxi. I was getting very fit from all this running, and very broke.

I went in to work deliberately late on Monday morning, but I knew I was safe from Oliver there. He wouldn't make himself look foolish in public. I cleared my desk, went home, packed, unhooked the answerphone and headed for my parents' home in Devon. It turned out that the disaster relief course had already started, but I persuaded them to take me on a few weeks late and moved to Basingstoke. Letters from Oliver began to appear in my college pigeonhole. They were alternately attacking and loving. They ex-plained about the weakness of my character, how I had made him feel trapped, pressured, because I loved him too much. How I was superficial, silly, looked at the world through rose-tinted spectacles. How I had ruined his life with my unwanted presence. How it had been my fault for not being stronger. Then there were the others extolling my virtues, telling me of all the things I had awoken in him, begging me to come back. I did nothing. Eventually he stopped.

The relief was overwhelming at first. It was wonderful to be quiet and alone, to get on with my work. But, still, I was very sad because I had lost my belief in love and in myself. The fact that I had eventually swung the seesaw with Oliver didn't help. What was the point of love if it was a game of see-who-cares-less, if it was such a ridiculous carry-on? What was the point of me, if I allowed my whole life to center on it, then mucked it up?

At times I got relief by turning Oliver into a monster in my head. Maybe there are just some men like that in the world, I thought. Men who have to be in charge, who have to punish those who awaken feelings in them which they cannot control. Men who will lure you with tenderness till you believe that you are safe, then slap you down. Men whom it is impossible for anyone to love without losing their dignity. Men who have to damage those who love them most. But, then, I had fallen in love with one, so what did that make me?

I decided to toughen up. I threw myself into the disaster relief course, poring over the books in the evenings. I kept in touch with Safila and with Edwina Roper at SUSTAIN. Miriam, who was the administrator at Safila, wrote to tell me the temporary assistant was leaving in August and promised to push for me to replace him. My tutor sent SUSTAIN a glowing reference. In June a letter arrived from them offering me the job. I let out my flat, said my good-byes, and left for Nambula.

Twelve

What've we been working for all these years, if they're just going to starve to death again?" said Debbie.

It was the day after I'd been to see André in Sidra. We were sitting round the table in the cabana, having coffee after supper. We had worked too late. It was getting on for midnight, and we were all frayed around the edges. We had nearly four hundred new arrivals now. They were starting to come from different regions of Kefti, all talking about locusts, and crop losses.

"I think what we have to do is just get on with it for a few days, get the system up and running, get used to the new situation," I said, trying to sound confident. "We're handling it well. I was very proud of us all when I got back yesterday."

The attempt at a rousing speech sat in the middle of the table like a big wet fish.

"That's all very well, isn't it, but we shouldn't be in this situation," said Linda, her mouth tight.

"It's not Rosie's fault," said Sian.

Debbie looked mortified. "I'm not saying it is. Of course I'm not. It's just a bit of a bugger, that's all."

"Quite so. Bloody Serena Sackville-System is to blame," said Henry. "Must say you're looking bloody sexy with that smudge across your eye, Sian. Making me a bit on the frisky side."

Sian looked upset, and started rubbing at her face. Even Henry's jollity jarred tonight. Poor old Sian, so fastidious and neat, hadn't had time to wash. Normally Henry would have known not to mention it. The whole chemistry of the group had been altered. We weren't sure of each other anymore. I thought that I should be a better leader, more capable of rousing the troops and getting something done.

"If I still can't get through on the radio tomorrow I'll go up to El Daman," I said. "Don't worry. We're not going to let another disaster happen." Rash words. "Meanwhile, we've just got to show what we can do."

"Show who? Who are we supposed to be showing?" said Linda.

She had a point. We were really alone. What were we supposed to do? We could try and control disease, but once we ran out of food and drugs, if these malnourished, infected refugees kept flooding in, we were scuppered. There was silence among us and we listened to the crickets out there in the blackness. A donkey was braying madly and forlornly like a car horn.

O'Rourke spoke eventually. "I think we're all seeing the blackest side because we're tired," he said. "We might well find that this all blows over in a few days and it is contained. Whatever, we have to let our responsibility stop somewhere. We are just a small group of people. There is only so much we can do, and we're doing it. Aren't we?" he said, looking at me. He was trying to be supportive.

"Yes," I said.

"Right, come on, team. Subject closed. Put in a box for time being. Time off," said Henry.

It seemed like a very forced occasion. I tried to join in the dinnertime chat, but wanted to be silent. Possibly everyone else did too.

"I wish we could call a grown-up." The words slipped out without me wanting them to, but for once they were the right thing to say.

"So do bloody I, I can tell you," said Debbie.

"Me too," said Henry.

"I *am* a grown-up, and I want my mother," said O'Rourke.

It was all better after that. Only Betty stayed silent. She went off as soon as the meal was finished, looking most unlike herself. It worried me. I left it a while, then went after her.

Betty was surprised to see me at the door. I rarely went into her hut. She ran a hand distractedly through her hair, knocking her glasses off-kilter. "Oh. Hello. I was just, er, having a little tidy-up."

I looked past her. There was a can of spray polish and a duster on the Formica table. Polishing Formica? Anxiety took people in the strangest ways. She was still standing there, blocking the door.

"Can I come in? I wanted a chat." She'd done this often enough to me.

"Of course, yes, come in. Would you like a glass of water?"

When she was turned with her back to me, pouring out the water, I saw her shoulders starting to shake. She was crying. I half got up.

"Betty—"

"Oh, don't, don't, please don't. Don't be sorry for me."

She turned back towards me, wiping her eyes on her sleeve. "I'm just a stupid old woman. A stupid, silly, useless old woman."

Part of me, I must admit, thought, "Well, you might have a point." Then I saw her looking so sunken and sad and felt real grief. I sat down next to her.

"I'm old, I'm old. Old and finished. Look at me. Everyone thinks I'm a silly old woman. You don't need me here. You have O'Rourke. Much better than me. You'll all be glad to see the back of me. Then you can all be young together. Just useless, useless."

"You're not useless. How can you say that? You're a brilliant doctor."

"What's the point? What's the point? We can't do anything about it all, can we?"

She cried for a bit.

"We can. We are doing. We'll do it."

This just made her cry even more. She was getting hysterical.

"Betty, look at me."

She looked at me hopefully. Her eyes were tiny and pink behind her glasses, like a little pig's.

"I came to see you to ask you to stay. We need you to stay."

Oh dear. This had just popped out of my mouth. It was a half-formed thought which seemed like the perfect way to cheer her up.

She brightened a little, then started to cry again. "You're only saying that to make me feel better. What have I got to go back to?"

"What about your husband—"

"That . . . that monster with his stupid young women. Nobody wants me. You wait till you get to my age. Nothing, nothing. On the scrap heap."

"Don't say that. It's so unfair. That's just the way women are made to feel. It's not true."

She sniffled some more.

"You *are* a wonderful doctor, you know how valuable you are—you know everything there is to know about medicine in Africa. They love you in the camp. We'll be lost without you if you go. I'm going to go to El Daman to tell Malcolm we have to have you to see us through this."

"But you have O'Rourke now."

"O'Rourke isn't you. He doesn't have your . . . your . . . qualities. Will you stay?"

She seemed calmer now. "Well," sniffle sniffle, "well, I suppose if you want me to . . . if Malcolm says I can." She gulped and pulled herself together. "You know, I know I'm a dreadful old busybody, but I really am so fond of you, so fond of you all."

When I left her she was calm and dozy, tucked up in bed to go to sleep. It occurred to me that if Africa needed us, sometimes we needed Africa a great deal more.

Thirty more refugees arrived in the night, and in the morning the radio still wasn't working. I decided there was nothing for it but to drive up to the capital and start kicking ass with Malcolm and the UN. Presumably messages had reached them by now, but they had to be made to take this seriously. By the time I hit the tarmac of the El Daman road, it was the busiest time of the day: five o'clock, when the desert came to life and the amber light glowed through the dust. The buses, trucks and rusting cars were joined by herds of goats and camels headed for their watering holes, pack animals, almost obscured by bales of straw, with thin comedy legs scampering beneath. Ahead of me the sun was dropping and dissolving like a vast crimson pill, touching the sandy wastes with redness and fire.

I was tense, watching. The lorries in Nambula were splendid beasts, decorated with fairy lights, paintings of jungle animals, and bits of tin and Christmas decorations. Their loose wheels wobbled precariously, their overloaded rears tipped at terrifying angles. Every few miles you would pass some garish testimony to what could happen—an upside-down truck lying with its wheels in the air; another broken down with a line of three cars squashed into the back; an overlong one collapsed in the middle with a small car underneath.

I didn't crash, but I was pulled over at two security checkpoints and had to bribe my way out. By the time I reached the outskirts of El Daman it was eleven at night. The traffic was heavy here, even at this time. I passed the first shanties of the city, dotted with fires; the great twinkling monolith of the Hilton, set apart from the smells and noise like some medieval castle. I skirted the center on the busy airport road and entered the quiet wide streets of the ex-pat area where the houses of government officials and aid organizations peeked out from behind concrete walls with their molded see-through patterns. When I drew up at the gates of the Malcolm Colthorne World HQ, or SUSTAIN office and residence, no one was up except the watchman. He was up in the sense of upright, but also asleep.

Eventually he was woken by my loud rattling and banging at the gate, and he let me in. I tiptoed into a guest room, and luxuriated in being in a real bed, surrounded by real walls.

I have a fear of ceiling fans. When I watch those heavy albatross wings whizzing round I imagine what would happen if they fell off. They would whang wildly round the room chopping off arms and heads. The fan in Malcolm's office had a wobble. I kept a vigilant eye on it, leaning my head back against the wall as I listened to his slow verbal forward rolls and back flips.

What Malcolm had been explaining to me, for what seemed like most of the morning, was that he had just been given a bollocking from head office for raising a false alarm about a bunch of orphaned children, ten thousand strong, ranging hungry, naked and armed with Kalashnikovs on the borders of the civil war in the north. When they were located by a Reuters journalist, there were in fact twenty of them, armed with little sticks. What Malcolm was working towards, in an extremely roundabout sort of way, was that he wasn't about to make an ass of himself with a second scare story in a fortnight.

I leaned forward calmly, resting my elbows on his desk and staring at him. It took him a while to wind down.

"Malcolm," I said, "in the four years we have worked together have I ever insisted upon anything?"

"Of course," he said, in his reassuring-the-troops voice. "You insist on things all the time, you're a very insistent person."

I began again. "I want you to understand that I mean this, and that I am completely sure that I'm right. The potential of the situation in Kefti is so devastating, life-threatening and serious that we must tell London about it now, not this afternoon, not on Monday. Now."

There had been a time when Malcolm was known as Malcolm the Invincible Man: an ironic title, as was never more obvious than that morning. Bossed and bullied by the harridan I became, he drafted the message, dictated by me, as I loomed threateningly over his shoulder. He muttered and whined as we went along. This was what we ended up with:

SUSTAIN EL DAMAN—LONDON.
URGENT FOR IMMEDIATE ATTENTION.

ROSIE RICHARDSON REPORTS 440 ARRIVALS AT SAFILA FROM KEFTI IN ADVANCED STATE OF MALNUTRITION WITH 24 CHOLERA CASES AND 19 DEATHS. THEIR REPORTS OF

LOCUST INFESTATION (BOTH HATCHING AND SWARMING)
IN HIGHLANDS, COMBINED WITH POCKETS OF CHOLERA
SUGGEST LARGE SCALE REFUGEE INFLUX MAY BE IMMI-
NENT IF SITUATION WORSENS. REPORTS APPEAR TO CON-
FIRM RUMORS CIRCULATING STRONGLY AMONGST RESOK
OFFICIALS FOR LAST 2 WEEKS.

HOWEVER [this was Malcolm's bit], EARLY WARNING
SURVEYS SHOW NO DEVIATION FROM NORMAL PATTERN.
YOU WILL UNDERSTAND REPORTS ARE IMPOSSIBLE TO CON-
FIRM AS SUSTAIN PERSONNEL FORBIDDEN TO ENTER KEFTI.

SHIPMENT FOR EAST NAMBULA OVERDUE AS YOU ARE
AWARE. ENTIRE REGION ON SHORT RATIONS. SAFILA CAMP
HAS FULL RATION FOR ONLY WEEKS. MEDICAL SUPPLIES
ALSO LOW, IN PARTICULAR REHYDRATION SALTS, IV FLUIDS,
ANTIBIOTICS, AND MEASLES VACCINE.

ROSIE REQUESTS LONDON APPROACH UNHCR AND EEC
RE SUPPLIES. REQUEST THAT DR. BETTY COLLINGWOOD BE
RETAINED IN ADDITION TO DR. ROBERT O'ROURKE UNTIL
THREAT IS RESOLVED.

PLEASE RESPOND, URGENT TODAY.

Malcolm was an old coward. He insisted the whole message
came from me, not him. Then, later in the morning, when I saw
what had finally been sent, he had added this paragraph.

I WOULD LIKE IT TO BE UNDERSTOOD THAT THIS TELEX IS
BEING SENT AT ROSIE RICHARDSON'S INSISTENCE. I PER-
SONALLY HAVE HAD NO OPPORTUNITY TO MAKE FIRST-
HAND ASSESSMENT AND AM RESERVING JUDGMENT.

In other words he was refusing to endorse my position. The
more I tried to argue my case the more Malcolm told me I was
overreacting. He reminded me of all the scares we had had in the
past. He pointed out the diplomatic drawbacks to crying wolf. He
told me to go back and do some more research.

It was Friday, the holy day, and everything was closed. I phoned round the UN, the other aid agencies, COR, the EEC. No one was in. My one stroke of luck was that there was a party that night at the home of the British consul, Gareth Patterson. Most of the people I needed to talk to would be there.

I hung around the office all day, writing letters, making phone calls, which were unanswered, watching the telex. I drove to the UN stores at the airport, but the guard wouldn't let me in. There was no reply from London. I was furious with Malcolm. This was his fault. He had turned it into a back-of-the-in-tray telex. And time was ticking away.

When Malcolm and I drew up at the British consul's residence at six-thirty the party was already in full swing. The house would have looked well as part of an African-village-style luxury hotel on the Kenyan coast. Patterson had designed it himself, plumping for open thatched rooms with cane chairs, squashy cushions, tumbling tropical plants, a parrot in a large wooden cage and a heavy emphasis on batik in the soft furnishings. The establishment was all on one level except for an exotic upstairs bedroom. Where the soft white sand and lapping blue waves of the Indian Ocean should have been, there were the sluggish brown waters and mudflats of the river.

There was a rather particular view on this section of the river. Some years ago Nambula had purchased a secondhand jet from Afghanistan Airlines. On its maiden voyage the pilot had brought it in over El Daman, spotted the lights of the runway and made a perfect landing. Only it wasn't the runway, it was the river. No one was hurt, the landing was graceful, if unexpectedly amphibious. The passengers waded ashore. Opposite the spot which Patterson had selected for his home was a little island where the plane had eventually come to rest at a jaunty angle. It was still there, giving him a permanent cue for an anecdote.

There were lights in the trees that Friday night. There were umbrellas in the drinks, which were masquerading as fruit punches—Patterson had managed to get hold of a crate of rum—and a steel band was playing on the terrace. It was clear that Patterson was overdue for some leave and had been browsing through too many long-haul travel brochures. For a moment, when we arrived, Malcolm and I stood at the end of the drive, watching the party across the lawn. You could spot the field-workers because they had all had the runs so often that their clothes were too big for them. I saw June Patterson lurch from one little group towards another, carrying a tray of umbrella-filled glasses which seemed not to be long for this world. Her blond curly hair cascaded down like a pile of doughnuts. She was dressed in a tight pale-blue nylon pajama outfit and sparkling sling-back stilettos. Everyone was pretending she wasn't there. I saw Patterson spot her, leave his conversation, hurry to her and tenderly take away the tray. Then he bent and spoke to her, looking like a primary school headmaster with a naughty five-year-old. As I watched, he drew her to him protectively, held her for a second, and kissed her on the forehead. A dipsomaniac wife was not the best asset for a British consul in a Muslim country—particularly a country which grew more fundamentalist with every week that went by—but Patterson loved his wife. I think he loved her more than his job, more than his reputation, more than he cared about what I, Malcolm, the French ambassador, the UN representative or any other bugger thought. It was the best thing about Patterson by some way.

I watched him as he disappeared with the newly rescued tray. With his blue safari suit, sideburns and daft good looks, there was something rather seventies about him. He reminded me of a game-show host, or one half of the kind of boy-girl singing duo who would perform dressed in flared catsuits on matching bar stools. Then I felt a tap on my right shoulder and turned round to look. There was no one there.

"Haha! Got you with that one, didn't I?" Patterson was standing on my left. He loved this kind of practical joke. "Hey, what are you guys doing without a drink? You are looking one gorgeous liddle laydeee tonight. Come and join the pardee."

"Hi." Caspar Wannamaker, from U.S. Arms Around the World: tall, blond, terminally boring Texan. "How goes it down on the farm?"

I told him, testing the water.

"Hell," he said. "You don't wanna get in a stew about it. Sure you wanna get it checked out in Abouti, alert your office, but come on, there are a hundred camps like Safila in the country. You can't start an international emergency every time a handful of refugees turn up in one of them with a problem."

"Four hundred isn't a handful."

"Oh, come on. It's happening all the time. Anyway. That ship's gonna be here within days. No problem."

Then he gave me a little lecture about getting too close to the refugees. "You've gotta stand back, you know, take an objective view. You can't let yourself be manipulated. You can't be one of them, salving your little liberal conscience."

I smiled politely and moved away. The workers from the European NGOs, the smaller nongovernment organizations like SUSTAIN, had all gravitated together. I approached a little group of French medical workers. They were the high priests and priestesses of relief chic: they wore fine cotton khaki, loose silk tops with interestingly cut necklines.

"It is ridiculous, perfectly typical," said Francine, a pediatrician, with a toss of her head, and an irritated little puff on a menthol cigarette. She had a clipped, nasal voice and looked like Charlotte Rampling.

"The system is completely stupid," said Jeanne, a tiny nervous creature. "It is worthless even to speak with this UNHCR. This idiot Kurt who is living down there is a complete disaster for an individual. At Wad Denazen they are hearing the same stories about this locusts. They are expecting arrivals too."

The French worked with the Italians at Wad Denazen. It was fifty miles north of us, also close to the border with Kefti.

"What are you going to do?" I said.

"Well, we are talking to our people in Paris, but you know we are a medical agency. We are not dealing with food. What can we do?"

"Do you have any IV fluids and antibiotics up here you could let us have temporarily?" I said.

"If we have we will send you, of course," said Francine, "but, you know, we are having the same difficulties as you."

"Thanks. We'll do the same for you one day." But I knew they wouldn't have anything to spare.

The man I really needed was Gunter Brand, the head of UN-HCR in Nambula: the man with the power in the aid community. He had a backslapping manner, a head as big as a horse's, and a very loud laugh. He had been booming around the party displaying his perfect English and overconfident social style. I found him talking to André.

"So then he said, 'Because of the vacuum inside their heads.' Waagh. Hahahaha. Ahahahaha. Ahahahaha," Gunter was saying.

I hadn't met him formally before. He had only been in El Daman for six weeks, but he had a very tough reputation based on a career in Central America.

"Hi!" said André. "Good to *see* you. Gunter, have you met Rosie Richardson, the administrator for Safila camp, with SUSTAIN?"

"Hey, good to meet you. One crazy party, huh? Have you ever seen such a *strange* house in Africa? You English have the most unusual tastes."

"Yes, I think Patterson had one too many piña coladas at the drawing board."

Gunter didn't respond.

André was trying to help me out. "I mean have you *seen* his wife's hairrr? What's going on with this woman, OK? I mean, I thought *I* was a dipso but really, my *Gaaaad.*"

Absurdly, I felt my hackles rise because a Canadian and a German were slagging off the English; it was like someone outside your family slagging off your aunt.

"Has André told you about the problems in Safila? We're very worried about it," I said.

André was standing slightly behind him, shaking his head frantically.

An irritated look flitted across Gunter's face. "Yes, André told me about the situation in Safila," he said.

"And what is going to happen about it?"

"As I expect André told you, the situation is being investigated."

"With respect, I don't think we have much time, Gunter."

He looked at me hard. "This is not the place to discuss this but I will tell you my view. I think you are right, there is a problem with locusts in Kefti. But it is not a serious problem. There will be swarms, there will be some crop losses. But they will be localized. Possibly you will have one or two hundred more arrivals in Safila and we will ensure that you, and all the camps along the border who are *in the same position,* will be provided for. Everyone is always saying it will be another nineteen eighty-four. Believe me. Watch my lips. It will not be another nineteen eighty-four. It is another scare. However, I will be most interested to read what you have to say, if you would care to drop a report into my office. Now if you will excuse me, it has been delightful to meet you," and he moved away, well away, to the other side of the party.

"Lead balloon, lead balloon. Dis*a*sterr," said André.

"Thanks."

"Let me tell you about Gunter, OK? Gunter is right about everything, OK? Gunter does not feel the need to explain himself professionally. Gunter will not respond to confrontations unless it is Gunter who is doing the confronting. Gunter will not talk work at social occasions. OK?"

"So I ballsed up on every count?"

"Every single one," he said, laughing. "Never mind, have a cigarette."

"No, thanks."

"Now, listen, don't worry about Gunter, OK? It's all in hand. I've talked to Wad Denazen about the possibility of them giving over some of their extra rations to Safila. They're pretty well stocked."

"And what did they say?"

"Not overenchanted with the notion but it'll be fine. OK?"

"But they're talking about getting arrivals too."

"Stop worrying so much. You're looking at the worst scenario. Have you told your head office?"

"I telexed them today. No reply."

"OK, fine. When are you going back?"

"Tomorrow morning. We've had four hundred and forty arrivals, from three separate regions of Kefti."

"How many dead?"

"Nineteen."

"My Gaad. Coffin city. OK, leave it with me. I'll pass by your office and talk to Malcolm tomorrow afternoon. You've heard the ship's due in ten days, OK? Are you going to be OK till then?"

"No. Well, it depends how many come and if we can contain all the disease. The problem's drugs as much as anything. We need measles vaccine, rehydration salts and antibiotics."

"OK, fine. Those I can get for you. I'll bring them down with me when I come."

"Plus the radio isn't working. And we've got cholera now."

"OK. Listen. This is not good. You are getting into a state. OK, fine. Now have a drink. Relax. I can see what's in your mind but it's not going to happen, OK. The ship is due. You are top of the list. You will have your supplies inside two weeks. OK?"

"Will you come and have a look yourself?"

"I will come and have a look myself."

Then he looked uncertain. "You really think you're going to have a big influx?"

"I really think we might."

André looked around him, then pulled me away from the crowd.

"Look, this is not on the record, OK? I think we're going to have to wait a long time for this ship. I think you're right to kick up."

"So what shall I do?"

"I think you have to have some more concrete evidence that we are looking at a big exodus, OK? There have just been a few too many people crying wolf over the last few years, and there isn't much love lost between the donors and Nambula just now. Our report from Abouti will help, but it's going to take three weeks, a month, to get here. The best will be if you can do something your end, try to get some concrete proof of the scale of this problem, OK? Can you get someone to go into Kefti?"

"You know what the problems are."

"Sure, sure. I know. Think about it anyway. But *don't go yourself.* OK? Send a runner. Now, come on, let's get a drink. Let's pardeee with Paddersurrrn."

"I can't face it, sorry. Try and come to Safila soon."

I said my good-byes and thanked Patterson. June had retired some time ago. Malcolm was settled in for the duration and said I could take the Toyota, he would find a lift. I crossed the lawn and almost walked straight past Jacob Stone at the top of the driveway.

"Leaving so soon? Come on, let's have a smoke."

We sat on the front of his car. Jacob, a big Jewish doctor with a thick black beard, had come to Nambula when it was a moderate Muslim state, when the elected prime minister was a British-trained lawyer. He had come as an NGO doctor, rather like O'Rourke. When he had been here two years everything changed, and Sharia law was declared.

Jacob was witness to a couple of amputations with a rusty sword. He was present at one of the public occasions when they hacked off the right forearm and the lower left leg while everybody watched. He had started a home for the thus disabled. And then, having seen enough horror and gangrene, he had offered his services to the fundamentalist government as a surgeon. He offered to perform the amputations under sterile conditions and anesthetic. And they took him up on it.

I told him about the problem as he rolled the joint with his usual incongruously dainty skill and expression of worry. His face had aged alarmingly since I had met him. I asked him if he really thought he was doing the right thing. Could you temper brutality and injustice with a measure of humanity and make things better? "Humanity is the bottom line, it's all we have." Jacob was flying—this joint was clearly not the first of the evening. "People like us can't move mountains. But we can go to the slopes of the mountain and do what we can. If we care in our hearts then . . . Rosie, look at the moon, right? It's like, just because we can't get to the moon it doesn't mean we can't drive to Sidra."

Dear Jacob. He is now in and out of the Cloisters, a tasteful private psychiatric home in the Cotswolds.

That night he told me to go away and keep true to my own sense of what was right and what was wrong. He said that we could only hope to do good in tiny ways; that if I saved just one life it was worth it.

"But we're talking about thousands of lives. And the system is just too slow and cumbersome. What am I going to do?"

And then he had his idea. "Use the celebrities."

"What do you mean? What celebrities?"

"The celebrities you told me about, that you used to hang out with in London. You're in a perfect position. Go back and look 'em all up. Make a little emergency appeal of your own, get it on the TV. Make a megafuss. That's the way to get what you need really quickly. Plus once Safila is big media profile nobody can afford to let an emergency happen. Think about it. Locusts. It's a great story for the media." He made a sudden champing motion with his jaw, flapping his arms. "It can't miss."

"But all that celebrity stuff is what I came out here to get away from."

"You can't get away from it. It's the way of the world now."

He took another long drag on the joint.

"Cause celeb," he said. He passed the joint on to me.

We smoked in silence for a while, then "How much do you care?" he said.

"How can you ask me that?" I whispered.

"Well, then, don't be picky. Do it. Be pragmatic."

When I got back to bed I lay awake for a long time. I thought of the camp as it would be now, the new refugees staggering down the hill in the darkness, the line of bodies waiting for burial in the morning, wrapped in sacking. I couldn't abandon the camp and go back to London. Surely that wasn't the only way? I hadn't come this far, just to go back with a begging bowl.

Thirteen

The morning after Patterson's rum punch party, I went into Malcolm's office and found him standing at the window reading a telex. He was wearing a pink T-shirt which said, "Skydivers Do It in Their Pants." He handed the telex over to me.

SUSTAIN UK LONDON

> WE NOTE WITH CONCERN YOUR COMMENTS RE: ARRIVALS AT SAFILA. AWARE OF DELAY IN EEC SHIPMENT. CONFIRM DR. BETTY COLLINGWOOD CAN STAY TILL FURTHER NOTICE. WE WILL DO EVERYTHING WE CAN HERE BUT NEED MORE CONFIRMATION AND CONCRETE FACTS. AWAITING RESPONSE OF UN, ODA. CAN YOU ENLIGHTEN US ON VIEWS YOUR END?

It was at least a response, but I wasn't sure how much SUSTAIN could do. Even if they have emergency food they wouldn't have the money to fly it out here and we'd end up simply waiting for another ship to get organized. I was running through treacle again. Nothing would budge.

I sat down and wrote my report for Gunter. I asked Malcolm to take it to the UN and get them to communicate with SUSTAIN UK. I had to get back to Safila.

Betty was delighted by the news that SUSTAIN wanted her to stay on. By the time we sat down for dinner that night she had become Mrs. Senior Cheerleader of Safila, determined to jolly everyone up.

"Now. What are we going to do about Christmas dinner? I think we should do it properly this year," she was saying brightly to the assembled incredulous stares as I entered the cabana.

"We can get a turkey from the market, like last year—as long as I don't have to kill it! Hahaha. Then I've got a super recipe for stuffing made with bread crumbs, tomatoes and garlic, with a bit of egg and lemon juice. Wish we had some mushrooms, though. Now, has anyone asked for a Christmas pudding to be sent out? We'll need two or three, I think."

O'Rourke had his head in his hands.

"Sweet corn we can get. Sausages from the Hilton. Oh, but what about sprouts? We can't have Christmas dinner without brussels sprouts!"

"Perhaps we could make some out of leaves and glue," suggested O'Rourke.

The other obvious development was a man with a fungus on his leg, who had taken up residence outside the cabana. Whenever anyone walked past, he shouted and jabbed his finger accusingly at the fungus.

"We keep sending him away but he just comes back again. He's from Safila village," Sian explained. "We can't do anything with his leg. It's too advanced. We've offered to take him to hospital in Sidra but he won't go, he thinks they'll amputate the leg."

"I'm going to amputate his leg with a kitchen knife if he carries on with this," said O'Rourke. "Betty, I've got a great idea for the stuffing."

"Robert, really," said Linda. "I do not enjoy the way you joke about the African."

Linda did tend to take things very seriously indeed. She was a thin, tense girl with a very straight back and an air of having been marvelous at hockey at school.

O'Rourke lit a cigarette and stared straight ahead.

Muhammad appeared in the compound, and I reeled when I saw him. His cheeks were sunken, the skin was pulling tight around his eyes. "Muhammad, look at you."

"We are on half rations, Rosie."

The thought crossed my mind that Muhammad might have made himself thin deliberately, to spur us into action. When I went down to the camp with him, I looked closely at everyone. Were they thinner already, weaker, or was I imagining it?

I went to the feeding center to pick up the weight-for-height charts and took them to Muhammad's shelter to discuss them with him. Instead of him, however, I found O'Rourke in there boiling the water for tea. He said Muhammad would be back in a moment.

I sat on one of the beds and began looking at the charts. O'Rourke came and stood behind me, looking at them over my shoulder. "Who did these?" he said. "That can't be right."

He pointed to a figure and his hand brushed mine. "It's nowhere near as bad as that. I think there's a certain amount of hype going on."

I turned round to look at him. He was looking straight at me. His eyes were hazel-colored today. I felt flustered and turned back to the chart.

"So the UN say wait, which is typical. What's Malcolm's line on all this?" he asked.

"He's being cautious as well. He thinks I'm overreacting."

O'Rourke shook his head. "A triumph of the embalmer's art, that boy."

Muhammad came back in and said, "We must act."

Layers of misinformation were shifting to and fro over the problem. I didn't know what to think. The Keftians were definitely hyping it up, the UN playing it down.

"André says someone should go up to Kefti and check it out," I said.

Muhammad had gone off to find some KPLF soldiers to discuss the idea with us. Officially the Keftian People's Liberation Front were not allowed in the camp out of uniform, but how were we to know who was a soldier and who wasn't? O'Rourke had walked to the other side of the shelter now and was standing opposite me across the room. I wasn't quite sure why he was here. He seemed always to be around now when anything important was happening. It was good, him being there.

Muhammad returned after a few moments. There were four beds in his shelter, made out of logs and rope, arranged in a horseshoe shape. The soldiers filed in and arranged themselves around the room, some on the beds, some standing behind.

Muhammad started to talk to the men, and translated for us. "They are saying that they can take us to these locusts and to see these people who are traveling towards us with no food. They can meet us at the border with their vehicles."

"How long will it take?" I said. There was some discussion.

"Maybe one day, or two." I trebled it.

"If we're going to go at all," I said, "we've got to go quickly, either tomorrow or the next day, take some photographs and get them up to the UN in El Daman."

"I will see if they can take us tomorrow," said Muhammad.

"Hang on, this is a war we're talking about," said O'Rourke. "Is this an acceptable risk? What are we looking at?"

"We have only three problems," said Muhammad. "The mines, the air raids and the ambushes from Aboutian troops."

"Oh, well, in that case, what are we waiting for?" said O'Rourke.

"How dangerous is it, really?" I asked Muhammad.

There was more consultation.

"We must drive from the border through the foothills to the gorge and then across the plain to the highlands. This road from the border to the gorge has been mined, but the mines are cleared now. It is being used regularly by the KPLF vehicles and there has been no mine for many months. They will send a truck ahead of us and we can drive in its tracks, so that if there is a mine they will detonate it first, and we will be safe."

"Pretty hard on the guys in the truck," said O'Rourke.

"They are soldiers, it is war," said Muhammad.

"And what about the air raids?" I said.

"They do not come close to the border, it is agreed with Nambula. Beyond the gorge we will travel at night. They are not flying
at night."

"And the ambushes?"

Muhammad said something to the men and they laughed.

"They are saying there are no ambushes. The road is well de-
fended."

"Is this reliable?" I said. "They want us to go, don't they?"

"I would not allow them to mislead you on this," said Muhammad.

"So do you think it's safe?" I said.

"I have told you what I believe to be the situation. I do not think
there is great risk, but I do not think you should make the journey.
I will go myself."

"But there's no point in you going on your own. You're a
refugee, they won't listen to you. It needs one of us as well."

"I'll go," said O'Rourke.

"No. I'll go," I said.

We both wanted to go. The purpose justified the risk, we had to
know what was waiting up there for Safila. But there are few real
adventures to be had in the modern world and this was a real ad-
venture. We were being as self-indulgent as brave.

"There is no reason for you to come, Rosie," said Muhammad.
"It is better that we take a doctor from the West to assess this situ-
ation, and in case of accident or sickness, and I will translate for Dr.
O'Rourke."

"I'm the one who's going to deal with the UN. If I'm going to
be convincing, I have to have seen this for myself, and taken photographs."

"It is better that we take a man."

"Why?"

"So we'll go the day after tomorrow then," O'Rourke said,
eventually. "All three of us."

Over supper there was much indignation over the attitudes in El
Daman. The plan to go into Kefti got a more mixed response.

"If you go in and get shot at, someone's going to have to come and get you out," said Linda. "And it's not going to look particularly good for SUSTAIN if it ends up all over the papers that their personnel are traveling with rebel enemies of the Abouti government."

"But it's not going to look very good for SUSTAIN if we end up with a starving Safila on the BBC news, is it?" said O'Rourke.

"It doesn't compare," said Linda.

"It's going to be much more of a job dealing with thousands on supplementary feeding than fetching three corpses out of Kefti."

"Oh, for God's sake, Robert," said Linda.

"Bloody hell, bit too much Terry Tension around here for my liking, I'll be the one under the bed wearing the flak jacket," said Henry, and wandered out.

"I just don't want you to get killed," said Debbie. "It's not worth the risk, surely?"

"We won't get killed," I said. "We've talked to Muhammad and the KPLF."

"I think it's a reasonable risk, given the end in sight," said O'Rourke.

"Well, dears, you know, that's all very well. But remember. It's a war," said Betty.

Henry reappeared with a bottle of brandy. He must have been saving it. There was a lengthy palaver, pouring it out into the orange plastic mugs. Everyone had some. Even Linda, even Betty.

After a while, O'Rourke said, "It's a dangerous, foolhardy, irresponsible, disobedient, roguish plan."

"Yes, it's completely irresponsible," snapped Linda.

"It's a rash, reckless, willful, ill-advised, perfidious scheme," I said.

"I think we should go," said O'Rourke.

The door of my hut rattled.

"Bloody hell, what's going on? Have you got a black man in there?" Henry barged in carrying a bottle of gin and a packet of dried orange juice.

"I say, have you got a bottle of water?" he said. "Thought we might have a last little drinkie together while you're still in one piece, all goddesslike limbs still attached, so to speak."

I suddenly felt very affectionate, possibly because I was scared, and hugged him.

"I say, steady on, old girl. Don't want Sir Horace Hard-on joining the party or where will we be?"

Henry had already had quite a few when he came in. When he'd had a few more he got uncharacteristically serious.

"You sure about this barking mad, foolhardy, gung-ho, misguided, mercy-dash-style excursion?"

We had a craze at the moment for using long strings of adjectives.

"Don't mince your words, Henry. Feel free to speak your mind."

"Road mined. Air raids. Job on line if you get caught. Camp left in lurch again for four days. Is it worth it, old thing?"

"I wouldn't go if I didn't think so."

He was swigging from the bottle now.

"Love to put absolute confidence in your judgment, old girl, absolutely love to. Choice of traveling companion worries me, have to say."

"But Muhammad's a great man."

"Not talking about Muhammad. Talking about bloody Cedric Sex God."

"Who?"

"Dr. Cedric Sex God."

So he was jealous of O'Rourke.

"O'Rourke is not a sex god." It was only half a lie. "He is a kindly, sensible, responsible, earnest, sturdily booted, borderline-bossy doctor. And you know why he has to come."

"Quite so, quite so. Need man. Need doctor to sew legs back on. Can't take me. Have to leave deputy in charge, anyway, not doctor. Can't take Betty, Betty doctor but not man. Also mad."

All memory of minor parts of speech had departed from the Montague brain.

"That's right. That's why he should come."

"Wicked seducer."

"Don't be ridiculous. There's nothing going on between me and O'Rourke and he is not a wicked seducer. Apart from anything else you're not in a position to cast aspersions, with your appalling romantic record."

He giggled. "Different."

"Not different."

"Think I better go 'stead of you."

I hadn't seen Henry properly drunk before. I'd forgotten how young he was. He looked frightened. Maybe it was being left in charge of the camp which was the problem.

"It's only four days. You'll be fine. We'll go over everything. You know exactly what to do."

Suddenly he flopped over and put his arms round my neck, nuzzling his head against me, as if he was a small child. "Scared, Rosie. Everything out of control. Don't want you blown up by bomb. Don't want everything all blown up, starving dead people all over the shop."

Henry: not so well sealed and varnished as I had thought. I liked him better for that. I stroked his head and soothed him like a baby.

It was about forty minutes after we had crossed the border between Nambula and Kefti. I could tell O'Rourke was tense because he was holding the wheel at ten to two, and gripping it tightly, instead of holding it at the bottom and leaning one elbow out of the window, which was his usual style. I was watching his knees in his jeans, next to my knees in my cotton trousers. I was doing that because it took my mind off what was happening. We were following the KPLF vehicle at two hundred yards, driving within its tracks. There were three soldiers in the KPLF truck and Muhammad, who wanted to ride with them until we got into the danger zone so he could speak with them. We had two soldiers with us in the Toyota, sitting in the back. When we got to the danger area we were going to park up till it got dark, then Muhammad was going to ride with us again and we were going to drive on with shades over the headlights. Now it was about three o'clock in the afternoon and the sun was still high.

The road was starting to climb, we had left the desert and there were bushes and trees on either side of the road. It felt damp and cooler and the air smelt fresh. The KPLF vehicle had disappeared out of sight round a bend in the road. What we heard was a low boom. O'Rourke hit the brakes. Black smoke billowed up above the trees. The two soldiers behind us shouted and jumped out of the back, running off into the bushes to our left.

I reached for the door handle.

"Stay in the cab," said O'Rourke quietly.

"It could be an ambush. We've got to get out." I was whispering too.

"Wait."

"We must drive on, Muhammad's in—"

"Wait."

And then there was a second explosion ahead. The air in front of us danced like the air above hot tarmac. We waited again, straining with the tension. It seemed unbelievable that this had happened so soon.

"OK," said O'Rourke after a while. He put the truck in gear and started up. We followed the tracks slowly, tensed for another shock till we rounded the corner.

"Oh, Jesus."

The cab had been blown fifty feet away from the rest of the vehicle. At the side of the track to the left I saw the bottom part of a leg lying by the road. The rear section of the truck was upright with a hole torn in the side and Muhammad's djellaba was hanging out spattered, bright red, with blood. One of his legs was hanging limply over the side of the hole and the stump of the other, below the knee, was bleeding heavily. O'Rourke was already halfway out of the truck with his bag in his hand. I started opening the door at my side."

"Come out this side and follow me."

I did as he said. We went to Muhammad, who was conscious but incoherent.

O'Rourke tied a tourniquet above Muhammad's knee. The stump was still pumping out bright red arterial blood. I turned away and threw up. There were blotches in my vision. I thought I was going to pass out.

"Just sit down where you are. Don't look at anything."

"I'll go and check out the cab," I said, and started walking past the truck towards the track ahead.

"Wait," O'Rourke said. I carried on. I thought I was behaving normally. I felt his hand on my arm. He turned me round to face him, put his hands on my shoulders. He was looking at me very calmly. "Just wait," he said. "Stand here for two minutes. Just stand here and watch me."

He went back and I saw him getting something out of his bag and giving Muhammad an injection. Muhammad was lying with his upper half on the bench seat of the truck, his lower half still hanging out of the gash in the side of the lorry. Then O'Rourke lifted what was left of Muhammad's legs and laid him flat along the seat. I saw that the back of O'Rourke's shirt had a huge dark patch of sweat and his arms were covered in blood up to the elbows. He wiped his hands on his jeans, then looked up at me.

"OK." He gave an energetic smile, as if we were performing some kind of challenge and doing very well at it. This time when he came up he put his hand on my back and guided me ahead towards the cab. "Now. Don't look in here until I've seen what there is."

The wheels were gone so the cab was resting on the wheel arches. O'Rourke opened the door and climbed in. I looked over his back and saw the driver's head which was smashed on the dashboard, leaking clear fluid and blood. The blood was coagulating in the hair. The older soldier seemed to be bent in half. I looked away again.

"They're both dead," said O'Rourke, coming out of the cab. "Where's the other one?"

We found the soldier in a thicket a little way away. The man had a piece of metal from the side of the truck stuck in his stomach. I helped O'Rourke with the soldier, getting him the things he needed out of his bag. It was starting to get darker. Together we carried the soldier back to the truck, me holding his feet. O'Rourke had left the metal in his stomach. The bloodstain in the dressing grew like ink on blotting paper, darker round the edges. We laid the soldier on the floor at the back of the truck and I supported his legs while O'Rourke climbed up into the back. Then I climbed up too and we laid him along the bench on the opposite side of Muhammad, whom O'Rourke had covered with a blanket. He was still unconscious from the painkiller.

I sat down on the bench seat beyond Muhammad. I lifted his head onto my knee and stroked it. He was warm and breathing heavily. I was glad he didn't know what had happened to him yet.

"Do you think he'll be OK?" I said.

"Maybe," O'Rourke whispered.

It occurred to me then that I had first suggested this trip, so it was my fault that this had happened and Muhammad had lost his leg. My vision broke up, and then a long time later I could hear O'Rourke saying, "OK now, OK." I was lying somewhere in the dark, covered in a blanket and I could just see O'Rourke in the light of a torch and I remembered what had happened. He was kneeling next to me, and gave me some water to drink.

"Shouldn't we get Muhammad back to Safila?" I said. "Can we move him?"

"Shh. Just take it easy for a while."

"Don't you think we should get back to the camp?"

"I've got a feeling we're only a few miles from Adi Wari. I think we should take him there and hope there's a hospital, and if not, pick up an escort and go back to Safila."

"What do you think about driving?"

"No."

"So wait until it's light, then start walking?"

"Guess so. Carry Muhammad."

"What about the soldier?"

"He'll be dead by tomorrow. If I take the metal out he'll die now, if I don't take it out he'll be dead by tomorrow."

There was the sickly metallic smell of blood in the truck and we couldn't smoke because there was kerosene all over the floor. So we stood outside for a while and had a cigarette. We could have lit a fire and made some tea, but we didn't want to risk being seen from the air. Instead we just ate a little bread and drank some water. We climbed back in the truck, sat down side by side on the seat next to Muhammad and wrapped the blankets round us. We would all have been more comfortable in the Toyota but we didn't want to move the injured men again. Muhammad was quiet but the soldier was delirious and shouting every so often.

We looked at the map and found that Adi Wari was only about four miles away. O'Rourke offered me a sleeping pill but I wanted to stay alert. Still, I think he may have put something in my drink because the last thing I remember before I woke up the following morning was sitting wrapped in the blanket leaning against him, with his arm round me very tight, really too tight. I felt a mixture of emotion, shock, guilt, dread, but at the same time I felt an odd form of elation, just because I was alive.

Fourteen

I woke with the first gray light filtering round the tarpaulin at the back of the lorry. When something terrible has happened, the second moment after waking is the most unbearable. You start with your mind washed clean by sleep, and then you remember.

Muhammad was comatose. So was the soldier. O'Rourke wasn't there. I climbed out of the truck and went into the bush for a pee. I was starting to have paranoid thoughts. I was thinking this was all my fault, and I was a bad person.

I walked back to the truck. O'Rourke was standing there, rubbing the back of his head. His hair was sticking up on one side like a duck's tail, and he needed a shave, but he had a clean shirt on. He looked as though he was in control, and civilization had not stopped.

When I came up, he put his arms round me and rocked me a bit, gently. "You OK, trooper?"

I said nothing. He took me to sit in the cab of the Toyota and talked to me. He was very good with me that morning. I think misfortune is hardest of all to deal with when you feel an element of guilt or shame about it. It takes away the option of a sustaining fantasy of yourself as a hero. I don't know how people manage to cope with accidents which are definitely their fault. But I know that people can emerge more or less intact from the most outrageous situations if they learn to think about them in the right way. I was

very fortunate that O'Rourke was with me at that time. He reminded me that everyone had made their own decision to go; we
had all weighed up the odds and decided that the end justified the
means. He told me that we knew that dreadful things happened all
the time, and that when one happened to you, or someone close to
you, you mustn't allow it to shake your confidence in the world,
because the world was still the same place. You were just beginning
to understand it better.

"I can't face Muhammad," I said to him.

"Yes, you can," he said. "You'll see. He will handle it better than
us. He'll turn it into an asset."

O'Rourke was right, as it turned out. Out here, the attitude
towards losing a limb was totally different from in the West. I once
heard a Red Cross prosthetics worker describe how in Switzerland
his patients were desperate that their artificial leg should look real so
that under trousers no one would know, whereas he would give a
Keftian the first crude attempt at a wooden limb fitting, and probably
never see them again. As long as the limb worked, they just wanted to
get on with their lives. It wasn't something they bothered to disguise.
Maybe this was because of the war and the proliferation of mines. I
suspect it had more to do with what they valued in each other.

When I climbed into the back of the truck Muhammad was
conscious and sitting up. It was a shock, in the light, seeing him in
a dirty djellaba. It was gray with smoke, and covered with great
caked patches of dry blood.

"Rosie." He held out his hand to me. "I have become one of the
war wounded. Will you love me the more for it?"

I took his hand but I couldn't speak.

"Don't be distressed. Please do not be that way. Rather you
should be rejoicing because I am still here. You see, I am still here
even though I have no leg now."

"Shut up. Quiet."

I thought this was rather rude of O'Rourke at such a sensitive
moment until I too heard the plane. It was a distant whine to the
east. Within seconds it was turning into a roar, growing until the

sound was unbelievable, as if the plane was in the lorry with us. I sat completely rigid. I was thinking: of course, this is what's going to happen, we're going to be bombed we're going to die now. The soldier, who had been lying comatose, started, then screamed at the pain from the metal. O'Rourke leaned over, and held him still. Muhammad was sitting with his eyes closed, arms folded over his stomach. We were tensed, waiting for the explosion. But the noise passed its peak, and the plane seemed to veer off, the sound fading until there was silence.

"I thought they weren't supposed to come this close to the border," O'Rourke said, with a ludicrous calmness.

"They must know we are here," said Muhammad.

"Right, we move," said O'Rourke.

"But how—what about the soldier?" I said. He was lying quietly now, but his eyes were mad. He was terrified.

"Leave him, leave him—he will die," said Muhamad.

The soldier couldn't understand English but the look in his eyes was awful.

"We can't leave him in this state—it's inhuman," said O'Rourke.

"You are not understanding death in Africa. This is war. He is a soldier," said Muhammad.

"But he's in such pain," I said.

"You can end that for him," said Muhammad.

O'Rourke said nothing. Obviously, he had the drugs.

"You can't kill him," I said.

"We are merely speeding a natural process," said Muhammad.

"We wait," said O'Rourke.

"Doctor, without your ministrations this man would already be dead. You are in the heart of Africa, you cannot apply your Western standards of medicine here."

"If I'd followed that tack, you'd be dead."

"That is a point quite irrelevant to the argument."

"How can you say that?" O'Rourke was angry now. "That is complete choplogic."

"I beg to disagree."

"Fuck it, Muhammad," shouted O'Rourke. "You are molding the arguments to suit our interests. It's not intelligent."

"The issue in question is the life of this man. My point concerns him. My own case is as irrelevant to the discussion as any other medical emergency."

"You're completely sidestepping any logical argument."

"But, surely, we must focus on our logic?"

"For heaven's sake," I yelled at them. "You're going round in circles. Come *on*."

We decided to take Muhammad a little way away, and come back for the soldier. O'Rourke sedated the man before we left him, and we set off with Muhammad between us, with an arm round each of our shoulders. It didn't work; his remaining leg was too painful to take his weight. So O'Rourke went back for a stretcher and we carried him. He was appallingly light.

We were in an area of woodland, with low, gnarled trees. The sun was gentle, shining through them, dappled, onto the grass. It seemed unreal. It didn't seem like war. After about half a mile we got to a big, round tree, like a mulberry tree, which gave a lot of shade. We left Muhammad there with some water and headed back.

It went against all instinct to go back to the vehicles. It seemed more dangerous than anything before. I was very, very frightened. I didn't say a word. When we were halfway there we heard the whine of planes again. We got down flat under some bushes. The noise grew, there were two planes, very low. They came right overhead, screaming. The whole area was bursting with the noise and vibrating. I was gripping O'Rourke's shoulder, digging into his flesh with my nails. I looked up and I could see the gray underbelly of a plane, filling the sky. And then there was a blast and we buried our heads in the grass feeling the whole world falling apart, shuddering, shaking, rebounding.

We were all right. We were still there. There was nothing left of the vehicles except bits of twisted metal in a crater fifty yards across. Odd how you think the selfish thing. I thought that I would get into trouble for bringing a SUSTAIN Toyota into Kefti and letting it be blown up.

"Well, that answers that little moral dilemma," said O'Rourke.

There was nothing left of the soldier. We looked all around for traces of the body but found nothing. O'Rourke, it turned out, had buried the other two soldiers in shallow graves in the woods very early in the morning. The graves were intact.

I had never seen Muhammad smile so much as when he saw us come back. He looked as though his face was going to crack with smiling. He embraced us both and actually wiped away tears.

"I think perhaps Allah was making a small point," he said.

"Oh yeah. What?" said O'Rourke.

"Only that I had logic on my side."

We had no supplies now, just water, O'Rourke's bag and a piece of cheese. It was nine o'clock. We knew we had to keep moving while the sun was still low. I felt uneasy about just going away. I thought we should do something to mark the deaths of the soldiers. Muhammad and O'Rourke thought I was mad. I made them say the Lord's Prayer with me. Then I searched for dimly remembered words, and said, "Lord, let thy servants depart in peace."

We walked until we could see the highlands of Kefti, blue-black and heavy, rising ahead of us. We were walking through a leafy glade, the sun was warm, birds were tweeting, and all at once it seemed as if we were taking a gentle Sunday afternoon stroll. I think we all felt the same sense of release as if there was no gravity anymore and we were going to float up into the sky.

Then O'Rourke started shaking with laughter. "Those last rites," he said. " 'Lord, let thy servants depart in peace.' That was wrong. They should be arriving. 'Lord, let thy servants arrive in peace.' " It suddenly sounded like the most ridiculous thing we'd ever heard and then Muhammad and I started laughing too, hysterically, saying, "Lord, let thy servants arrive in peace." We were falling about, completely helpless, so that O'Rourke and I had to put the stretcher down, doubled over, crying with laughter. And then there was a burst of machine-gun fire a hundred yards ahead.

It was Keftian soldiers from Adi Wari, looking for us. There were eight of them, They took us to a good path and carried Muhammad's stretcher. He was beginning to look very ill and tired. The land was rising more steeply now, we walked for two hours and then joined the main track again, the one we had been driving on. It turned a corner, round a hill with smooth, round rocks protruding through the trees, and for the first time we could see the landscape ahead: undulating, wooded, dark, and gashed by a deep red gorge, with the mountains as backdrop. On the edge of the gorge was the small patch of rooftops which made up Adi Wari, with glints of bright light where tin roofs were reflecting the sun.

We were met by a KPLF truck which took us straight to the hospital. The hospital was cleaner and better ordered than the hospitals in Nambula, built in a square round a large grassy courtyard. The Keftians were organized, well educated. O'Rourke was talking to their doctors about Muhammad. Once we knew that he was settled, I told O'Rourke I wanted to go and discuss the locusts with the KPLF. He asked me if I was sure I didn't want to rest for a bit, but I said I was fine. I was glad he let me go and didn't fuss me.

As I was leaving one of the nurses came after me and said that Muhammad wanted to speak with me. He was in a room on his own lying back on the mattress. There were bullet holes in one of the walls and a square hole open to the outside, with a grille half hanging over it.

"I need to speak with you," he said furtively.

I sat on the bed.

"There is a woman," he whispered. "Her name is Huda Letay. Will you remember that? Huda Letay." He seemed feverish now. "I thought . . . that perhaps . . ."

"What?" I said.

"I want you to ask for her and look for her when you are in the highlands."

"Of course. Who is Huda?"

"She is a woman . . ."

"Yes?"

He closed his eyes.

"Don't worry. I'll ask for her."

"Her name is Huda Letay. And she is a doctor of economics."

"Where will I find her?"

"I thought that perhaps she might be among the refugees in the highlands. I thought that I would find her."

"Don't worry. I'll look for her."

"She was a student with me at the University of Esareb."

"And why do you want me to find her?"

He looked away as if he was ashamed. "She is the woman whom I wished to marry."

Wished to marry. I knew how he hated loss of face. "What happened?"

"Her parents arranged for her to marry elsewhere. To a man who was wealthy. And she was not able to go against their wishes."

"How will I find her?"

"She is very beautiful."

"Could you tell me a little bit more?"

"Letay is her family name. Her married name is Imlahi. If you find her, I merely wish to know that she is safe. She is from Esareb. She has long dark hair, unusually shining, and she is always laughing. If you find her, perhaps, if she is ill or she is alone . . . you might . . ."

"I'll bring her back," I said. I knew all about having fantasies.

"Thank you."

He looked so unlike himself. All his spirit had gone. He had to remember his personality or he would sink.

"Don't you want to send a poem?" I said.

Something promising flickered in his eyes.

"'Locusts to the right of us, locusts to the left of us'?" I began—this was a favorite game of ours.

"'As I walked out one evening, walking down Bristol Street,'" he said smugly. "'The crowds upon the pavement, were fields of—'"

"Locusts," I finished. He started to smile. "'Shall I compare thee to a—'"

"Locust. 'Thou still unravished—'"

"Locust. 'I wandered lonely as a—'"

"Locust."

It wasn't the proper deep laugh, but it almost was.

"October 'is the cruelest month,'" he began. "'Breeding—'"

"Locusts 'out of the dead land,'" I finished. It wasn't funny anymore. I held his hand tightly for a while, then I left him there, and went off with the soldiers to the KPLF offices.

I was seated in front of the military commander for the region, who cannot have been more than twenty-six. He had come into the town especially to receive us. The room was long, thin and empty except for a desk, with the commander sitting at one side and me at the other, a bookshelf full of worn, thin pamphlets and a table at the back. Half a dozen soldiers were in the room, two of them standing behind the commander, the rest lounging around the table. I felt slightly ridiculous in a room full of large armed men in uniform, and unexpectedly physically vulnerable. The commander had a thin, intelligent face with a beard, and Muhammad's courtly manner of speech.

He apologized profusely for the mine and the aerial attack. He stressed how thorough the mine-clearing operation had been on the road; that they had not had a mine incident between Nambula and the highlands for six months; and that ours was a most unfortunate freak incident. The Abouti planes must have been alerted by the smoke: they never strayed into the Nambula border region as a rule. He knew all about our mission and was most keen that it should proceed.

I explained that we could not risk going farther, but he said that he would give us two vehicles to travel ahead of us, and a truck to travel in with a full armed escort, and that we would move only at night. They had vehicles traveling that route constantly, whereas the route where we had hit the mine was underused. The area where the grasshopper bands were gathered was only four hours away. If we went a little farther to Tessalay we could see the refugees beginning to move down from the highlands. It was a question of one night's drive. Surely, having got this far, it was worth achieving the goal of the mission? I said I would have to go back to the hospital and discuss it with O'Rourke. The commander excused himself and went out of the room.

When he was gone I realized that I was going to continue, even if O'Rourke didn't want to. It seemed too pointless to go back, with all this mess, and nothing achieved. The commander returned with a girl soldier, Belay Abrehet, who was to be my guide in Adi Wari. She looked slightly bored and didn't smile.

I made some more inquiries about the route and the risks. All the bridges over the gorge had been destroyed, so we would drive north to a crossing place, then down into the gorge, up the other side and farther north to another riverbed, this one dry, where the locusts were hatching. Then, if we wanted to go on, we could turn east and go up into the mountains. I started asking about the extent of the locusts and the crop damage and about the cholera stories, but the commander said I should talk to RESOK, the Keftian relief society. I told him that we would go on with them, and said I would go to the hospital after I'd been to RESOK and that we should meet here again between four or five. It was two o'clock now.

Outside there was a different kind of midday heat from that of Nambula. The sun still burned the skin, but the air was cool and in the shade it was actually chilly. Adi Wari was built on a slope leaning toward the edge of the gorge. A wide stony track ran downhill as the main street, and the buildings were rough stone and concrete with tin roofs. There were people, dogs and goats in the road and soldiers hanging around in little groups. The scene looked very different from a Nambulan town because no one was wearing a djellaba. The civilians wore cheap-looking Western clothes, or cloaks in dark colors. There was no garrison in Adi Wari: it was too obvious a target. The Keftians kept all their military accommodation and hospitals underground.

We walked down the hill and stopped at a building, which was blackened inside, with a fire burning. The man at the entrance leaned into the furnace and shoveled out four rounds of semiblackened bread. I hadn't eaten for a long time, and it was just the right kind of foodstuff: warm, soothing and unworrying. I felt absolutely fine—almost better than normal, in a state of heightened energy. I suppose it was some kind of preservative shock.

Belay lightened up a bit as we walked to RESOK. I offered her some of the burnt bread and she laughed. She was twenty-four and spoke a little English. She put her hand up to my face, touched one of my earrings and asked if she could have them and I, used to this, gave them to her. I asked her if she had taken part in the fighting and she said, "A little," and looked straight ahead as if she didn't want to discuss it. There were a lot of soldiers about and they greeted her as we passed as if they were schoolmates.

It wasn't like I expected, being in a war. At home I had vaguely imagined, without thinking it through, that a war meant fighting all the time, like in the First World War trenches, and that if you went to a war zone you would run a continual gamut of bullets. This was probably because the only bits you tended to see on the news were the shootings. Here, it felt as though life was more or less normal apart from danger spots, places you didn't go, things you didn't do—like playing on motorways. Of course it was the unexpected, the blast from nowhere, that made it lethal. But, in between, you just carried on as normal and bought bread.

We followed the main street right down to the edge of the gorge, and there I saw the remains of the bombed-out bridge, a thick concrete column set into the rocks below, with a tangle of rusting steel supports sticking out. The cliff did not fall sheer: there was a footpath down to the bottom two hundred yards below, crisscrossing the red rocks like a mini–mountain pass. The river was a frothy ribbon, meandering between shingle beaches and broad stretches of grass. I thought, for a split second, that it looked a nice place to camp.

We turned left along the edge and then back up the slope again and into a compound where I saw the RESOK sign and a couple of Land Rovers parked outside. Inside, the walls were covered with Keftian art, primitive drawings of the war. I had seen these paintings before. Sometimes there were Keftian art exhibitions in a community hall in Sidra which had been built by the Japanese in the sixties.

The man I needed to see was the head of RESOK for the Adi

Wari region, Hagose Woldu, whose name had often come up in discussions in the camp. It turned out he had just left to go to the KPLF office. So we went back there to find that he had left to come and meet us at RESOK. So we set off again. When we got back to RESOK he gave me a most warm and gratifying greeting.

"Miss Rosie, it is my great honor to meet you. We are most grateful for your work with our people in Safila."

Hagose was a very tall man indeed, dressed in brown polyester trousers, which were much too short for him, and a very old mock denim shirt with floral cuffs and collar.

He took me to a room where a relief model of Kefti was laid out on a large table, the highlands forming a doughnut shape, the desert in the center, and lowlands on the outside, crossed by the riverbeds. You could see the Adi Wari gorge where we were. The highlands beyond were crevassed with great fissures. An extraordinary oval plateau was surrounded by cliffs on all sides.

Hagose had placed model huts in various sizes, like Monopoly houses, all over the mountains and lowlands to show the population distribution; with red flags to show the current areas of fighting, and green flags to show where the locusts were hatching. There were green flags all over the desert area in the center and the low-lands which ringed the mountains. They were in clusters along the coast, in clusters at the river mouths, and following the course of the riverbed in the plain beyond the gorge. I asked him how he had gathered all this information without aerial surveillance. Hagose claimed it was by word of mouth. He said that the locusts in the desert center were swarming and moving west and crops were al-ready disappearing in the western highlands. He said that the pop-ulation was already beginning to move the length of the country.

It was difficult to know how much to believe because he had everything to gain by sending me back in a breathless state declar-ing an emergency. I thought about what Gunter had said at the em-bassy party and wondered. But all I needed to know about was the area which fed Safila. If I saw refugees moving there on the routes to us, then I would know what I was dealing with.

Directly east of Safila there was a break in the first ridge of mountains—the Tessalay pass. This was where some of the most dramatic scenes of the mid-eighties exodus had been filmed for TV.

Hagose made much of their lack of wherewithal to deal with the infestations. The Keftians didn't have any pesticide and even if they had had planes, it was too risky to fly. At the moment they were trying to deal with the swarms by beating them off with sticks, digging trenches in between the crops and filling them with fires. Apparently, the Aboutians had bombed two villages making these sorts of preparations. Hagose wanted an amnesty to be declared, and the UN to come in and spray. Too late, too late, I thought. It would take three months to set that up.

Hagose was going to send a RESOK official into the highlands with us, and send word ahead to the villages we were going to visit. He said he would go over to the KPLF and talk to them about the route.

Belay and I went to the hospital. Muhammad was asleep, they told me, and O'Rourke had gone off to find us. It was a typical afternoon of confusion. I left a message that I would be at the KPLF ready to go between four and five. And went shopping.

I bought bread, tomatoes, grapefruit, and tinned cheese. It was cloudy now, and gray. I caught a gust of wind and shivered. I bought some blankets as well. Belay left me to visit a relative. As I walked up to the KPLF I could see O'Rourke with a group of soldiers, peering under the back of the vehicle, checking something.

"So you reckon you can get another truck?" O'Rourke was saying to one of the soldiers, as we approached.

"Yes, I think it is possible."

"How long will that take?"

"I think we will be finding one at Gof."

"No. Not at Gof. What I am saying is that I do not want to set off in this vehicle. The back axle is fucked. Do you have another vehicle in Adi Wari?"

"It is possible."

O'Rourke saw me and nodded. His patience seemed to be wearing thin. There was a heated discussion in Keftian among the soldiers. They were all leaning down and peering at the back axle. We edged away so we could talk without being overheard.

"I came to find you at the hospital," I said. "What do you think about going on? They say it's only four hours to where the locusts are. You don't have to come, if you don't think—"

"No, no, that's fine," he said. "I've talked to them. It sounds OK, but I'll believe this four hours business when I see it. Listen, are you all right?" He touched my arm and rubbed it. "You're frozen. Here take this." He took off his jumper.

"What about you?"

"I'm fine."

"But—"

"Just put it on, you're shivering."

It was a soft gray woolen jumper. I put it on. It smelt of him. I liked that.

"What's happening with the truck?"

"It's a heap. It'll pack up within five miles. We'll have to wait for another."

It seemed Muhammad was all right. O'Rourke had operated on the stump that afternoon. He had managed to save the knee. For just a moment I thought, Oh, God, are we being mad going on? Will that happen to me?

It was dark by the time they brought another truck. O'Rourke inspected it thoroughly with a torch, got them to change a tire and put another spare in. He was being very good.

It wasn't four hours to the locusts, of course. We drove at a snail's pace, with shades over the lights so that you could just see a dim glow on the ground directly ahead and two red glows beneath the taillights of the trucks in front. It was very, very cold. O'Rourke and I were in the cab of the third truck. I was in the middle, between him and the driver. We put the blankets round us and I tried to sleep by leaning my head back against the seat. He said, "You can lean on me." I tried laying my head on his shoulder but it was uncomfortable and he sat up and put his arm round me and I slept then.

I woke up when we reached the crossing point. The road tipped at an unfeasible angle, the gears and engine straining. We stopped at the bottom and got out. There was no moon. It was chill and dank down there with the great cliffs looming above. I could hear the river off to our right. It sounded shallow, like a stream. I had bad pins and needles so that I could hardly bear to move my legs. I was very stiff. The back of my neck was jarred, and my mouth tasted filthy. I got back in the cab and ate some grapefruit and bread and drank some water and shivered. We set off again in convoy, forded the river and climbed the other side of the gorge. When we were back on the level I dozed again.

At 4:00 A.M. we reached the dry riverbed where the grasshopper bands were supposed to be. It was still pitch black. We parked and waited. I got the camera ready.

The blackness was diluting. A patch of gray appeared ahead on the horizon. We were pulled up on the edge of a small hill with the shallow river basin before us and a broad escarpment, about fifty feet high, half a mile beyond.

Slowly detail edged out of the darkness, drained of color. I strained my eyes to see what was ahead and recoiled, stunned. The whole of the basin was alive, moving in waves. There was a carpet of insects half a mile across, covering the earth and the road ahead. They lay there, like something from a horror movie, glinting in the growing light.

A thin orange cusp appeared on the horizon. And as it rose the clouds tore open, letting color flood into the scene. As the first rays hit the carpet a shower of insects right across its surface fluttered up, dancing in the light like a snowstorm.

Fifteen

We drove both ways along the edge of the escarpment, looking down onto the insect carpet. It stretched for five kilometers. At one point we walked down into it. The most unnerving thing was that the locusts didn't react to us at all. They stayed put, clinging doggedly to the earth, even if we walked over them. They were like aliens with a secret common purpose. Occasionally, as the sun rose higher, a whole area of them would heave and shift for no clear reason. The man from RESOK picked a couple up and showed us their wings. They were ready to fly.

I was beginning to worry about how all this would translate into hard evidence. I wondered if our description and some odd-looking photographs would be enough—a carpet of insects is not ideal as a photographic subject. We put a few of the insects in a polythene bag to take back with us. I decided I should get some signed affidavits as well. Ideally, they should have been from disinterested parties. The trouble was, there were no disinterested parties.

The soldiers were getting jumpy about air raids so we drove five kilometers westward, to a village where there was an underground shelter. The village was fairly large: a huddle of about two hundred huts set in a little valley below us, with the dry yellow stalks of the crop growing in terraces all around. The people had started to harvest even though the crop was not ready, because as soon as the locust swarm moved, the wind would bring it this way.

There was frantic activity. The whole village was out in the fields. From a distance their curved backs moving up and down in the crop looked like maggots. They were harvesting strips in each field, starting to dig trenches in the bald patches left behind and filling them with straw, so if the locusts came they could light fires to protect the rest of the crop. The village sounds rose up at us, as we approached: a babble of voices, animal sounds, high-pitched cries from the children, a cock crow. It all seemed feeble and hopeless when you thought what they were up against. A couple of hours with a light aircraft and some pesticide could have solved it for them.

We were sitting in the KPLF compound, drinking tea in the shade, when a cloud passed over the sun. And at once a great cry went up outside, the high whooping sound the Keftians make when someone has died and we knew it was the locusts. We went outside the fence and saw that a shadow was creeping over the whole area.

Everyone was running towards the crop. The cloud came around us as we got there. The locusts felt like chips of wood, hitting your face, and any exposed part of you. Flames rose up from the trench directly ahead, and thick smoke followed as someone threw damp straw on top. It was almost completely dark. I abandoned the photographs for now, pulled my blue shawl over my head and ran into the field. There were figures everywhere, flailing at the air with beaters made from long sticks with a bundle of twigs tied at the end. Someone thrust a stick into my hands. I stopped to stare at a plant in front of me. Each of the narrow yellow leaves, and the pod of grain at the top, had seven or eight insects teeming over its surface. I watched one leaf disappear, with the locusts dropping below or fluttering up as it was finished. I started hitting the plant with the stick, over and over again, making it shake. The insects clung on, I couldn't dislodge them. There was a great rushing roar all around. Immediately ahead, through the smoke, flames and darkness a thin old woman was beating at the plants. The brown cloth around her body had slipped down, her sagging breasts flapped in time with her beating. As I watched she let the stick fall from her hand. She raised one hand, formed it weakly into a fist and raised it. Then legs folded under her, as in a curtsy, she let herself fall to the ground, and rolled her head in the soil.

Four hours later there was nothing left of the crop. The people were out in the fields whooping, wailing, tearing their hair, beating their heads, raising their hands up and falling down to the ground in traditional histrionic public mourning. And as the sun bore down in the white midday heat, scorching the dry earth, shimmering on the horizon in a vicious mirage of water, you could understand their terror. The earth had nothing more to give for six months now. There was no more food.

We were supposed to be relief workers, but we were helpless. There we were, crawling on the surface of those tracts of dryness, watching a whole nation's food drain away. What could we do? O'Rourke treated a few cases of burns and heat exhaustion. I took more photographs, feeling like a voyeur. We could only warn that there was little food to spare at Safila.

We slept in the underground shelter and drove on when it was dark. I hated the darkness now. Beyond the foothills, the road started to climb steeply. There were high mountain peaks all around us. The air smelt alpine. We climbed for a long way, then cleared a summit and dropped down again into a narrow valley, running at right angles to the road. We had the headlights on now that we were in the mountains. The Aboutians would not risk flying here at night, particularly when there was no moon.

Our driver suddenly held up his hand and said melodramatically, "Tessalay."

Ahead of us was a wall of rock higher than anything we had come across before. A dip in this first range of peaks formed the start of the Tessalay pass—a four-mile corridor through the highest section of the western highlands. At this end the rocky corridor was closed off by a low ridge which formed the dip in the range. The road snaked up it and down the other side to enter it.

Before we even started to climb we were aware of figures moving along the edge of the road. A little group would be caught in the lights, with one of them leaning out into the road, hand raised, trying to flag us down. They did not look as though they expected us to stop since all they saw was KPLF trucks. The military had nothing to offer them. As we climbed the bends of the pass the numbers increased until there was a group every fifty feet or so at either side of the road. They all did the same thing as we passed, straightening up and raising a hand halfheartedly to stop us.

At the top of the pass all the vehicles stopped. I wished there was a moon, then, because it would have been an extraordinary view with the whole pass stretching below us, and I wanted to see the scale of the movement. The drivers tried to angle the lights so that we could see the figures climbing up from the floor of the pass. The people we were passing were not as bad as I'd feared. They were thin, but not starving, and they had possessions with them. I thought that maybe they had learned lessons from last time and decided to move while they were still strong enough to travel—but they had a long way to go to Safila. Tessalay was a dangerous place to be, because the Aboutians knew about the refugee movement and there were air raids most days. The road was impassable for vehicles now because of the bomb damage. The refugees traveled as far as they could at night and made for the underground shelters in the valleys off the pass, well before daylight.

It wasn't long till dawn now. We thought we should set up in one of the shelters and do a survey. We found one just over the top of the ridge. It was cavernous, big enough to take all three of our vehicles. The ground at the entrance was covered in black engine oil and spare parts and military vehicles were everywhere. It was more like a mechanic's shop than an air raid shelter. People were smoking even with all the oil about. I thought it was a death trap. I didn't want to stay there. I said this to O'Rourke and he agreed.

In the end we drove as far as we could down the other side of the ridge until we came to a crater. We got out then, to walk to the next shelter, and left the drivers to take the trucks somewhere where they would be hidden and safe. It was a bit of a mistake to set off on foot, because as soon as the people saw that we were foreigners, who might have money or food we were mobbed. A crowd gathered around us quickly: crabby hands grabbed at my flesh and people were jabbing their fingers at their mouths aggressively. I

wasn't afraid because I had seen this before and it wasn't that anyone meant us any harm. It was more of an elaborate pantomime.

The soldiers started hitting at the crowd with sticks. They
weren't hitting hard but, all the same, it meant that O'Rourke and
I, caring angels from the West, were setting out through the mob to
save the starving, while our soldier escorts cleared our path by
thwacking at malnourished women and children. After fifteen seconds O'Rourke stood stock still and roared with the full depth of
his voice: "WILL—YOU—STOP—THAT—BEATING."

There was a stunned silence and the crowd fell away immediately around him.

"Put those sticks down," he said, gesturing to the soldiers. "Put
the sticks down."

They looked at him as if he was mad, and held the sticks by their
sides.

"Now clear a path," he said, gesturing ahead of him at the crowd.
"Make a path here, look," and the crowd parted like the Red Sea so
that we could make our way along. As we walked, I turned round
to see that, sure enough, the soldiers had resumed their thwacking
behind us, and some of the crowd were laughing.

The shelter they led us to was like a broad tunnel dug into the
hillside, orderly inside with people sleeping in lines on mats or low
wooden beds. There was an open area in the center where those
who were not asleep were milling around. We set up a table,
weighed and measured the kids, and asked questions. The height-
for-weight ratio was about eighty-five percent on average, which
wasn't bad; eighty percent was the danger point. It meant that the
people would be in a poor state when they reached us, but not as
bad as the last time.

The refugees were coming from a fairly limited area of the western highlands within a band of about forty miles either side of
where we were in the Tessalay corridor. So far, the crop losses
seemed to be focused in this one band. That backed up what
Gunter had said to me at the embassy party. But, then, this was only
the start of the swarming season and it was hard to know what was
going on elsewhere in Kefti. From the picture we were building up,

we estimated that between five and seven thousand refugees were on the move, heading for Safila.

I asked everyone about Huda Letay but they said that no one was here from Esareb because it was a large town and the crisis was not affecting the towns as yet.

O'Rourke had set up in a corner, examining people who were sick. There were all the usual illnesses which went with hunger: diarrheas, dysenteries, respiratory problems, some measles cases, but nothing unexpected and no meningitis. Even so, if we didn't have the drugs we needed it wouldn't take long for these people to turn Safila into a death camp again.

We asked RESOK to make an announcement, warning the refugees about the food situation in Nambula, and saying that they might be better staying put, but these people just shrugged or laughed. It was obvious to them that where there were Western agencies and the UN they had a better chance of getting food than here. I remember looking round at the people, when RESOK were giving the address, and thinking—yes, I will see you all again and your skin will be tight over your faces, so that your mouths are trapped in a grin, and your hair will be thin, and you will not be able to walk and your children will be dead and there is nothing any of us can do about it. It is awful to feel responsibility and have no power. We set off back to Adi Wari at the end of that day, when it got dark.

When we reached the hospital, we found that Muhammad had already been taken back to Safila. O'Rourke stayed to look at some cases in the hospital, and I walked to the RESOK offices. I explained to Hagose about the low supplies in eastern Nambula. I suggested he try to disperse the refugees amongst the villages here which had food. But he gave me a familiar look which said, "Don't try to kid me that the West can't come up with food when it wants to. We know about the wine lakes and the grain mountains." When I got back to the KPLF, O'Rourke had found a Land Rover, which we could take back to Safila, and had arranged for a truck to escort us to the border. From there we would continue on our own.

The air was getting warmer, and the soft earthy smell of Nambula drifted through the open windows. The truck ahead stopped, and O'Rourke pulled up too. After a few moments the truck set off again, branching off from the track we had been following. It was clear that we must be close to the border. The KPLF knew where the line was. Half an hour later the truck stopped again, and this time the soldiers got out. We got out too, and said rather over-the-top good-byes, shaking their hands, sharing embraces, full of camaraderie as if we'd met on holiday and it was time to go home.

"Any second now we'll be swapping addresses," O'Rourke muttered to me as he extracted himself from the second effusive embrace with the same soldier. "If this goes on much longer, I'll be bearing this man's child and washing his socks."

When the sound of their engine had died away we stood for a while in the open desert. The sky was a huge arc of stars, bursting with light.

"You did good up there," he said, nodding back towards Kefti.

"Not as good as you."

The air was heady. We were standing on sand which felt cool underneath my feet. We were standing very close, looking at each other.

"Shall we drive on then?" he said.

He was right that we should get away from the border because it wasn't too safe around there. Besides, it was already ten o'clock and we were a good five hours from Sidra. I drove for a while. Then we swapped. We were both very tired. I think it was the relief at being out of Kefti which let the tiredness out. I could only just see him in the glow from the instrument panels. His shirt was rolled up over his forearms. His arms and wrists were strong, adult-looking. I had never really thought about wrists before, but suddenly these seemed like the most beautiful wrists I had ever seen, such strong wrists, such manly wrists, such brave wrists, such wondrous wrists.

"How far do you think we should go tonight?" he said, then looked slightly embarrassed, realizing what he'd said.

"You're driving."

A little later he brought the truck to a halt, and cut the ignition.

We lit a fire and sat by it on a piece of tarpaulin. O'Rourke brought out a bottle of whisky.

"Where'd you get that?" I said, surprised.

"KPLF."

He had some dope as well. We watched the fire. There was one big black log, becoming white and dimpled underneath, crumbling into the embers. When he passed me the joint our hands brushed. We didn't talk at first, then I lay back on the tarpaulin and he lay back too, away from me, and we talked.

He told me that his father had been a diplomat and he had been brought up in various parts of Africa and in the Far East and had been in the Peace Corps when he left medical school. His father was dead now and his mother lived in Boston. He had become disillusioned with medicine and had worked in New York for a long time making corporate films and commercials for drug companies and a lot of money.

"Then it all fell to pieces."

"How?"

He didn't say anything for a while, then, "I don't want to talk about that . . . if you don't mind."

"All right."

"Tell me why you came out here," he said.

I told him a certain amount because I was stoned. But I didn't tell him about Oliver. We fell silent. He passed me the joint and our hands touched again. We were alone. It was so tantalizingly close. We mustn't, I thought. I thought about Linda. I thought about going back to Safila. I lay back on the tarpaulin and looked up at the stars, feeling my brain swimming from the joint. I took another drag, and started to wonder if anything we did tonight really mattered at all.

"Look up there," I said, after a few moments. "Look at those stars. Makes you feel so tiny, powerless. Tiny beneath the stars." I moistened my lips. "What do you think our purpose is here on earth, O'Rourke?"

"You're away with the fairies, aren't you?"

"I am a fairy," I said, handing him the joint.

After a while, he said, "To live right, I guess."

Later he got up and went to the truck. The door opened. He was moving about. The door closed. He came back with some bedding and handed a bundle to me, bending over me. He kissed me lightly, as if to say good night. He kissed me again. When he kissed me the third time it was with finality.

"I'm going to sleep over here," he said. "If you need anything, just whistle."

I woke again at two o'clock. I had somehow moved closer to him. I sat up and looked around. The fire had burned down so that it was almost all white, with a bit of the big log still black in the middle, red underneath. You could see plants in the glow, with big, round leaves, like we had in Safila. O'Rourke was asleep, breathing heavily with one arm over his head, covering his face. I lay back and looked at the stars for a while. It was still warm, with just the lightest of breezes every now and then. I pulled the cover over me and turned to face his back. He was wearing a thin khaki shirt. My face was so close I was almost touching him. He rolled onto his back, adjusting his head and his arms. When he settled back there was a change in his breathing that told me he was awake. I lay still, with my heart thumping. I looked up at the outline of his chin. Then I saw one eye open, look down at me and close again. He turned slowly to face me. He reached out and put his hand on the small of my back, his fingers touching my waist. I held my breath. Our mouths were so close they were almost touching. Then, using the palm of his hand, he moved me towards him, pressing me into him against his jeans where he was hard. He moved his mouth just slightly closer and our lips brushed, and this time it was not possible to resist, in the firelight, all alone together after the terrors.

CHAPTER

Sixteen

When I awoke, in a euphoric glow from the night, O'Rourke was already up, boiling water in a billycan on the fire. It was still very early. The sun was only just clearing the horizon. I took one look and shut my eyes again. We shouldn't have done it. It had been wonderful, but we shouldn't have done it. Maybe Linda wasn't involved with O'Rourke anymore, but she certainly wanted to be. I didn't want her to be upset, I didn't want to be upset myself, and I didn't want O'Rourke to be in an awkward spot, not when so much pressure was building up for us all. The trouble was, romantic feelings were beginning to creep out and run around with no respect whatsoever for the scale of the crisis we were facing.

He didn't know I was awake. I looked across, and took in every detail of him as he stared into the fire, the khaki shirt stretched across his back, his forearm resting on his knee, the thoughtful, quiet profile, and I knew what was happening to me. Out here, the absolute coexistence of opposites: tragedy and comedy, the serious and the superficial, had long ceased to surprise me. Even when the grimmest events were taking place, trivial matters continued to annoy, and affairs of the heart, far from retreating into insignificance, seemed to be whipped up, heightened.

Since the Oliver debacle I had four years of romantic aridity, but emotional peace. And now, just when I needed to be calm and to concentrate—this. I had to get a grip. I didn't want to go back to all that turmoil I had had with Oliver. This was not the time, even without the complication of Linda. O'Rourke and I would just have to brush away what happened last night, be mature about it, and go on as before.

I made a bit of a fuss of waking up, yawning and stretching.

He looked over at me.

"I do apologize for last night," I said. "Can't imagine what came over me."

He looked relieved. "Do you want a cup of tea?" he said.

"In a minute." I stood up and looked around. "Not a bush in sight," I said.

"Try behind the Land Rover. I'll shout if anyone's coming," he said, with the quick smile, looking at the featureless circle of the horizon.

We were fantastically mature on the drive back to Sidra, *fantastically* mature. We talked about every aspect of the locust crisis and went through all possible options for dealing with it. It was almost as if the night had never happened. O'Rourke was unexpectedly relaxed. I had been expecting him to be all tense and in a bad mood. I had automatically assumed that he would regret what we had done, and start pushing me away: the legacy of Oliver. In fact, he seemed perfectly normal. After about two hours of driving across flat sand we saw an object on the horizon. As we got closer we realized it was two lorries which had crashed head-on. We started to laugh. They had managed to drive straight into each other on a stretch of track with neither a bend, nor an obstacle, nor indeed any feature whatsoever for fifty miles.

"I guess they must love each other," said O'Rourke. "They met by accident."

They did look endearingly affectionate, pressed together, nose to nose. It must have happened some days ago. The cargo had been taken away and there was no one around except an Englishman on a bicycle. He was wearing a safari suit and a pith helmet and had a pack on his back.

"How, in the name of *arse*," bellowed the man, as we drew alongside, "did this absurdity happen? I say. Am I going the right way for Kefti?"

"This," murmured O'Rourke, cutting the ignition, "is why I never go back home."

"I was just thinking exactly the same thing."

We were still laughing, and saying, "What in the name of *arse* . . ." when we drove away. It turned out that the Englishman was on a sponsored lone cycle ride, crossing Africa from west to east to raise money for a donkey sanctuary in Norfolk. He was surprised by the news that there had been a war in Kefti for the last two decades, but would not be persuaded of the need for a detour.

We were only about an hour from Sidra now. Soon we could see the shape of the weird red mountains rising up on the horizon. On the surface I probably seemed as relaxed as O'Rourke did to me. I kept taking out little moments from the night of passion, like new purchases wrapped in tissue paper, remembering. I felt rushes of affection and vulnerability. Deep inside I could feel something ridiculous going on. As we drew closer to Sidra, and I realized the intimacy of the last few days was about to be broken, it got worse and worse. It was no use. I couldn't help myself. I was starting to want to know where the relationship was going. And we weren't even late for anything.

The arrival in Sidra brought welcome distraction. I suggested we drop off the photographs to be developed, find something to eat and then report to André at the UN. We sat in a dirty café on the main square and had a Coke while we waited for our food. We sat in silence. I tried to concentrate on the scene. A horse and cart was clopping by, carrying charcoal, looking as if it had had a bag of soot emptied over it. From across the road, a boy dressed in a sack with sand smeared on his face was making his way towards us, begging as he went. Apart from the sand on his face, it wasn't clear what was wrong with him. The people he approached all put money into his bowl as if they were used to him.

"Do you think he's crazy?" I asked O'Rourke, in a matter-of-fact voice.

"Dunno. Could be schizophrenia."

It was no use. I felt it welling up again. O'Rourke looked so ir-resistible to me now. Such a good man, so self-possessed, so purposeful. And now we were going to be separated by other people. I kept thinking about what we did last night. What did it mean to him? Did he care about me as much as he seemed to? What was going to happen to us now? It was going to burst out. God, I wished I was a man. I sat on my hands and clamped my lips tightly together.

"Er—Rosie. Are you all right?" he said.

"Fine. Why?" I said in a strained voice.

"It's just, you look—rather peculiar, that's all."

"I'm fine."

He leaned over and put his hand on my forehead. "Hmmm."

That just made it even worse. What do you feel about me anyway? I wanted to shout. What's going on?

"I'm just going for a little walk," I said instead. He looked at me, puzzled.

I came back when the food was ready, feeling rather more composed. The crisis had passed. I was going to be the iron woman again now, with a bit of luck.

A third of the photographs hadn't come out at all. There was a whole collection of entirely black ones. "Night," we decided they should be called. Then there were the blurred ones. "Fog?" O'Rourke suggested. "Fur?" Some of them were fine. Enough of them were good enough.

We ordered a dozen prints each of the good ones, and set off to find André at the UNHCR. As we were driving there, I started thinking about the implications, here, of the explosion. I didn't know how much trouble we were going to be in.

"What did I say to you?" André said, when we walked into his office. "Don't go there yourself. Are you OK?"

I handed him the photos.

"My Gaaad."

"Ten days till the ship, then?" I said.

"I wish," he said grimly.

"What, you mean it isn't coming?" said O'Rourke.

"It's coming, but not in ten days."

"When, then?"

"Mother of God, I wish I knew. They say another two to three weeks."

O'Rourke handed André a cigarette, and lit his own. The delay with the ship wasn't the worst of it. There had been arrivals in other camps farther north along the border.

"I'm sorry, guys. I just don't know what to say."

This was no longer the reassuring André I knew, the man with the invincible light touch. This was a man with a quarter of a million people running out of food on his hands.

"I know it's not your fault," I said. "But I just can't understand how these government organizations can go through so much, be publicly humiliated, like they were in Ethiopia, and still fuck up."

André just put his hands in the air and rolled his eyes.

The conversation moved on to the Security forces. Apparently Abdul Gerbil, the Security chief in Sidra, was apoplectic about what we had done. He was an insanely bossy man, who always wore Blues Brothers–style sunglasses with his djellaba, and sported a Coco the Clown hairdo.

"It's not the fact of the trip itself, it's the fact that he didn't find out about it first," said André.

"The problem will be if it gets in the press," said O'Rourke. "That will really piss him off. Has anyone picked it up?"

"No. I think it's fine," said André. "I've told everyone to keep their mouths shut."

"And what about Malcolm?" I said.

"Haven't heard anything."

"Only a matter of time, I suppose," I said.

We decided we had to go to the Security office. But the heavens were smiling upon us, and Abdul Gerbil had gone north for the day. We made very certain that everyone of note knew we had come, and we left a formal letter for Gerbil saying that we had come to discuss the most unfortunate events with him. Then, trying not to break into a run, we jumped into the Land Rover and got the hell out.

We dropped André back at the office and he promised to send a report, and the photographs straight to El Daman. "I'll see if I can get a message to Malcolm before he causes too much trouble, calm him down a bit."

"Thanks," I said. "Do you think he knows about the Toyota?"

"Probably not. I didn't know."

"Good. Don't tell him, then."

"Oh, sure, I'm going to tell him. OK. Look, if you're stuck you can take one of ours, we've got a couple of spares, OK? Do you want to do that?"

Unbelievable that they had spare vehicles hanging around. "Yes, please."

That was much better than driving around in a KPLF Land Rover, even if it was unmarked. I knew where the KPLF had their base in Sidra, though it was unofficial. So we took the Land Rover back to them and set off to Safila in the UN pickup.

"Knock, knock, anyone at home?" Betty was tapping playfully on the top of my head. I looked up, startled, at Henry, Linda, Sian, Debbie and O'Rourke sitting round the cabana table with the remains of dinner in front of them.

"Sorry, sorry. I'm just a bit shell-shocked."

"Literally, poor old sock," said Henry.

"You should get an early night," said Debbie.

It was good to be back in the warmth of the cabana chat. Fungusman was still there, but he had decided he wanted the leg cut off now. Henry had got drunk and dyed one of the dogs purple using iodine. It was all very amusing, but underneath we were all taut and nervous. In the camp a third of the children were below eighty-five percent, weight for height. There had been three hundred more arrivals since we left, and the daily deaths were rising.

"I think if you don't mind I'll get an early night," I said. "I need some sleep."

O'Rourke, seated nearest the door caught my hand on the way out. "You OK?" he whispered.

"Yes, fine, just . . . tired. I'll see you tomorrow."

I wondered if the others noticed anything odd.

The next day was not good. I overslept: it was eight o'clock when I eventually got myself up and showered. I emerged, wet-haired and wrapped in a towel, to find the giant horse head of Gunter Brand staring across the compound at me. Gunter was being harassed by Fungusman, who was making sawing motions across his leg, jerking his chin up and shouting. Gunter had evidently struck him as the perfect man for the job. Meanwhile Psycho, the dog Henry had dyed bright purple, was barking and running round the two of them in a circle. What was Gunter doing here? And where was everybody else?

I shot into the hut. If Gunter was here this was our big chance to get something done. I dressed in two seconds flat, and came out again, sporting a confident smile.

"Gunter, how nice to see you. Psycho, sit!" I said authoritatively, as if it would be a completely normal, everyday occurrence for Psycho suddenly to sit down. "Phew, I was just having a little freshen-up, it's been a long morning! Would you like a drink? Come on in." I motioned him towards the cabana, placing myself between him and Fungusman, who stuck out his leg at me and mimed a chopping action. "Shut up and go away," I hissed, gesticulating at him. "Go away. Go away."

Psycho was following Gunter into the cabana, rushing at his ankles and barking. Gunter, clutching his briefcase, did a little dance to avoid the dog.

"Why is this dog purple?"

"Haha," I laughed merrily. "Now. What can I get you? Cold drink? Cup of tea?"

Kamal the cook wasn't there and the kettle had disappeared.

"A cup of tea would be nice, thank you."

"Ah. Actually, I'm not sure where the kettle is. Would you like a Coke while I have a look for it?"

As I opened the fridge two packets of Brie fell out into my hands. The interior looked as though it had been filled by a wealthy, dipsomaniac mother of twelve who had just been to the *hyper-*

marché. Bottles of O'Rourke's Pouilly-Fuissé, raspberry vodka, boxes of Lindt chocolates, tins of pâté and quarters of Stilton were crammed onto the shelves. I stuffed the Brie back in quickly, and shut the door, turning round to find Gunter staring. The sound of a vehicle coming up the road reminded me of the UN pickup which André had loaned us. Gunter must not be allowed to know about it or the blown-up Toyota. He might just overlook the fact that we'd been to Kefti, but not if he knew about the mine. It could turn into a diplomatic incident.

"Shit." Gunter was looking down now, furious, shaking his leg. Psycho had decided to shag Gunter's foot.

"Psycho! Stop it." I grabbed his collar and tried to restrain him. "Would you mind just popping into the other room?" I said. "He seems to have taken a fancy to you, I'll get rid of him."

I dragged Psycho out, flung him towards the edge of the hill and ran out into the road to flag down the UN pickup. But it wasn't the UN pickup, it was one of our Toyotas, driven by Debbie.

"Gunter's here from the UNHCR," I hissed. "Can you go down and tell them to hide the UN pickup?"

"OK," she said cheerfully. "I've just got to stop off at the store on the way but I'll tell them."

Back in the cabana, Gunter was striding irritably around the sitting area. I opened the fridge a crack to get out a couple of Cokes and took them to him, out of breath.

"I'm sorry no one was here to greet you when you arrived."

"It was a somewhat unusual reception."

"So André isn't with you?"

Shit. The end of a joint and a packet of rolling papers with a square torn out lay in an ashtray on the table.

"No, he has gone up to the port."

I put my hand over the roach and the rolling papers and picked up the ashtray. Had he seen? He showed no sign.

"Oh, really? What's he doing there? Why don't you sit down? I'll just have another scout around for that kettle!"

The drug paraphernalia disappeared into the bin. The kettle had not returned. Unaccountably I picked up a grapefruit and took it back to Gunter, who was now sitting down. He looked at me oddly. We had a somewhat strained conversation. He appeared to be on a whistle-stop morale-boosting tour. I started to tell him about the problem. Then there was the sound of a vehicle again. I prayed it would be O'Rourke or, at least, not Betty.

"So, you see," I was saying to Gunter, "we're really only OK for three more weeks as we are." There were slamming doors. A female voice. A male voice. O'Rourke's voice. Good. Except that the female voice sounded angry. They were heading for the cabana, getting louder. I realized that if Debbie had missed them while she was at the store, nobody would know that I was still up here.

"You're sleeping with Rosie, I just know you are."

It was Linda. They were outside the cabana. I looked at Gunter with horror. He was staring straight ahead.

O'Rourke's voice came again: quiet, reasonable; but what he was saying was indistinct. "Just because . . . Kefti with Rosie . . . sleeping with Rosie."

"I don't know how you can say this. I don't know how you dare!" shouted Linda.

"But . . . what . . . to do with you?" I still couldn't quite make out what he was saying.

"Everything." They were heading into the cabana, now. I was frozen to the spot.

"But you're not my girlfriend. I don't have a relationship with you. I never said I was coming here to be with you. This isn't right." My mind was racing. They were entering the kitchen area.

"You've slept with her, haven't you? Admit it. You have."

"Linda. Don't do this."

"All my instincts tell me that you have been fucking our administrator on your reconnaissance trip to Kefti, and given my past relationship with you, and given that I have to work with both of you, I have a right to know whether or not this is true."

"You don't." They were heading for the sitting area, where we were.

"You've slept with Rosie. I know you have. When did you do it? Where?"

"All right. Have it your way. Yes, I slept with Rosie. I slept with Rosie, two nights ago. In the desert. On a piece of tarpaulin," he said, as they appeared in the doorway, to find Gunter and me staring at them, open-mouthed.

O'Rourke tried to get us out of the situation by pretending it hadn't happened. It wasn't a bad try.

"Hey, a visitor. Hi! Pleased to meet you. My name is Robert O'Rourke, I'm in the process of taking over as MO for Safila. This is Linda Bryant, nurse and nutritionist."

"O'Rourke. Linda. This is Gunter Brand," I joined in valiantly. "The UN High Commissioner for Refugees for Nambula." O'Rourke's eyes met mine, horrified. "Gunter, this is Robert O'Rourke, our new doctor, fresh from the States, and Linda Bryant. Linda's been with us for two years now. Has anyone seen the kettle?"

I was trying to get either Linda or O'Rourke to follow me into the kitchen so that I could tell them to get rid of the UN pickup, but Linda seemed on the verge of bursting into tears and was rooted to the spot, and O'Rourke was doing some sort of maniacal old boy's act with Gunter. I had never heard him talk so much. He was holding the keys in his hand, jangling them. I brought them drinks. I wondered if Gunter was going to go berserk. I went back to the kitchen. Did this mean there was nothing going on between them, after all? Were we still going to be able to work together? I came back to the living room. Suddenly I heard another vehicle. Henry was out of it and in the cabana bellowing before I could do a thing. "Hi. I've brought the UN pickup up as ordered pronto. Is this our visitor? Bloody nice of you to lend us the truck. Bloody good of you. Thanks a lot."

It was O'Rourke who took the initiative and told Gunter the truth about Kefti. Funnily enough, he seemed more impressed than angry. He listened to us, looked at the photographs and the figures with some concern and asked a lot of questions. He clung to the view that the locusts were in limited areas and disputed our estimate of the numbers heading for Safila. But the very fact of his presence showed that he was acknowledging a problem on some scale.

Down in the camp Gunter's tour was going well. We were in the feeding center. The mothers were sitting in ordered lines spooning something into their children's mouths out of orange plastic cups. We were standing at the back, behind the cooking pots, when I heard a voice behind us, clear as a bell. "Are you sleeping with Rosie?"

It was Sian, on the other side of the rush matting wall.

"Are you?" she said.

I was flabbergasted. What on earth had got into everyone today?

"Of course I'm not bloody well sleeping with Rosie, you mad-woman," said Henry's voice. "Old as the bloody hills."

"You seem to spend all your time with her."

"Sian, old girl, I am Rosie's assistant."

"*Why* can't I move into your tukul?"

"No room, old girl."

"It's because of what's happening with Rosie, isn't it?"

Gunter was looking at me very hard.

"Sian, I am not sleeping with Henry. Henry, I am not as old as the hills," I said through the wall, then smiled graciously, in queenly manner. "Shall we move on, Gunter?"

As a grand finale, while Gunter and I stood watching the dry ra-tion distribution, Abdul Gerbil appeared, djellaba flapping, sun-glasses askew. Popping with rage, he ran through the whole story of Kefti: the dead soldiers, the wrecked Toyota, Muhammad's leg, and my total irresponsibility, recklessness, willfulness, disrespect for au-thority, and unsuitability for my post.

Henry drove Gunter back up to the compound, and I said I would follow. I had a couple of things to sort out. As I was walking back to the jeep, Linda was coming the other way, heading for the hospital. "I hope you're feeling pleased with yourself," she said.

"I'm really sorry. I didn't mean that to happen. It was a very ex-treme situation."

She looked at me. "I don't entirely blame you," she said. "He is irresistible."

"I didn't intend to do it."

"It's him I blame. The bastard."

"But is he a bastard? Were you going out with him?"

She looked as if she was going to cry. "Apparently not."

"But you used to?"

"We did have a sort, of, well, an affair, I suppose, in Chad. It ended after a few weeks, and then I left and went to Niger. But, then, when I heard he was coming here, you know how it is sometimes. You imagine that—"

"I know," I said, "believe me."

"Do you?"

I nodded, feeling shitty.

"And what about you and him? What's going to happen?"

"It was just— It's not going to continue," I said firmly.

"Good," she said. "Thanks."

And then I thought, Oh, shit, did I really mean that?

Back in the compound, Gunter asked if he could speak to me in private.

"Of course, I'll be with you in a moment."

I went back to my hut and hit myself hard on the forehead. Everything was in tatters. Gunter wouldn't give us special help now. Gunter could get me fired.

"Fuck, fuck, fuck, fuck, fuck, fuck, fuck," I said.

There was a rattle at the door and Sian appeared. "I'm so sorry about what I said to Henry. I don't know what got into me—"

"It doesn't matter. I'm sorry I can't . . . I've got to—"

She had sat herself down on the bed. "It's just with all this happening I feel so insecure, I—"

"I understand, it's just— right now I can't talk. But why on earth did you think that—"

"Well, you two are so close, and he's so odd sometimes."

"But he's my assistant. I'm sorry, I really have got to go. Can we talk later?"

"I just wanted to say I'm sorry. It's just . . . everything's so worrying at the moment."

"I know. I feel the same. Look, I've got to go and be disciplined by Gunter."

"Oh, no. I'm so sorry. I just—"

"Don't give it a second thought. I'll talk to you later."

Gunter was standing staring at my hut as I came out, flicking his thumb against his finger, irritated. I hoped he hadn't heard.

"Shall we go talk at the edge of the hill?" I said, walking towards him. "It's quiet there."

We walked in silence till we reached the spot. I knew what was coming. I stopped and looked him straight in the eye.

"I have several things to say to you," he said.

"Yes?"

"I have worked in relief camps too, you know, for many, many years. Once, in Cambodia, I was sleeping with three nurses at once and not one of them knew about the others." He threw his great horse head back and roared with laughter. "Now, your mission to Kefti was ill-advised, and may cause us some great diplomatic problem in El Daman, as I am sure you realize. You will not be able to claim for the vehicle on the insurance."

"I know."

"But you showed initiative. And you showed your commitment. And you were brave. You have taken photographs and gathered data?"

"Yes."

"So, now we will go and look at this information." He put his hand on my arm. "Your operation here is extremely intelligent and efficient. And I am most impressed with the, er, energy of you and your staff."

He threw his head back and roared again. He had got one over me and he knew it.

Seventeen

Before he left, Gunter looked at the photographs of Kefti and listened to what we told him with ostentatious gravitas. I hoped he would be convinced now, and promise to get something done. Instead, he reassured us that the UN in Abouti knew all about the situation, and did not consider it serious. It was nothing we couldn't deal with in Nambula, he said, since the ship was due to arrive at any moment. I was frantic. I argued that if the ship didn't arrive, it would be disastrous, and we needed extra supplies anyway. Gunter promised to look into it. Henry and I spent the afternoon reorganizing the reception center, and starting up a new cemetery.

At five o'clock, Sian came over to find me. She couldn't look at me. "I think you should come to the hospital. Hazawi and Liben Alye are there."

I cursed myself for not singling them out, and asking someone to make sure they were all right when I was away.

Hazawi was a heap of skin and bone in Liben's arms. She had severe diarrhea, vomiting and fever. He was wiping her bottom with a piece of rag. Two lines of tears were flowing down the furrows in his face. He looked up and saw me, and for one second there was accusation in his eyes. It was enough.

Hazawi died at eight o'clock. Liben would not accept that she had died. He became impervious to everything around him. He washed the small body and dressed her in the green frock she had always worn. Then he placed her on his shoulder and walked very slowly out of the hospital, playing with her cheek as he always had done. I walked with him, but he did not know I was there. It was dark, and there were high mourning cries coming from the hospital. Liben suddenly squatted down at the side of the path and placed her in the crook of his arm like a baby, straightening her dress, smoothing what was left of her hair.

I sat down beside him and took his hand, but it was limp and cold. I sat there for a long time. Eventually I went to find the home visitor for Liben's village, and she brought some Keftians who knew him. They lifted him to his feet and took him back to their hut. Liben would have to be made to bury Hazawi in the morning.

There was no communal comfort that night. We all got back from the camp at different times, late, grabbed what we could from pots in the kitchen, and went straight to bed. O'Rourke was still down at the hospital. Everyone else was in bed. I lay face down, unsleeping, stretched out, crucified, feeling as if a stave were being driven through my back. I had seen what was about to happen and there was nothing I could do about it. I felt as if we were surrounded by brick walls. It was the blackest night.

When, eventually, I got to sleep, I dreamed of high dark mountains all around, and Jacob Stone shining a big blond light, such as you get on movie sets, at the mountains, and a glass staircase with lights at the side, and then I woke up. I shone my torch at my watch. It was four o'clock. The mice were rattling. They were in the ceiling, but they sounded as if they were on the floor. I got up and lit the hurricane lamp, lay back on the pillow and thought about the dream. I thought about what Jacob Stone had suggested, after Patterson's embassy party in El Daman.

I sat up all night, thinking.

As soon as it was light I drove down to the camp. The mist was still hanging around the river. A cock was crowing. People were just beginning to emerge from the huts, women in white shifts with mussed-up hair, children clinging to their legs, rubbing their eyes, bewildered.

Muhammad was lying on his bed, reading.

"So, at last we can talk."

"I'm so sorry. I—"

"No, but do not apologize, of course."

"Don't get up."

"But I must make the tea."

He already moved well with his stick.

"You will find the tea slower than ever now," he said, turning round with a sly grin. "But you see, you cannot complain, because I am disabled."

The tea was even more disgusting than usual.

"I came to tell you I'm going back to London," I said.

He didn't react.

"I'm leaving the camp this afternoon."

"Really?" he said casually, after a pause.

"Yes." There was another pause.

"Might I ask why?"

I told him my plan: there was a flight from El Daman the next morning. I was going to go back, try to get the story in the press and persuade some famous people to do an appeal. I was aiming for a slot on TV. That way, I could raise enough money or find sponsorship to airlift some food out immediately.

"And do you really think this is possible in so short a space of time? Will the famous people do as you ask?"

"Oh, I dunno." I stared glumly into my tea. "I used to know some of these people. It does happen sometimes. It's the only way I can think of to get the food quickly. What have I got to lose?"

"Forgive my many questions. Is it wise to leave the camp now?"

I would be sacked, of course, if I did that. So, I told him, I would resign instead. If the plan worked, maybe SUSTAIN would take me back. We had, perhaps, three weeks till the big influx arrived. The camp was organized now, and I thought Henry could cope if Muhammad helped. If I could get the appeal up and running in London, then I could come back in time with the food.

Muhammad stared into the embers, thinking.

"What do you reckon?"

"This ship is not going to come in ten days," he said.

"No."

He thought some more. His cheeks were very drawn now. "I think you are right, you should try."

I relaxed. "Thanks."

But Muhammad still gazed into the fire and suddenly I remembered about his friend, Huda Letay. I should have made time to talk properly before.

"You remember asking me about Huda when you were ill?" I said.

"You did not find her."

"No."

He got up miserably, and took the sugar back to the shelves.

"They said there was no one from Esareb amongst the refugees. They said the locusts are not affecting the towns yet. I'm sorry."

"No. That is good." He turned, his face composed now. "She will be safe. And now you must press on hard with your plan."

"Would you like me to bring something back?"

"Yes—about five hundred tons of food."

"I mean for you."

He thought for a while. "I would like a copy of *Hamlet*."

"Are you planning to perform in this TV spectacular?"

Out came the throaty laugh. "Perhaps. I must think of my public."

Everyone was gathered for breakfast, looking white and shattered. I told them what I was going to do.

"It's the UN that's got to sort it out," said Debbie. "It's good that you're trying, but you're not going to do much with a few sacks of grain and some stars hugging babies."

"Fewer people will die if we get some food here quickly," I said.

"We can't have celebrities crawling all over the camp at a time like this." Debbie pulled a face: "Just imagine it. It'll be a bloody nightmare."

"I think it's worth having a go," said Linda.

"What have I got to lose?"

"We need you here," said Sian.

"How long would you be away?" said Linda, eagerly.

"Maybe three weeks. You can manage without me, can't you?"

"Course we can, old sock," said Henry. "Don't worry about that. We'll make sure they all die in an organized manner."

This was unexpectedly grim from Henry. "Well, that's what'll happen when we run out of food and drugs," he said.

"Exactly," I said. "Doesn't it make more sense at least to have a go at getting some supplies?"

"What are SUSTAIN going to say?" said Debbie. "You'll lose your job, and then what if these celebrities won't listen to you?"

"I'll have to risk it."

O'Rourke was conspicuously silent, staring into his tea.

"Well, if you pull it off, old sock, it'll be fanbloodytastic," said Henry. "If you don't, well, you'll look a bit of a Charlie."

"Well, I think it's a marvelous idea, Rosie dear." Betty. "Absolutely super. When in doubt, do something rather than nothing, that's what I always say. And, besides, I remember Marjorie Kemp in Wollo in nineteen eighty-four. They'd been screaming about the famine for six months and what help did they get? None. It was only when the BBC came out that it got moving. If the celebrities do come out here, well, I'm sure we can manage to make them welcome. I'm sure they'll bring out a few goodies for us as well. Ask them about brussels sprouts."

Oh, no. Betty welcoming celebrities. I almost changed my mind.

O'Rourke came into my hut as I was packing.

"I don't think you should go," he said.

I looked at him. "Why?"

"Look, it's not that I think you're irresponsible. I can see your reasoning. You've set everything up here very well. They can manage for a couple of weeks."

"What, then?"

He rubbed the back of his head.

"Do you think it's letting the UN and the donors off the hook?" I said.

"No. It's doing the opposite, if anything. It will embarrass them."

"So what in the name of *arse* is it, then?"

He smiled quickly, then looked serious again. "I don't think media stars should be involved with this. I certainly don't think we should have celebrities at large in Safila."

"Why not?"

"Because I think the notion of celebrity is completely absurd. All it proves is how gullible everyone is."

"It's not the celebrities' fault."

"Quite so. It's the whole world that's mad. Everyone wants to imagine it's possible to achieve wealth and power out of all proportion to what they do. So they pay to see and read about stars who've managed to do that. But the reason the stars managed it was because people would pay to see them and read about them doing it. It's completely nonsensical."

"Isn't it good that they want to put something back?"

"Come on. Who's helping who? Caring's a requisite part of the image these days if you're a celebrity."

We were standing at opposite sides of the hut, facing each other. I'd hoped he would back me.

"Do you think I haven't thought about this?"

"So what have you thought?"

"I think there's a fine line," I said. "On the one side are the celebrities who are helping the cause more than they help themselves, on the other side the celebrities who are helping themselves more than the cause."

"You can't make simple distinctions like that with aid. Look at the mixture of motives you get even in this place. Anyway, you're not going to be able to pick and choose celebrities in that space of time."

He was probably right there.

"It might not be an ideal solution, but what harm can it do if it gets us the food?"

"It's a question of human dignity." He rubbed the back of his neck. "You know, and I know that the north/south divide should be lessening and it isn't. Putting out images of celebrities wandering amongst famine fields is an obscene symbol of the divide. It's like saying, 'Hey! the status quo is acceptable. All we need to do is put out a helping hand here and there and we've done our bit.' It's an emollient. It's a lie."

"Isn't it better than doing nothing?"

"Maybe or maybe not—if it makes people think something's being done, when nothing much *is* being done."

"It could save Liben Alye's life."

"But what does his life mean without Hazawi?" He saw my look. "I'm sorry. But celebrity campaigns are always, by their nature, too late. They are reactive. You know that."

"Not every time. Maybe not this time. We've got three weeks. And maybe we can put that message across, about being too late."

He shook his head, looking at me. "You are very naïve sometimes."

"It's you who's naïve. This is the way of the world as it is. We can't change it. The public will listen to celebrities."

"Why don't you just get an airlift sponsored? You don't have to get involved with show biz."

"Because it's not just Safila that needs food. What about the other camps? If we get media attention focused here the governments will have to react."

He shook his head.

I turned back to the bed and carried on with my packing. He was confusing me. "I've got to get on."

"Fine," he said, and let himself out.

After he'd gone I sat down and thought. I knew he had logic on his side, but it was the only way I could think of to get the food here in time, and that seemed more important. But, still, it worried me that he thought I shouldn't go.

The door rattled. It was O'Rourke again, carrying the Kefti photographs and the notes we'd taken.

"Don't go without these."

"Thanks. I'll leave a photocopy with Malcolm."

He sat down on the chair. "If you're determined to do this, then I'll support you."

"Thanks."

"Do you need some money?"

"No."

"Think about it—flights, clothes, taxis, London. You're sure?"

"I'm sure, but thank you."

He looked at me. His eyes were hazel green, searching. "Are you all right?" he said.

There's nothing like someone being nice to you to make you want to cry. Suddenly I just wanted to lean against him, and feel his arms round me. But he had given no sign, since that night, that he wanted that.

"I'm fine," I lied.

"I wanted to say—that night in the desert, that absurd conversation with Linda. Are you feeling all right? You're not angry or unhappy?"

Don't lay yourself open, I told myself. Don't risk it, not now. "I'm fine."

"I just didn't want you to go off to London feeling—"

"Are you involved with Lin—?"

"No. We were, briefly, three years ago. But not since, except—"

"It doesn't ma—"

"—except that since I arrived it's been a bit like being hit over the head with a valentine. I didn't even know she was here when I got the job." He looked troubled. "But I—"

"Listen, it's fine. Forget about it." I didn't want to hear it. I knew what he was going to say: "I don't want to get involved with anyone else, either." Meaning me. I felt close to tears.

I got up again. "If you don't mind, I've really got to pack or I'll never get going."

I turned round to the bed and started folding clothes, because I didn't want him to see my face.

He stayed where he was, and I carried on packing. After a while he said softly, "You seem very defensive."

I didn't reply.

"Did someone hurt you?" he said.

I wiped my eye with the back of my hand and carried on with the packing. "I've got to finish packing," I said. "I'll come and say good-bye before I go."

He hesitated a moment and then he let himself out, lifting the corrugated iron and replacing it.

Eighteen

*G*eldenkrais, Arimacia, Beth-Luis, enter now the aura hole and heal. Let the Jade Warrior guide. See . . . feel . . . experience."

Bill Bonham was floating in a dimly lit tank of water beneath a turquoise pyramid trimmed with seaweed. "THE TRANCE OF THE SHAMAN TANTRA!" he thundered. His portly form rose from the tank, white robes dripping. "WHERE? WHERE ARE THE HOPI?"

Already I was starting to wonder what I had done. It was the first night of an unusual one-man show *The Healing of the Chakra Energies,* billed as "A theatrical first for the nineties and the New Age. An exploration of man's spiritual potential through Performance Art." I remembered Bill as a cynical leather-jacketed friend of Oliver's who made a great thing about not suffering fools gladly and was always disappearing into the toilets to snort cocaine. Apparently, between being commissioned for his one-man show and producing the script, he had gone stark raving mad. He now believed he was descended from the Aztecs and destined to reveal the Route to Ecstasy through wearing turquoise.

It's fine, I told myself, a very good use of time. The Famous Club was out in force, the search for the Hopi merely the price to pay. Four seats away, Kate Fortune, dressed in something ludicrously frilly as usual, was gazing raptly at the stage, shiny lips reflecting the dancing purple lights, flicking back her long hair from time to time.

The tiny wizened pixie director, Richard Jenner, sat with his teenage girlfriend, Annalene. I hadn't seen them since I was sick at their dinner party. Corinna Borghese, the acerbic girl who had presented *Soft Focus* with Oliver, was fidgeting in her seat and rolling her eyes, her hennaed crop so short now as to be almost shaved. She was wearing sunglasses. Couldn't say I blamed her. Across the aisle, the distinguished profiles of Dinsdale Warburton and Barry Rhys looked impassively forward, as if they were watching an RSC *Lear.* Beside me, Julian Alman was fiddling miserably with his electronic personal organizer.

I had arrived at Heathrow in the early hours of that morning, stayed at Shirley's and spent most of the day asleep. In the afternoon I called Julian Alman. Julian and Janey: out of all Oliver's friends I had been closest to them. Julian, the nation's happiest comedian, was now in a state of wallowing moroseness, in the throes of a separation from Janey and he had eagerly invited me along tonight as his date. It was the perfect opportunity.

The sound of waves, seagulls and whales filled the auditorium. Bill Bonham was prostrate at the front of the stage. "The Spirit Horse!" he enunciated. "Where, where is the Spirit Horse?"

Damp fronds of hair framed the bald patch above the puzzled face. "Seek, seek, seek," chanted an Aztec chorus over the PA system.

There was silence. Then a gong and a high insistent peeping filled the air around me.

"Blast," whispered Julian. "My phone. Blast." He fumbled in his coat and dragged the phone out, its green lights twinkling. "Hi, Julian Alman here."

"Shh," hissed Kate Fortune, without taking her eyes off the stage.

"Turn the phone *off,*" I whispered.

"Shh," said a voice behind us.

"Janey, look we can't keep on—," Julian was whispering into the mouthpiece.

"THE SPIRIT HORSE IS ARRIVED."

Kate Fortune stared at Julian with her eyebrows raised, then turned quickly back to the stage, flicking her hair over her shoulder.

"Look I've told you, I need to unify my personality before—"

I took the phone from Julian. "Janey, it's Rosie. Julian's actually in the theater. He'll ring you in half an hour." I turned the phone off and put it in my bag. Julian looked at me, anguished.

Where was Oliver? Was he here?

Bill Bonham reappeared now, dressed in jeans and leather jacket. He was spotlit at the front of the stage, sitting on a pile of bones.

"You laugh, of course, chakras, gobbledegook, crap. But then you think, Christ, *who's* laughing. *Is* it me? Or is it the wounded child within?"

Across the aisle I saw Dinsdale's shoulders beginning to shake reassuringly.

There was darkness.

"RELEASE THE BLOCKAGES."

The stage lighting changed to pink.

The pyramid and the platform were vibrating, and suddenly Bill Bonham appeared on the platform, hands at either side, palms raised upwards.

"Open to the Channeling."

A rush of dry ice rose around the flotation tank. People in the front row started to cough.

"Fertilizing the Star Seed!"

The platform, and Bill's arms were rising.

There was a flash of red light and, across the auditorium, above us in a box, Oliver's face was illuminated for a second, grinning broadly at the stage, before it disappeared back into darkness.

When the houselights went up the box was empty.

Crowds were pouring out of the theater into the startling noise, rush, lights and cold of Piccadilly Circus. Dinsdale and Barry, possibly the two most famous actors on the British stage, were standing in the middle of the pavement, projecting at each other, oblivious to the crowd gathering around them.

"Bloody load of hogwash," roared Barry. "Errant, woolly-minded, self-indulgent, and *poorly enunciated*. Absolutely crazy."

"Don't, my darling, don't," said Dinsdale. "I absolutely can't *beaaaar* it when you get like this. The boy looked divine and you know it. Those rrrobust little thighs silhouetted thrrrrough sodden, clinging, heavenly rrrrobes. Oh, look, there's that *divine* young Indian, writer poetry chappie," said Dinsdale, spotting Rajiv Sastry stomping towards them, shoulders hunched in his Oxfam overcoat.

"How are you, darling boy?" shouted Dinsdale flirtatiously.

"Fucking angry, actually," said Rajiv. "Sends me tickets to the show then doesn't invite me to the fucking party. Fucking classist unnecessary manipulative—"

"But, my darling boy, do not fret! You must come as my escort. What in the *world* could be more charming?!"

Dinsdale feigned surprise as a pair of elderly ladies asked him for an autograph. "My autograph? But I would be honored, I would be thrilled, I would be delighted. Bless you, my darlings. But surely you would like to ask my distinguished friend and colleague here too? Barry Rhys?"

"Oh, for God's sake, you bloody fool," thundered Barry, furious. "You've been doing this to me for forty bloody years. It wasn't funny the first time and it's not funny now. I'm going to the bloody party."

"Hello, Dinsdale! How are you?" I said when the ladies had gone.

"Hello, my darling, what can I do for you?" He turned to me, expecting an autograph.

"Rosie Richardson," I said.

He looked at me blankly for a second.

"Rosie Richardson. Ah, er . . . I used to do your publicity at Ginsberg and Fink?"

He threw open his arms and grasped me in a theatrical embrace. "My darling, how *maaaa*rvelous to see you! You look wonderful." He still didn't remember. "And have you met the most gorgeous, the most talented boy in the whole world?" he said, gesturing vaguely towards Rajiv.

"How are you, Rajiv?" I said.

"Great. Yeah. It's going really well. We've got the first read through on Thursday."

"What did you think of that *maaaa*rvelous show? Wasn't it simply the most divinely, exquisitely outrrrrageous thing you have evah, evah seen? Of course, my darlings. Bless you. Who is it to?"

Another old lady was asking him for an autograph.

"Lovely to see you, my precious," he said in a tactful dismissal, over her shoulder. "Bless you."

"Bye," I said, obediently, with a sinking heart. Dinsdale had been one of my big hopes. I made my way over to Julian, who was still standing in the entrance to the theater, anxiously rubbing the portable phone against his chin. A young girl in leggings and a bomber jacket was about to corner him, holding out a notepad.

"You really cheer us up, right?" she was saying. "It's like when you're on, like, everything seems, like, really funny, right? Like, no worries, right?"

He caught sight of me over her shoulder. "Janey just doesn't understand that I have to be whole within myself before I can form a relationship," he wailed. "But hang on." He started dialing the number again.

I took the phone from him. "Let's go to the party," I said.

"Hey, thanks, right?" said the girl, looking puzzled.

"Awesome to make himself spiritually naked in that way. I was humbled, genuinely."

"Totally lost it . . . end of his career . . . like, I really love that man."

"Veree, veree rare to see that kind of raw courage on stage."

"What an asswipe."

"I mean, what do you say to the guy?"

The walls of the banqueting room in the Café Royal were lined with stands selling New Age merchandising, crystals, runes, feather items. A Perspex pyramid was suspended on wires above one of the most spectacular Famous Club turnouts I had ever seen.

"I don't know where to start," I said to Julian. "Who do you think I should ask?"

"The thing is, it *is* very nourishing when we're together," Julian replied, "very nourishing. But then, I wonder, why do I need this support in my life?"

We had been talking about Janey since Julian rang my doorbell, only interrupted by *The Healing of the Chakra Energies*. Janey had a baby now. She had discovered she was pregnant just after they had split up. Julian had insisted on calling the child Irony. My efforts to bring up the crisis in eastern Nambula had been met with distracted stares.

"Oh, my angel!"

Heads turned as Kate Fortune fell on a young girl holding a baby, threw back her hair, seized the baby, and cradled it in her arms. Flashguns flashed, cameras clicked, the paparazzi surrounded her in a scrum.

"It's Romanian," said Julian. The phone rang. "Excuse me a minute. I'll catch you up later," and he scurried off into a corner.

I spotted Corinna Borghese curling her lip at Gloria Hunniford's back, running her hand over her spiky head. Let Corinna try to do her patronizing right-on number on me now, I thought. I wasn't just Oliver's bit of stuff anymore. I'd done things.

I made my way over to her.

"Hi, Corinna. How are you?"

She peered at me. "Sorry? Have we met?"

"Rosie Richardson."

"Oh, yeah. Yeah. Hi. Haven't seen you around for a while."

"No. Been in Nambula actually, working in a refugee camp," I said airily.

Corinna tossed her head. "Oh, God, not more neocolonialism. Do you realize we're on the brink of a third world war because of these patronizing Western attitudes to the Arab states?"

"Excuse me. Do you mind?" Kate Fortune was trying to get past me, with the nanny following on, holding the baby.

"Hello. How are you?" I said.

"I'm sorry?" She flicked back her hair and looked at me, distracted.

"Rosie Richardson. I used to . . . be with Oliver Marchant," I finished lamely.

"Oh, oh. Yes, of course," she said doubtfully. "I know, isn't she gorgeous? I brought her over here from Romania, as I expect you've—I can't tell you how she's changed my life. How are you? I'm sorry I'm just trying to find my—"

"I'm fine. Listen, have you got a minute? I wanted to ask you about an appeal I'm trying to organize for Africa."

"Of course. If you talk to my agent she'll send you something, now I'm sorry I have to find—"

"No, the thing is, I've been working in a refugee camp and we've got a problem and I'm wanting to get everyone together to do a fund-raising program and I wondered—"

"Well, I'm really putting all my energy into Romania now, with the baby and so on, but if you talk to my agent . . ."

"But it's a real emergency."

"Sweetie, give my agent a ring in the morning and I'm sure you know . . . Anyway, lovely to see you again. *Really* good to see you. Ciao."

I turned back to find Corinna staring at me. This was going to be harder than I'd thought.

"Mmmmmm. Give me a hug, my darling. Give me a hug." Richard Jenner's wiry little body thrust itself against me. "Now, darling. What was your name again? Tell me, remind me."

"Rosie Richardson, I met you when I was with Oliver."

"Of course. Of course. You were the girl who was sick on the table! Hahaha. Let me get you a drink. Don't throw up this time, will you? Hahaha! What did you think of Bill? Isn't it just garishly tragic? Paul and Linda are here. Have you seen? Over there. No, look over there. Oh, my God, there's Neil and Glenys. We must say hello. Come along."

He seized my hand.

"I need to talk to you," I said. "The last few years I've been working in a refugee camp in Africa and we've suddenly got a famine on our hands. No one seems able to help us." He was pulling me along towards Neil and Glenys.

"I'm listening, I'm listening, keep talking."

"No, stop a minute."

Richard stopped and turned around.

"It's urgent. It's why I've come back to England. I need some help from . . . you and the people here that you know," I finished lamely. I was starting to feel a bit of a fool.

"What kind of help? Are you looking for money, or what is it that you want help with?" His eyes were flicking towards Neil and Glenys, who were moving away.

"We need money but more than that we need publicity. I want to do a TV appeal—maybe take some people out to Africa."

He caught hold of my arm. "Look around the room. No, just look, darling. Look around the room."

I looked.

"You see Kate Fortune over there with the baby."

I nodded.

"Romania. Dave and Nikki Rufford?—rain forests. Hughie?—Terrence Higgins Trust. Benefit show on Friday. I'll give you a check, my darling. I'll gladly give you a check. Call my office in the morning and they'll sort something out. But a benefit? No, darling. No. Unless you've got months and months to do it properly. No. It'll crater. Completely crater. No. Anneka! Give me a hug, sweetie. Mmmm, mmmm." He winked at me over Anneka's shoulder. "Call my office in the morning, darling. I'll let them know."

This was awful. I decided to head for the stands at the edge of the room to give me something to pretend to be doing, then try to find Julian. I was almost at the edge of the room and then, through a clear parting in the sea of heads, I found myself looking straight at Oliver.

His head jolted back as if he had stopped suddenly. We stared at each other like rabbits caught in headlights. Then the crowds closed in again and he disappeared. I turned to the stand beside me, shaken, and pretended to look at the crystals, feather items and leaflets. "Interior design with FENG SHUI," offered one. I picked up another, which said, "FASTING WALKS AS A ROUTE TO PERSONAL DEVELOPMENT." I suddenly had to get out of the room.

I pushed my way out through the throng, and into the cool and quiet of the ladies' loos. I found myself a cubicle, locked the door, put the seat down and sat on it. Then I heard the door open outside and someone come in.

"Have you seen that girl's back?" It was Corinna's street-cred drone.

"Oh, you mean that girl who used to be with Oliver," came the sugary tones of Kate Fortune. "Isn't it embarrassing, poor thing?"

"Crippling. Like, anyone would think she's the first person to go and work in a relief camp."

"Oh, it's a complete nightmare. You know, you want to help, but really . . . one can't do everything."

"Quite. And, like, talk about Roberta Geldof. I mean puh-lease."

After they'd gone, I sat staring at the cubicle door for a long time, traumatized. I could see how they felt. Arrive at a first-night party and some git you hardly remember turns up with a suntan and starts demanding shifts in your diary. A vision of the camp came flooding over me: O'Rourke's advice, the refugees on their way. Debbie, Henry, Betty, Muhammad, waiting to see what I could do. And it wasn't going to work.

I went out feeling anguished, and stupid, and looked for Julian. I couldn't find him. I decided the best thing to do now was go home. I had just put on my coat and was walking towards the stairs when Oliver emerged from the gentlemen's cloakroom. He was the same—the face had filled out a little, the hair was a touch longer, but the same.

"Rosie!" He came towards me, smiling, poised, charming, no sign of the earlier loss of composure. "You look wonderful." He bent to kiss me and the familiar Oliver scent, the dark stubble on his cheek, the lips just touching mine, set off the old chemical alert. Atoms and particles started rushing around, WARNING! WARNING! All systems to throb again.

Oh, no, I thought. Oh, no. Not this. Not now. Not still. Please, no.

I moved a few feet away. "Hello." Unnatural squeak. I cleared my throat. "Hello," I said, in a very deep voice now. "How are you?"

"Plumpkin," he said, and folded me in his arms. "I've missed you so much. How was Africa?"

He was all tenderness. We caught up. I told him why I was here.

". . . and so the upshot was there was nothing more I could do out there, I'd tried every single thing I could think of. This seemed like the only option left."

His eyes were kind. He was biting his bottom lip and putting his head on one side sympathetically. "You're right," he said simply. "We should do something."

I looked at him in astonishment, my mind racing. He must have changed. If Oliver was willing to help, then I could probably pull off the appeal. He was the one person I knew I ought to avoid, and he might turn out to be my best chance.

"What do you need?"

"An airlift. Two, three airlifts if possible, maybe more."

"How long have you got?" he said gently.

"Three weeks," I said, and that was when his mood completely turned.

"Three weeks?" he said. "Three *weeks?*"

That tone. He looked and sounded as if I was the most loathsome, pathetic, despicable person who had ever walked this earth. I had forgotten what this was like.

"I have to say I think you're completely insane," he was going on, authoritatively, dismissively as if he was in a board meeting, demolishing the opposition. "It's a completely absurd thing to try and do in three weeks. And, frankly, I hear you've made a complete fool of yourself tonight."

Keep calm, I told myself, don't rise to it.

"Don't you remember the rules I taught you?" he said. "Hmmm? Friends of the famous? You have to recognize the boundaries. You must accept the inequality without drawing attention to it. Don't behave like a member of the public. Don't stare, don't look around the room for the famous ones and make a beeline, don't put them on the spot, don't demand famous-person favors, reassure, don't lecture. You got back in the club, then broke all the rules. I saw you, you did it to everyone. You were in a perfect position to pick up again—you're an old friend now, so you make them feel loyal. You do something nonmedia so you make them feel deep. But you ballsed up. You forgot everything I taught you." Then his eyes were caught by something ahead. "Plumpkin," he said, but this time not to me.

It was Vicky Spankie, the actress who had been married to the rain forest Indian. Her dark glossy hair was cut in a bob. She was wearing what may well have been a rain forest robe.

"Can we go now, Olly?" she said, coming up to him and fingering his lapel.

"Vicky, you remember Rosie, don't you?" he said, taking hold of her hand as if she was a five-year-old. I wondered what had happened to the Indian.

"Rosie's come back from Africa with a bit of an unrealistic plan, unfortunately," he said, laughing. "I was just explaining to her about the horrible real world we live in."

"Good night," I said, and headed for the stairs.

"Good night" was no good. As the taxi made its way along Regent Street I blinked at the lights and thought about what I should have said. "Good night, scumbag." No, "asswipe" was a better word. Who'd said that tonight? "Good night, asswipe." "Sod off, you little toad." "Still having the mood swings, then? Would you like the number of a psychiatrist?" No. I should have been more lofty. I should have chipped in, after the friends-of-the-famous speech, "I think you're being rather hard on your friends. I think these people are better than that, don't you?" As we left the lights of the West End, and headed out towards north London, I calmed down. Maybe it was better that I hadn't got involved in a confrontation. Better just to walk away and leave him be. I should have done that from the word go.

CHAPTER

Nineteen

*A*ll my teeth were falling out. I was holding some of them in my hand and trying to keep my mouth shut so that the ones that were left would stay put and no one would see. I opened my eyes. I ran my tongue round my mouth to check the teeth were still there, but then the memories of the party started seeping back into my head. It was a monstrous night. I kept dropping off, waking, having bad dreams again. Shirley was sleeping on the other side of the bed, her long hair spread all over the pillow. I lay motionless, trying not to wake her, remembering what had happened. I should never have left Safila. The refugees were on their way, there was no food waiting for them. I had abandoned them for an arrogant plan which would come to nothing.

The party had rocked me far more than it ought. Out in Africa I thought I had become a new, strong person, and that all that humiliation with Oliver could never have happened to the new me. But twenty-four hours back in London had made me wonder. Maybe the chemistry between two people was something you just couldn't change. I stared miserably at the ceiling. Oliver and the Famous Club were central to what I was trying to do and I couldn't handle either of them. Everything was negative. Bad thoughts charged about in my head. Moments from the party, visions of the camp, loomed up, and, encouraged by the rest, the memories of the Kefti trip crept out and danced grotesquely about me. I wished

O'Rourke were here. Though it might have been just one complication too many, what with all three of us in the bed.

Shirley woke up at one point.

"Are you all right?" she said.

"Kind of."

"Don't get involved with that madman again," she said. "Promise me. Or you'll never sleep again."

"I promise," I said uncertainly. It had been such a ray of hope when I thought Oliver would help. But he hadn't changed and I had to keep away from him. But what was I going to do? I'd blown the whole thing. It was hopeless.

At about 5:00 A.M. I finally dozed off. An hour later I was woken by a fearsome grinding and roaring, the sound of tearing metal, of knives scraping on tin, of ancient, rusty, groaning motors. I sat bolt upright with terror. A light, high whooping joined the grinding—dooweeedooweeedoweeedowee. Then there was silence. Then the loudest bell I'd ever heard. The grinding stopped, then started up again, louder, nearer.

"Sorry," Shirley said sleepily. "They've privatized the dustbin lorries. There'll be two more before eight o'clock. Every shop has its own personal refuse collector and they still don't take our sodding bags away."

"What about the bells?"

"Burglar alarms," she said. "Dustbin lorries set off the burglar alarms. Stupid dustbin lorries," and she laughed and put her arm over her face. When she had gone back to sleep, I tried to snuggle up to Shirley without her noticing.

In the morning, of course, it all seemed like paranoia. I decided I had to get the project on a sounder footing: get the story in the newspapers for a start and go and talk to SUSTAIN. It was early days, I still had three weeks.

"And it's the UNHCR you're dealing with?" said Peter Kerr, from *The Times*'s Foreign desk.

"Yes, mainly, as well as SUSTAIN, and the Nambulan relief commission but the UN supply us with food."

"Fine. Geraldine," he shouted across the room, "call the library, love, will you? And *PA* and see what there is in the last six months." He looked at me questioningly. I nodded. "Last six months on Nambula and Kefti. Refugee story. Try under Aid and Locusts as well."

He started leafing through the photos. "What's your relationship with SUSTAIN now?"

"Fluid. I'm going to see them later today. I just put in my resignation in El Daman and left."

"I have to say this is not a great time for a famine story."

"What do you mean?" I said. "When is a great time?"

"Come on. You know how these things go. All eyes are on Eastern Europe and the Gulf now."

"But does everyone think the problem's solved? It's not. Look at this."

I picked out a photograph of Liben Alye lowering Hazawi into her grave. "This is my friend," I said emotionally. "This was last week. It's outrageous to start applying flavor-of-the-month thinking to this."

He looked to either side, then picked up the photograph shiftily and put it down again. "Listen, love, I hear what you're saying. I am just explaining—how—these—things—tend—to—work, all right? This is a newspaper." He scratched the back of his neck.

"Course, you could do a personal piece for the feature pages—what about that? My experience in the relief camp, my mission, personal quest sort of number."

"No, it needs to be a news story."

"Well, I think we'll be the judge of that, shall we?" he muttered. Then he banged a hand down on the desk. "Leave it with me, love. I'll check it out, but I wouldn't hold your breath."

I emerged, despondent, from the meeting into the fridgelike world of the London docklands, and a blast of wind hit me, howling round the high concrete and glass buildings. A man bumped my shoulder and hurried on, sporting an ugly purple and green track

suit. A lorry groaned past, changing gear, and splashed muddy water on the coat I'd borrowed from Shirley. The skies were heavy and
gray. I thought of Safila at sunset, of the red earth, the hot wind, the
sound of it filling the empty acres. Maybe it was all just too different and far away for people to imagine.

Back at Shirley's I wiped the mud off her coat, made a cup of tea
and wondered which way to turn. I had envisaged front-page news
stories, featuring my photos. I had thought it would be easy to talk
to the celebrities. Always before, in this celebrity world, I had been
the other half of Oliver. I had forgotten how alone and insignificant
I was going to be. I looked at the phone. I wanted to ring SUS-
TAIN but I really needed something concrete to offer them first to
prove this celebrity plan might work.

What could I do? I certainly shouldn't go around begging favors
anymore from celebrities who didn't remember me. It was behaving like Hassan's girl in the Safila village, who always barged straight
up to us demanding earrings. Muhammad had figured out how to
fit in with the ex-pats and make us work for him. I thought hard.
Now, if this was Muhammad, trying to get help for Kefti at a series
of ex-pat social occasions, what would he do? The answer was not
what I'd done last night. He'd never try to pull off a trick like that
at a UN drinks party—too crass, too difficult. He'd get a friend
who was an ex-pat to help him. I had to get someone, or something, to help. But what? Who? I decided to ring some more newspapers.

A little red light was flashing on the answerphone. I pressed
PLAYBACK.

"Hi, Rosie. It's Oliver. Listen, I got your number from your
mother. I just wanted to say I'm sorry I was a bit over the top last
night and wish you good luck with your plan. That's it. If there's
anything I can do, give me a call."

I was excited for about four minutes, then I calmed down. It was
just part of a pattern. He'd be nice. Then he'd be horrible. Then he'd
be nice again. And then he'd be horrible. He was a lunatic. He had
a bad effect on me. Still. He was definitely my best shot. He'd told

me last night he had a new job as some flash executive at one of the ITV companies. He was still presenting *Soft Focus,* which had moved to ITV with him. He had the power to get us a TV slot and the celebrities would probably come on board if he asked them. They trusted him—professionally, at least.

Why should he do it, though? He was such a cynic. Conscience. Now there was something. Most of the time, socially and professionally, Oliver put up a very convincing front as the good guy, strong, moral and fatherly. Somewhere inside he must *want* to be that way, or imagine that he was. Maybe I could work on that. Then there was me. I wondered if I still had any power over him. I had rejected him once. He was a control freak, he probably wouldn't quite be able to reconcile himself to that. But was it a sound plan to get food for the starving by attempting to manipulate a powerful loony? No, really not at all.

Half an hour later I got out the phone book and dialed the company number.

"Oliver Marchant, please." I was up against it. I had to play every card I had.

"Just putting you through."

The world was imbalanced, half of it was vulnerable and if that meant people's lives relied on unreliable things, like politics, like accounting, like fashion, like Oliver Marchant's moods then that was the way it was.

"Oliver Marchant's phone." Oh dear. It was Gwen. He still had the same supercilious PA.

"Hello, it's Rosie Richardson here. Could I speak to Oliver, please?"

"Oh . . . oh. Hello. Well, he's really very busy."

"I realize that. But he did call me and ask me to ring."

"I see . . . um, well, he's in a meeting at the moment. Shall I ask him to call you?"

"Actually, what he said was to fix a time to pop in this afternoon." Slight lie but never mind. A phone call wouldn't do.

"Hold the line, please," she said in a cold, skeptical voice. Damn, she was going to ask him. I waited. Our relationship didn't need to come into it. I could simply ask him as one professional to another and appeal to his better nature.

"He has a window at four-thirty."

"Four-thirty will be great. Thank you."

At four twenty-five, I arrived on the seventh floor at Capital Daily Television. Gwen was waiting for me outside the lift.

"Hel-*lo*, Rosie. My, you have changed."

What was that supposed to mean?

"Just along here. You won't be able to have him for very long. You're very lucky he's managed to pop you in. Are you enjoying it in Africa?"

"I'm not sure *enjoying* is quite the word."

"Have a seat," she said. "He won't be a moment."

I sat watching Gwen type for twenty-five minutes. I was very nervous. He was cleverer than me. He suddenly opened the door, looking at his watch. He didn't acknowledge me. "Call Paul Jackson, will you, and tell him I'm running late? Come in," he said, still not looking at me. "Did Sam Fletcher call?"

"Yes. Oh, and Greg Dyke," said Gwen.

"I'll get back to them when I'm through with Rosie. I'll be ten minutes."

Ten minutes? Was that all?

The office was a large white room with a wooden floor, soft black-leather sofas lining three of the walls and plate glass windows behind the desk with a panoramic view of the city. There was a matte-black staggered plinth in the center of the room with golden award figurines neatly placed at various levels. Oliver sat down behind the desk. There was nothing on it except a flat black phone, a flat black ashtray and a black hardback notebook open at a pristine thick white page. The wall to Oliver's right was covered with pictures of Oliver with celebrities: Oliver with Mick Jagger, Oliver with Kenneth Branagh, Oliver between Margaret and Denis Thatcher.

I sat down on the upright chair opposite.

"So, then. Where are we? Sorry, haven't got much time here."

He was entirely detached and formal. His hands were flat in front of him on the desk, dark hairs on the sides, long familiar fingers.

"What is it you want to talk to me about?" he said, glancing at the matte-black watch we had chosen together. I might have been a stranger pitching an idea for a series. This was no good.

"You know what I want to talk to you about," I said.

He blinked at me.

"You rang me this morning. Have you forgotten already? Have you gone senile or something?"

He looked down, then he gave three slow laughs through his nose, and leaned back in his chair, putting his arms behind his head. "Well. You haven't changed, have you?" he said.

"I think I have," I said. "It was very good of you to ring me today."

"That's all right."

"You're the only person I know who can make this work. I think you're a kind man. I want you to help."

I was watching his face. He was flattered. It was working.

"What are you suggesting?"

"Nothing complicated. We just need to get a handful of celebrities to agree to do a simple program. You're quite right. I was going about it the wrong way last night. But if you approach them, they'll say yes."

"To what?"

"A TV appeal. Just a short show."

"But you say you need to do this inside three weeks."

"It's enough. Couldn't it be done in the *Soft Focus* spot?"

He got up and walked into the middle of the room, thinking. Then he turned toward me, shaking his head. "I'm sorry, love. I'd like to help but it can't be done. Not in that space of time."

I looked at the plinth, then got to my feet, walked over and picked up one of the awards. "Do you remember when you won this? Do you remember how long it took you to put that program together? Ten days."

"I remember," he said softly.

He was looking down at me, into my eyes, holding the look for too long, as he used to do. I broke the moment, moved back and sat on the chair and saw his face change.

"It can't be done," he said. "You might get the money for your first lot of food. I'll give you a few grand. Dave Rufford's got millions he doesn't know what to do with. If you posed as a therapist you could take Julian for everything he's got. Bill Bonham's completely barking now. You could probably get the whole lot from him if you convinced him it would heal his aura. How much do you need?"

"The food is no use without a cargo flight. And I can't get a flight sponsored without publicity. The problem's bigger than just our camp. We need public pressure and we need to explain why it's happened. I don't just want to tug heartstrings."

"Have you tried the newspapers?"

"I tried *The Times* today, but famine's out at the moment apparently."

"You went to *Today?*"

"No. I said I tried *The Times* today."

"You want the tabloids. I'll give you a name at the *News*. They could make a big thing out of it. 'Ministering Angel Twists Arm of Former Lover to Save Starving.'"

"Oh, come on," I said angrily.

"It's a great story, great picture. Just undo another button, love."

I shot him a furious look.

"Sorry, sorry. Just arsing around," he said.

"Don't."

"You *have* changed, haven't you?" he said disparagingly.

"Yes."

"Look. I can't help you. I know it's a heartwarming idea but it's unrealistic. You can't just stick a bunch of performers in front of a camera like that."

"I'm not saying we should. It needs organizing properly. That's why it needs you, and an office and some staff."

"It won't work. What can I say?" He raised his hands and let them fall.

"You could say you'd try," I said. "You're a good person, aren't you?"

"I'm in a new position in a new company here. I can't come in at this stage with an idea which is going to go off at half cock."

"Oliver, I know this is difficult for you, but try. Just try to get a grip on the idea that there might be some things in life which are more important than your career." I got up. "I can't pull this off on my own, but if you won't help me, someone else will. I'll do it. You watch."

Right, no more pressure, just leave. I picked up my bag and headed for the door.

"Thanks for talking to me anyway, that was good of you. I'll see you in a couple of years. Bye."

When I got back to Shirley's, sure enough the little light was flashing on the answerphone.

"Oh, Rosie, hi, it's Oliver here." Excellent. Excellent. "Listen, if you want to talk about this idea some more I'll be in the Groucho at eight o'clock. Maybe see you there."

I sat back and sighed. Thank God.

B arrrurrrrr!" Dinsdale got the evening off to a splendid start, bellowing across the room like an old she-elephant.

"Barry, do tell me, are you going to be the chairman? I absolutely can't bear it if you are. I'm desperate to be it. Absolutely wild for it."

"Oh, shut up, you bloody old fool, do. Absolutely crazy. You know perfectly well who the bloody chairman is. Where's the bloody drink around here? That's what I want to know. Bloody crazy."

When Oliver decided to move, he moved. It was just five days since I'd seen him in the Groucho club, and now over a dozen major celebrities were assembled in a conference room at Capital Daily Television for our first meeting. It was the Famous Club, acting branch, with certain key additions. Edwina Roper and the bearded figures of SUSTAIN's press officers were standing in a little group with Oliver, Vicky Spankie and Julian. Vicky was wearing a khaki combat jacket and peaked cap with a hammer and sickle on it.

Oliver was in his most charming, authoritative mode, working the room, relaxing everyone. He was talking to Edwina Roper, touching her arm, looking at her as if she was the most interesting person in the world. Edwina was coloring slightly, charmed, putting her hand to her throat.

The Irish actor Liam Doyle was standing in another group with three actors donated by the RSC. Bill Bonham was already seated at the table, mouthing something, his mantra presumably. Rajiv Sastry and his friends were talking in low, bitter voices and looking around the room. Behind them Corinna Borghese was lecturing a group of *Soft Focus* personnel. And Dave Rufford, the wealthy ex–rock star, was handing round photos of his five-year-old son, Max, sitting on a Shetland pony and dressed in full fox-hunting gear.

I was talking to Nigel Hoggart, a very clean young man in a gray suit, who was the representative of Circle Line Cargo. They had more or less promised me a sponsored flight to take out the first lot of food, provided they were happy with the publicity.

There was a commotion at the door and Kate Fortune fluttered in, followed by the nanny, the baby and two aides. She swooped across the room and positively fell upon Oliver, taking hold of her hair and throwing it back into the eyes of Barry, who was coming forward excitedly to greet her.

Dinsdale caught hold of my arm. "D'you know, my darling. I'm so sorry. I'm such a senile old *fool*. I did not have the faintest glimmer of a *clue* who you were the other night outside the theatah. I only remembered when you'd disappeared and I was agonized. You must think I'm the most frrrrightful boorish old nincompoop."

"No problem. I'm very glad—"

"But could you help me out, my darling, could you? Could you bear to? Where is it we're raising the money for? Do you know? You could possibly bear to tell me? Could you?"

"Nambula."

"Oh, Nambuuuula." The brown eyes fixed on me concernedly. "Ah yes. Nambula. Bossy neighbors, bothersome borders. What is it? Refugees? Keftians? All that again? We must gather round and support. We must help. We must."

"Yes, Keftians. Didn't know you were an Africa buff, Dinsdale."

"Oh, I read the papers, you know. Every day, my darling, cover to cover, never miss. *Barry!*" he roared.

"What is it now, you bloody fool?"

"It's Nambuuula. Nambuuula."

"Yes, all right, all right. No need to make a bloody song and dance about it."

Edwina Roper tapped me on the shoulder. "Rosie, this is terrif, what a turnout! Well done. Isn't Oliver Marchant the most charming man?"

"This is Nigel Hoggart from Circle Line Cargo, who are going to help us with the flight—we hope!" I said, smiling creepily at Nigel.

"Yes, I know. Been twisting our arms all week, this lady has!" said Nigel. "That's what's been occurring." He winked at Edwina.

"Have you heard anything from the government?" I asked her.

"Yes, I've spoken to the ODA. Not good, I'm afraid. They're aware of what's happening in Kefti. They're concerned, but they don't have the funds at the moment. They'll need an additional budget before they can do anything, especially as it has to be a question of airlifting now."

"Have you heard anything from Safila?"

"Nothing recent, I'm afraid. There's still no radio contact and Malcolm has been away. But we're getting reports of arrivals in Wad Denazen and Chaboulah."

"UN made their minds up what they think yet?"

She shook her head. "I think what we have in this room is our best shot."

Oliver gave good meeting, relaxed and authoritative.

"Right," he was saying, looking round the table. "Acting? Acts? Africa? What are we going to call ourselves?"

"Act on Africa," said Vicky looking at him hopefully.

"Arms Around the World?" said Kate Fortune. "Hearts? Hearts of Africa?"

"Bleeding Hearts for Africa?" said Corinna dryly, lifting off her sunglasses.

"Africa Crisis," said Julian. "Blast no—Drama. Drama out of a Crisis. Must be something in there."

"Love Aid," said Kate Fortune. "Love the Children Aid? Arms Around the Children?"

"Luvvie Aid," said Rajiv.

"Now that's not bad," said Oliver. "Luvvie Aid. What d'you think? Bit flip?"

"Completely crazy."

"Acts, acting, come on," said Oliver. "African Acts, relief, famine, charity, Charitable Acts." He turned to me with a long, smug look. "Charitable Acts. What about it?" Charitable Acts it was.

"I can put it into the *Soft Focus* slot in either two or three weeks' time, but ten P.M. on a weekday is not ideal. Vernon Briggs will have to approve it, and if we want another slot it'll have to come from him."

There were a number of childish noises from around the table. Vernon Briggs was Oliver's boss, from the old end-of-the-pier school of TV entertainment. Not a popular man with the younger celebrity.

"Like, OK, if I have to work with Vernon, then I'm, like, out of here," said Rajiv.

"Now, come along," said Oliver.

"Do you really think this is appropriate to a *Soft Focus* spot?" said Corinna. "I mean, it's not exactly arts, is it?"

"We're artists, aren't we? Aren't we? Is theater not art?" said Vicky. "I mean, I certainly think of myself as an artist. Aren't we artists too?"

"Bloody crazy. Sitting here talking about this, that and the other," roared Barry. "Is this art? Bloody nonsense. What is the performance? What *is* the performance? None of us has got a blind idea what the hell lines we're supposed to be learning. Absolutely crazy."

"Take no notice of him, my darlings. Mind's completely gone. Vanished totally, years ago."

"Well, it's a fair-enough point," said Oliver. "What is the heart of the show going to be? It has to be something short—we can't count on more than an hour. The viewers have to feel they're getting their money's worth if they're going to send cash. They want to see you doing something you wouldn't normally do. It's got to be simple and it needs a theatrical connection—"

"Can I just say something here?" said Eamonn Salt, in his flat monotone. "Obviously we're very grateful for this turnout tonight."

"Absolutely," said Edwina Roper. "It's fantastically generous of all of you to give up your time and energy to this wonderful cause. Thank you."

"Yes," I said. "I'd like to thank everyone too, on behalf of the camp at Safila."

"Excuse me," said Corinna, "excuse me. I find it rather odd that charity professionals should feel they have to be sobbingly grateful to a group of performers for a few days' work. I think the gratitude should probably be the other way around."

"Well, let's say we're all grateful to each other and try not to break down, shall we?" said Oliver, after an awkward moment. "Now what were you saying, Eamonn?"

"Yes, indeed," Eamonn went on in his droning tone. "I think it would be helpful if the content of the program could somehow mirror what the appeal is about. The money raised will help in the short term, but essentially this is a political issue. There are things it is difficult for us, as a charity, to say, but you could say them for us."

"Excuse me?" said Corinna. "If we all get up in front of the camera are we supposed to be saying what *we* think, or what *you* think? I mean, you know, like, everyone's always saying we shouldn't be ill-informed mouthpieces. So are we allowed to say what we think?"

"Well, let's hear what SUSTAIN think first," said Oliver.

"Yes, indeed. In the first place the Keftian people's movement has arisen because of a war, and the war has arisen because of a corrupt autocracy in Abouti. In the second place the reason why provision has not been made for these refugees is because of a certain slowness to react and cumbersome bureaucracy from the UN, but also—and essentially—because of the slow responses of governments. The reason why food is not in place, actually, is because our government, and the French didn't send what they were supposed to send when they said they would."

Kate Fortune was looking very intently at the nail on her index finger. She bent it towards her and starting picking at it with her thumb. Julian was starting to play with his electronic organizer. Eamonn was not one of the world's great orators.

"If you look beyond that," Eamonn continued, "if Nambula wasn't saddled with a massive foreign debt, because of the loans made by the World Bank during the oil boom in the seventies, then they wouldn't be using all their fertile land to grow cash crops and would have more than enough food to deal with their own refugee crises."

"Well, that should be easy enough to put across entertainingly in half an hour," said Rajiv.

"Oh, but listen, everyone. Don't you think, really, for all that, it's the children who really get through to people?" said Kate Fortune. "I don't think we want to get all bogged down in politics, do we? It's the children we should be thinking about."

"Stupid woman," muttered Barry.

"Honey, what about Elizabethan-style playlets?" cried Vicky Spankie, looking at Oliver with sparkling eyes. "The roots of famine personified—War, Debt, Bad Governance!!"

This hugely amused Barry.

"Lo! I am Bad Governance! Begotten of a fat greedy despot in a gold-plated Roller," he thundered, in that famous overenunciated delivery.

"Lo! I am Incompetence—" Dinsdale began.

Kate Fortune got to her feet, blinking back tears. "I'm sorry. I really don't think we should be making jokes when . . . when children are dying."

"All right. Yes, let's all settle down," said Oliver, glancing at Vicky, who was looking red-faced and furious.

Bill Bonham piped up, "What about trying to do something more with what's preoccupying the world at present, linking the whole thing with a spiritual karmic quest? Doing good, feeling good about yourself. It could be presented as more of a journey."

"Yes, thank you, Bill," said Oliver, adding under his breath, "Any more completely lunatic suggestions while we're at it?"

"I have to say I don't think we should be doing this at all, actually," said Corinna.

There was silence.

"I really think it's, like, counterproductive," she went on. "This is a Tory cock-up and then we say, 'Oh, it's OK, guys, we'll fill up the gaps, no sweat, you know.' I mean, puh-*lease*."

"And, of course, we're only giving the illusion of filling the gaps, aren't we?" said Oliver. "Aren't we talking drops in the ocean?"

"It is true that the total amounts raised by Live Aid and Band Aid was less than five percent of the government overseas aid budget for that year," said Eamonn Salt.

Everyone stared at him, taking it in.

"But Live Aid did a lot of good, didn't it?" said Julian, looking hurt.

"Yeah," said Dave Rufford expansively.

"Of course, Live Aid was a tremendous help," said Edwina Roper. "It completely changed the face of giving. It was tremendous fun. It opened up a new sector of young donors which didn't exist before. It did tremendous things for all the agencies."

"Yeah. It was like this rebellion. We were telling the Tories, 'Look, cunts, we're not 'avin this,'" said Dave.

"Oh, yes, it had its moment"— Corinna was yawning through her nose— "but the moment has passed. Now every two-bit model in the business is gushing around the world doing photo shoots with the starving. It's gross. I mean, it's cultural imperialism at its absolute worst. It's, like, we the celebs save the little monkeys, you know. Self-congratulatory crap."

A crestfallen air fell on the table.

"Yeah, that's right, actually," said Rajiv. "I'm with Corinna on this. I'm having no part of it."

"So you think there's no point?" said Julian, dismayed.

"Well. It's something we do have to consider," said Oliver. "All this 'Make way, let me help, I'm famous.' Maybe it *is* irresponsible." He looked almost relieved. I couldn't believe this. It had all been there and now it was slipping away.

"It's, like, crap. It's like a false reassurance for the public," said Rajiv.

"Exactly," said Corinna, looking smug. "*Why* isn't that ship there? *Whose* cock-up is this? This is what we ought to be asking, not demanding fivers from pensioners."

"Right. Robbin' the poor to bail out the cunts," said Dave Rufford.

"Well, quite," said Corinna. "I mean puh-*lease.*"

"Absolutely crazy!" said Barry, rising to his feet and thumping his hand down on the table. "Have you all completely taken leave of your senses?" He stood motionless, staring around the room with one eyebrow raised. "Have you gone mad? A camp," he said, raising one hand in the air, and staring ahead, "a camp in darkest Africa, thronging with people, starving to death. They ask us for help. . ." —his voice dropped to a whisper— "and we say no? If you stood before a dying child and he held out his hand, and asked you for food, which you had, would you say *no*?"

He paused, turning his head from one side to the other, glaring round the room. "Well, let's bloody well get on with it then," he roared.

"But this is exactly what I'm saying," said Kate Fortune. "It's the children—"

"Oh, puh-*lease*," muttered Corinna. "I mean, that's just propagating the neocolonialist—"

Dinsdale jumped to his feet. "First word of sense I've heard from the old fool in fifty years," he bellowed. "Of course we must do what we can, my darlings, what can you be thinking of? We must help! We must *thrrrow* ourselves to the fore!"

"Yeah, I'm with you on that, Dinsdale. No point being bleedin' right-on about it when the poor fuckers are starvin' to death," said Dave Rufford.

"Yeah."

"Absolutely."

"I agree," said Julian. "I'd love to do something. Oh, blast." His phone had started ringing again.

It was plain sailing after that. Oliver was growing more and more ambitious. He was talking about doing a satellite broadcast from the camp. He was being absolutely wonderful. Even Corinna was beginning to come round.

Kate Fortune rose fussily to her feet. "Well, I'd like to say here and now that I would be more than happy to go out to Nambula."

Barry's head crashed down onto the table.

"We can discuss who's going to go out later," said Oliver. "What about the main show? We can have a few people's party pieces and monologues, but we need something central and theatrical."

"Shakespeare," said Barry. "It should be the Bard."

"What about a Shakespeare sketch?" said Julian. "A comic one."

"Like it," said Oliver. "Maybe speeded-up Shakespeare. A fifteen-minute *Hamlet*? Obviously we'd have to have other things around it, but that could form the core."

"I'd love to do my Ophelia," said Vicky.

"Oh, yes! So would I," said Kate.

"Surely you're more of a Gertrude, darling," someone murmured.

On it went. I didn't care. It was all going to happen now, that was what mattered. And the thought crossed my mind that if Muhammad and the representatives of RESOK found themselves in the Famous Club they would be just as bad. The Keftian tent moving, the political engineering was all part of the same thing. The Keftians wanted not to be hungry, not to be sick so that they could live, improve their lot and their status, and show off, indulge in life's little vanities like everyone else.

"So"—Oliver closed his large matte-black notebook and banged his hand on top of it— "thank you, everyone. We meet again here, at the same time, next week, by which time we will have a running order and scripts on the way."

"Hang on. Who's doing the casting?" said Liam Doyle.

"Me," said Oliver. "Thanks very much, everyone, meeting adjourned."

Under the table Oliver slipped his hand onto my knee. I lifted it and put it back on his own.

Immediately afterwards, he cleared his throat and said, "By the way, before we all get too excited remember this all has to be cleared by Vernon Briggs or we can't go ahead. And this is a man who thinks *Hamlet* is a small cigar, and a comic sketch means a mother-in-law, a banana skin and three racial stereotypes. We'll keep you posted, anyway. Thanks very much, everyone."

Now why did he cast a dampener like that, just when we were all fired up?

Twenty-one

Things were beginning to happen at CDT. Oliver had found us a spare office four doors down from him. A PA and researcher, drafted from the *Soft Focus* team, came in and made phone calls from time to time. It was my job to sort out sponsorship for the flights, liaise with SUSTAIN and produce fact sheets for the celebrities. I turned up every day to find the room slowly filling up with the stuff of television production, charts and files and bits of paper, but there was a diffident air. The day after that first big meeting Oliver was curiously unavailable. He put his head round the door once but he was too busy to talk. We had two weeks left.

The days were painless enough, crowded and straining with tasks and people, but I dreaded the darkness, when the stars were the same stars they were seeing over the camp. I'd hated it getting dark ever since the explosion in Kefti. Whenever I thought about that, it was like hitting a new bruise. Bad chemicals rushed through me and took a long time to seep away. At night I lay awake, seeing Sefila. There was still no contact with the camp. Maybe messages had been sent, lying in a pouch on the backseat of a Land Rover, pushed under a pile on Malcolm's desk. The silence meant nothing. Horrors could grow secretly in those inaccessible places, then burst on the world fully formed, as if they had grown overnight.

Every morning I rushed to the newsagents, and scanned the papers. Always there was nothing. I had spent two hours with Oliver's contact on the *News*. She seemed keen. I had told her about the Kefti crisis and about what I was hoping to do with the fund-raising, and she'd rung me back about it later in the day, but after all that nothing had appeared. No news was coming out of Nambula. It made me nervous. Sometimes it made me wonder if I was going mad and had imagined it all.

The next day there was a tiny piece in the News in Brief column in one of the broadsheets.

NAMBULA REFUGEE CRISIS

Relief workers in Eastern Nambula are reporting threats of an influx of over 10,000 refugees displaced by civil war and locust plague from Kefti, a rebel province of Abouti. Workers say that relief supplies are inadequate and warn of a disaster on the scale of the 1985 famine.

The day after, there was a two-column piece on the foreign news pages of *The Times* under the byline of a correspondent in El Daman. He put the numbers on the move at twenty thousand and quoted nonspecific "aid workers" as saying food supplies in the camps would run out in two weeks. There was a slightly pointless quote from me, followed by the fact that I had resigned from SUSTAIN because I was frustrated with the inactivity. There was a quote from the government in El Daman giving the usual line about Nambula not having enough food to feed its own people let alone anyone else's. Then there was a statement from the UN.

"Reports of a movement of displaced people from the highland areas of Kefti towards the Nambulan border are impossible to verify at this time because of the instability of the region." A UN source spoke today of a "heads-in-the-sand" attitude amongst officials and bungling bureaucracy.

Maybe this would provide some momentum. I rushed into the office with a new confidence. No one was around. I called Oliver to tell him but Gwen informed me he was in conference all morning and would talk that afternoon.

The phone rang. It was Eamonn Salt.

"Have you seen *The Times*?" I said, excitedly.

"Yes indeed. Doesn't reflect too well on SUSTAIN, does it?"

"Why? What do you mean?"

"They mention that you resigned from your job and there's no quote from us."

"But I told you I'd been to *The Times* and the *News* when I first got back. Did you call them?"

Silence.

"What's the problem?"

"I think we should get the press side of things sorted out. We need a proper press launch. Can we talk to Oliver about it?"

"He's busy this morning, shall I fix a meeting?"

"Yes, indeed. And in the meantime I think it's best if you call all the celebrities and make sure no one shoots their mouths off till we've worked out the policy."

I rang round all the numbers I had, some of them agents, some of them answerphones, asking everyone not to talk to the press, so as not to steal the thunder before the big launch.

I spent the rest of the day working on the fact sheets, and talking to Circle Line about the airlift and the sponsorship deal. It was all going well on that front. If we gave them assurances about coverage and got hold of the first consignment of food, they would have a flight ready to go in a fortnight.

But still the *Soft Focus* staff drifted in and out, oddly aimlessly, and no one seemed on the case. Everything seemed on hold.

At five o'clock Oliver rang.

"Hi, can you come in for a moment?"

He was leaning back on the L-shaped leather sofa with his arms behind his head. He wasn't wearing a jacket.

"Come in, have a seat."

I sat down on the other leg of the L, and handed him *The Times* report.

"Great, isn't it?" I said, as he read.

"Well, it's not great for the refugees," he said, and handed it back to me.

There was a knock at the door and Gwen appeared with two cups of tea.

"You can go if you like, Gwen," he said. "Isn't it your French conversation tonight?"

"Super, thanks," she said lovingly.

"You doing anything tomorrow night?" he said when she had gone.

"Why?"

"Good. We'll have dinner."

"Why?"

"I want to talk."

"What about? Talk now."

He sighed, stirring his tea. "I've had your Eamonn Salt on the phone, talking about a press launch," he said.

"I know. When do you think it should be?"

He suddenly got to his feet and strode over to the plinth. "Do you pay any attention to what I say?" he said.

I looked at him.

"I told you nothing was definite. We have simply been looking into an idea and that is as far as it goes. It's most unlikely that it will work. The idea of having a press launch at this stage is ridiculous. I never told you this would go ahead." His mouth was twitching. "I feel harassed. I feel my hand is being forced."

I could feel myself breaking out into a sweat. If this failed it was too late to try anything else. I couldn't believe it. We'd held that meeting, a dozen major celebrities had agreed to take part. We had an office, we had people from *Soft Focus* starting to gear up. The PA was looking into having a satellite dish sent to Nambula from Nairobi. But it was in his power to stop it. I said nothing. This was how he had always been. One day he'd be talking about spending the rest of his life with me, then the next day he couldn't even be bothered to phone.

"So we'll have dinner tomorrow and talk," he said.

He was looking at me very oddly. What was going on now? I said nothing.

"I am asking you to have dinner with me tomorrow night."

I put my head down.

"ROSIE, I AM ASKING YOU TO HAVE DINNER WITH ME."

Unbelievable that we could get back into this, as if it were a dance, a game of computer chess. He would do this, and I would do that and off we went. I did know what I was taking on. But surely he couldn't behave like this with all his program commissions?

"What exactly is the problem with the program?" I asked.

He turned and looked at me blankly.

"Why is it most unlikely that it will work?"

"Ah," he said. "Vernon Briggs."

"Vernon Briggs."

"Yes. It's just not his bag—actors, arts, messages about debt. There's no slack in the budget and we're gearing up for the franchises. There's no way he's going to agree to this."

"But he must know it's happening. You must have talked to him. What did he say?"

"It's not his sort of thing."

"Have you spoken to him?"

He said nothing. A little idea popped into my head.

"Oliver. Have you spoken to Vernon Briggs?"

He kept his head down.

"Oliver. I am asking you a question. Have you spoken to Vernon Briggs about Charitable Acts?"

Silence.

"Have you?"

Still nothing.

I picked up the phone and dialed the switchboard.

"Vernon Briggs's office, please."

Oliver looked at me, aghast but curiously impotent.

"Ah. It's Oliver Marchant's office here. Could Oliver pop in and have a word?"

"One moment, please."

I waited with my heart thumping. It was awful to have believed it was all going to happen and then have it whipped away.

"Vernon can see him in ten minutes."

"Thank you. And Rosie Richardson will be coming too."

I looked at Oliver, sitting with his head down.

"We're both nuts, you know," I said. "If anyone saw this they would lock us up."

He looked up and grinned sheepishly. "I know."

"Come and sit on my knee," he said then.

"Oh, sod off, you revolting old madman."

Vernon Briggs heaved himself up from behind the black, gilt-edged desk and came to greet us, clapping his hands together and rubbing them.

"Hello, playmates!" he said, in the hoarse Yorkshire voice. "Bored to tears up 'ere. Fancy a drink?"

"No, thanks. You remember Rosie Richardson?" said Oliver.

"Oh, lawks a' mercy! The woman who could have been the mother of my child if she'd played her cards right. What a sight for sore eyes. You two getting back together, are you? Come to ask for Uncle Vernon's blessing? How are you, my love?"

Vernon Briggs had not improved with time, apart from the addition of a Bavarian-style handlebar mustache.

"Like it?" said the program controller, fingering the waxed tip. "It's a cunt tickler."

The carpet across which he was proceeding was deep pile and black, with a mock zebra-skin rug in the center. I glanced back at it quickly. I hoped it was mock zebra-skin. "Hello, son," said Vernon, reaching up to clap Oliver on the shoulder. "Nice to see you. To see you . . . ?"

Oliver said nothing.

"Eh, eh. None of that, son. None of your sulky sulks. Not till you've done your time, come up through the ranks, shown you know your public-school arse from your Oxbridge elbow. That was a load of old cobblers you came up with the other night. Seen the ratings, have you? Two point four million! Gah! Bums on seats, boy. Bums on seats. That's what we want, not your pseudo-intellectual twaddle."

On the walls were gilt-framed seventies-style prints in shades of pink and purple. They featured long-haired, long-legged girls and pink items: girls getting out of pink sports cars, girls sipping pink cocktails out of triangular glasses, girls leaning on pink cocktail bars, buttocks outlined through tight pink dresses. It was such a shame that Corinna wasn't at the meeting.

"Take a pew, take a pew."

We sat before him, on black lacquer and gold Chinese-style chairs.

"Come on now, dicks on the table, what's up?"

Oliver sighed. "You and I have been talking about the franchise bids," he began. I had been very firm with him in the last ten minutes.

"We have that, son. Quite right. We have that. Ten out of ten," said Vernon, winking at me. "Sharp as a needle, this boy. Tell you what, son, I'll let you off your Latin prep tonight for showing promise."

Oliver straightened his tie uncomfortably.

"As you know, with the franchises in mind, I've been looking for projects which we can get on the air quickly, showing a commitment to public service broadcasting and obviously worthwhile issues." I'd never seen him so unconvincing.

"Eh oop, eh oop. He's coming on. Starting to learn to do what he's told at long last."

Oliver shifted his long legs in his finely cut suit. "I have, er, a definitive project which could achieve that for us."

"Well I never!" Vernon put on a posh voice. "He has hay definitive prowject which will aychieve all that for hus. Give me names, son, names."

"Barry Rhys, Dinsdale Warburton, Vicky Spankie . . ." Oliver was saying.

"Aye aye? Spankie wanky. Keep it in the family."

"Julian Alman, Liam Doyle . . ."

"Don't tell me, let me guess. *It's An Arty Farty Knockout?*"

"Kate Fortune . . ."

"Now yer talking. Ooof. 'Scuse me. Just adjusting me kegs. And where does the worthy bit come in, then?"

"Er, well, Rosie's just come back from Nambula where she's been working in a refugee camp. They have seven thousand malnourished refugees about to descend on their camp and no supplies. They need an airlift of food quickly. The idea is that we should do a one-off live performance of a specially written speeded-up *Hamlet* using all these names, and on either side we do an emergency appeal. It might seem a bit derivative but—"

"Keep going, lad, keep going."

Oliver glanced up at him for a second, nonplussed.

"The problem is, if it's going to be worth doing we have to get it on the air in an unfeasible amount of time, actually within the next two or three weeks."

"Ah. I'm with you. Bit of a bugger that. Yeah. Bit of bugger. Naah, forget it. Too short notice . . "

"It *is* possible to do it in the time," I said. "We've been offered a sponsored flight to get the food out to Nambula, and Nambulan Airways could give us some free flights if we wanted to take a crew and some artists. It would save thousands of lives, maybe tens of thousands of lives."

Oliver was sitting there like a sack of potatoes. I trod on his foot. He jerked upright. "I wondered about putting it in the *Soft Focus* slot," he mumbled. "Also there's a mobile satellite dish sitting in Nairobi at the moment."

"If we leave it longer than that it will be too late," I said. "We've got twenty thousand already in the camp, starting to go under because we haven't enough food, and when the others arrive . . ."

Vernon's bloated face grew troubled. "Kiddies in a bad way, are they?"

"I just wish you could see it."

He looked away misty-eyed. The cunt tickler trembled. Vernon sat for a while, fingering it.

"It always gets to the children first, that's the worst of it."

"We'll do it," he said. Then he jumped to his feet. "We'll do it. Get that dish up there. Get 'em on the phone. It's only fartarse and fannying about for Global Whatsit."

Oliver looked as though he was trying to swallow an oyster which was still in its shell.

"Get a banner done—THANK YOU CAPITAL DAILY TELE-VISION—get the little pickaninnies to hold it up."

I opened my mouth to speak and shut it again.

"Get Kate Fortune out there in a little safari suit. What about Tarby? What about Monkhouse? What we need, boy, is someone with heart."

Oliver was rubbing the back of his neck.

"Forget the *Soft Focus* spot. That load of old fartpantsbollocks. This is mainstream. Get those kiddies right up against the mid-evening surge, where everyone can see them. Don't want a dry eye in the house. Might even do it myself, if you're lucky."

He plodded into the center of the zebra-skin. He stood there deliberating, tugging one end of the mustache pensively.

"Now, *that* might just be a very good idea. I'll do it myself. I haven't been in Africa since nineteen forty-two. I fancy a trip. Might even say a few words while I'm at it."

He turned to me. "Don't you worry, luvvie. I'll see it right for the kiddies. Right, lad. Get on the phone. Call Ian Parker in OB Ops. Tell him Vernon Briggs told you to call and I want that satellite out of Nairobi and on its way to that camp, with a crew, this time to-morrow. Leave the slot with me, son. You go and get your cast list smartened up. We don't want any more of this Alas, Poor Yorick brigade. Get me some decent names on board, then we'll be up and running."

Come on, Oliver, I thought. Make a stand. Tell him what we're trying to say. Tell him it's not supposed to be a tear-jerking jamboree. But he sat completely mute. It was extraordinary.

"Cat got your tongue, lad? Come on, step to it." Vernon opened the door and gestured us out. "I'll see you same time tomorrow, see how you're doing. Put your dick back in your pants and get moving."

Oliver attempted to saunter out, followed by me.

"Don't you worry luvvie, leave it with me," said Vernon and slapped me on the bottom.

Halfway down the corridor I burst out laughing. "What are we going to do?" I said, helpless. "It's great that he's behind it, but—"

"I know," said Oliver, starting to laugh as well. "We can't have him directing it out in Africa."

"Not through his cunt tickler."

"Don't worry," he said. "I'll handle him."

"But that's what's so funny," I said. "You can't," and collapsed again.

"Come on, let's go for a drink," he said, grinning foolishly.

So we did. We talked, and it was nice. Friendly. Equal.

When I got home I was very happy. It was all going great. Vernon was behind the broadcast now. Oliver was back to sanity for the time being. The sponsorship was in place. SUSTAIN thought they could get the first lot of food on tick till we raised the money. The scripts were coming in. The celebrities were being helpful. I'd been home for an hour, having a bath, eating cheese on toast in the kitchen. At nine o'clock I went to put the television on and saw a message from Shirley on the mantelpiece.

CATHERINE KELLY CALLED FROM
THE DAILY NEWS.

Catherine Kelly was Oliver's contact on the paper. I'd seen her for an interview the day after I first saw Oliver in his office before Charitable Acts existed. I'd told her all the details of the Kefti story, and she'd been very interested, but nothing had appeared.

I picked up the phone and dialed the *News*.

"You want Catherine. Hang on, I'll just get her. Sorry, she left five minutes ago. Can I give her a message?"

"Just say Rosie Richardson returned her call." I left the office number.

The next morning I rushed to the newsagent's as usual and leafed through the *News* excitedly. Nothing, nothing, nothing. Then I opened the center page and nearly dropped the paper. There was a full-page spread with a picture of me in evening dress, together with a cartoon of a giant-fanged insect, superimposed over a photograph of starving African children. The headline was:

I'LL MAKE THE STARS HELP,
SAYS JILTED LOCUST HEROINE

"Actually, can you make that twenty Rothman's as well."

Beneath the locust was a picture of Oliver with his arm round Vicky Spankie and at the bottom of the page tiny pictures of Julian, Liam, Dinsdale and Barry.

I immediately thought of all the phone calls I'd made to the celebrities the previous morning. Don't talk to the press, I'd said, don't steal the thunder before the launch. Oh, no. Where *had* they got the photo of me? I was wearing the black shepherdess brides-maid's dress. It must have been that awards ceremony I went to with Oliver. Oh, shit. *Shit.* What had happened? I'd told her about Kefti but nothing about the celebrities. There weren't any celebrities involved at that stage.

> The former live-in lover of TV's *Soft Focus* chief Oliver
> Marchant, 38, flew into London this week in a dramatic
> mercy dash to save the lives of thousands of refugees
> threatened by a terrifying locust plague of biblical pro-
> portions. Rosie Richardson, 37 [I was *not* 37, I was 31],
> was devastated 4 years ago when Marchant refused to
> marry her and ended their relationship. [Where had they
> got all this?] Swearing never to return to England, she left
> to work in a refugee camp in Nambula, East Africa,
> where she has remained ever since. In recent weeks,
> though, the camp has been dogged by terrifying swarms
> of locusts many miles across, blotting out the sun, pancak-
> ing down on the refugees and their crops. Frustrated by
> the inaction of the aid agencies, Richardson left the camp
> vowing to return to England and extract her pound of
> flesh from the lover who had spurned her.

"When I got back I found it terrible trying to adjust to the luxury here compared to the poverty I had come from," said Richardson.

(I never said that. Oh dear, maybe I did, but that was only half of what I said, and I was talking about the first time I got back in eighty-five. Also, that wasn't in the interview. It was when we were just chatting before she left. What else had I said?)

Still reeling from the trauma of seeing an elderly friend, Libren Aleen, lose 26 children in the famine, Richardson said, "These rich stars have a duty to help."

(Maybe I had said celebrities *feel* they have a duty to help.)

"They are given so much wealth for their talent. This is their chance to give something back and I'm going to make them do it." [Never said that.]
    After training as a relief worker in Basingstoke, Richardson became a worker for SUSTAIN, running the 20,000-strong camp in Safila in the East of Nambula . . . refugees displaced from Kefti [fine, fine . . .] defying death in a perilous lone journey deep into the war. "The UN are completely incompetent," says Richardson. [Oh, *God*] . . . furious with SUSTAIN's refusal to believe her story and send more food she made her dramatic resignation and caught the next plane to London. "The celebrities and the British public are all we have left to rely on."

It got worse.

At first Marchant, who friends say complained at being "harassed" by Richardson after the relationship ended, refused to help, saying the plan was impractical at such short notice. But Marchant's current girlfriend, *Last Leaves of the Indian Summer* star Vicky Spankie, 26 [she was

30 if she was a day], was moved by Richardson's plight and persuaded Marchant to help.

Vicky Spankie. It must have been her. They had most of the names of the celebrities, bar Kate Fortune and Corinna. It *must* have been the wretched Spankie. I peered more closely at the African picture. It wasn't Nambula or Kefti. It looked as though it might have been Mozambique. There was a quote from the UN at the bottom saying they were still verifying the reports and everything possible was being done. And then another quote.

SUSTAIN spokesman Eamonn Salt confirmed yesterday that Richardson was no longer employed by the agency. "SUSTAIN personnel are strictly forbidden to enter Kefti for reasons of security and diplomatic relations. Any defiance of this edict by an employee would be treated with the utmost seriousness." Neither SUSTAIN nor CDT, where TV hotshot Marchant is program controller [Vernon wasn't going to like that], claimed any knowledge of the Charitable Acts appeal today.

Friends of Marchant's expressed concern that Richardson was using the crisis as a means to win Marchant back from TV's Vicky. "Of course everyone wants to help the starving Africans," said one, "but sometimes you mistrust people's motives." The two stars are expected to marry early next year.

CHAPTER

Twenty-two

I lit a Rothman's and nearly choked. I walked back to the flat in a daze.

The phone was ringing when I got in. I sat down at the kitchen table and let it ring. It stopped and then started again. Brrr brrrr. Brrr brrrr. Brrr brrrr. Brrr brrrr. I took the little bugger off the hook. A faint noise, like a car burglar alarm, started. Then a voice said, "Please replace your handset." Dooweedooweee. "Please replace your handset." I replaced my handset. The phone rang immediately. I bent down and unplugged it, lit another cigarette, choked, put it out, laid my head on my arms and wanted to cry.

Get a grip, I thought suddenly. My shoulders are narrow, but my bottom is broad. I wiped my face with a piece of paper towel, shoved the *Daily News* in the bin and set off for work trying to look tough.

The phone was already ringing when I got into the office.

"Is that the Jilted Locust Heroine? Welcome to the Famous Club." Oliver.

"Shut up. It's horrible."

"Horrible? Don't be ridiculous. You just see what happens. All publicity is good publicity, remember?"

"But I've told all the actors not to talk to the press. They'll think I was just trying to get all the attention for myself."

"I think you'll find they're smarter than that. Now calm down."

The phone rang again.

"Rosie Richardson, please."

"Who's calling?"

"Pat Wilson, *Express.*"

"Could you call the press office, please?"

"I just did. They told me to call this number."

"Could you—could you call them back and say—"

"No. I'm not playing musical telephones here, love. We want an interview with Rosie Richardson today, and a photo. Have you got a number?"

"I'm sorry, you will have to call the press office, this is a different . . . this is not, I can't help you." Gulaaarg.

"All right, if that's the way CDT wants to play it. I'll remember that. Bye."

The phone rang again. "Hello, it's *Woman's Hour* here. Could I—"

I had a brain wave. "I'll just transfer you to the press office."

The phone rang again. "Hello. Is that Rosie Richardson?"

"You need to talk to the press office. I'll just transfer you."

"This *is* the press office."

"Ah."

At that moment Oliver put his head round the door.

"Oh dear . . . sorry. Yes . . . yes . . . oh dear . . . I see . . . yes . . . Melissa. Could I just interrupt one second . . . yes, I'm sorry . . . oh dear."

"Give it to me." Oliver took the phone from me.

"Oliver Marchant here. What's the problem? Yip. Yip. Yip. So what's the problem?" He rolled his eyes at me. "Which is exactly what, as a press officer, you are hired to do. Yes. Was there anything else? Fine. Bye."

The phone rang again. He picked it up. "Hi. Yip. Yip. Oh, come on, Corinna, for God's sake. It's happened to you often enough. Of course she didn't do it deliberately. Yep. Yes, I think it probably was something to do with Vicky. OK. I'll tell her. Fine. See you tomorrow."

"Corinna sent her sympathies," he said, "after a little persuasion. Now don't give it another thought."

The phone rang again. I picked it up this time.

"Hello, is this Charitable Acts?"

"Who's calling, please?"

"Hi. Good to speak with you. My name is Mike de Sykes. I represent Nadia Simpson."

There was an expectant pause.

"Nadia Simpson?" I mouthed at Oliver.

"Supermodel."

"What?" I whispered.

"Very famous."

"Oh, hello. What was it you wanted?" I said into the phone.

"Actually, we're very surprised you haven't rung us."

"I'm sorry?"

"Give it to me." Oliver was trying to take over again. I shook my head and held him back.

"You did realize Nadia is Nambulan?"

"She's Nambulan," I mouthed. Oliver threw his head back and laughed. "Born in Huddersfield."

"Shhh. Shhh . . . No, I didn't, actually."

"Look, Nadia wants to help. Nadia is very upset at what's happening to her people. The girl is destroyed. Now, listen, have I got something for you! Nadia Simpson is telling me she's ready to go out to Nambula."

"Oh."

"She wants to come to Nambula," I mouthed.

Oliver slit his throat both ways with his finger.

"I'm going to bring Nadia in to see you this afternoon. She's got a window at three, OK?"

"It'll have to be the end of the day, I'm afraid."

"Make it the Groucho. Six-thirty."

"Six-thirty, Groucho club. Fine, I'll be there."

Oliver shook his head. "You're wasting your time."

The phone rang again. He bent forward and pressed buttons.

"Gwen, take Rosie's calls for a while, will you? Thanks."

He sat on the side of my desk. "Now, my little jilted locust heroine. As the story is out, we'll go with it. Fix a press call for Thursday—for either ten or three in a conference room here. I'll have a word with Melissa so she can help you. I'll brief the celebs if you give me all the stuff. And we'd better get moving on this Africa broadcast and sort out who's going out there. I've had Kate Fortune on the phone about it twice already. She's got the hide of a Timberland boot, that woman."

"It was *my* idea," a bald man in horn-rimmed glasses, between me and the bar, was whining loudly. I was watching the scene in the mirror, as London's smarter media types gathered in the Groucho club for their end-of-the-day drinks, sinking into soft dark armchairs, and asking each other how they were.

"I thought it was Jeremy's idea. Hi, Roland, how are you?"

"Roland, hi. How are you? Jeremy put in the initial treatment. But it was my idea. We were in here. We were sitting with Rory, where Jerome and Simon are now. And I'm saying, 'What about social workers? Twelve-part series Inner London, housing project, battered babies, deportation, solvent abuse,' and with Jeremy it was like, 'Oh, God, yawn yawn, wor-*thee*.'—Hi! How are you?—Then, next thing, Jeremy's taken it to Jonathan, and suddenly it's, like, he's got the commission, and it's all happening. I mean, I seriously feel justified in ringing Jonathan up and saying something. The point is—Hi! How are you?—it was *my idea*."

"*Voilà.*" Mike de Sykes, a small, plump man in a white suit placed our drinks on the table. "Nadia won't be a moment. Just popped downstairs to freshen up. Ah, here she is," he said, looking up at the door. "The girl herself. You're gonna love this girl, Rosie."

Nadia was a very beautiful girl, with sculpted Arabic features, but there was something about the way she had done her hair, scraped back severely from her face, then ringleting down weirdly from two high bunches, which reminded me of a sheep. A few minutes later, we were deep in conversation. Well, I say deep . . .

"So Mikey's saying, 'Nadia, you should go to Nambula.' And I'm thinking, Why? And I'm pissed at him. You know? Then I see the pictures. And Mikey's saying, 'Nadia. These are your people.' And

I'm looking at these pictures, of these children that are dying, and I'm thinking, This feels real, you know? This just feels so real. These are my people. And then I'm saying, 'Mikey I think I'm going to Nambula.' "

"Nadia's a very caring girl," said Mike, grabbing a handful of Twiglets and shoving them into his mouth.

"And Mikey's saying, 'Nadia, it's not enough to weep.' And I'm looking at these pictures, and I'm thinking, I really think I am, you know? I'm going to Nambula."

"Which pictures were these?"

"The ones in the *News*, hon," said Mike, grabbing another handful of Twiglets. "Nadia was just destroyed when she saw those pictures."

"If it's the same article I'm thinking of, there was only one picture and it wasn't of Nambulans. I think it was taken in Mozambique, though no one was to know."

"Nambula's part of Mozambique, huh?" said Nadia.

"No. No. It's a separate country to the north. About two thousand miles to the north, actually."

"So they put a picture of someone else instead of my people?"

"Nadia, don't get upset."

"I am upset, Mikey. You're saying, don't get upset. I am upset. This is real for me, you know? They put a picture of this Mozambique, instead of my people. This is why I have to go to Nambula."

"Were you born in Nambula?" I asked.

"This is what I said to Mikey. I wasn't born in Nambula. Why am I going to Nambula?"

"But your parents are Nambulan?"

" 'Mikey,' I said, 'my mother is British, my father is British,'" and the accent was mid-Atlantic, "'so why am I Nambulan all of a sudden?' "

"Your father is Nambulan, hon. His father was Nambulan."

"So your grandfather was Nambulan?"

"Her grandfather was Nambulan. Nadia feels very close to the Nambulan people."

"But you realize the people we're trying to help are Keftian?"

"Huh? Mikey, I don't get it."

"Wait a minute," said Mike, jutting out his chin aggressively. "You're telling me these people who are starving are not Nambulan?"

Half an hour later, Nadia was beginning to come to terms with the Keftians' infiltration of her people. "I'm really bored with my life, you know?" she was saying. "I really want to change my life. This feels real to me, you know? And I figure if I go out there and we take the pictures then something good will come."

"What do you actually want to do in Nambula?" said a voice behind me. It was Oliver, standing with a smirk on his face. What was he doing here?

"Hey! Oliver Marchant. Sir. The main man. Let me get you a drink, sir," said Mike, jumping to his feet. "Oliver Marchant, this is Nadia Simpson."

"Pleased to meet you. Go on, go on, don't let me interrupt," said Oliver, drawing up an armchair and motioning to the waiter. "Large Scotch, please, Hannes. Anyone else? Go on, Nadia."

"Nadia wants people to be aware of what's happening."

"And what is happening?"

"People are suffering," said Mike.

"Why?" said Oliver. "Come on. It's important. This is a political issue."

"Huh?" said Nadia, suddenly nervous. "I don't want to get political. I'm not a political person."

"Nadia's not a political girl."

"I'm not a political person. But, you know, I figure it's not enough just to, like, get upset."

"It's not enough just to weep," encouraged Mike.

"I know, she wants to weep in front of the cameras," said Oliver, laughing. "Well, that's sweet, but I'm afraid it's not that sort of program."

Nadia looked rather hurt and very young.

"But it's great that you want to help," I said hurriedly.

"Wait a minute. I don't get this," said Mike. "I don't get it. Nadia Simpson is saying she will give up her time, and go out to Nambula for you, waive her fee, expenses only, and you're saying, don't call us we'll call you?"

"Precisely," said Oliver, leaning back with his Scotch. "We have a lot of artists wanting to take part, and we're choosing carefully. If performers are going to stand up on television, in a refugee camp, with messages for the public, then they ought to be informed, and have something responsible to say."

"Come on, Nadia," said Mike, getting to his feet.

"But Nadia does want to find out about it," I said.

"Come on, hon. I'm not having you spoken to like this."

"Hey, wait, Mikey, I wanna talk to this lady. I wanna talk to the lady. OK, Mikey? I wanna talk to the lady."

She rearranged the sheep hairdo. "People like to be negative, you know? People like to be negative about doing good. I don't know why they like to be negative, when people are doing good. They like to be negative."

"They like to be circumspect," said Oliver.

"Come on, Nadia. We're wasting our time with these people. We're out of here."

Mike was helping her to her feet, leading her towards the door.

"But you said, go to Nambula."

"You're going to Nambula, hon. You're on your way to Nambula."

He was opening the door and bustling her out. "The whole fucking world's gonna know you're going to Nambula."

"Did you have to be so rude?" I said, when they'd gone.

"I wasn't rude. I just nipped it in the bud. Come on. You're a busy girl. You haven't got time to waste with these idiots."

"You might at least have thanked her."

"For what? Why should she expect undiluted gratitude? What has she got to offer us? I tell you what. It's a two-way exchange, this business. If the charities toughened up and asked a few more questions before they went slobbering all over the stars they'd have a lot less trouble."

"You were crushing a butterfly under a millstone, or whatever the expression is."

"Oh, come on, sweetheart, lighten up. Have another drink. I've done a bit of a script for Africa. I want you to have a look at it."

He'd drawn it up in two hours. It was brilliant. I lightened up.

It wasn't simple, me and Oliver. I knew his bad side and I didn't trust him. But the charm of the boss man, of a man more capable than you, who is helping you, is very seductive. Over the few days that followed in London, as I watched him using his brain and his power to drive the program along, as everything came together, the press launch, the sponsorship, the food, the program slot, the scripts, as I found him right behind me whenever I was in difficulties, I felt Safila growing safer by the moment, and myself on ever more uncertain ground.

Twenty-three

We were kissing in Oliver's flat, ravenous. His hand was inside my shirt. It was the night after the press launch. We had been bashing the phones all day, talking to sponsors, artists, engineers, cameramen, journalists. At that moment I wanted nothing more than to escape into sensual release with Oliver. He was sliding his hand round my back, unclipping my bra in one smooth move, pulling my shirt up with the other hand.

"We mustn't do this," I said with my eyes closed, breathing unsteadily.

"I think we must," he whispered into my neck.

I twisted away.

"Why not?" he said, holding my arm.

I moved away from him. "You know why not."

I sat, rubbing my forehead while he went to get a drink, straightening my clothes, fastening myself up, trying to work out how I'd got into this. He'd asked me again to have dinner with him. We were getting on so well, he was being so good, and had done so much, it seemed churlish and oddly conceited to refuse.

He wanted to go to the movies before dinner, he said, so we could wind down and "forget about work," for a while. The only film we could get into was some Vietnam war spectacular. I thought it would be fine, but when the first machine gun went off, and the first khaki-clad stomach turned red, it hit my mental bruise like a cudgel.

I got up, apologized my way along the row, walked out, down the stairs, into the tackiness and kids of Leicester Square. I leaned against a wall, trying to make the goblins lie quiet. I could see Oliver looking for me outside the cinema. I wasn't going to tell him about the land mine. Horrific experience evolved too easily into anecdote. Events which, as Nadia Simpson would say, were real to you, and painful, got turned into entertainment for everyone else. It was a good way of making yourself seem more interesting, but pretty cheap.

In the end, though, I did tell him. He was very understanding. And because, he said, I was too upset to go to a restaurant, he took me home to his flat and said we'd get a pizza. And we both, I think, felt a pang at the memory of all the old Oliver and Rosie pizza jokes. Then, when we got into the flat and the door was closed behind us, he dropped his coat on the floor, and took me in his arms. And, shaken and shook around, lonely, aroused by so much proximity, by my practical need for him, by the chemical rush which had never left us, I didn't resist.

He came back in with the drinks, and lit a cigarette. He was angry.

"You realize I can't do this?" he said.

"I know. We mustn't."

"I don't mean *that*. I mean Charitable Acts."

I felt as though all my insides were shuddering. "What are you saying?" I said. "How can you not now?"

"It's up and running. Vernon can direct it."

"But you know that would be hopeless. It's shaky enough as it is. It would fall apart. We're relying on goodwill. They all think he's awful."

"He'll take over whether I'm there or not. He's coming out to Africa. As you yourself said, I can't handle him."

"Why are you saying you can't do it?"

"If Vernon's going to get involved—which he is—I'll be better off out of it. I haven't got the time, anyway."

"But you'll do the London end?" I said, trying to keep my voice steady.

"No."

"Why? Why have you decided this now?"

"Like I said, I haven't got time."

I thought for a minute. "If I had said yes to you just now," I said carefully, "would you have found the time?"

His face was thunderous. "You have no idea, have you? No idea. You come back full of self-righteousness, with your dying people and your cause. I thought you had come back for me. You're playing games with me to get what you want. I love you. I can't be expected to work with you on this basis. I can't go out to Africa if we're playing this stupid game of just being colleagues."

He was lying, wasn't he? He hadn't been misled at all. When had I misled him? He didn't love me. He just had to make sure he could still have me if he wanted.

"What about Vicky?"

"Blah. Vicky. That's over."

"And if I say I will sleep with you?"

Surely nobody, not even he, could play this dirty?

"Then it would be easier for me."

He could.

He stormed into the kitchen. It was eleven o'clock. I knew we couldn't do the program without him. I stared at the rain, driving against the window. The camp would be in darkness now, apart from the hospital and feeding center. We had twelve days left till the broadcast. They had ten days' worth of food. The new refugees would be arriving any day. They would be starting to cross the desert to Safila, pouring out of the highlands heading for the border. There were five, maybe ten, thousand of them, and they didn't have anything to eat. It occurred to me that my romantic life didn't matter very much. Neither did Oliver's or Vicky Spankie's. Maybe I should just do it.

The phone rang twice, and the answerphone clicked on. Vicky Spankie's voice echoed over the wooden floors.

"Olly. It's Vicky. I know where you are. You're not with Julian. You're out with Rosie, aren't you? Or *Kirsty.*" There was an indeterminate noise which may or may not have been a sob. "Phone me when you get in. Please."

Oliver strode in from the kitchen, dived for the phone, clicked off the answerphone. "Hi, I'm here. What are you talking about?" He was walking with the phone into the bathroom, trailing the long cord, shutting the door behind him.

Unaccountably, Vicky's voice rang out again. "Olly, please call me when you get in."

I walked slowly over to the machine. He had put it on ANSWER PLAY instead of turning it off. I was going to stop it, then another message began.

"Hi. It's Kirsty here. Just ringing to see . . . um . . . just ringing because you said you were going to call me after . . . and . . ." The beep went.

"Olly, where are you?" Vicky again. "You said we . . . I called Julian and he said he wasn't seeing you tonight. Why do you keep doing this to me? I feel so stupid and wretched and reduced. What are we doing this weekend? I can't bear this."

I remembered that feeling so, so well.

"Oliver, it's Mummy. Please just give me a little call, darling. I keep leaving you all these messages, and I haven't even had the briefest little chat with you for two months."

There was a beep, then someone obviously rang off, then another beep and a different woman's voice. "Hi, pervert. Just called to say crisis averted. The Big Pig swallowed it. I'm working late at the office Monday, OK? Hope you can make it. Don't call me at home tonight. I'll ring you tomorrow. Mmm. Dirty kiss you know where."

I left the tape still playing, put on my coat, and left.

He caught up with me in his car just as I reached the bus stop on the King's Road.

"Get in," he said.

"I'm waiting for the bus."

"I'll take you home."

"No, thanks."

"Look, I'm sorry. At least let me drive you home."

It was pouring rain. I got in the car. We set off north in a particularly filthy silence. Halfway through Hyde Park, he swerved the car into the car park beside the Serpentine, and turned off the ignition. A Japanese couple were walking by the side of the lake, his arm around her shoulders. A pair of ducks were making a purposeful wake through the black water.

He looked sad, beaten. "I am very unhappy," he said.

As he knew, many women have quite a strong urge, when confronted with a broken man, to try to mend him. Messing about with Oliver was not what I had come back to England for.

He rubbed his head with his forearm miserably.

On the other hand, I thought, we're going to be in a real mess without him.

"I hate myself," he said.

And, actually, it was ridiculous to think he had been doing all this work just so I would sleep with him.

"I feel so wretched."

"Will you please put the heater on?"

We were all human. He'd probably just lost his temper, and allowed the control fetish to have its head. At least I should give him a get-out clause.

"You didn't really mean you weren't going to do the program, did you?"

"Yes," he said, uncertainly.

The car was starting to fill with warmth again.

"You've been wonderful these last two weeks," I said. "You've sorted it all out, you've got everyone together, you've driven it along. The whole thing is only happening because of you. Every time I think about the camp I think about them all depending on you, and you being so good."

He was brightening like a child. It was all true, that was the stupid thing.

"I know you care about those refugees. You've put your other work on one side to do this, and stuck your neck out with Vernon. You're not going to abandon it now."

I hope, I added silently.

I watched him weighing it up.

"You don't really want to get into a mess with me again. We're fine as we are."

He was staring at his hands. "I do care."

Maybe he was changing.

"I feel . . . I've really loved doing this, you know. It's . . ." He looked down and rubbed his thumb against his fingers. "It's really good to be doing something that's doing good. Oh, Jesus, it sounds so corny. I mean, it makes me feel good."

"So you'll carry on?"

"Yes," he said. "I want to carry on."

And he leaned across and gave me a little kiss on the lips.

"I would have done it anyway," he added smoothly. Bastard.

Twenty-four

It was Sunday morning, six days before we were due to leave for Africa. The Charitable Acts cast and production team had decamped to Dave Rufford's stately home for the first full rehearsal. They were mooching about his recording studio in the Great Hall, waiting for things to start moving. Vernon had found us a juicy one-hour spot, mid-evening, a week on Wednesday. Ten days to go. I looked around and wondered if we were going to get it together in time.

The artists were sitting around happily on sofas, tucking into smoked salmon and cream cheese bagels, cappuccinos and Buck's Fizz, reading the papers. A little group was gathered around the cast list for the speeded-up *Hamlet,* laughing and giggling. Corinna was staring furiously at a row of stags' heads, which were all wearing sunglasses. Oliver was striding around, telling people off like a schoolmaster, then staring madly at his script. The Oliver Marchant as saintly savior concept seemed rather to have gone to his head. Dave Rufford was playing with a remote control switch, making the gilt-framed old masters, decorated with false mustaches, sink back into the walls. Wood panels whirred up and down as he pressed his buttons. I watched as Oliver shouted instructions to a PA, walking straight into five-year-old Max Rufford, who was driving a miniature Aston Martin, with a full petrol-fired engine, over the polished wood floor.

"Jesus Christ," he said. "What is this? We are trying to raise money for the starving."

One of the *Soft Focus* PAs handed me an envelope. "This fax came for you from SUSTAIN."

It was a copy of a telex from Henry. It was the first word I'd had from Safila since I left.

HOPE ALL GOING WELL WITH APPEAL. NEED IT, CAN TELL
YOU. ARRIVALS STILL COMING. NO MOVE FROM UNHCR.
STILL NO SHIP. NO MED. SUPPLIES FROM ANDRE. RESOK
PANICKING RE: MAJOR LOCUST EXODUS. DAILY DEATHS
CLIMBING TO DOUBLE FIGURES. BRACING OURSELVES.
NOTHING HERE FOR THEM WHEN FLOODGATES OPEN.
COUNTING ON YOU, OLD GIRL. HENRY.

I had never had such a terse message from Henry. I looked at the date. It was sent from El Daman five days ago. It must be at least a week old. Maybe more. I tried to imagine what was going on out there now. I looked anxiously round the room.

"Darling boy! We have a *disaster* on our hands." Dinsdale was gesturing dramatically up at the cast list. "Exquisitely cast. A per-*fection* of a casting. But where? Where is the *ghost?*"

Oliver looked up, distractedly.

Dinsdale's brow furrowed. "I shall step in. Do not fret, dear boy. I shall rise to the occasion and brrrrrridge the gap. I, Dinsdale, shall be the ghost! It will be the performance of my career."

"You're supposed to be bloody Claudius, you fool. You can't play the bloody ghost and the murderer of the bloody ghost. Absolutely bloody crazy," bellowed Barry.

"That's fine. Good idea. Family likeness," said Oliver, returning to his script.

"Absolutely crazy," said Barry.

"Oh, shut up, you fearsome old spoilsport. Just because I have two parts and you merely have the one."

"Oliver, could I have a word. I'm sorry, I'm just *not* happy about playing a woman of this age. I mean, I've gone, love. I'm sorry, I've just gone."

"One minute, Kate. Come on, everyone. Read through, please, pull up some chairs in a circle."

Everyone carried on talking.

"Where's Julian?" said Oliver, bearing down on me, looking at his watch.

"He must be on his way. I've tried his car phone, and it's engaged."

"If he was being paid for this, he'd be here on the bloody dot. It's charity, so he's late. Try him again."

"Look, I don't want to be fockin' queenie but my character wouldn't say this line," said Liam Doyle, hurrying after him. "It's not right."

"Shut up, please, Liam."

"I've just had a call from Jerry Jones about Natalie D'Arby," said Dave Rufford's wife, Nikki. "He said he spoke to you and you thought there might be a part for her."

"A part *in* her was what I said."

"I am *so* furious," said Kate at me, looking resentfully at Oliver. "This is some scheme of Vicky Spankie's to force me into playing a woman twice my age."

"I'm sure Hamlet's mother was very young," I said. "They used to have children before puberty in those days."

"Did they? Did they really?"

"Max. Outside," said Nikki as her son narrowly missed her leg in his car.

"Leave the little bleeder alone. 'E's not doin' any 'arm," said Dave.

"Will everyone *please* pull up a chair, and let's make a start," shouted Oliver. "It's like trying to plot *Aïda* with a flock of sheep."

I was leaning on the piano, going through the mail which had come in since the press launch on Thursday. It made the *Evening Standard,* the BBC and ITN news and most of the papers the next morning. By Saturday there was a sack of letters waiting in the office. The response was extraordinary: pound coins taped to drawings from eight-year-olds, twenty-pound notes from pensioners. Dinsdale, Barry, Julian, Oliver and Nikki had all discreetly made out large checks that morning. We would probably have nearly enough to pay for the first planeload of food before we set off.

The process of getting everyone on chairs in a circle was not moving so quickly. Scripts had been unaccountably mislaid or fallen into the wrong hands, spectacles had to be retrieved from cars, glasses of water fetched, lavatories visited, nannies telephoned. Oliver was standing amid the mayhem shouting, "Come ON, everyone, please. *Where* is Dinsdale?"

Barry's voice reverberated round the great hall, making mincemeat of the acoustic panels. "'Angels and ministers of grace defend us!'" he bellowed. He was staring aghast at the minstrels' gallery where Dinsdale was entering wearing a sheet and a pair of half-moon spectacles.

"'Be thou a spirit of health or goblin damn'd?'" roared Barry.

Dinsdale started to remove the sheet and spectacles peevishly from his head. "How dare you steal my thunder, you frightful old tart? Fiendishly mean of you on my first entrance. Absolutely fiendish. Shan't forgive you. Never speak another *word* to you as long as I live."

"'Oh, earth! What else? O, fie! Hold, hold my heart.'" Barry was clutching at his chest and stumbling dramatically. Everyone was laughing.

"This whole thing is turning into a farce," shouted Oliver. "Stop this *now.*"

They stared.

"I think we should all have better judgment than to act around like schoolchildren when lives are depending on us."

There was silence.

"Yes. You see? I think we should all remember why we're doing this," he said primly.

I was waiting for him to add, "It's not funny, it's not clever, it's just silly," but he just walked furiously back to his chair and sat down, drumming his fingers on his script.

I rubbed my forehead with the back of my arm, worrying. I decided to get on with my sack of letters, and try not to think too hard.

"Are you all right, m'dear? You look exhausted. Have you had some breakfast?" Nikki Rufford came and leaned next to me on the piano. I was going through the press clippings now, ready to photocopy them for the celebrities. "Oh dear, I do wish Dave wouldn't do this," she said, looking up at the false mustache and beard on the Holbein above her.

"You must be done in yourself, after the rain forest do. It's very good of you to have everyone here."

"Oh, it's fine. Dave loves all this." She laughed affectionately. "He's so excited about being a gravedigger."

We looked over at them plotting the sketch in the background. It was extraordinary how quickly it had come together, once they got going.

"Halas, poor Yorick. I knew him well! Don't break off, playmates. Don't break off. Just come to inspect the troops. Carry on. Have I missed To Be or Not to Be?"

The rehearsal ground to a halt as Vernon Briggs strutted into the great hall shouting, "Carry on. Don't mind me. You carry on, lads."

He started waddling towards Nikki and me. "Ladies! Ladies! Hello, my loves. Nice to see you, to see you . . ."

"Nice," we muttered foolishly as he arrived.

"Load of bloody old bollocks, this, isn't it?" he said too loudly, jerking his head backwards at the actors. "Don't you worry, my love," he reached out and patted my bottom. "I'll see the kiddies right. I'll get it sorted out with some decent names. Tarby. That's who we need. Someone with a bit of heart. We're not having old Michelangelo Marchant getting bossy-side-out in Africa either, lecturing everyone on the siege of bloody Omdurman. Now, I'm not here for long. I want to be at Newbury for the four-fifteen. I want all this lot that's coming out to Africa gathered for a little talk. Get 'em to frame themselves, will you, love?"

Corinna, Julian and Kate were glancing nervously from Oliver to Vernon. This was the celebrity combination which was to take on the dark continent in the name of Charitable Acts. It was perhaps not the ideal choice, given Corinna's antineocolonialist fervor, Julian's emotional state and Kate's confidence in baby-hugging as an infallible route to world peace, but with two weeks' notice it was the best we could get. At least Julian's portable phone wouldn't work in Safila.

"So my intention is that we provide an introduction and three main inserts, each presented by a different one of us in a different area of the camp, the feeding center, the hospital and outside one of the huts," Oliver was saying. "They can all be cabled. We talk to the refugees, we try to explore their sensibilities in relation to Western aid, and their perceptions of the roots of the poverty and the north/south divide and—"

"Yeah, you do that, lad, if you can keep yerself from nodding off. I'll be pointing a camera at Kate Fortune holding those kiddies with a bit of music in the background and the phone numbers running underneath. 'When a Child Is Born' that's what we want."

Julian, Oliver and Corinna all started to speak.

"But—"

"I really must—"

"I absolutely cannot—"

Only Kate was beaming fondly at Vernon.

He ploughed on. "Now, lad, who's looking after the show in London while we're away?"

"Er, I'm going to record the *Hamlet* and the special performances this Wednesday, and Marcus Miles will direct the live links on the day."

"What? You think you're gonna have this load of bollocks in shape by Wednesday, do yer? Rather you than me, mate. Anyway. The dish is on its way. What's happening with the flights? We've got the food, have we? When's that cargo plane going?"

"It's leaving on Friday morning with the food and the camera crew," I said.

"All free?"

"We have to reimburse the cost of the food out of the appeal and

Circle Line are giving us the first flight for nothing, provided we give them a credit."

"And we're flying out Saturday?"

"Yes, two P.M. Heathrow."

"Everyone jabbed up, all got your kit, have you?"

"Oh, Rosie, I was going to ask," said Julian. "Do we have to take the water bottles that you've bought for us? Because, you see, I've found this one with a leather holder that you can fasten to your belt. And it holds the same amount."

"Have you got those fact sheets ready yet?" said Corinna. "I want to know what I'm talking about."

"You'll have them by the end of today."

"There will be somewhere to plug in my hair dryer in the camp?" said Kate.

"Was it the pills in the white jar we were supposed to take every day?"

"Which airline are we flying?" said Oliver.

"Nambulan Airways."

"Are they, I mean, are they all right?" said Julian.

"Eh oop, 'Fly me hi-gh, on a coconut air-way,'" sang Vernon.

I bit the side of my thumb. I wasn't sure whether they, or Safila, knew what they were in for.

Twenty-five

"If we crash, can I eat you?" asked Oliver.

It was Saturday and the Nambulan Airways jet had heaved itself into the air only five and a half hours after the scheduled take-off time. A range of unnatural engine sounds was making the cabin shudder, and a high tinnitus whine, which the stewardess had announced would cease after takeoff, was surprising no one by failing to cease.

A shot of our plane appeared on the video screens now, only to plunge to the bottom of the screen with the rest of the shot, followed by a flickering white line and a new shot of a glamorous waterskiing man, dark hair blowing back in the wind, taking one hand off the rope to wave and smile at the camera. The shot widened to reveal the water skier skimming past the mudflats of the river in central El Daman. He was balancing on one leg now, with the tiny figures of basking crocodiles just recognizable in the background. For a moment I was mesmerized by this vision of Nambula as a playboy's hot spot, until the water skier suffered the same fate as the plane, to be replaced by the flickering white line, and, this time, a desert sunset, Arabic music, a nomad silhouetted on a camel, and the mountains of Sidra behind. I felt a great rush of joy at the sight. I glanced across at Kate Fortune, wondering if she was sharing my joy.

Possibly not. Kate was wearing the same pale, shocked expression she had been wearing since she entered the plane to find herself seated beside a wizened man in a very dirty djellaba, who was holding a newspaper parcel full of eggs. She was playing a complicated psychological game with him over the armrest. She took hold of the peach gabardine of her sleeve, moved it away from the once-white cotton of his sleeve, and lifted her eyes to his face, pointedly. The man looked at her, looked down at his sleeve and back at her with puzzlement. Then still looking at her, he reached into the fold of his djellaba, took out a handful of leaves and put them into his mouth.

"Excuse me."

Julian was sandwiched between two Nambulan women who were even larger than him. They were swathed in the colorful, musk-infused robes of newlyweds.

"Excuse me." Julian was trying to get the attention of the stewardess, who looked at him with a bored expression and stayed where she was.

The djellabaed old man was reaching into his mouth now, which was stained red, with bits of leaf protruding from his lips. He stuck his thumb and forefinger inside, took out a gobbet of chewed-up leaf, smiled endearingly, and offered the gobbet to Kate. For a moment I saw the Fortune face break into the first natural smile I had ever seen on it.

"Excuse me."

Julian was attempting to squeeze his enormous body past one of the brides. Through a combination of climbing and squashing he managed to extract himself and made his way up to the stewardess, who, along with everyone else in the cabin, was watching him suspiciously.

"Excuse me? Is it possible to move up to first class now?" said Julian discreetly.

"No first class," said the stewardess loudly.

"Shhh. Yes, there is, I can see it through the curtain," said Julian, looking nervously around the cabin.

"No first class."

"The lady we spoke to at the check-in desk, Mrs. Karar, said we could move up to first class after takeoff," he said, out of the corner of his mouth.

"You sit down."

"We're with the television." Julian did an incomprehensible mime. "Me very large. First class?"

"Where is your ticket?"

Julian fumbled in his pocket. "Blast."

A roll of twenty-dollar bills fell onto the floor. A thin man in a brown polyester jacket with a hole in the elbow bent down and gave them back to him.

"Thanks. Blast."

Eventually he produced the ticket, and handed it to the stewardess.

"Television. We raise money for refugees," he said, rubbing his stomach hungrily. "First class?"

The stewardess was staring at the ticket.

"Mrs. Karar . . ." Julian began again.

"This free ticket," said the stewardess.

"Yes. That's right. You see Nambulan Airways gave me a free ticket because we're doing a broadcast to help Nambula, which is why Mrs. Karar said I could go into first class," he said, bright red now.

"You are not having paid for this ticket. You sit down now."

There was a ripple of laughter from the cabin, as Julian struggled back to his seat, looking mortified.

"Excuse me."

The stewardess lifted her chin at Oliver.

"Could you bring me a Scotch and soda?"

"No alcohol."

"I'm sorry?"

"Nambula is Moslem country. Alcohol is not allowed."

Oliver looked at me with a gleam of pure panic in his eye.

"Have we got any Scotch with us?"

"No."

"WHAT?"

There was a pause.

"I've forgotten my sunglasses," he said.

"Oh dear," I replied.

Another pause.

"Damn," he said.

I sighed. "What is it now?"

"Sunblock. Forgotten it," said Oliver.

"Just wear a hat."

A docile calm had settled over the cabin, as happens in the mysterious rhythm of airline journeys. Corinna Borghese was sleeping under an eye mask which was smeared with pale-green gel. Vernon was dozing, with a half bottle of whisky openly resting on his paunch. I had seen him paying off the stewardess. Oliver was beside himself with mixed emotions, wanting some of the whisky but not wanting to admit that Vernon had been smarter than him, still going on about his sunglasses.

It was a curious bridge between the two worlds—this apparently modern jet where nothing worked anymore, odors of goat and musk wafting around Marks and Spencer's business suits, and un-fathomable objects wrapped in newspaper and string tumbling from the overhead lockers onto the heads of the passengers below. It was around this point when every item in your bag became pre-cious and irreplaceable; when you remembered that total availabil-ity of all things at all times was not a universal state, and started to panic slightly. It was the beginning of the slippery slide away from bursting schedules, clockwatching and rush, as well as order, effi-ciency and logic.

I settled back, enjoying a hiccup of freedom. No phone call could reach us here. Ten hours in which to rest. The day before had been a bloody nightmare, every minute bursting with too many tasks. At five-thirty, stuck in a traffic jam in a taxi with a list of eighteen things to buy before six, I had torn a hole in my tights with my own hand.

Just as everyone had got off to sleep, the stewardess appeared with an evil-smelling trolley. Oliver lowered his table and drummed his fingers on it expectantly. As the stewardess reached us, she handed me my food and banged Oliver's down on the table.

"Excuse me," he said to her retreating back, removing the lid without looking. "Excuse me."

I saw it happening too late. The table was not level. The tray was just leaving the edge. I made a lunge towards Oliver's lap and my hand was covered in what I can only describe as loose brown stools.

Our Nambulan fellow travelers were enjoying the entertainment very much. Oliver was standing in the aisle, dabbing angrily at a brown stain which extended from halfway down his crisp white shirt to the crotch of his fine dark navy trousers.

"Where is the senior steward?" he was saying to the stewardess, who was holding out a grubby napkin impassively. "Where is the airline representative? This is completely absurd! I can't travel like this! I need a change of clothes!"

"First class." Julian was standing behind him supportively. "You must move him to first class."

"Come on, get your kegs off, lad, give us all a laugh," Vernon beamed. "Get one of them Nambulan nighties on."

At that moment Corinna appeared behind the stewardess looking alarmed.

"The lavatory's blocked," she said. "The stench is intolerable."

"First class?" said Julian, hopefully.

The next morning I awoke in the El Daman Hilton, three weeks to the day since I had left Nambula. It was a Sunday. The broadcast was scheduled for four o'clock the following Wednesday. The performances had all been recorded. And Dinsdale and Barry were going to present the show live from London, with inserts beamed live by satellite from Safila, all being well.

It was a worry. Too much was hanging on it. The refugee column should be arriving any time now and rations would be more or less on naught. With the food we had brought we could save the situation for, maybe, a week. After that everything depended on us—unless the long-promised ship managed to turn up. Circle Line had another plane standing by in London. Food was ready to be loaded. All we needed was enough credit-card donations on Wednesday night and then regular airlifts could run till the danger was over. If the broadcast went smoothly, everything should be fine.

The El Daman Hilton had given us rooms at a discount, which was a treat for me. The foyer was the epicenter of the better-off expat community in El Daman. Airline crews, diplomats, UN and EEC aid officials met in this little haven of the West to play tennis, swim, drink fruit punch and swap gossip. Among the nongovernmental aid workers, spending time at the Hilton was considered a sinful sellout. It was deemed much more appropriate to hang out in the dubious and stenchful restaurant of the Hotel El Souk. But given a respectable excuse, like a foreign journalist to meet, we'd all be straight in the Hilton pool like a shot.

I came down to the foyer at eight o'clock, having made full use of all toiletry items including the bubble bath and shower cap, asked the chambermaid for extras, and secreted them in my bag for the Safila showers. The celebs were asleep in their rooms. I was looking for the camera crew, a cameraman, a soundman and an assistant, and the *News* photographer. They, together with Edwina Roper, our minder from SUSTAIN, had drawn the short straw and ended up having to travel in the cargo plane. They should have landed yesterday afternoon, but none of them had checked in. I asked for any messages at reception. There were two. The first was from Malcolm.

GREETINGS TO YOU AND THE FLYING CIRCUS. SORRY HAVE
HAD TO DEPART, URGENT, PORT NAMBULA. NO TIME TO
ARRANGE PERMISSIONS. BEST OF LUCK. MALCOLM.

Great. The second was from Patterson, the British consul.

YOUR CAMERA CREW AND SENIOR PERSONNEL OFFICER
HAVE BEEN DETAINED AT THE AIRPORT. SORRY, UNABLE TO
ASSIST TODAY AS MY WIFE IS UNWELL. HAVE ARRANGED
FOR YOU TO SEE GENERAL FAROUK, HEAD OF SECURITY AT
THE CENTRAL SECURITY OFFICE AT 9:00 A.M.

I looked at my watch. Eight-fifteen. Better move, I thought, but we hadn't organized any vehicles yet. Just then, André from the UNHCR appeared through the revolving door.

"Hi. How *arrrrre* you? Good to *see* you again, OK."

We kissed each other on both cheeks.

"And how is the Jilted Locust Heroine?"

"Oh dear. So you saw that."

"*Saw* it. There was talk of nothing else for a week, OK?"

"Lies, all lies."

"Don't knock it. It did a lot of good. It incensed Gunter, for a start."

"I've got a message from Patterson to go and see Farouk."

"I know. I've come to take you, OK? Farouk's expecting you at eight-thirty."

"Patterson said nine."

"Patterson is a total prick."

"What's happening in Safila? Has the ship come?"

"OK, fine. The ship is not here. OK? And for reasons I will explain there are unlikely to be further ships for some time. OK, fine. The refugees, as you predicted, are on their way, not just to Safila but to all the camps along the border."

"So what's the situation at Safila?"

He said nothing for a moment.

"OK, fine. Put it this way. How many tons are on that Circle Line plane?"

"Forty."

"Get it unloaded and down there today."

That bad. I found myself blinking very quickly.

"Morning, sweeetheart." It was Oliver. "Great night, eh? Call to prayer every half hour. I open the minibar to find it contains apricot nectar only. At four-thirty the reception rings to tell me my plane has not been delayed. Project for today is hunt the Scotch, I feel."

I stared at Oliver aghast for a split second. I didn't want him here.

"Oliver, this is André Michel from the UNHCR. André, this is Oliver Marchant who's . . . who's . . ."

"The director of the show. Pleased to meet you, André. What's happening?"

"Don't you want some breakfast before we start?" I said to Oliver, pointing to the coffee shop.

"Have you found the crew?"

"No. Er. No."

"Have they checked in?"

"No."

"What? Where the fuck are they, then?"

"OK. This is another problem," said André.

"Give it to me straight," I said nervously.

"Your crew and personnel officer are in the cage at the airport."

"A cage? Jesus Christ," said Oliver. "What kind of place is this?"

"It's not a cage," I said, trying to calm him. "It's a cell."

"A cell? Oh, well, that's all right, then. As long as it's only a *cell*, that's fine. If my crew are locked in a cell at the airport, that's perfectly all right. Lovely. A cell, no problem."

We were driving through El Daman to the Security office, heading along a dust road with crumbling colonial buildings on either side and a mass of tangled wires overhead. Everything was peeling, cracked and covered in dirt. Horns blared, donkey carts and camels dodged the crazed zooms of trucks and taxis.

"OK. At nine o'clock on Saturday night, Patterson calls me," André was saying. Oliver was sitting in the back, staring out of the window and releasing periodic blasphemous expletives.

"Patterson tells me there are three Charitable Acts representatives and a SUSTAIN official held at the airport," André continued. "OK, fine. 'Patterson,' I say, 'why are you calling me? What does this have to do with me?' It turns out Malcolm is in Port Nambula and Patterson can't leave the house because his wife is drunk. OK, fine. I go to the airport. I locate your camera crew and Edwina Roper, who are in the cage. By this time it is eleven P.M. I wake up Security. There is no problem with the visas. OK, fine. So why are they in the cage? The government do not want any more non-Moslem aid workers in Nambula, they say."

At one side of the road a group of children were sitting in a sewer, screaming with laughter as they ducked underwater, splashed and swam.

"Jesus Christ," said Oliver.

A man was sitting cross-legged beside a pyramid of Benson and Hedges packets. The man's djellaba was hitched up to air a pair of grotesquely swollen testicles, each one the size of a small football.

"Oh, my God. Jesus, that is disgusting."

Ahead a new poster showed a grinning President Rashid, Nambula's military ruler, embracing Saddam Hussein.

"And presumably all this is pissing off the donor governments?" I said, nodding at the poster.

"Too right. This is a love affair, OK? This is the real thing. Saddam and Rashid are expected to marry and have each other's children any moment. Rashid's latest obsession is that there are too many whites in Nambula. He wants the aid and the money, but not them."

"So the donors are saying no deal?"

"You've got it. Particularly the Americans. They haven't officially frozen all further shipments. But they ain't leaving the States."

"I see."

"Rashid's anti the Western press now, he doesn't want the media here. Which is why your lot are still at the airport."

"Oh, my God. What is that child eating?" said Oliver.

"So how come the rest of us were allowed in?" I said.

"Good question. OK, it could be because they think you're fund-raising rather than press, or maybe it's because your camera crew said the wrong thing. But, whatever, it's all pretty dodgy. I'd watch out for Gunter too. He doesn't want you lot here either. Not until he's got his ship in. You've got a satellite dish waiting for you, did you know that?"

"Oh, shit. I'd forgotten that. When did it arrive?"

"This morning. It's in the SUSTAIN compound. I think the boys are having breakfast there, then heading for the Hilton. I'd keep an eye on it if I were you, OK? Rashid would just love to have a satellite dish, to force everyone to watch his dreary military parades."

We were turning into the road which ringed the souk. The earth sank down into a pit in the center of the square, crammed with rows of wooden stalls with filthy awnings. Flies buzzed round the pieces of dark meat suspended from the counters. As we passed, an ax banged down and severed the head of a live chicken.

"Oh, no. Oh, please," said Oliver.

A dirty hand took hold of the neck, blood spurting between the fingers, while the body twitched and the claws scampered angrily.

"Oh, sweet Jesus."

"Have they started unloading the plane?" I said.

"They hadn't at seven-thirty this morning," said André.

"But Malcolm got the trucks there as we arranged?"

"The trucks are there. I don't know how much Malcolm had to do with it."

"But the crew are still in the cage?"

"They are still in the cage."

"Just pull up for a sec, will you? I just want to grab a pair of sunglasses."

Oliver had spotted a stand selling mirrored Michael Jackson–style models. André pulled up sharply by the edge of the square.

"Oliver, we haven't got time—"

"Shan't be a sec." He was already halfway out of the door.

"We are in a real hurry—"

"Look, I just need a pair of sunglasses, OK?" The thunder look had survived the journey. I watched, anxious, as Oliver set out through the blinding heat towards the throng. He was dressed in a Panama hat, a pair of cream linen trousers and a pale green silk shirt. For some reason best known to himself, he had a gentleman's clutch bag tucked under his arm.

"I'd better go after him."

"Leave him, he'll be fine," said André, adding, with a sly look, "He's the director."

Every child within a two-hundred-yard radius was now running towards Oliver shouting, "Hawadga!" He was staring down, horrified, at a beggar with no legs who was propelling himself forward on vast muscular arms. People were closing in aggressively from all directions, holding out snakeskins, creosote, sheep's bladders.

"Oliver, watch the ba—" I started to yell out of the window, just as a tiny boy whipped it from under his arm and ran. I saw Oliver turning to us, looking as if he'd just been asked to decapitate a chicken, as the crowd surrounded him.

"Come on, André, don't muck about."

"OK," he said sulkily, and started up the engine, driving slowly through the crowd, honking the horn. They parted to let us through, but Oliver had completely disappeared.

"Stop the car," I said, and jumped out.

There was a hard knot of people at the center of the throng. Where was he? A Nambulan boy grabbed my arm, and pointed at the ground. A brown Gucci loafer was visible through the djellabas.

"Get out of the way!" I yelled.

He was lying in a pile of rubbish. The people were pressing forward leaning over him, concerned. I bent down. His eyelids flickered.

"What happened?" I whispered. "Are you all right? Are you hurt?"

He opened his eyes.

"I think I, er, fainted," he said foolishly. Then a look of horror passed over his face. "Oh, *Christ!*" he said, looking down, appalled, at the cream linen trousers. "Is there a loo around here?"

We dispatched Oliver to the Hilton in a taxi, but by the time we reached the Security office at nine-thirty we had missed General Farouk. He had gone to the airport to receive an important state visitor. After two hours of shuttling to and fro between five different ministries, we emerged, sweating, with a bumper haul of rubber-stamped papers. We had permission to start unloading the plane, permission to release the crew from the cage, permission to travel, permission to take photographs, permission to change money, and a rather uncertainly worded permission for all members of the group to emit satellite waves.

At twelve o'clock, with all this accomplished, we roared up to the airport and hurried to the Security office, only to discover that Edwina Roper had already been sent back to London and our permission to release the crew was invalid because it had not been signed by General Farouk. It took several hours to sort that one out, and by the time the disgruntled crew had departed for the Hilton, muttering about overtime payments, the heat had gone out of the day, the drivers for the trucks had disappeared and there was no one around to open up the plane.

It was 10:00 P.M. when André dropped me back at the hotel. As I turned to wave him off a convoy of white government limousines was sweeping into the driveway, little flags fluttering on the hoods. Before the cars had stopped moving, the doors opened and two soldiers jumped from each one, jogging in formation to form a guard of honor outside the revolving door, rifles cocked. Next, the tall, uniformed figure of General Farouk emerged from the second car. He turned graciously and handed out a tall, slender woman in brightly colored Kenyan robes, with an enormous headdress. A small fat man scrambled after them, clad in a tight, rumpled white suit. He looked like Mike de Sykes. He looked back for a moment and I caught a glimpse of his face. It was Mike de Sykes. Mike de Sykes and Nadia Simpson. So these were the honored guests of the state whom General Farouk was meeting at the airport.

The concierge looked at me oddly as I entered the lobby.

"Can I help you?" he said with some alarm.

I realized I must look a bit of a mess. I cleaned myself up briefly in the ladies', then headed for the bar where Vernon, Corinna and Julian were sitting around looking bored. Four giant golden balls were suspended above the bar area where huddles of neatly dressed aid officials talked in hushed, urgent tones, and the light-aircraft pilots and engineers, recognizable by their burnt faces and dry blond mustaches, looked around, bored. Dotted between them, sipping at tall fruit punches, were men with guns in dark-green uniforms.

I glanced at Vernon and choked on my mouthful. There was a half bottle of Scotch between his leg and the chair.

"Ahm, Vernon. You do know all these men in uniform are the Security forces?" My voice came out unexpectedly high.

"Don't you worry, my darling. I've got plenty of dollars in my back pocket."

"*Please*, Vernon, hide the Scotch?" Please, please, don't let's get done for alcohol, I was praying. Please let's not have any more Security dramas.

"Naah." Vernon was reaching for the bottle, unscrewing the top.

"Vernon, get rid of the Scotch."

He looked up sharply at my tone. "You'll get a slap in a minute, my girl."

"Oh, puh-lease," snapped Corinna.

"Where have you been, anyway?" said Julian plaintively. "Oliver's in bed with his stomach. And Kate is very upset about what they've done to her hair. I told her it looked fine but . . ."

I explained.

"You'd better get your act together, my girl," said Vernon. "Any more messing about like this and we won't get this show on the road."

"The trucks will be loaded in an hour," I said. "They're going to stop by here, to confirm it's all gone OK, then head off down to Safila. They should be there by dawn."

"Yer what?" said Vernon.

I repeated the sentence.

"Listen, luvvie. Those trucks are going nowhere tonight."

"What do you mean?"

"Call me old-fashioned. But I thought we were here to make a television program about a famine. Now when those trucks set off to that camp, we are going to film them setting off to that camp. And when that food arrives at that camp, we are going to film it arriving at that camp. *Comprende?* This is what we in television mean by making a television program."

"Oh, puh-lease," said Corinna.

I took more deep breaths. Then went over the situation again.

"The trucks must leave tonight."

"No, no. The longer we leave it the better. Can you see those pictures when we roar into that camp, six bloody lorries in a convoy, CDT breaks through with the food to end the famine?"

He was just drunk. He wasn't thinking straight.

"The lorries are going tonight," I said, dangerously.

"The lorries, my love, are going nowhere without us."

"Then we'd better all start packing. We leave in an hour."

"Blast. Right," said Julian. "Right. Absolutely right."

"Sit down, lad," said Vernon. "We can't film nothing in the dark."

We were getting nowhere. He wouldn't budge. It was Corinna who saved the day.

"Vernon," she said, leaning towards him. "Have you thought about the children?" She put her hand on his knee. "The kiddies? Little kiddies, hungry and dying because you're drunk?"

Five minutes later Vernon was still wiping tears from his eyes and we had a deal. There were six lorries. Three would leave tonight, loaded. The other three would leave at 7:00 A.M. tomorrow with the rest of us.

Twenty-six

O h, look at that. Blast, I've missed it. Oh, look another one," said Julian, staring out of the window at the passing desert.

"Another what?"

"Camel. Look. I say, I don't suppose I could stop and take a photo, could I?"

"You've already got twelve pictures of camels."

"But, you see, the sun's behind me now which is much better because—"

"Wait till we stop again for Oliver."

Poor Oliver kept having to trek across the sand to squat behind skimpy bushes with a toilet roll.

"Do you think if I gave the people in this camp some money it would help them, or is it only the food they want?" said Julian.

"It would help, but you have to do it in the right way."

"Could I have another boiled sweet, please?"

"Of course you can. Here you are," I said, and let him put the wrapper in my bag.

We had been on the road since 7:00 A.M.. The air above the tarmac shimmered in the heat, the desert spreading flat to the horizon on either side. To the left a group of huts was soft brown against the sand. To the right, a quarter of a mile away, the camel which had attracted Julian was tugging at a tuft of thorns. A nomad clad in soft blue and gray was sitting motionless on its back.

"Braargh! Oh! Oh!" Kate Fortune screamed.

The truck ahead of us had braked slightly. She put one hand against her chest and the other on her forehead.

"Heurgh. Oh, I'm sorry. Oh!"

The driver, Fayed, looked daggers at her from under his turban. We were the second vehicle in the convoy.

"I'm sorry. I really think . . . you know I have a child who is dependent on me at home, and this really isn't safe."

She reached for her hair to flick it back, and an expression of anguish crossed her face. Kate had decided to have a light body wave at the hotel hairdresser's. This single casual decision had transformed the once long, straight, silken tresses into a dry-ended frizz, reminiscent of old ladies in markets with more on their minds than hairstyles. Kate had been combing conditioner through the frizz throughout the journey, but the combination of goo and dry heat only served to coagulate the fraying mass.

She let out a sob, and grabbed a handful of frizz, yanking at it madly.

"I can't believe this has happened to me. It's too awful. I can't go on screen like this. I'm going to sue them, *sue* them."

She turned to me beseechingly. "Does it really look awful?"

"You could always wear a hat," said Julian.

Kate broke into a wail. Fayed looked round at her furiously.

"Or a scarf," Julian finished helpfully.

"It's nice, Kate, honestly," I lied. "It's good to have a change of look for a program like this. It suits you."

"Do you really think so? Really?" She grabbed at the rearview mirror and turned it towards her. Fayed muttered something unintelligible, grabbed the mirror and twisted it back. He kept glancing across at her now, as if she were a dangerous mental patient. She burst into tears again.

Actually, I did feel sorry for her. Just because there was a famine it didn't mean your own problems stopped existing. "It's not what you look like that matters. It's what you're like inside," I ventured vaguely.

"So it does look awful," she wailed.

Fayed changed violently to a lower gear.

Soon, we were driving through a sand cloud which seemed to have been thrown up by the wheels of the convoy. We closed the windows, and turned off the air-conditioning, but the dust filled the cab so that we had to wrap cloth round our heads to keep the sand out of our eyes and stop us coughing. Kate was trying to take out her contact lenses under a piece of white cotton.

"What's that?" said Julian.

The lorry in front of us had groaned to a halt, and then started reversing towards us. I looked where Julian was pointing and saw a naked body, curled up in a fetal position lying in the lee of a rock. The wind was rolling the body slightly. It had stiffened, and a layer of sand was blowing over the ribs.

The whole convoy was pulling up, and I asked Julian to let me get out past him but he climbed out before me. The drivers from our truck and the truck in front went over to the body. I walked down towards the other vehicles. We were in one of the areas of rocky out-crop, which dotted the desert floor like giant molehills. Sandstone rose on either side of us, worn by the wind into smooth sculptures, with boulders and smaller rocks forming stationary avalanches in the gulleys. The dust hung around the mountains like mist. The wind was blowing the sand quite hard now so that it stung my skin and I had to pull the shawl over my face. The next vehicle behind us was the Land Cruiser where Corinna and the TV soundman were traveling. Corinna was wearing dark glasses and listening to her Walkman. I asked the soundman to tell the rest of the convoy to stay in the vehicles because it wasn't good if everyone crowded round the body.

As I walked back, the drivers were wrapping the body in a piece of sacking. When I got close I asked them to stop and unwrap it again. It was an old woman who was very thin. She had died with her mouth and eyes wide open. She had no teeth and the gums were jagged and dry and full of flies. The drivers wrapped her again and lifted her into the back of the lorry at the head of the convoy.

"What do you think happened?" said Julian, as we started up again. His face was sweating.

"I don't know. They don't leave their dead unburied here. She might have been a madwoman."

"Why a madwoman?"

"Sometimes villages turn mad people out into the desert. That might be why she died alone. I hope so."

"Why?" I didn't answer.

"Why, Rosie?" he said again.

"Because if not, then she's a refugee from Kefti, and refugees from Kefti don't usually abandon the dying or leave their dead unburied."

"So why would they abandon her?" Shut up. Please, just let me think.

"Because they were desperate," I said. But to cross that psychological barrier they would have to be very desperate indeed. She didn't even have a shroud.

"But why should they—"

"Please. Just be quiet now. Look, there's a desert rat— Look where my finger's pointing."

The road was approaching a bend and after that we would hit the open desert again. I was afraid of what we would see, because after this the road ran parallel with the Kefti border and our route would merge for a while with that of the refugees. The truck ahead had disappeared round the bend and we were turning now. My breath was caught in my stomach. As we cleared the bend, the desert unfolded itself under the thick yellow sky, flat, featureless, empty. I was stunned. Where were they? If not even stragglers were left on this part of the route they must have brought a very sudden disaster to Safila.

We had been driving for perhaps another half hour when we heard the whine of a plane, quite a way off.

"Hey! What's that?"

"A plane, Julian."

"Who do you think it is?"

"Probably the UN," I said, with more confidence than I felt. The driver glanced across at me. Planes this close to the border made us very nervous. We could not have been a more obvious Aboutian target: nine vehicles in open desert bringing food for the Keftians.

"I say," said Julian, turning to me with huge eyes, "I say, it wouldn't be any of those rebel fighters, would it?"

"Oh, no. I can't believe this." Kate Fortune was hyperventilating. "I was told it was safe. I can't believe this. I have a child at home. I was told it was safe."

"We are safe. It's fine. We're in Nambula," I lied in a gay voice, trying to listen to the engine as the plane got closer. It didn't sound like a MiG. It wasn't a MiG. It was a small plane: quite low. It was overhead now. We all peered up through the windshield. It was a Cessna: dark green with the insignia of the Security forces painted on the side and heading for Safila. Now what did that mean? Nothing was making any sense.

An hour from Safila we stopped at a village where there was a restaurant—or, rather, an indescribably filthy area of boiling cauldrons and soda crates. The ground here was covered in dry yellow grass, dotted with failed spindly trees. It was still cloudy, with an oppressive heat unrelieved by breeze. It was three o'clock. I wanted to get to Safila in time to distribute the food before dark. Oliver was already rushing off across the scrub clutching a loo roll. Everyone else began getting out, putting their hands on the small of their backs, stretching their arms. People in djellabas were appearing from nowhere, gathering round the trucks. I could see us getting involved and losing time. Now we were so close, I was desperate to be back. I asked the restaurant manager if he had news of what was happening at Safila. He said he had heard that things were very bad there, but that was all. It was hard to believe that Safila could revert to the way it was in 'eighty-five but I knew it was possible. It didn't take very long for things to spiral out of control.

"'Ere, is it all right to eat this muck?" asked Vernon, gesturing towards the cauldron.

"Depends how hungry you are," I said.

Corinna was sitting under the rush shelter on a metal chair. She was still completely withdrawn behind her shades and her Walkman. It seemed very odd, but I guessed she was just a bit thrown and trying to keep herself together. Kate was posing for the News photographer, crouching down with a little crowd of kids, ordering them to put their arms round her. Suddenly they all looked in one direction and rushed off. They were heading for Julian, who was completely surrounded. He was bending down, beaming like Santa Claus, then putting his hands on his ears and making a noise like a donkey to make the kids scream.

He looked across at me radiantly. "Aren't they super? Blast. Hang on. Run out." He did the donkey impersonation again.

Oliver was leaning over one of the Land Cruisers. He looked in a very bad way. He must have lost half a stone. I walked over to him.

"Have you had anything to drink?"

"No."

"You must. I'll go and get you some salts."

"No, no. I don't want any salts. I don't want anything to drink."

"You must, you've lost so much fluid."

He looked at me with the expression of an ax murderer. "I said I don't—want—anything—to—drink, all right?"

The Nambulans near him started to laugh. He treated them to the thunderous look and they laughed again. Bad temper was taken so seriously here that you hardly ever saw it. They wouldn't understand a temper which flared up like this, without apparent cause.

"Jesus Christ!" he shouted at them. The Nambulans threw back their heads and roared appreciatively.

"Fucking hell." He banged his fist down on the Land Cruiser, occasioning another great shout of laughter and delighted round of applause. Quite a little group had gathered about him now, waiting eagerly to see what he would do next. I glanced nervously around our team, wondering how we were going to cope with Safila in the grip of a famine. There was a tug on my sleeve. It was one of the cooks from the restaurant.

"This very bad man," he said. "Very bad man." He was pointing towards Vernon, who at that moment was reaching out to pat a young Nambulan woman, dressed in purdah, on the bottom. The cook, who I thought was probably married to the woman, hurried back towards Vernon. Kate was sitting in the Land Cruiser now, gesticulating at a group around her window.

"Stop staring," she was saying, pointing at her eyes. "Stop staring, it's rude to stare."

"Rootastair," repeated the crowd.

"Stop it," she said, almost crying now. "Stop staring at me."

A great shout went up from the kids around Julian, and people started to run in his direction. He was handing out dollar bills. I hurried towards him again.

"Don't give them any more money," I shouted.

"Why?" If he said "why" just once more I was going to eat my fist.

"Because every time a Westerner appears they'll start begging. Give the money to the headman, quietly."

His face crumpled, which made me feel like a bossy harridan. They were all at it now. The camera crew were giving out pound coins and sweets. The *News* photographer was taking Polaroids of everyone and giving them away.

"Fucking hell, just GO AWAY, WILL YOU!" yelled Oliver, occasioning another cheer.

"Rootastair," went the crowd around Kate.

The restaurant manager was standing a little distance away, beaming contentedly. "They are being very funny people," he called to me. "They are making very much laughing."

I didn't know what to do. There was no point asking the villagers to leave them alone. It was far too entertaining. I went back to Oliver who was leaning on the Land Cruiser, silent, with his head in his hands, the crowd still surrounding him expectantly.

"I think we should get everyone together and have a talk before we get to Safila," I said. "It will be easier for everyone if we explain a few things."

"Well, don't look at me," he said. "I want to go home. Now."

I decided to try Vernon instead. He was eating meat stew from a metal tray with a piece of bread. Gravy was dribbling down his chin and a piece of gristle had lodged itself in the cunt tickler.

"I think we should get everyone together and tell them what to expect before we get to Safila."

"Bloody right," he said pushing the plate away. "Bloody right. Look at 'em. Bloody shower. Look at that bloody Oxbridge wanker lying on the Land Cruiser. Let's kick some sense into 'em. Basic rule with Johnny African—show 'im who's boss, don't converse except to give orders, don't give 'im a bloody penny. Don't you worry, my love. I'll give 'em a good talking to."

"On second thoughts," I said looking at my watch, "maybe we'd better get moving and do it when we get there. Yes, I'm sure that's best. Jolly good. Excellent. I'll get everyone going."

I put myself in the cab of the first lorry. When Safila village came into view on the horizon I stopped the convoy, got everyone out and started my speech before Vernon knew what was happening.

"So, to recap," I was explaining to a resentful-looking team, "we are going into a very extreme situation and we should be prepared to see some very upsetting things. There could be five, ten thousand people starving in the camp. They have no food other than what we have brought, so you might see some fights over the distribution, but try to understand why that happens. They are utterly dependent on the success of our broadcast. But we must remember that they are human beings and individuals who deserve to maintain their dignity. They will expect you to treat them with the same respect which the SUSTAIN personnel have been showing them for many years. The SUSTAIN team are extremely sensitive and absolutely exhausted—so please try to treat them delicately too. Thank you."

"I look forward to meeting your team of sensitive, exhausted neocolonialists," murmured Corinna, with a smile as everyone dispersed. "Maybe they'll make me alter my view."

"Rosie, old girl!" Henry was bellowing, charging across the compound with a grin stretching from ear to ear. Kate, Corinna and I had speeded on ahead of the rest of the convoy.

"Bloody marvelous to see you," he went on. "Bloody goddess-free zone without you. All gone to rack and ruin down the old black hole of Calcutta. Hello!" he said, seeing Kate and Corinna. "Ding dong! More goddesses. Welcome to Safila."

Corinna had stopped in her tracks and was staring disbelievingly at Henry. "Kamal!" he bellowed towards the cabana, where our Kamal was crouched over the stove. "Dish up some tiffin, old boy, will you?"

Kamal beamed and waved. "Very good," he shouted. "I am making tiffin for you. Welcome, welcome."

Corinna removed her sunglasses, looked at me, looked at Kamal and then back at me.

"Henry," I said hurriedly. "This is Corinna Borghese and Kate Fortune. Kate, Corinna, Henry is our assistant administrator. Henry is running the camp," I said, remembering I had no job now.

"Absolutely charming, delighted, delighted," Henry said, putting out his hand to Kate, who seemed not to notice. She was staring distractedly at the huts, her hands fluttering everywhere, like moths. I wanted to go straight down to the camp. I didn't want to mess around. I could hardly bear to ask Henry how bad things were. He was trying to put his old brave, flip face on things but I could tell he was struggling. There were bags under his eyes and he was pale and drawn.

"How is it down there?" I said quietly.

"Pretty damn good, actually," he said, brightening. "Bloody lot better than when you left, in fact. You heard we got some food from the EEC?"

I stared at him, speechless.

"We got a big delivery five days ago. Just when we were running out. They'd found it in a grain store in El Fayed. So we've put everyone on supplement."

"Why didn't you let us know? Why didn't they know in El Daman?"

"Because it came from somewhere in the north. The radio's still down. I sent a message in the pouch but—"

"Haven't the new refugees arrived?"

"No. Bloody odd, actually. Haven't seen hide nor hair of 'em. Muhammad reckons it's because as soon as they started trying to cross the plains, the Aboutians started bombing them. So they've bedded down in the highlands. Have you got Security with you, by the way?"

"We've got a couple of minders. Why?" I was trying to make sense of what he had told me. It didn't add up. I'd seen those people. There were too many of them just to bed down. Maybe some foreign aid had reached them through Abouti. But *how*, if the Aboutians were attacking them?

Henry was still talking about Security. "Their plane landed near the village a while ago. I thought they'd come to meet you."

"What did we get from the EEC?" I said.

"Dried milk powder, oil, soya mix and the drugs."

"How much?"

"We should be able to hold on till the ship comes."

"How come they didn't tell us it was there before?"

"They didn't know. Stocktaking error or something."

Corinna laughed incredulously. "Well," she said. "Shall we turn round and go home now?"

Kamal was walking towards us beaming. "You are welcome," he was saying. "Your tiffin is ready and waiting."

Corinna took off her sunglasses and looked at me hard. "Is this man," she hissed, "your servant?"

Twenty-seven

J pulled up at the top of the hill overlooking the camp. Some children were running along a path towards the river. Goats were sprawling over a hummock, tugging at a bush. Figures moved lazily across the plain. It all looked much the same as before the crisis. I was glad that they were safe—but I didn't half feel a prat.

I had left Henry trying to find somewhere for Kate to plug in her hair dryer, with strict instructions for him to keep the Charitable Acts contingent busy in the compound when they arrived and not to let any of them come down to the camp yet. I put the truck in gear and started down the steep track, skidding slightly in the sand. As I got to the bottom the kids started running towards the truck, cheering and waving.

I parked and walked towards the hospital surrounded by boisterous kids. They weren't back to normal yet, still too thin. But Henry was right, they were much better. Once everyone was eating properly, and drugged up, and the organization was back on course, you could bring things back under control pretty quickly. Henry had done a good job. Maybe they didn't need me anymore.

Betty appeared fussily at the entrance to the hospital. She was wearing her best pink souk-tailored pajama outfit. "Hello, dear. Did you have a wonderful time? Do you know, I can't tell you how dreadful it's been for us here. Quite dreadful. We've been working right round the clock, *hardly* stopping for meals. You look marvelous. Did you have a good rest?"

"Well, not exactly," I said.

"You've timed it beautifully. We've just got ourselves sorted out, so we can take it a bit more easy. Did Henry tell you about the EEC food? He's been wonderful. He organized the most marvelous feeding program as soon as we got delivery. He's been working his fingers to the bone, that boy. O'Rourke's been wonderful too. What a strong, capable man he is. Have you brought your celebrity friends to see us?"

"Yes. And forty tons of food."

"Well, I'm sure it'll all come in useful," she said, without much conviction. "It'll be super to meet our famous chums anyway. We're going to make them ever so welcome—give them a taste of bush life! Kamal's going to make us a picnic to take to the river, just like old times."

I forcibly removed from my mind a vision of Corinna participating in this event. "How's the hospital?" I said, walking towards the entrance.

"Oh, *much* better now," she said.

Debbie and Sian came rushing out and we hugged each other. "Have you heard about all this food appearing out of thin air?" said Debbie.

"Yes, I heard."

"Have you brought . . . ?"

"I've brought the celebrities. And a planeload of food."

"Sod's law," said Debbie. "Well . . . you know . . . if the EEC food hadn't come, or if the refugees had, then we would have been desperate for it."

"But it has, and they didn't, so it looks like we're not," I said, ruefully.

"Well . . . it was still a nice thing to do."

"Thanks," I said, trying to sound grateful.

"That food'll be gone in two weeks. You've done the right thing," said Debbie.

The three of us went round the beds. The crisis may have passed but people were still in a bad way: there were cases of diarrhea, pneumonia, malaria, meningitis, three marasmic babies, and some malnutrition which had gone beyond help. "At least they can do their film in here," said Debbie. We exchanged a wry look.

"It's worse in the cholera hospital," said Sian helpfully.

"I'll go and have a look," I said.

I could see the rush shelter of the cholera unit, standing on its own away from the huts on a slight rise. I was walking along a hard earth track and then I saw O'Rourke. My heart did a great heave and sigh. I wanted to break into a run towards him.

I kept walking along the path. He was lighting a cigarette, thoughtful and absorbed, looking out towards the river, round over the camp, towards me. He saw me and started, stubbed the cigarette out under his foot, raised both hands in the air. I saw him smile and gesture towards the river. He started walking down the slope where he was pointing, with the slight limp. A track led off to the right ahead of me in that direction. I hurried along it. He was hidden by huts now. A big earth mound rose ahead to the left, the track following its base, the big red rocks and the river ahead. I turned the corner. He was standing there. We both rushed towards each other then stopped, embarrassed.

"So you've really done it—you've brought celebrities out?"

We were walking back up towards the main bit of the camp.

"Yes. Funnily enough, just when you no longer need it, I've brought four celebs, forty tons of food, a journalist, a photographer, a full television team including at least two certifiable maniacs and a satellite earth station."

"Well—well done. Good on you." That was nice of him, considering he'd been so against this. "Where are they? Not down here yet, I hope."

"No. Henry's entertaining them in the compound."

"Good. That's good."

"Don't worry. They're very committed, and they've been very well briefed. I don't think they'll give us too much trouble," I said, "but I don't know what we're going to do with them now we don't have a problem anymore."

"Well, we need some new latrines digging," he said with the quick smile, then added, "But, of course, there is still a problem."

"Well, I must admit, I found it hard to—" I began.

"You and I both saw that exodus in Tessalay," he said. "Where have they gone? They can't just have disappeared into thin air. I'm deeply uneasy about what's happening up there."

Just then we heard raised voices a little way ahead.

"They're not starving, Mikey. You say to me 'Nadia, your people are starving,' and I come out to be with my people, and see my people starving and my people are not starving."

"The people are thin, Nadia. The people are very thin."

"You say to me the people are thin. I'm looking at myself and I'm thinking, 'Nadia, you are thin. You are very thin. You are not starving.' The people are not starving, Mikey."

"Now don't get upset, hon."

"I am upset, Mikey. I am upset. My people are not starving. I am upset."

We came out into a clearing, surrounded by huts. Nadia Simpson's feet were encased in soft leather sandals, laced up her calves. Her long brown legs were bare. She was wearing a very short uneven sarong made from animal skins. Her hair was piled high on the top of her head, held in place with a large bone.

"Is *this* one of your celebrities?" said O'Rourke, staring at me aghast.

"The people are hungry, hon," Mike was saying, encouragingly. "They are very hungry."

"You say to me the people are hungry. I am hungry, Mikey. I am very hungry. I have not had anything decent to eat since we left the office. I am hungry, Mikey."

Nadia and Mike were standing with their backs turned to the clearing. At the other side of the clearing a group of Keftians were staring at Nadia. A plump white woman with big gold-flecked glasses and a wet-look khaki boiler suit was crouched in front of a child taking a photograph. Beside her was Abdul Gerbil from Security in Sidra. They must have brought Nadia to Sidra in the plane. He was wearing his dark-green uniform instead of a djellaba but he still sported the Blues Brothers sunglasses and Coco the Clown hairdo. He was jabbing at the crowd angrily with the handle of his pistol, pushing them back. A bored-looking white girl wearing leggings and a tight white T-shirt, which revealed her midriff, was sitting beside an open toolbox full of makeup.

The woman in the wet-look boiler suit straightened up, and peered over at Nadia and Mike with a coy smile.

"Nadia?" she said. "Nadia?"

Nadia turned sulkily.

"You feel something special for the children, don't you, Nadia?" she said. "Would you like to hold one of the children for me, Nadia? Would you? Would you like to give the children their Care Bears?"

Mike de Sykes took out a small aerosol and began to spray Nadia in preparation.

A deep laugh gurgled out. Out of the corner of my eye I spotted a familiar, white-djellabaed, vertical-haired figure watching the proceedings and grinning from ear to ear.

"Where are we going now, Mikey?"

"The hospital, hon."

"The hospital. That should be gross, huh?"

The whole group, Nadia, Mike, Abdul Gerbil, the makeup girl, the woman photographer from *Hey!* magazine, and Keftian onlookers, were trooping along the path. O'Rourke, Muhammad and I were bringing up the rear.

"I need a hospital. I do not feel good, Mikey. I really think I'm gonna get sick."

"You won't get sick, hon. You are not going to get sick. I am not going to let you get sick."

"You say I'm not going to get sick. I am sick, Mikey. But wait a minute, wait a minute." Nadia brightened suddenly. "If I get sick it means a whole lot more people will get to hear about Nambula."

"That's right, hon. They'll get to hear about Nambula. You're getting into it now, hon. I can feel you getting into it."

"This feels real to me, Mikey, you know? It feels a lot more real than London, Mikey. It feels real to me."

"That's good, hon, that's very good."

Nadia's sarong was riding up so that the firm crescents of her bottom were just visible as she walked. Muhammad was walking behind, watching. He had not bothered with an artificial limb, and was hauling himself along efficiently on his stick.

"I am not having that woman in the hospital," said O'Rourke as we followed along.

"But, Doctor, you yourself have said that it benefits the patients to be distracted and entertained." Muhammad chuckled.

"Not like this," said O'Rourke, staring straight ahead. "It is an insult to the dignity of the refugees."

"But I am a refugee, and I have felt my recovery gallop apace ever since I caught sight of that woman, and particularly that bone in her hair," said Muhammad. "I am a new man."

"I don't think we've got any choice anyway," I said. "If Security say she can wander round the camp, she can wander round the camp."

"You might be right there," said O'Rourke grimly.

"I am firmly behind her," said Muhammad, staring delightedly at the bottom.

"You are a filthy lech," I said. "I'm going to give you your copy of *Hamlet*. That will keep your mind on higher things."

"You remembered," he said, taking my hand. "You remembered. Such kindness."

I had the book in my bag. It was a leather-bound version of the complete works, but I wasn't going to give it to him here. A Keftian woman caught hold of my arm. She thrust a fold of fabric into my hands and pointed towards Nadia, patting her thighs, and putting her hand to her mouth to indicate hunger and poverty. I opened the fabric up. It was a dress. The woman pointed towards Nadia again with a concerned expression, and said something in Keftian which I couldn't understand. Muhammad exploded into laughter again.

"She is thinking that Nadia is very poor that she must wear animal skins which do not cover her body. She is wanting to give Nadia this dress. It is her best dress and she says that if she will visit their homes, they have food for her."

He said something to the woman. She listened, then started to laugh too, hooting at the joke, banging her forehead, bending double, regaling the women around her so that they all started laughing too.

"I told her that Nadia was rich and that rich women in the West like to dress like refugee woman, and that this is how she think refugee woman dress," said Muhammad.

"Very amusing," said O'Rourke, "but I am still not having that woman in the hospital."

He hurried ahead and caught up with Abdul Gerbil. I could hear them conversing angrily as the party marched forward.

"Birra belly bra. Wibbit."

"Dongola fnirra."

"Sinabat. Fnarraboot. Wop."

The lady from *Hey!* magazine was getting anxious about the light. There was no sunset because of the clouds, but it would be dark in an hour. As we approached the hospital I saw that another of the Land Cruisers from the Charitable Acts convoy was parked next to mine. I hoped it was Henry. I hoped the others had not escaped from the compound. O'Rourke and Abdul Gerbil were still arguing in Nambulan, outside the entrance to the hospital.

"Guys, I can't hang around here. I'm losing my light," said the photographer, bustling ahead. "Sharee, come on, sweetie. Matte her down, sweetie. Matte her down."

Nadia, Mike, the photographer and the makeup girl were heading for the hospital entrance now. O'Rourke and Abdul Gerbil, still arguing, hadn't seen them. I rushed ahead to try to stop them.

"Mikey. What's *she* doin' 'ere?" Nadia's mid-Atlantic drawl had slipped at the sight of Kate Fortune.

Kate was sitting on a low wooden bed just inside the entrance, with her hair wrapped in a peach-colored turban. Cradled in the crook of each arm were two of the marasmic babies. The *News* photographer was lying on the floor in front of them, looking through his camera. The mother of the third marasmic baby was holding the child out at an awkward angle, just above Kate's lap.

"Can you just cheat it up for me, love?" the photographer said to the mother. "Up a bit. No, that's too far. Split the difference."

"GET OUT."

There was not a sound. The population of the hospital, Jane, Linda, Sian, Kate Fortune, Nadia Simpson, both photographers, Sharee the makeup girl stared at O'Rourke open-mouthed.

"GET OUT. ALL OF YOU. NOW."

"Hey, listen, mate, we've got an exclusive—" began the *News* photographer, trying to get up from the floor.

O'Rourke bent down, grabbed him by the back of his shirt and shoved him towards the entrance. He turned back to the assembled group.

"You heard," he said. "Leave."

"But—" began the *Hey!* photographer.

"Mikey—" began Nadia.

"I WILL NOT," O'Rourke roared again, "HAVE MY PA-TIENTS USED AS FASHION ACCESSORIES. Now get out. All of you."

As the invaders filed out huffily, Kate Fortune handed back the babies to their anxious mothers and hurried out after the others, adjusting her turban.

Ruffled feathers had been smoothed to some extent. Abdul Gerbil had been persuaded that things were much worse at Wad Denazen, and Nadia, cheered by the notion that her people were more starving elsewhere, had agreed to depart. Kate and her photographer had returned to the compound. It was dark now. The frogs in the river had begun to make their astonishingly loud belching noises. There were still a few lamps lit, but the refugees were turning in.

"I'd better go back up to the compound," I said to O'Rourke. It was almost seven.

"You're very tired," said O'Rourke. "Why don't you stay down here for a while? Sit with Muhammad. Unwind."

"Because I've got to get everything organized. They've all got to find places to sleep and be sorted out."

"Henry can deal with the sleeping arrangements. There's plenty of beds."

"But we have to organize the food and the showers and everything."

"Save your energies for keeping that broadcast within the boundaries of taste. I'll go up there and tell them you have things to do down here."

So I sat with Muhammad. It was tranquil in his shelter. He had a pot boiling on the embers, incense burning and lamps flickering all around. I gave him his Shakespeare. He was very pleased. People I knew dropped in to sit with us for a while.

Liben Alye came. He smiled and nodded and took my hand but his eyes were dead and he seemed finished. I had brought him a pair of trainers. He seemed pleased. All the refugees wanted trainers. But I felt shabby giving him these, when the only thing which gave his life meaning had been taken away.

We sat in silence for some time, as was the way. I asked Muhammad to explain to Liben about the broadcast and to say that it was to remind people in the West that famine should not be allowed to happen again. His eyes came to life for a moment but then he seemed to sink back in despair.

When Liben had gone, Muhammad said something to a boy outside then came back in, and said, "No more. Rest now."

But he didn't give me a rest. He limped over to where he had pinned a map of Kefti to the rush mats which made the wall.

"These of my fellow countrymen, for whom I sacrificed my leg—" he began melodramatically, then turned to see if he was having the desired effect.

"Ye-es . . ." I said.

"Where have they gone?" he whispered. He looked very dark in the lamplight. One side of his face had a line of light down it, highlighting his cheekbone. "The Security forces tell us that they have dispersed because of the evil bombing of the Marxist autocrats."

"Dispersed where, though?" I said. "I thought they had no food reserves up there."

"That is the reality," he said. "There is no food."

"So what's happening?"

"I believe they have dispersed widely across the lowlands, but are still traveling by night. Their progress is slowed as they reach the open desert because of the need to construct camouflage for the daylight hours."

"When will they come?"

"I am waiting for news."

"You have people looking for them?"

"I am waiting for news."

"Cannot reveal your sources, eh?" I said.

"Perhaps your team will have their starving babies in abundance," he said, ignoring my question. "And we will have more sorrows. The broadcast is on Wednesday?"

"The day after tomorrow, yes. I'd better get back up to the compound, I suppose."

"And I had better start work on my lines. You will let me speak? You will let the Keftian people speak for themselves? Or must we have these Western women with bones and turbans in their hair who understand nothing?"

"That's not fair. They've done their research. But of course you can speak." I thought of Vernon Briggs and lost my confidence. "At least, I hope so, but it's not me who's in charge."

"But always," he said, glinting in the half-light as he showed me out, "in the end, it is the woman who is in charge."

"I wish it were true."

"Then let it be true this time."

Twenty-eight

*I*t was very late when I got back to the compound, but the lights of the cabana were still on, and O'Rourke and Corinna were standing in the shadows round the side. I felt a horrible jealous lunge. Surely he wasn't going to fall for Corinna? She was still wearing her sunglasses, for God's sake.

"Oh, puh-lease," she was saying. "This is cultural imperialism in its most blatant form. I cannot, in all conscience, stay here."

"I completely understand. Perhaps you'd like me to drive you to the village?" said O'Rourke, politely.

"Is there a hotel there?" she said, huskily.

"There's a little place, yes. It's pretty much free of any form of colonialism, neo or otherwise, and not at all racist. You have a mosquito net? And a torch? I'll get you some water. And take your own sheets, of course. It's open to the sky but I don't think you need worry about rain. It's a dormitory room. They don't get many women there but they do have an equal opportunities policy—so keep all your clothes on."

It hadn't taken him long to suss her.

"Hello," said O'Rourke, as I walked up to them. "Corinna is wanting to stay elsewhere."

"Yes, I heard you saying. You're going to the village, then?"

Corinna tossed her head. "I'm afraid I find it completely abhorrent to be waited on by black servants."

"Kamal isn't a servant. He's a cook."

"Oh, yes, it's easy to hide behind semantics, isn't it? Is this where donations go? Is this why we're out here? Asking the public to pay up to have you lot waited on? So you don't have to lift a finger? I have to say I'm appalled."

O'Rourke started lighting a cigarette.

"Please do not smoke next to me."

He walked half a dozen paces away and lit the cigarette.

"Did O'Rourke explain why we have staff?"

"Nope," came his voice, out of the blackness.

"The people in the village need the work."

"Oh, excuse me," said Corinna. "I've found out how much these people earn. It's a pittance. It's slave labor."

"The trouble is we can't pay much above the going rate, or it mucks up the local economy."

"Oh, puh-lease. Why don't you wipe your own tables if you don't want to muck up the local economy?"

"It's stupid having nurses doing housework, when they're over-stretched in the camp and someone else needs the work."

"Oh, come on. It doesn't take that much effort to run up a bit of supper."

"Good. You can cook the chicken tomorrow night," said O'Rourke, appearing back out of the darkness. "You'll have to kill it. That's OK?"

"I am, as you know, a vegetarian," hissed Corinna.

"Does it ever occur to you," he said mildly, "that you might be missing the wood for the trees? Now, shall I run you to the village?"

"Oh, don't be ridiculous," she said. "It's obvious I can't stay in that place."

I wasn't sure I wanted this sparring to continue between them. It was just a touch too sparky-warky for my liking.

"Shall we go back in, then?" I said. "Is there anything left to eat?"

"I'm going to bed," said Corinna. "With Kate Fortune, apparently."

"Night, then," said O'Rourke. "I take it you won't want to be woken with tea."

"Depends who brings it," she said throatily, gave him a long, un-ambiguous look, and sashayed off. I stared after her. I'd never seen her coming on strong to anyone before.

"Hmm," said O'Rourke, when she'd gone. "Did you talk to Muhammad?"

"Yes." I wanted to talk to O'Rourke now, too, but I felt unusually tongue-tied.

"You must be tired," he said.

"Yes."

"Well, get a good night's rest." He hesitated. "Night."

Then he went off into the darkness, and I wondered where to. Most people had gone to bed. At the far end of the cabana Betty was rabbiting on at the camera crew, still wearing her pink outfit. A bottle of gin stood in front of them. Betty's face was almost as pink as the outfit and she was gesticulating even more than usual. Julian had found a new victim for his Janey stories in Debbie. The two of them were bent over the kitchen table.

"You see, I think I was afraid when Janey had Irony—that's our child. I couldn't deal with the child because I still felt I was a child myself."

"Surely not," said Debbie.

"Ah," he said, beaming at me. "I was just telling Debbie here how I felt with the children today. You know, today, with those children, I felt for the first time that I was needed for myself—by the children," he said, looking at me, thrilled, obviously forgetting all about the dollars.

"That's great. Is there any stew left?"

After I had eaten, I looked for my bag but I couldn't find it any-where. It wasn't in the Land Cruiser or in the cabana. It was one of those tiny, stupid irritations that completely floor you when you are tired. I wanted to scream, and bang on everyone's doors with a stick. I would have to go to bed without brushing my teeth. I made my way to the hut, trying to keep control. I let myself in without a torch, and felt my way across the room, fumbling for a match to light the hurricane lamp. As the flame flared up I heard someone stir behind me. I spun round and let out a scream.

Oliver was lying on the bed, stark naked. "Hi, sweetheart," he said, with a lazy smile.

"What are you doing here?" I shouted. I was nearly in tears. I was so tired. I picked up a towel from the chair and threw it to him. "Cover yourself up."

He swung his legs to the floor, wrapped the towel round his waist and moved towards me. "I just thought you might need a cuddle. Don't you?"

"What I need is sleep."

He was moving close to me now, towering above me with the lamp behind him. I couldn't see his face.

"I thought you might be frightened," he said. "All this pressure building up for the broadcast, all alone in a mud hut. Wouldn't you like me to sleep with you?"

"NO. No. I just want to be quiet, and rest."

"But you're all alone, with insects and rats and snakes everywhere." His voice wobbled slightly. "I heard drums outside, and something that sounded like, like a hyena."

I suddenly understood and tried not to smile. "Are *you* worried about sleeping on your own?"

"No, no, of course not," he said, too quickly. "It's just I find it . . . well, it is rather—"

There was a bang as the corrugated iron flung open. "SHE SAID NO."

O'Rourke was standing in the doorway. "You heard her. She said no."

O'Rourke, too, was naked, except for a towel wrapped round his waist. I was waiting for Oliver to lose his temper, swear at O'Rourke, but he just stood weakly in the middle of the room.

"What kind of man are you?" said O'Rourke, looking at Oliver incredulously. "What kind of low behavior is this?"

The two men stared at each other for a moment, in their towels.

"Get out," said O'Rourke. He seemed to be making rather a habit of this today.

Oliver picked up his clothes from the table, still holding the towel round his waist, and started to shuffle out, saying, as he went, "I've got nowhere to sleep now."

"You can sleep," said O'Rourke, "with me."

The next morning we organized a supervised tour of the camp, dividing the party into groups. The crew stayed up in the compound, working on the equipment. Corinna had stayed up there too, saying she didn't want to gawp at human beings as if they were animals in a zoo.

The clouds had gone today and it was hot—even for Safila. I was walking towards the hospital with Julian and Oliver. Oliver had been in a state of traumatized silence all morning. He was pale and odd, shrinking from contact with the refugees. At first I had thought it was a sulk because of what had happened in the hut last night. But then, watching him, I remembered what it was like when you first came across all this: the stenches, the faces covered in flies, the gungy eyes, the amputated limbs.

As we entered the hospital, the *News* photographer was sitting in exactly the same position he had been in an hour and a half ago, with his lens pointing at the head of a woman patient.

Sian came hurrying up to me, wide-eyed and anxious. "I think we must ask this man to leave," she said.

"What is he doing?" I said.

"I think he's waiting for her to die."

"Jesus Christ," said Oliver, and walked unsteadily back into the air.

"Come on, darling," the photographer was saying to me, as we stood outside, in heat that threatened to take the skin off our faces. "You don't want me taking pictures of Kate with the kids. You don't want me taking pictures in the hospital. What am I doing here? There's a story to tell, love. It's got to be done somehow."

Vernon Briggs was making his way up the path towards us, sweating, panting and wiping his forehead with a red handkerchief.

"There isn't a bloody story to tell, that's the bloody truth of it," he bellowed. "This is a right bloody carry-on, this is. Sod this for a game of soldiers."

Kate and the cameraman were following after him, with Muhammad and Henry. Betty was bringing up the rear, talking to the soundman.

"We can't make a bloody emergency appeal out of this lot," Vernon was going on. "Nothing bloody well wrong with 'em."

"What are you talking about?" said Oliver. "Just look at them. This is no way to live. Look at them."

"Don't you start waxing poetical with me, lad. You can see this sort of thing every day, the length and breadth of bloody Africa. Crisis? This isn't a bloody crisis. As far as they're concerned, this is bloody luxury."

"Well, I must admit I'm disappointed," said Kate.

"Disappointed? It's a bloody shambles. Crying wolf is all these aid agencies ever do," said Vernon.

"It's not crying wolf," I said. "It could all still happen."

"Not in the next two bloody days, it couldn't. Listen, luvvie, I'm not fart-arseing and fannying about with ifs, buts and maybes. There's some expensive time being wasted here. We've got that bloody satellite dish up from Nairobi. We've got a technical crew, a camera crew, we've got Kate Fortune, Julian Alman, Corinna Borghese, the head and deputy head of programming from CDT out here on a wild goose chase, with the world's press looking on, the network cleared on Wednesday night, the franchise and my credibility hanging on it and nothing to put in it. If we weren't stuck in the middle of bloody nowhere, I'd put a call in to London and pull the whole thing now. It's a bloody disaster."

"A disaster you say?" Muhammad was standing very, very still. "It is a disaster that there is no disaster?" Vernon turned round slowly. The rest of the party stopped.

"You are disappointed. Why?" Muhammad glanced witheringly around the group. "Did you come here to make your success out of our misery?"

After lunch, at Muhammad's suggestion we assembled in his shelter for a meeting. Through the entrance you could see the satellite dish perched on the edge of the hill above the camp.

"The salient question is this. Is there a need for the appeal? Do we have grounds to make an appeal?" Oliver was asking.

"Yes," said Muhammad.

"Are you mad?" said O'Rourke. "There is no question. Do people have to be on the point of death to deserve help?"

"An appeal saying what?" said Vernon. "They're doing all right 'ere? They've got one lot of food from the EEC. They've got another lot from us. They've got another lot coming from the UN. They don't do a stroke of work, just sit on their arses waiting to get fed. What's *this* appeal going to say: could you send some money so this lot can buy themselves ghetto blasters?"

"That's completely unjustified," said Oliver.

"Oh, don't give me that namby-pamby, middle-class, bleedin'-'eart carry-on. It's dicks-on-the-table time, son. You've cocked up."

"It is you who is cocking up," said Muhammad. "And it is fortunate for you that your dick is not on my table."

"Eh, eh. Don't you give me that, Sambo."

"SILENCE," roared Muhammad. "You are in my home now, and you will listen. You have come here, seeing nothing, hearing nothing, understanding nothing, and now you will listen."

He moved into the center of the earth floor, leaning on his stick.

"Do you believe that we want to beg for food? Do you believe that we have no pride?" he said. "What has caused this situation, that we are reduced to beggar men? Tell me," he said, looking at Vernon.

"Drought, war and a bloody lazy waiting-for-handouts attitude," said Vernon belligerently.

"Did you starve in England when you had to fight for your freedom? Do they starve in Arizona when there is drought? Do you understand what it is to live balanced on the blade of a knife?"

Kate Fortune coughed uncomfortably.

"Lazy? *Lazy?* You call us *lazy?* Do you know what it is to walk for five miles to find water, to carry it home for five miles, fastened in an earthen pot to your back? To work all day, from the gray, smoking mist of dawn, to the last red rays of the sun . . ."

Don't overdo it, Muhammad, I was thinking, don't overdo it.

". . . coaxing the dry earth with your bleeding, callused hands to bring forth food for your children? To scour the barren mountains for firewood to keep your family alive through the freezing night, knowing that every branch which is cut, every tree which dies, is causing the earth to die with it, the desert to creep towards us? And to rejoice when the first green shoots burst from the dust, knowing, still, that if the rains fail, then we will starve, and if the rains come, then the insects may come too, and we will also starve?"

"Well, you don't have to start a bloody war, to add to your troubles, lad, do you?" said Vernon.

"What little we had was taken in taxes. The army came in tanks and took our children to fight for them, raped our women. Our land was taken. We were persecuted for our beliefs. Would you not fight? If you were in the same position as us, would we not help you too?"

Muhammad paused, and touched his forehead with his fingers. "Had we been given a little help—had we been given seeds, pesticides, hoes, medicine . . . then we could have stayed in our villages, and survived. But the West would not help the country of Abouti to develop. They were opposed to the Marxists. They did not want them to develop. We, too, were opposed to the Marxists. But to the West we were Aboutians, too."

"But you're here now, aren't you? You're all right now."

"For how long? If the refugees come, and there is no more food, then in a few weeks we will die. We are like lamps in the wind. It takes only a breath to snuff us out."

"You've got a river. In fact, you've got two rivers. There are bloody weeds growing down there. Why don't you get off your backsides and grow yourselves some food, instead of asking everyone else for it?"

"We are not permitted."

"By who?"

"The government of Nambula. They do not permit us to cultivate lest we stay."

"Well, it's their fault, then, isn't it?"

"Is it? When they cannot afford to feed their own people?"

"Nambula gets enough help from the West."

"Not anymore. But even before Saddam, what kind of help? A tractor factory—to furnish contracts for Germany. A cement production plant from Holland. The people cannot eat cement."

"It's all very well, lad, but we're talking popular television here. They don't want to sit there watching an economics lesson. It's not the Open bloody University."

"The West is rich. The third world is poor," said Muhammad. "It is obvious, it is stupid. It is the obvious, stupid truth. Is that not simple enough to explain?"

"They won't buy it, lad. They need to see the kiddies starving before they get their checkbooks out. It can't be done. We'll just make ourselves look bloody idiots."

"That's not altogether—" Oliver began.

But Muhammad was looking up ahead of him, as if he was alone. He looked despairing and sad: sadder than I had ever seen him.

"I understand," he said. "I understand." Tears were starting to form in his eyes. "As far as the West is concerned, if they cannot see our children starve on their television sets, in their homes, if they cannot see them trying to stand on their skeletal limbs, and failing, if they cannot see them reaching out to the camera and crying for pity, if they cannot see them writhing, as the walls of their stomachs begin to digest themselves, then there is no problem. And for us, when we see our children starving to death in our homes, then it is too late."

Muhammad gave the assembled group a terrible look, then turned and limped slowly out of the shelter, leaving silence behind him.

"I wish we'd had the camera running," said Oliver angrily, and rubbed at one of his eyes.

I went out after Muhammad. He was standing with his back to me, looking over the camp. I did not know what I could say to him. I did not know how to explain, how to say sorry. I reached out nervously, touched his arm.

Muhammad turned. He smiled wickedly. "How did I do?" he said.

By nine o'clock the next morning, lines of thick cabling were running all over the camp, along the path to the feeding center, up to the food depot on the hill. The TV mobile control room was parked outside the hospital with the technical crew climbing in and out, fiddling with switches. The dish was working, but seven hours from transmission the Charitable Acts team were still up in the cabana, arguing about what they were going to do. Thanks to Muhammad's outburst, Vernon was now putting the full force of his personality behind the broadcast, which was precisely the problem.

Oliver was attempting to take control. "Each of us, Kate, Julian, Corinna, me, does a different insert from a different location, the hospital, the cholera clinic, the feeding center, explaining how it all works, and why they need help."

"What about Muhammad?" I said. "We have to let him speak."

"Now, wait a minute, wait a minute," said Vernon, getting to his feet. "Don't start talking bloody daft. I've said we'll go ahead but we're not going to go all silly. The public want people on that screen who they know and who they trust. We're not having every Abdul Doodah in the camp doing his party piece. And we're not doing this by bloody committee. I'm in charge. You do and say what I tell you to."

"Well?" said Oliver after a moment. "Go on, then."

"We stick that camera in the hospital with those sick kiddies and it stays there and we play some sad music over those shots and there won't be a dry eye in the house."

"What music?" said Corinna.

" 'Hello,' by Lionel Ritchie," said Vernon. "It's a cracker. Beautiful song. Fabulous." He cleared his throat and began to sing it.

"Jesus Christ," said O'Rourke.

"Oh, puh-lease," said Corinna.

"We don't mention the EEC food,"Vernon continued, ignoring us. "We show a shot of our lorries and we tell 'em this whole camp was starving to death before we arrived. *Comprende?*"

"Listen, old boy." It was eleven o'clock, we were down in the camp and Henry was trying to reassure O'Rourke. "Bit on the Tania Tasteless side, no two ways about it, but all in a good cause, end justifies the means, etcetera, etcetera. No point getting in a stew about it."

"I WILL NOT HAVE IT." O'Rourke was in an uncompromising mood. I respected him hugely when he got like this, but it also made me want to laugh.

"Is there no such thing as a gift anymore? Banners for Capital Television, logos for Circle Line Cargo, the jeep company. This isn't giving, this is using the misery of the disadvantaged world to make commercials."

"BE QUIET." Vernon was shouting at the crowd of kids he had assembled, and banging with a thick stick on an oil drum. They stared at him now, wide-eyed and silent.

"Now, hold it up," he said, gesturing with his hands. "Hold it up."

In the center of the crowd a long red roll of fabric appeared.

"Hold it up," he yelled, raising his arms above his head to reveal two oversized rounds of sweat.

The long red roll unfurled into a banner which read, "THANK YOU CAPITAL DAILY TELEVISION."

"Oh, my bloody God and fuck," said O'Rourke.

"Now, cheer," Vernon shouted. "Come on, hip, hip, hurray, hip, hip—"

"Hurray," went the kids uncertainly.

"This is gross," said O'Rourke. "This is obscene."

"I say, steady on, old boy," said Henry. "It may be a bit Christabel Crass, but it's not *obscene*."

"Come on, hip, hip . . ." went Vernon.

"Hurray," the kids said again.

At that moment Muhammad appeared.

"I have news," he said, dramatically.

"Gauuuurgh! What is it now?" said Vernon, angry at his little tableau being interrupted.

"If you do not wish to hear the news there is no necessity for it," said Muhammad, petulantly.

"Oh, come on, Muhammad," said Henry.

"Spit it out, lad," said Vernon.

"It seems that your problems may be over and ours just beginning. I have had word that the refugees from Kefti have been gathering within the Dowit mountains."

Dowit was about ten miles from the border with Kefti. The mountains there were the same red sculpted shapes that jutted out of the desert at Sidra and on the road to El Daman, but at Dowit, rock walls formed a ring round a sheltered area in the center. It was used sometimes by the nomadic tribes during sandstorms.

"Why there?" said O'Rourke.

"It was agreed. It is a landmark. It is safe from the air raids, it is hidden, and there are springs in the mountains. They are in a very severe state having walked for many days and nights with no food. They are assembling at Dowit hoping to receive help there but they have nothing. Their condition is very bad."

My first reaction was rage at the UN. What had they been doing when we were away? We had warned them. They had seen the photographs. Why hadn't they been monitoring the border? Supplies in Nambula were low but plainly not finished. There was no excuse for people being ten miles inside the country with no food.

"So," Muhammad continued matter-of-factly, "it seems that you will have your starving babies, after all." He was very controlled. I knew what he must be feeling. After all this, after all we had tried to do, the worst had happened anyway.

"Thank God for that," said Vernon excitedly, looking at his watch. "How long's it take to get there?"

"Two hours," said Muhammad.

"And they're really starving like in Ethiopia? Fanbloodytastic. Well done, lad. Right, let's get this banner rolled up and we'll set up the shot in Dowit. Can't you just see it? With the food being doled out in the background. Get those cables packed up and that dish on its way. All hands to the pump. Change of plan. Fanbloodytastic."

I was suddenly terrified. This program was our only chance now. It was already eleven-fifteen. How could they get all the equipment moved to Dowit and working before four o'clock? It had taken them two days to set it all up.

"Are you sure we have time to do this?" I said. "Won't you have to reset the satellite if you move it?"

"Eh, eh. Don't start. You'll get a slap in a minute, my girl," said Vernon.

At this O'Rourke suddenly turned and strode off furiously towards the hospital.

"We'll set off straight away. Get this banner rolled up. Get the girls ready in their safari suits and those food lorries. We can have Kate Fortune at the head of the convoy, breaking through with the first food for the starving."

O'Rourke reappeared now carrying three bottles of American beer.

"I think this calls for a celebration, don't you?" he said.

"Where did you get that?" I said.

"Never you mind," he said, smiling at me strangely. "Why don't you go up to the compound and tell everyone what's happened?"

"What . . . ?"

"Just go," he hissed.

I did as he said, leaving him, Henry, Muhammad and Vernon behind. It worried me. Something was up. But I trusted O'Rourke. At least, I thought I trusted him.

I drove up the hill to the compound, trying to imagine what we were going to find at Dowit. The thought of Vernon getting his hands on real hunger and despair had a unique horror of its own. The first person I saw at the compound was Oliver. Oliver had always seemed like two people but out here it was more pronounced than ever. He wandered around looking pale and shrunken with no presence whatsoever, and then suddenly he would click back into his old authoritative, charming professional self. He took the news about Dowit in his authoritative persona.

"Do you think we'll be able to get all the equipment working in time if we go?" I said.

"Possibly, sweetheart. I'll check it out with the crew. Don't worry about it. Get everyone into the cabana as quickly as you can."

At half past eleven we were trying to get everyone assembled around the table. I went off to look for Kate.

I found her lying face down on the bed in her hut, sobbing.

"It's all right," I said, sitting down on the bed beside her. "It might not be as bad as we all think in the end. It's all right." I had lived in Africa for four years, and seen starvation many times before and still I was scared. How must she feel?

"It is *not* all right," she said, sitting up, staring at me furiously. "It is not all right," she repeated, pulling at her hair, fluffing it out then pulling at it again. "Look at it! How can I go on screen like this? It's not all right at all. It's ugly. Ugly, ugly, ugly," and she flung herself back on the bed and sobbed.

I got up and walked to the door without a word.

"Rosie," she wailed. I turned. "Could I borrow that hat you're wearing? Just to see if it looks—"

I opened the door, walked out, and stood breathing deeply for a few moments. Then I came back in. It wasn't as simple as vanity. Her whole sense of herself had been whisked away by the hotel hairdresser.

I took off the hat and gave it to her, watching as she tried it on. "It looks great," I said. "Really good."

"Does it?" she said. "Does it really? Do you have a full-length mirror anywhere?"

As I walked back to the cabana Henry and O'Rourke were unloading a sack of grain from the back of the truck. When I looked more closely I realized that it wasn't a sack of grain. It was Vernon.

"What happened?" I said, hurrying towards them. They were unsteady under his weight. O'Rourke was holding him by the shoulders, Henry had a chubby leg under each arm.

"I think it must have been the beer," O'Rourke said shiftily.

"Doesn't seem to be able to take his liquor," said Henry, grinning delightedly.

"What did you put in it?" I said, feeling rapidly growing elation. "Come on, what have you done?"

"I don't think he'll give you any trouble for twelve hours or so," said O'Rourke sheepishly.

It was now eleven forty-five. We had just over four hours to go before transmission and we were still sitting in the cabana, deciding, now Vernon was knocked out, whether we should go or stay.

"So, as long as nothing breaks or comes unstuck, you don't have to reset anything, you just park up and turn it on?" said Oliver. He was perched on the edge of the table looking cool and in control. The sight of Vernon knocked out and snoring with his mouth open had done wonders for Oliver's confidence.

"That is correct," said the chief satellite engineer, Clive, who always talked as if he was on the radio, and not allowed to say yes or no.

"But if something breaks on the way, we're fucked?" said Oliver.

"If there was a malfunctioning or, indeed, an actual breakage of one of the components of the earth station during transformation, then it would be technically impossible to regain satellite contact."

"And is that likely to happen?"

"Well, as I said previously, given the erratic nature of the terrain—"

"Come on, Clive," Oliver interrupted impatiently. "You drove over here. What're the odds? Shall we risk it or shall we stay here?"

There was an expectant pause with all eyes on the beard and wire glasses of Clive. Only Clive could point us to a decision. Clive made no move to speak.

"Did anything break when you drove up from Nairobi?" I asked.

"There were no breakages or severe malfunctionings as such on the journey in question," said Clive.

"Don't you think we should just stay here?" the cameraman said. "If the satellite won't work after we've moved, we can't transmit anything. And if we get to Dowit and find there's nothing there then we've nothing to transmit. We've got to broadcast something this afternoon or the whole thing will be wasted. Why can't we just stay here and let the refugees say what's happening at Dowit?"

"Look," said O'Rourke, "we are now four hours and ten minutes away from transmission. We must make a decision."

"I've just got a feeling that we should go," said Oliver. "I know it's living dangerously, but I say we risk it."

The technical crew were organizing the satellite dish. We decided to take two food lorries with us, and another loaded with water and medical supplies. O'Rourke, Henry and Debbie were going to come with us. Betty was supposed to stay behind and look after the hospital with Sian and Linda, but this was not a plan that pleased her.

"Oliver, dear, I know you're in charge and what you say goes," she flapped at him, "but I do think I should be there too. If this is a serious medical emergency, then we really do need all the doctors we have, don't you think? Besides, you know, although it's only silly old me, I have worked in Africa for many, many years, and you just might find you need that seasoned old voice of experience somewhere along the line."

"I think she's right," said Roy the soundman. Everyone looked at him in surprise. He was a funny, helpful little man, who had never been heard to express an opinion before. "Betty knows what she's talking about better than all these kids put together. She should be in the program."

"Ooof, no, it's only silly old me," said Betty, rolling her eyes.

"It is now twelve fifty-five," said Oliver. "I don't give a flying fuck who comes, but will everyone who is coming just get in the vehicles and on the road."

Twenty-nine

*J*t was cloudy again, and out in the open desert the wind was getting up, carrying a lot of dust with it. Kate and Corinna were side by side in the front of the Land Cruiser. O'Rourke was driving. I was in the back with Oliver. The rest of the convoy were behind.

"Shit," said O'Rourke, braking. A small goat trotted away ahead of us. "Where did that come from?" It was getting increasingly difficult to see anything—it was like looking through a yellow fog.

"This weather isn't doing us any favors, is it?" said Oliver.

"That depends. Sometimes it looks rather striking when the sun shines through this stuff," said O'Rourke. He and Oliver seemed to get on quite well at times. Maybe it was sleeping together that did it. "I'm not happy about rolling up straight away with these food lorries," he went on.

"Neither am I," I said.

"Why not?" said Corinna. "What's the matter with you now? You can't turn up to a famine without bringing something to eat."

"Frightfully bad form" murmured O'Rourke.

"It depends how many Keftians there are," I said. "We don't want to start a settlement there."

"Isn't that better than them coming to Safila?" said Oliver.

O'Rourke let out a tsking noise.

"No," I said. "The water supply's not up to it, and it's too close to the border."

"But you can give them some food to keep them going?" said Oliver.

"Yeah, but we have to do it right. We don't want a riot," said O'Rourke.

"Anyway, let's wait and see what we find," I said. "There might only be a couple of dozen. It might be a false alarm."

"Jesus, it had better not be," said Oliver.

"What's that?" said O'Rourke, starting to slow down.

"Oh, my God," said Kate Fortune, straightening up and looking ahead. "Oh, my God."

What she was looking at was a group of corpses, lying at the side of the track.

There wasn't anything we could do except cover them up. They were young men who had starved to death, which suggested that they might have been sent ahead to warn us that the refugees were coming. The place was about a quarter of an hour's drive from Dowit. We left the two food trucks there. We knew now we were going to find a very bad situation and we needed to assess it first, and make a plan for the food. As we drove away, I glanced back and winced at the sight of trucks of food from England parked beside the people who had already died of hunger.

The red shapes of the Dowit mountains loomed ahead. I wondered whether, if I had just been driving past them as usual, I would have been able to tell that something terrible was happening there, or if they only seemed so forbidding now because of what I knew. The dust was growing heavier in the air, as if there would be a sandstorm soon. The sun was trying to break through, but it was with a weak, watery light.

A track led off the road to the left towards the mountains, and passed by means of a short corridor through the rock into the plain in the center. The convoy stopped where the track met the road. The sound of a drum was coming from the mountains. It was a slow, single, hollow beat.

Clive said that he thought they should keep the satellite dish and equipment here as they would not be able to get a signal inside the mountains. Then I saw figures appearing through the dust. They looked as though they were moving in slow motion because they were trying to run towards us but their legs, which were as thin as the bones beneath the skin, were not strong enough to carry the weight of their bodies.

Muhammad was already hurrying towards them. The skin on their faces was pulled back tight as though they were grinning, but they were not grinning. O'Rourke and I started walking towards them too. The expression in their eyes was terrible, because it was so human, in bodies made unhuman by starvation.

A boy who looked about seventeen had reached Muhammad now and was talking to him. The boy was talking slowly, trying to concentrate, as if he was dizzy. His teeth looked very big in his mouth and the top of his head was unnaturally large because there was no hair on his scalp, and no fat or muscle on his face, only skin. He had a piece of brown cloth like sacking wrapped around him and you could see the sockets of his shoulder above it.

"He is coming from my region," said Muhammad. "He is saying that there are many thousand refugee inside the mountain."

The boy started to speak again, touching slowly between his eyes with his thumb and first two fingers as if he was trying to clear his head.

"He is saying they have no food now for many day. He ask if we are having food for him."

Muhammad was not speaking in perfect English as he usually did. O'Rourke and I looked at each other, registering the line of decisions which lay ahead.

"We go and look, and then go back for the trucks?" O'Rourke said.

"Yes. I think so, yes."

We gave the people who had come out to meet us some high-energy biscuits which we had put in the back of the Land Cruiser.

Oliver was speaking to the crew of the satellite dish, and he told us they were going to park between the road and the mountains and try to set up the link.

As we drove along the track which led into the mountains, we passed more and more people but we kept driving now. Some of them turned round and followed the truck when they saw that we would not stop. Others stood still, looking bewildered.

Kate Fortune had started hyperventilating and making noises. She put her hand on O'Rourke's arm as he was driving, and told him that she felt ill, and he said, "Look, shut up."

As we drove into the narrow opening in the mountains it was very eerie because the dust was swirling around the rocks and the people were still coming towards us, jabbing at their mouths with their fingers. We drove through a very short corridor, like a fissure, with the rock rising sheer on either side, then the track turned a corner and opened onto the plain in the center of the mountains. It was about three-quarters of a mile across and not flat, but dipping down and uneven and surrounded by the high walls of the mountains. Smoke was hanging above the ground from all the fires, and below it the whole of the plain was covered in people, sitting on the ground, thousands and thousands and thousands of people. There was very little movement but the sound was immense: it was the sound of a great number of people crying. I remember looking out of the window of the jeep and seeing the face of a young girl. I remember being shocked that her tears were so full and wet because the rest of her body looked so withered, dried up and finished that you could not imagine where the moisture had come from for the tears.

Everyone started to climb out of the vehicles. Muhammad was talking to a group of men who had come forward to meet him. They looked as though they were village headmen although they might have been RESOK. I was looking over to my left where the sound of the drum was coming from, and I started walking very slowly through the people towards it.

In a clear area to the left, which rose in a slope towards the base of the mountains, they were laying out the dead. There was a line of about twenty or thirty bodies, with people mourning all around them and, behind, a group of men were using a pole to dig a grave. And people were coming from different directions, carrying bodies in their arms. When I got to where the corpses lay a man was placing the body of a child in the line. The child was in a sack and the body was so frail that the man seemed only to be laying down the weight of a rolled-up towel. Some of the bodies were on stretchers and they were all covered with something. One was wrapped in paper sacks, on which was printed, "A Gift from the People of Minnesota." Further down was a blue blanket with a woman's feet sticking out of the bottom and between them two tiny feet.

At the end of the row a woman was squatting next to the body of her son. She had taken the cover from him and she was clapping her hands above his head as if she were trying to wake him. She looked as though she was trying to do everything she could think of to stop her pain. She was shaking her hands as if she was trying to get water off them, then covering her eyes, then holding the sides of her head, then holding her son's head and talking to him, then trying to bring him to life again by clapping above his head, but nothing could alter anything. When I looked at the body of the boy lying in front of her, useless and dead, I can remember thinking that it was stupid that he had died of starvation. It seemed stupid that all that grief had happened, not because of some sudden accident or unavoidable illness but because the boy had no food, when there was so much food, in the world.

Most of the people were just sitting or lying on the ground in groups. They were so weak and dazed that they were not responding to our presence or to anything. I had never seen people so malnourished and still alive. I made my way back slowly through them to where Muhammad was still talking to the headmen. I realized that I was crying and made myself stop.

As I walked past the Land Cruiser I paused because Corinna was leaning against the back of it. Both her fists were clenched very tightly and her shoulders were hunched. She was crying in a way that forced her face into dreadful shapes beneath her sunglasses and wrenched her body. I saw her crying and did not try to comfort her. I watched her groaning and racked and I was glad, because she was not made of concrete, or Lycra, or Perspex as I had thought.

She saw me looking and pressed her forehead against the back window of the Land Cruiser. Then she said, "Could I have a cigarette?"

I gave her a cigarette and lit it. Kate was sitting in the Land Cruiser with her head in her hands. Julian and Oliver were both standing alone looking dazed. I could not see Henry or Betty or Debbie. O'Rourke was crouched over a child. He was not making any sound, and looked exactly the same as he always did when he was treating the children except that there were tears streaming down his face.

I did not know what to do. I stood dazed like the others and stared at it all. It was such a monumental horror that it felt as though nothing should be the same anymore, and nothing should continue: none of us should speak or do anything, the sun should not be moving across the sky, and the wind should not blow. It did not seem possible that such a thing as this could be taking place without the world having to shudder to a halt and think again.

Thirty

*T*he only way of dealing with it was not to think too hard but simply to do one task after another: to do one thing and then to do the next thing.

O'Rourke, Henry, Muhammad, Betty and I gathered by the vehicles. There were somewhere between ten and twenty thousand people on the plain. The sun was breaking through the dust now and there were thick shafts of light, like girders, lighting up great areas of the people.

"This place is just asking for epidemic," said O'Rourke.

We decided that, while Muhammad and I started on the rehydration and feeding, Henry would check that the water supplies were clean, and set up defecation zones. Betty would organize measles immunization. O'Rourke and Debbie would start a clinic for the worst cases.

"What about the broadcast?" said Betty. It was one-thirty. We were due on air at four o'clock.

"Those forty tons of food are not going to last long here," said O'Rourke.

Oliver and Julian were still standing staring at the crowd. I made my way over to Oliver. "Come on," I said. "Come on. You have to go and organize the broadcast. You have got to make it work. Take the Land Cruiser back to the satellite dish and tell them what you've seen."

He looked at me blankly.

"Go on, Oliver," I said.

Corinna was walking towards us. She was wiping her eyes and looked as though she was pulling herself together.

I looked at Oliver. He was still staring around helplessly.

Muhammad came and joined us. He placed a hand on Oliver's shoulder and took him a little way away, talking to him.

"I'll help," said Corinna. "Tell me what I can do."

I asked her to drive back to where we had left the food lorries and bring them back here.

"Ask them to wait outside the mountains till we're ready. Will you be all right with the four-wheel drive?"

"I'll be fine," she said.

"I could ask Henry to go instead."

"No. I'll be fine. You need him here."

"Wait, look, I'll come with you," said Julian.

"You stay here," she said. "It doesn't need two of us."

"Tell me what I can do," said Julian.

"We need to organize the food next," I said.

After a while Oliver and Muhammad came back. Oliver looked better and said he would drive back to the satellite dish and start working out what we should do.

The village headmen were gathering around Muhammad.

"Will these men organize the distribution?" I asked Muhammad.

"Yes, of course."

I looked around trying to work out where we could start. "Are the people in any sort of grouping?"

"Yes. They have tried to stay in their villages."

"How many villages are represented here?" I asked.

He spoke to the men again.

"Perhaps five hundred villages."

"We'll start with the under-fives. And the most serious cases. And we'll set up a feeding center here and rehydrate them at the same time. Then maybe we can start getting food out to the rest later."

"We must feed the mothers too," said Muhammad.

"Yes, we'll feed the person who comes with the child."

"I will talk to the headmen," said Muhammad. "They will orga-nize it."

I was trying not to imagine anything except what was before us, and not to imagine it getting worse so as not to let dread come out or panic. I looked around for Julian, and said that we needed to build three enclosures out of stones.

"Yes, right, good," said Julian, bending down to pick up a large stone. "Here?" He looked as though he was ready to do it himself, single-handed.

"We have to get some people together to help."

I started to ask the people around us, the ones who were strong enough, but it was hard to explain what we wanted to do.

"What are the enclosures for?" said Julian. And I told him we needed separate areas for the immunization, for giving out the high-energy biscuits and for feeding the really bad cases with a wet ration.

"We need walls round them so everything stays under control," I said, but I didn't know if that were possible, since there were so many desperate people. Then Julian started miming out what was to be done, which made the people laugh in spite of what was hap-pening but they understood and started gathering the stones. A man came up who spoke some English and that helped us, because then the Keftians could take over the organization. We were work-ing on the area which was immediately to the right when you en-tered the mountains, so it would be easy to unload the trucks. Soon about three hundred people were collecting stones and starting to build the walls.

I kept looking over to where all the vehicles were parked at the end of the rocky corridor. The television crew were milling around agitatedly. A thick cable was lying along the track, and they were frantically attaching more to the end of it. Oliver kept driving up and down the corridor, going back to the satellite dish. They were like wasps going in and out of a nest.

At three forty-five the enclosures were built, and each one was crammed with children and sick people, sitting or lying on the earth, waiting in lines. The village leaders were arriving all the time with new cases, supporting them or carrying them. Every so often a group of people would suddenly run in one direction, because some of the food had been spilled and everyone would scrabble on the ground, picking up whatever they could find, and eating it. Outside the walls there were crowds of people, pressing forward, looking in. There was the sound of high agitated voices above the wailing. It was difficult to keep calm because outside the walls people were crowded a dozen deep, holding out their children to us to show us that they were dying and begging us to let them in. Fights were breaking out, because it was so unfair to be on the wrong side of the wall.

I kept looking at my watch, then down at the camera crew, but the situation still seemed the same. People kept driving off down the corridor and coming back again. I couldn't understand what was going on. I thought Corinna and Julian should be down there, rehearsing by now, but they were in the next enclosure, helping with the distribution of the biscuits.

"I think I'd better go down and find out what's happening," I said to Muhammad.

As I walked across the slope towards the vehicles, Oliver was coming up to meet me. "It's not working," he said, as soon as he was close enough. His face was screwed up in a scowl, self-pitying.

"Why not?" I said, swallowing hard.

"There's a problem with the dish."

"What?"

"It's got dented."

"Dented?" I was blinking very quickly. "What happened?"

"I don't know. They reckon a stone must have hit it when they were driving."

"Is there anything they can do?"

"They're trying to hammer it out but it's a delicate job. It has to be absolutely smooth."

"Will they do it, do you think?"

"To be honest, Rosie, we're stymied."

I rubbed my forehead frantically. We didn't have enough food. There was another Circle Line plane waiting at Stansted. It could be loaded and here in twenty-four hours. We could have airlifts every other day till the crisis was over, but not if there was no broadcast. The lives of all these many thousands of people actually depended on a piece of television equipment which was dented. It seemed a stupid way for the world to be but there we had it. And now there was only half an hour to go.

"Do you know what you're going to do in the program, if they can get it working?" I said.

"Yes. I've worked that out at least," he said.

"Don't you need Corinna and Julian here? Where's Kate?"

"She's in the Land Cruiser. There's no point bothering with her."

I looked over. She was sitting sobbing, pulling at her hair.

"Yes, you might as well send Corinna and Julian down. But you carry on with the feeding. I think that's going to be more use, to be honest. We'll call you if we have any joy."

I tried to carry on but it was very hard to concentrate. I knew that we had just one hour between five and six to blast this horror out to the world and it was our only chance. But there was nothing I could do.

At ten minutes to four, a shout went up from the camera crew. I saw the cameraman starting to point the camera at Julian and Corinna. Corinna was looking towards me, giving a thumbs-up. I stuck my fist in the air, made my way out of the enclosure and started running towards them. As I drew close, panting and stumbling over the stones, Oliver roared out of the corridor in the Land Cruiser.

"We can't get the fucking signal," he was shouting as he strode across the sand. "The dish is working but we can't get the signal. We're in the shadow of the fucking mountain. Fuck. Fuck. Fuck. Fucking Vernon. We should have stayed where we were." He was banging one fist against the other, striding around, uselessly. It was five past four now. The show would be on the air in England, with no link from Nambula.

"Muhammad," Oliver said suddenly, "is there any way of getting a vehicle higher up?"

"Yes, there is a track but it is very steep. If you go out and follow the edge of the mountain to your left, you will find it after two hundred yards."

"Where does the track lead to?" said Oliver. "Is there anywhere we can drop the cable down?"

Muhammad pointed to the mountains above the enclosures, squinting into the sun. They were almost sheer: great curves of red rock. "The road is climbing up there on the outside behind the ridge, but you will find there is a place where you can look over the plain. Perhaps you can throw the cable down there, above where they have built the enclosures."

"OK," said Oliver, already striding towards the vehicles. "I'll go up there with some of the lads. Get the camera over there in the feeding center and we'll drop the cable down to you."

At twenty past four, with forty minutes to go before the broadcast ended, Julian and Henry were waiting at the foot of the mountains, holding the end of the cable, looking up, hopefully, surrounded by crowds of Keftians. The rest of us were a hundred yards away on the other side of the wall, inside the wet rations enclosure. We were working out where the camera should be, and what we should do. I kept looking around the plain at all the people and thinking how much we had wanted this not to happen. We had brought the cameras to it too late, and still we couldn't make the program work. A man came up and spoke to Muhammad, and he looked as though he was going to collapse.

"Huda is here," he said. "Will you come with me?"

It was Huda Letay, the woman he had asked me to find up in Kefti. Muhammad was kneeling beside her, holding her hand, moving the blanket higher over her chest to where the bones of her shoulders stuck out through the skin. Her hair was reddening and frizzy, only clumps of it remaining because of the marasmus. At the other side, Huda's mother was holding her twin babies. They were screaming and the skin was wrinkling on their legs because there was no muscle underneath. They were about a year old, two little boys, with big eyes. When they stopped crying they had grumpy expressions, which were very appealing. Huda was lying with her head back, her bulging eyes staring up at the sky, moving her head from side to side. I think she knew who Muhammad was because as he spoke to her she made a little noise.

I turned back to see what was happening on the mountain. Julian and Henry were clambering up the boulders which lay at the bottom holding their end of the cable, and looking up all the time. The rock rose in a clear, smooth sweep above them. Then the mountain fell back through another area of boulders and loose rocks, before rising up in a perfectly smooth shoulder to the summit. High above us, standing at the top of the loose rocks, were Oliver and one of the crew boys. Two more of the boys appeared round the side of the rock carrying a large coil of cable on a metal frame.

It was going to be difficult to get the cable down to the sheer drop, unless they carried it over the area of loose rocks, but that was steep and looked as though it would shift if they walked on it. Oliver joined the men bending over the cable and I watched as they started lifting something. They brought it a few feet off the ground and started swinging it. They swung, once, twice, three times, and then they threw it. It was a boulder in a net. It bounced down over the loose rocks, dragging the cable behind it, towards the sheer drop. As it bounced it loosened the rocks below which were falling with it. Six feet from the edge it stuck behind a pinnacle of rock. An avalanche of stones began to roar over the precipice, crashing down onto the rocks below, making the people scatter.

Oliver started to make his way, gingerly, down over the loose rocks and boulders towards where the cable was stuck. Suddenly a whole section began to move underneath him. He was sliding with it towards the sheer drop. Corinna screamed.

More stones were falling over the edge now, Oliver was grabbing with his hands, trying to get a hold, then he flung himself sideways and caught hold of the pinnacle, kicking at its base. He clung on, as the rocks rushed beneath him over the edge, and as they fell, among them was the boulder attached to the cable, which was snaking down the drop now.

Oliver was still clinging to the pinnacle. I couldn't see what was happening at the bottom of the mountain, because the refugees were all crowding around. Suddenly there was a commotion behind us. I turned and saw the cameraman blundering towards us, pointing the camera. Corinna was following. "Go go go," said the cameraman to no one in particular. "Go. We've got the link. Go go go. Go go go. Twenty seconds. Stand by."

The soundman was holding out an electronic box and an earpiece. I grabbed the electronic box, shoved it in Muhammad's hand, and the earpiece in his ear. The cameraman pointed the camera at Muhammad and the soundman picked up the boom and held it over Muhammad. "You are on a wide shot, yes?" Muhammad said to the cameraman coolly. "If you raise your hand when you are ready for me to speak I will speak."

I glanced at my watch. Ten to five.

"Ten seconds till they come to us," said the cameraman.

"A really wide shot first," ordered Muhammad, "so that the viewers can see the whole plain."

I could hear angry voices coming out of his earpiece.

"But I am the man on the spot," said Muhammad indignantly. "You must play music over the wide shot then fade it when you come to me. You have music there?"

There was more angry shouting from his earpiece.

"They want one of the celebrities," said the cameraman. "Corinna, come on love where are you?"

"Let Muhammad do it," Corinna said.

The cameraman looked at her.

"Let Muhammad do it," she said again.

"Yes, let him do it," said Julian.

I looked up at the mountain. Oliver was slowly hauling himself back up towards the crew on the end of a rope.

Muhammad was speaking to Huda and her mother, and watching the camera out of the corner of his eye. The camera was panning round the feeding center as Muhammad had ordered. Huda was weak, but listening to what he was saying, nodding slowly. The cameraman started to raise his hand and Muhammad looked at Huda for a count of two then slowly turned to stare straight into the lens.

"Nearly twenty years ago," he began, "Dr. Henry Kissinger made a proclamation to the World Food Program in Rome. 'We must,' he said, 'proclaim a bold objective: that within a decade, no child will go to bed hungry. That no family will fear for its next day's bread. And that no human being's future and capacity will be stunted by malnutrition.'"

He paused, and helped Huda to sit up higher.

"For six weeks now, the United Nations, the EEC, the aid agencies and the Western governments have known that tens of thousands of people in the highlands of Kefti had no more food. They knew that they were traveling here to seek help, walking day and night with empty stomachs, watching their children and old folk die on the way. The Keftian people were starving to death as they walked but still traveling in hope that they would find sustenance here on the borders of Nambula. And what have the UN done in that time? What have the Western governments sent? What is waiting for these people here? Nothing."

He gestured out towards the plain and the cameraman followed his arm.

"Year after year you have seen—and you will see—pictures like these on your screens. Year after year your governments, your organizations, with their grain mountains and colossal budgets, fail to help us in time. Year after year, you, the ordinary people like us, are asked to reach into your pockets to save us when it is too late. And now we are asking you to save us again. Why?"

He turned to Huda.

"This is Dr. Huda Letay, who was my college friend when we studied economics together at the University of Esareb."

He waited for the camera to find her. Huda's head was rolling on the earth. Her mouth was open as if in a scream.

"She is twenty-seven."

Muhammad reached round and put his arm behind her shoulders. He beckoned the microphone to come closer. Huda's mother laid the twins beside her. And Huda raised her head to speak. "These are my children," she said, in a voice that was scarcely a whisper. "One week ago their sister has died of hunger. Four days ago their brother the same."

The soundman was looking at the cameraman, trying to get the boom lower, closer to her head.

"Yesterday their father too."

She was leaning closer to the camera now, staring straight into the lens. A movement caught my eye. Kate Fortune was standing behind the camera, gesticulating, wearing her peach turban.

"Half the world is rich and half the world is poor," Huda continued. "I am not resentful of you, who live in that rich half, only I wish that I and my children live there too."

She paused to cough. The babies had begun to cry, and the soundman was still trying to get the boom closer.

"I was born in the wrong half of the world," she said. Her voice was hoarse now. "I do not wish to die. And if I must die I do not want to die like this, without dignity, lying in the dirt like a beast." She started to cough, and closed her eyes, leaning back against Muhammad's arm. He eased her up a little, whispering to her.

She opened her eyes again and lifted her head. "I was born on one side of the line and you on the other. I will die here. My children and my people need food and so I must abase myself and beg." The coughing overcame her again. "We need help from everywhere and every place. *Really* we need that help. Not for to dance or to feel . . . comfortable, only to live."

And then her eyes closed and she sank back against Muhammad's arm again, coughing, then lying still as he stroked her head.

Thirty-one

*A*bsolutely definitive." The director's voice, two thousand miles away in London, was still beaming down to us from the skies. "Seriously moving to have a live death." It was beyond sunset now, and the desert was red. Oliver and I were in the control van, which was parked outside the mountains at the foot of the track leading up to the satellite dish. The broadcast had been over for an hour and a half. Credit card donations were flooding in, and so were the accolades. The back of Oliver's shirt was torn and his forearms were covered in cuts from the rocks.

"Oliver, I think you should tell him that Huda's in a coma. She's not actually dead," I whispered.

". . . Vernon with you?" crackled the voice of the director over the sound system.

Oliver pressed a button and spoke into the microphone. "Not at this precise moment," he said. "Vernon is a little unwell."

"Tell him we've had a call from the Independent Television Commission congratulating CDT. Looking good. Looking good."

There was a pause while the line crackled.

"Just had a phone call from Stansted. Circle Line plane took off five minutes ago. Should be with you . . . twelve hours' time. Oh-oh. Hang on. New total, two million three hundred and ninety-seven thousand pounds aaaaaaand counting . . ."

There was the sound of a champagne cork popping. "Oh-oh. Hang on. Wait a moment. Wait a . . ."

Oliver broke into a smile. "Two million three hundred and ninety-seven thousand pounds," he said to the group which was gathered outside the door.

"Hey! I've got the *News* on the phone," said the director's voice.

". . . want to airlift out the twins. The dead woman's twins." More crackling.

I grabbed the microphone, and pressed the switch.

"Can you confirm that they want to evacuate two infants out of twenty thousand people?"

There was more crackling.

"Affirmative," said the director.

"And does it have to be those two?"

"Affirmative. The dead woman's kids."

"What if they've died already?" I said. "Will they take a different two?"

"Confirming that it must be the kids of the woman who died on the program . . . twins . . ." More crackling.

"But she isn't dead yet."

"OK . . . *Daily News* guy here in the studio wanting to talk to his photographer . . . got the photographer with you?"

Outside there was the cry of an animal, somewhere far away over the sand. The photographer appeared in the doorway and came up the stairs. Oliver pressed the microphone button for him.

"Steve Mortimer here," said the photographer, turning round with a flourish and hitting Oliver in the face with his camera bag. There was a pause for the time lag.

"Steve, hi, Rob here," said a different voice over the talkback. "How yer doing, mate? Listen. We want the kids. You got the pictures? You got the live death?"

"Sure," he said.

"But—" Oliver began.

"OK, that's enough. We lose the line in five. Big thank-yous to everyone. Absolutely fantastic. Out of this world. Oh-oh. Hang on. One last thing. The guy that spoke at the end, the one holding the dead woman. They want him brought over . . ." The line was lost in crackle. "Natural . . ." Crackle, crackle . . . "Want him as regular on CDT before the franchises. Get him brought back with you or send him with the kids. OK. This is it, Nambula, we're losing you. Well done again, everybo—"

And then there was nothing more: just the hollow note of the drum and the loud, ringing silence of the desert.

The mountains were dark shoulders against crimson. A jeep was drawing up. Doors opened and slammed shut, voices rang out through the dusk. Julian, Muhammad, Betty and Henry were all emerging.

"Rosie!" Julian was making his way towards me, his face furrowed with concern. "Rosie," he said. "I know what I want to do."

"What's that?"

"Well, first of all I want to give all the money I can. And I'm going to really work when I get back to keep the campaign going. But I want to do something more. I'm going to adopt those babies," he said. "The little twins, you know, the orphans. You know the mother's dead now?"

I looked for Muhammad. He was limping away from the vehicles, on his own.

"I want to help the family," Julian went on. "I'm going to bring them back to live with Janey and Irony and me."

"I'm having those babies," snapped Kate Fortune.

"But you've already got a Romanian baby," said Julian indignantly.

"Sorry, loves, the *News* has got 'em," said the photographer.

"Er. Don't want to point out the Orville Obvious," said Henry, "but surely there's enough babies to go round? I mean, even if it's orphans you're after, probably a good few more up there. No reason why everyone has to have the same ones, is there? Or am I being a total thicko?"

Corinna was leaning against the caravan, smoking a cigarette. She saw me looking at her and gave me a sympathetic smile. She had been a different woman all afternoon, warm, sisterly, supportive. She walked over towards me now, leaned forward, brushed some-

thing away from under my eye and said "Tired?" I hoped the famine hadn't turned her into a lesbian.

Betty was trying to get all the jeeps parked in a cozy circle.

"Come along," she was saying. "We must eat. Nobody's eaten a
thing since breakfast. An army can't march on empty stomachs. No
use to the refugees if we can't get on with the job. I made sure Kamal put some bread and corned beef in before we set off. Should be
enough to go round, I think. I've even got a tub of mustard. Mind
you, it's English. I prefer a milder mustard myself."

"What a woman. Thank goodness we've got Betty to look after
us," said Roy the soundman, reverently.

A hundred yards away, in the gathering darkness, Muhammad
was leaning on his stick, staring towards Kefti, where the clouds
were like coals against the red glow. I picked my way across the
scrub towards him.

"I'm sorry," I said, when I was beside him.

After a while, he said, "It is very hard to bear." And then, "But she
was wonderful, was she not?"

"Yes, she was."

"And if there's a time when it is true to say a person did not die
in vain . . ."

". . . then this was it."

"But still, it is very hard."

We were standing in complete darkness now, but it was the
warm, enfolding darkness of those nights. There had been headlights approaching for some time from the direction of Safila, and
now the vehicle was drawing up. Inside Betty's circle of vehicles,
the faces were lit by torches and firelight. All the group were together except O'Rourke, who was still with the refugees. The
doors of the jeep opened and the troll-like figure of Vernon
emerged fulsome bottom first. We could hear the tone of his voice
but not the words. He sounded defensively blustery.

"Do you know what I fear?" said Muhammad.

"Tell me."

"That even after all this, very quickly, for everyone else, it will be
as if it never happened."

"I know."

We stood in silence for a while.

"They want you to go back with them, the television people, did you hear?" I said.

"No."

"Would you want to?"

"And collude in that corrupt sickness?"

"Corrupt sickness is not confined to the West," I said, "as we both know."

"I mean the sickness of the chosen few," he said. "If I despise the unfair division of the world, the uneven granting of gifts, then when I have my chance to be plucked from the anonymity of the disadvantaged and placed within the enclosure of the privileged, when the gifts are about to shower down on me, do I say yes, or do I say no?"

"What will you achieve by saying no?"

He thought for a while, and then said, "Spiritual treasures."

"Well, I think that might be the length and breadth of it."

He shook his head.

After a while I said, "If you go to London now you might be able to do something. You're being invited to join the Famous Club. You'll get lionized by the media, and you'll have a measure of power. If you get the mass of ordinary people behind you, then sometimes you can change things a bit."

"Do you really believe so?" he said. "Do you? This is the third famine which has smitten and destroyed us in my lifetime, and it is always the same. Afterwards the cameras and the journalists come, and then the officials make plans, and they promise it will never happen again. Then all is well for a while, they grow bored, and then it happens again."

"Maybe we have to keep trying. Maybe it gets a little less bad each time, there's a bit more development each time, it makes you a bit less vulnerable. Maybe you have to go to London and push to speed it up."

"And sacrifice myself?"

"It's not much of a sacrifice. You'll be pretty comfortable. You'd get a bit rich. You'd know you'd never risk dying of hunger again."

"But of thirst," he said, "spiritual thirst. I would be accepting the inequity of the system. I would be Britain's tame, one-legged African refugee, a novelty, a token. No longer myself."

Someone was making their way from the group towards us. It was impossible to see who it was, but we could hear them stumbling over the scrub. It was an uneven patch of ground.

"Hi." Oliver emerged from the blackness. He looked very thin now.

"Well done, my friend," said Muhammad. "You were a hero."

"They're all going now," said Oliver. "Back to El Daman."

"Now?" I said.

"Yes. They want to drive through the night and get back there tonight."

"I will leave you," said Muhammad.

Oliver and I stood looking at each other in the darkness.

"You did a very great thing," I said.

"I made an heroic gesture. Anyone can do that once. Doesn't last long, everyone sees, makes you feel fantastic."

"You could have been killed."

"Well, I wasn't. It's the O'Rourkes of this world who are the heroes, slogging away unsung, surrounded by diarrhea. He's still up there, isn't he?"

"This wouldn't have happened without you. All the work in the world would have made no difference without any food."

"Don't be ridiculous."

Then, after a moment's thought, he said, "But actually it wouldn't, would it?"

"No. You made it happen at every stage."

"I feel . . . very . . . oh, I don't know. Thanks anyway. Thanks for . . . I mean, God, I sound like Julian. I think—"

"What?"

"I think. I dunno. I'm sorry I've been . . . This has been great for me. I feel . . . Jesus, what do I feel? I feel . . . good. I feel more . . . good than I've ever felt. Maybe I'll be different now. Maybe everything will be different."

And there was a moment of real closeness between us. I thought how much we had both learned.

"Rosie, I want to ask you something."

"Yes?"

"I want to ask you to come back with me."

I glanced across at him nervously. "Er. You know I can't do that."

"I am asking you to come back with me."

"I can't. I have to stay here."

"Rosie." He was beginning to raise his voice. Footsteps were starting towards us across the scrub. "I am ASKING you to come back with me."

"You don't really want that. You don't really want me. You know you don't."

"It's O'Rourke, isn't it?"

"I've got a job to do."

"Rosie, I am asking you to come back with me."

"No."

"I've done this thing, and we've saved the situation and now I AM ASKING YOU."

"Of course I'm not sodding coming back with you," I burst out. "You've seen what's going on up there."

"You love O'Rourke," he said, "don't you?"

"Oh, puh-*lease*, Oliver." Corinna appeared out of the darkness. "Can't you see the girl's got more on her mind than bloody men? Here you are, little one, I've brought you a sandwich."

"I'm going back to the fire," said Oliver.

"Oliver," I said, catching his arm, "thank you."

"Do you know," said Corinna when he had gone, "I think we have all gained more than we've given, here. I think we will all be profoundly altered by this."

I said nothing.

"Don't you think so? Weren't you completely altered when you first came out here?"

"In some ways," I said. "But in some ways I think people always stay the same."

We could see the taillights of the departing convoy, long after we had ceased to hear the sound. Betty, Henry, Debbie and I stood watching them, not knowing quite what to do now. I was trying to imagine what life was going to be like in Safila without Muhammad. He had decided to go with them.

"Dears, I must tell you the most marvelous news," said Betty.

There was a pause while we tried to lift ourselves out of our thoughts.

"What's that, Bets old thing?" said Henry, after slightly too long. "Don't tell me, you're going to adopt the twins as well?"

"No, silly," said Betty coyly. "Well. Roy. You know Roy the sound engineer?"

"What, the one you were talking with behind the caravan before he left?" said Debbie.

"Charming fellow," said Henry. "Bit of a Crispin Crashingbore at times, but by and large, absolute charmer."

"He's asked me to marry him."

"That's wonderful," I said.

"Don't like to throw a dampener on the proceedings," said Henry. "Bloody marvelous, couldn't be more delighted. But aren't you already married, old sock?"

"Oh, yes, of course I know. But when all this trouble with the famine's sorted out here, and Dr. O'Rourke takes over I'm going back to England and start divorce proceedings, and start again with Roy."

"What's that?" said Henry. Ahead of us a white djellaba was just visible, approaching with a limp.

"Is that you, Muhammad?" I called.

"No, it is an apparition," came his voice.

"I thought you were going to London to speak for your people."

He swung towards us on the stick. "I decided it was better to stay with my people here," he said, breathing heavily. "We must fight from within, we must insist that we may cultivate, we must demand that food be kept in storage in our highlands, so that when disaster strikes again we need not leave our homes."

"Bloody hell, Muhammad," said Henry. "Turned into a bloody saint-style person. Throw up your chance of fame and fortune to insist on the right to grow tomatoes."

"The shallow and flippant nature of your character never ceases to appall me," said Muhammad, joining us where we stood and leaning an arm on Henry's shoulder.

The others set off back to the camp, and I drove back to pick up O'Rourke. As I reached the end of the rocky corridor and emerged onto the plain, the moon was coming up over the mountains, throwing a white light onto the scene. On the rising ground to my left, the dead were still being carried to the burial ground, the bodies were still being laid out and the graves still being dug. I could see the lamp still lit, over in O'Rourke's clinic, where he was working. I walked over to him.

"Have you nearly finished?"

"Finished?" He could hardly keep his eyes open.

"Come on. You'd better get some sleep. You've got to start again tomorrow."

I left him to finish off, and walked over to check on the feeding centers. When I came back he was packing up his equipment into boxes. I helped him load them into the jeep.

As we drove out of the rocky corridor and down to the main road, the lights of the convoy were just visible in the distance heading for El Daman.

"I feel like five kinds of shit driving away and leaving this," said O'Rourke.

"At least you're coming back in the morning."

"It worked then, did it, your broadcast?" he said, with the quick smile.

"Yes," I said. "Bit late, but it worked."

After the broadcast there were three months of hard labor for us. The population of the camp doubled and there were journalists and cameras constantly at large. There were frequent rumors that Fergie was coming out on a mercy dash to bring royal jelly and ginseng, that Elizabeth Taylor was coming with Michael Jackson and a mini-fun fair, or that Ronnie and Nancy Reagan were planning to spend Christmas with us. Most of them proved to be false alarms, but still it was unsettling and nerve-racking for staff and refugees alike.

All the publicity, time-consuming as it was, meant that questions were asked publicly. The European and American governments and the UN came in for a lot of flack. Even we had completely underestimated the sheer magnitude of the disaster in the highlands: for two months people continued to pour down in unimaginable numbers. The scene we had witnessed at Dowit was reenacted time and time again along the length of the border.

Safila was better off than most of the camps because of the food from Charitable Acts and because we had raised our profile right from the start. The journalists always came to us first. We were in the center of the media spotlight and the big shots could not afford to let the situation get too bad for us. Elsewhere it was appalling.

Safila played host to all sorts of political dignitaries and discussions about how to stop disaster happening again. The latest plan is that there are to be grain stores positioned and kept stocked all the way along the border, and an agreement with Abouti that the aid agencies can take food into Kefti if ever the harvest is threatened again. As Muhammad put it, "If ever that comes to pass then I will both marry Kate Fortune and become her hairdresser." Stranger things have been known, of course.

Betty stayed on for a couple of months to see us through the worst of it, then departed for a desk job in London and Roy the soundman. Parcels of candied peel and decomposing date and walnut loaf have started arriving with touching regularity. Linda asked to be sent back to Chad and left about six weeks ago. Henry became very serious and adult for about a month but is now once again preoccupied with the contents of Fenella Fridge and Sian's Boris Bra.

And O'Rourke: he's asleep now, actually, in my bed under the mosquito net. I keep glancing up from the desk, watching him, in the glow from the hurricane lamp. He snores a bit, but I'm getting used to it.